TH

DOCK ROAD

A seafaring tale of old Liverpool

by

J.Francis Hall

PRINTWISE PUBLICATIONS LIMITED

1992

© This edition published 1992 by
PRINTWISE PUBLICATIONS LTD
47 Bradshaw Road, Tottington,
Bury, Lancs, BL8 3PW.

Warehouse and Orders:
40-42 Willan Industrial Estate, Vere Street,
(off Eccles New Road),
Salford, M5 2GR.
Tel: 061-745 9168
Fax: 061-737 1755

Originally published 1939 by Hutchinson & Co (Publishers) Ltd
in their First Novel Library No.130
Illustrations from Herdman's of Liverpool, by W.G. Herdman

Thanks to Tony Thorlby for his kind help and photographic
knowledge in reproducing the drawings in this book.

Reprint chosen and additional illustrations selected by

Cliff Hayes

ISBN No. 1 872226 37 X

Printed and bound by Manchester Free Press,
Paragon Mill, Jersey Street,
Manchester, M4 6FP
Tel: 061-236 8822

INTRODUCTION

I am constantly looking into the past, and especially into the history of the North-West. Printwise have re-published three successful novels that have been both historic fact mixed with fiction for added dimension and interest. Under the banner 'Northern Classic Reprints' these books have helped to bring to life the true events, and of the people involved.

After publishing 'Lancashire Witches' for Lancashire and two books for Manchester I naturally set my sights on Liverpool. The city is well served by the Helen Forrester novels, which I have read and re-read. And of course 'Our Benny' is always available, so the search was on for something else. I wanted something that was full of facts and atmosphere and yet not too heavy. I talked, I asked, I read, and I mithered.

Then I was told about a book called 'The Dock Road'. Liverpool Central Library let me have a look at the one copy they have and it looked good. So off I went to get a copy. I searched second-hand bookshops, and Mike Royden was very helpful in searching at Book Fairs for me. People had heard of it, and said they had read it and liked it, but there didn't seem to be any copies about. I asked Billy Mather to put out an appeal on his great 'Memories' show one Sunday, and although people telephoned to say they remembered the book and how enjoyable it was, no-one actually had a copy.

Then that unlikely duo — the Batman and Robin of Merseyside — Billy Butler and Wally Scott mentioned it on their show, and that's when Ron and Dot Whitely heard my plight and came forward with a copy for me. They even brought it down to give it to me personally. Now I could read it for myself.

Well, it stood the test. It was enjoyable and it was fascinating with it historical details. The characters in it were full of life and personality. It was a really good read.

Now after negotiating with the original publishers and finding suitable illustrations it is ready. We very proudly present an illustrated edition of what I hope you agree is a novel that captures perfectly an exciting era of Liverpool past.

Cliff Hayes

A story of Liverpool shipping and commerce
in the early 1860's. While all characters are fictitious,
the background is based on incidents and events which
were common to the times, and amidst which the
foundations of a great shipping industry were laid.

ABOUT THE AUTHOR

Not a lot is known about the author J. Francis Hall.

We do know that his full name was John Francis Hall and that he was known as "Jack". He worked as a lead writer for the *Journal of Commerce* in Liverpoolin the years leading up to and during the second World War, and it was there he developed his skill in writing. He was President of Liverpool Royal Naval Reserve and leader of the "Sea Urchins", an organisation to help young naval recruits. He was for many years a member of the Liverpool Press Club which used to meet at the Adelphi Hotel. Described by his colleague Jim Pearce, who worked with him on the *Journal* as a very likeable friendly workmate, stocky and fair haired.

This was not his only novel and he completed his second novel 'Atlantic Interlude' shortly after the War. It is believed he moved to the Blackburn area in connection with a family business, and probably still lives in the area.

We thank Jim Pearce of Wallasey for the above details.

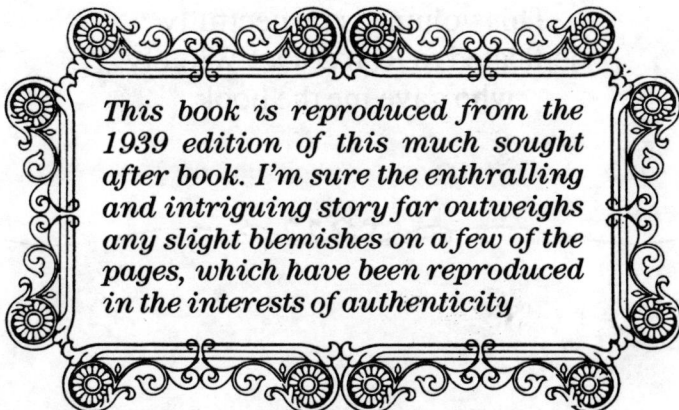

This book is reproduced from the 1939 edition of this much sought after book. I'm sure the enthralling and intriguing story far outweighs any slight blemishes on a few of the pages, which have been reproduced in the interests of authenticity

ACKNOWLEDGEMENTS

To all Liverpudlians who believe in this great city, who work to let others know how proud we are to be part of Liverpool, and plan for a better future. To Linda Carr and Charlie Corless at the Tourist Board; Billy Butler & Wally Scott who keep Merseyside smiling, and who are great champions of Liverpool. Bob Azurdia and the whole team down at Radio Merseyside who all try that little bit harder to do the best for the city. Gerry and Roger Phillips at Radio City; David Stewart at Charles Wilson's Bookshop and the work of the Civic Society; Paul McCue for being Paul McCue; Phil Young and his Scouseology — one of the nice guys of Merseyside; Mavis Adams for all the work she has put into the Maritime Museum Shop; Miss Danby at W.H. Smiths, Church Street Liverpool for always trying to help all local books, and many other people I know I'll regret leaving out.

This volume is respectfully
dedicated to Ron & Dot Whitely
who gave me the book

CONTENTS

St Nicholas' Church

CHAPTER 1

MEETING CAPTAIN BRADY

NIGHT was falling on Liverpool, that progressive, aristocratic port of the Palatine County, and along the Dock Road the noise of the horse-drawn traffic was but a thin dying echo of the vast turgid roar which, throughout the day, had marked the port's flourishing trade.

Away out on the river, ships lying at anchor were beginning to hoist their riding lights, their feeble rays pricking the gloom like so many fire-flies, and, as though that were a pre-arranged signal, lights began to appear, one by one, in the taverns and buildings that stretched along the road that fronted the docks and the river.

It was late October in the year 1861. The wind, blowing keen and fierce from off the landing-stage, whistled and eddied up Water Street and carried on even as far as Lime Street station, and passengers bound for the ferry clutched their hats and bent their bodies forward as they forged along. The first seething rush was over and now the patter of hastening feet came from the last few remaining clerks who, eager to leave the bonds of their daily servitude behind, directed determined footsteps towards the landing-stage. Their principals, the merchant princes, immaculate in white cravats and top hats had long since set the example, and now the last ledger was being closed, and the last counting-house locked and bolted as all official commerce closed for another day.

In the mud and mire of the Dock Road, however, the business of the night was just starting. Sailors from the ships in the docks were beginning to drift ashore, while out on the river little cockle-shells of rowing boats, laden down to their gunwales, were bringing off sea-faring men intent on a spree. Except for a few belated flat drays lumbering ponderously along, the road was empty of vehicular traffic. But on the rough sidewalks the sprinkling of people was steadily thickening and the constantly swinging tavern doors gave notice of the way in which pedestrian traffic was going.

The great steam-organ in the dance hall at the back of the 'Duke of Wellington' public-house was bellowing and wheezing with ever-increasing confidence as the steam whistled through its pipes. It had things very much its own way, for it was still too early for dancing, and it snorted and brayed and gasped unchallenged by the hilarity of the patrons lining up before the marble-tops and gilded mirrors of the glittering bar. The scene in the 'Duke of Wellington' was one which was common to all the other bars as they prepared to hand out liquor and entertainment in exchange for the swollen purses of the seamen of all nations.

The foundation of the port's greatness had been laid in the previous century, but all the ignominy of the slave trade and the fact that Liverpool had drawn its shipping trade from London and Bristol through cutting sailors' wages and manning its ships with poor-law apprentices was long since forgotten by the citizens, who were justly proud of their civic reputation. All that mattered to them was the wonderful sight of docks crammed full with the cream of the world's maritime commerce—tall, graceful ships, whose masts made the docks a towering forest of spars and brought wealth and romance from the most distant parts of the world.

The port *was* Liverpool and the whole life of the town centred around it. The local newspapers were full of shipping information and reports; the coming and going of ships were occasions in which all proud citizens took a deep interest. Record passages, epic tales of ship-wreck and disaster; each day brought its full quota of shipping intelligence; it was the very life-blood of Liverpool, and few conversa-tions were held in which ships and seamen did not figure.

This one-time little fishing hamlet had prospered into one of the world's greatest ports, its industry had flourished and along with it many immense personal fortunes had been made. But it was not only mercantile business that prospered, for alongside it there throve an underworld of vice. Into the port's water-front ebbed and flowed the scum of the world. No vice was too vicious but what it found an outlet in the shady furtive alleys lying at the back of the Dock Road or off Paradise Street. Cesspools of iniquity were but thinly disguised. Vice, as well as commerce, was a money-spinner, as both men and women found out when they peddled it around the docks. Foreigners of every colour and creed sought forgetfulness and pleasure in the excesses which for the most part they imported. Colonies of Chinese, Lascars, Africans sprang up, and always there were the Irish, 60,000 of them pouring into the port, year after year, hard on one another's heels.

Steadily the foreign colonies in and around sailor-town increased as the trade of the port prospered. In those areas promiscuity was so general and child-birth so casual that the traffic in human bodies was the major business of the night. Fortunes were made there, too, but as far as the majority of the population was concerned, poverty was the great denominator and virtue stood little chance of reaping a reward.

In one of the smaller, quieter taverns, two men sat talking and, very occasionally, drinking. One was an elderly man with thinning grey hair and heavy untidy moustache. His face was weathered and lined and the loose flesh on his neck hung angrily over the top of his stiff collar as though protesting against that formal article of fashion. Perched near the end of his large nose was a pair of steel-framed spectacles. Why he wore them it would be difficult to state, for he went to great pains to avoid looking through them, and as a result his face carried a sort of permanent downward tilt. He was dressed in a thick, dark blue pilot cloth, and although it was a cold night outside and barely warmer in, he nevertheless continued to mop his perspiring brow with a large brilliantly coloured silk bandanna.

His companion was a much younger man, dark complexioned and of medium height, and since he was a ship-chandler he had that easy suavity of manner which is the first essential of that trade. He was showing unusual deference to the elder man, and any observer would have had no difficulty in recognizing the occasion as a master mariner being touted for ship's stores. Yet the two of them were so deeply engrossed in conversation that there seemed to be something more behind their talk than the question of stores. In fact the question of where the old sea captain was going to buy his sea stock had not been entered into at all, and they were discussing the circumstances which had led to their meeting again after a period of five years.

Five years earlier they had met in Bombay; the young man was just embarking on his career as a water clerk and the old shipmaster was just setting off on his last homeward voyage to go into retirement.

"I never thought to see you back at sea, Captain Brady, after forty years of it," said the younger man.

"Forty-two years," corrected the other gravely, "forty-two years of hard work, bad food and poor pay."

"And still you can't keep away."

"Aye, I tried it out on shore, but bless you, lad, in less than a month I'd found out that a ship's bunk was the only bed I could sleep a wink in. It was a queer business, I tell you."

"Where did you settle?"

"I took a little place near Robin Hood's Bay," the captain explained, peering over the top of his spectacles. "It had a tidy piece of land just as I always figured it should, so that after I got tired of looking at the ships at sea I could go and do a bit of digging."

"Sounds like a sailor's dream of heaven!"

"Nay, Mr. Stewart, that was where I made the mistake. I was too near the sight and smell of the sea. What I should have done was to have gone away inland until I met up with someone who'd never heard tell of ships. But there you are, I didn't, and after six months of watching the ships reaching towards 'the High' I felt my anchors were dragging, so I slipped my ground tackle and got myself this job aboard the *Bellerophon*; it was easier than finding a new anchorage. Mind you, she's nothing to some of the ships I've been master of, but she floats, and—man alive, it's grand to feel a ship's deck beneath your feet. But how about yourself? I thought you'd have been an Indian Nabob or whatever they call 'em. Didn't get the sack, did you?"

"No," laughed Stewart easily, "I came home to set up in business for myself and, Captain, if there's anything you want from a Liverpool pantile to a bower anchor, I'm the man to supply you."

"How on earth did a young fellow like you get the money to start on your own?"

"You can't stay seven years on the Indian coast without picking up a bit of cash here and there as you should know, Captain."

"I'll be bound you never saved any money out of the wages that old skinflint paid you," the captain said suspiciously.

"I'm not saying I did, Captain, but it was all made honestly, at least for a ship's-runner, and, anyway, here I am in Liverpool with sufficient cash to give me a start, and I'll make my fortune yet, see if I don't."

"You're in the right business for that, anyway."

"You've hit it, Captain," said Stewart complacently; "with a bit of luck I'll give some of the other chandlers a run for their money."

Captain Brady looked at him shrewdly for a little while, then, lifting his arm, he drained his tankard and very deliberately placed it back on the table.

"Yes, luck," said the captain musingly, and passed his bandanna over his lips. "There's some folks they say are born lucky and there's others who ain't. But for my part I think it works both ways. Take these sailors here"—and he turned and waved his hand towards the men lolling at the bar—"now they think they're lucky because they've got money in their pockets and they're ashore. But see them tomorrow morning when their purses are empty and they're outward bound with nothing to show for it but an aching head. You see, young man, luck doesn't last, particularly good luck, and you've got to pin your faith on something more than that."

"All the same," persisted Stewart, "you must have luck to make a fortune."

The old man took off his spectacles and started to polish the lenses slowly, and then he said softly, as though to himself: "I came across another young fellow much the same as you a matter of ten years ago. His mother kept a little baker's shop up in Duke Street. 'I'm lucky,' he said, and all his friends said, 'Aye, Jimmy, you're lucky all right,' and so he was; everything he touched turned to gold. Last year he owned eighty ships, employed more than 3000 sailors and drove a four-in-hand all over the town."

"There you are, then!" said Stewart triumphantly.

"Perhaps you've heard of him?" continued the old man gravely. "James Baines the name, owner of the Blackball line. Well, you'll notice he isn't driving a four-in-hand now!"

"Yes, but it wasn't his fault that Barnard's Bank failed," protested Stewart.

"I'm not suggesting that it was; but all the same, I don't remember that wonderful luck of his saving him. Take that skipper of his, Bully Forbes—there sailed a lucky man if ever there was one. He believed in his lucky star, and right well it served him in the *Marco Polo* and the *Lightning*, but I reckon the clouds must have covered it up that night he put the *Schomburg* ashore. Forty-three thousand pounds she cost to build, and there she was, cast away on her maiden voyage. Yes, it was an expensive star all right."

"What about Paddy MacGee, the ragman," said Stewart defensively, "or Mr. Leyland, or that Hull shipowner, Mr. Wilson, and a score of others? They're all as rich as Croesus, yet if the stories about them are true it's not so long since they hadn't two halfpennies to rub together. Surely they've been lucky?"

Brady put on his spectacles again and looked at the young man pityingly. "That's not luck," he said, "that's industry and perseverance, as far removed from luck as the sun is from the moon. If you'll take a tip from me, young man, you'll profit more by following their example than you will by relying on luck. Anyway, how are you getting on so far?"

"I'm not complaining, Captain, I've been in Liverpool three months and I'm making a living, and that's more than you can say of a lot of Lancashire people in these unsettled times."

"It is that," said Brady gloomily. "I'll tell you what the trouble is, there's far too much Government interference in business. These politicians, I reckon, spill more wind without cause than a French brig close-hauled. Look what they're doing to shipping with all their fancy regulations!" He spat eloquently into a near-by cuspidor, and over the top of his spectacles he glared round at the steadily increasing number of carefree boisterous men crowding the bar. "Look at 'em," he growled disgustedly, "all the regulations in the world will never save them from the crimps and harpies they've got around 'em now. Shipping reforms! Bah! What happens? The Government passes an Act and puts another runner into the Custom House to see that it's carried out, and they issue a lot of official forms with so much writing on them that every man jack before the mast has become a proper sea lawyer. It's such nonsense that they've even made a shanty out of it—'According to the Act' they sing. I wonder where it's all going to end?"

"But surely, Captain," said Stewart thoughtlessly, "everyone admits the industry needs reform. Why, hundreds of lives are lost each year through the ignorance and incompetence of those in charge at sea."

Captain Brady gave him a look of astonishment and indignation. "Why, boy," he spluttered, "you still smell of pap. What do you know about it?"

Stewart backed down hastily. "Nothing, Captain, of course; it was only something I read in this morning's *Shipping Albion*."

"*Shipping Albion* fiddlesticks! What does a damn' printer know about the sea—or ships and seamen for that matter?"

"I think it was a Government report they were quoting," said Stewart nervously, wishing he had never mentioned it.

"More like it was that drunken reporter Sam Sharp in his cups again," said the captain querulously. "I've never heard such nonsense in all my life. Acts of God, my boy, that's the cause of losses at sea." And as though that dictum settled it for once and all, he stood up indignantly; a short, sturdy figure with all the marks of the sea upon him. Believing firmly in the integrity of his fellow shipmasters and disdainful of landsmen who ventured to criticize their professional character, he looked what he was, a ship's captain of the old school—conservative, dogmatic, infallible.

SETTING UP AS A SHIP'S CHANDLER

By the sixth decade of the 19th century England was well in the grip of that acquisitiveness which founded so many private fortunes and secured for this country so great a share of world trade. In this mad scramble to be in amongst the money, men were inspired by the examples of others. Coal-masters, iron-masters, cotton-masters, unknown men, became magnates over-night. They were the first of those Englishmen to whom money and business were the be-all and end-all of existence. The inventions and discoveries of the century were just beginning to prove their profitable worth, and it was easy for England, with her immense coal resources and established shipping industry, to seize the trading opportunities of a waking world. Europe was a disorganized continent, poor from endless wars. America, the only serious rival, was in the throes of a bitter civil war with no thoughts for foreign trade, and so the market was clear for British enterprise, and trade rolled almost of its own accord into the ports of London and Liverpool.

It was into that golden age of British commerce that Stewart, following the example of many others, launched himself. He had scraped up a matter of £200 whilst he was out in India. Very little of it had come from the wages paid to him by Surtees and Fenton's, for they were not a philanthropic institution like the old East India Company. However, there had been ways of adding to one's income, little bits of cargo bought and sold, and at the end of seven years he found he had £200 to his credit. It was sufficient for him to start on his own and though there was nothing to bring him back to England, for he had never known his parents, he read the signs and portents correctly and decided that England offered the opportunity to a man with only a little capital. The thought of staying out in India and becoming a passably rich man made no appeal to him, for he was ambitious and preferred the immediate risk of a venture in England to the long prospect of years of service and ultimate security in a climate that would certainly impair his health.

When he arrived in Liverpool he knew no one, but he speedily set about making himself known to those who could put him in the way of business. Most of his time he spent in wandering round the docks going

Supplying the ship's stores — Liverpool Dock Road, 1860

from ship to ship looking for commissions. There was nothing he would not do even though at times it cost him money to do it. His principal line was selling stores and victuals to ships ; he felt he knew that business inside out, and it was a profitable affair if only you could manage to get the orders. Captains of ships did not mind the quality of the goods so long as they got their backhander. The trouble was that it was too profitable and competition was severe, for Stewart was only one of many who realized that supplying ships with inferior food and gear at high-grade prices was good business.

He persevered, however, and by dint of hard work had managed to get a few reasonable orders to supply ships, and it was on the strength of these that he optimistically left his lodgings in Charlotte Street and moved into his own establishment in Chapel Walk. True, he only occupied the basement and courtyard of a private house, but it served as both warehouse and lodging, whilst giving him the added respectability of a business address. In the courtyard were the disused stables and out-houses which he planned to fill with stock as soon as ever he could persuade the wholesalers to let him have it.

The rest of the house belonged to Joe and Fred Eastwood, coasting shipowners. The two brothers lived and managed their business from the other two storeys. They operated little sailing schooners, bringing china clay up from Fowey for the potteries. In their time they had been profitable enough, but during the past few years the coasting business had felt the full impact of steam, and little steam coasters were ousting the sailing vessels from the short sea trades. For well over fifty years the little sailing schooners of Eastwoods had made a good living, and somehow their owners just could not understand the implications of the rise of steam-driven competition.

Believing that the phase would soon pass they hung grimly on to their ever-decreasing business, but the sign of the times was apparent in their dusty, silent offices, and above all in their leasing of the basement premises and courtyard buildings for a miserable five shillings a week. But it was just the place for Stewart, and full of enthusiasm he commissioned a sign-writer, under the promise of several pints of beer, to print him a board with his name 'James Stewart' written in large gold letters, and underneath it in smaller type 'Ship's husband'. The finished article he hung proudly on the iron railings which enclosed the flight of steps leading down to his premises. He spent a morning in an old marine-store dealers' yard and picked up a desk, a table, a couple of chairs and, to his great delight, a letter-copying press, and took them back with him.

There were two rooms opening off a dark dismal passage which connected the front door with the courtyard at the back. They were large damp stone-flagged rooms, but they had fireplaces and the dampness could soon be remedied. The front room he decided would do as an office-cum-store-room, and he managed to take away some of its bareness by fixing shelves around the wall and stowing on them the small stuffs which ships needed and which he hoped to sell. In the corner he placed his newly acquired desk and a couple of chairs and the letter-copying press, and after a week of hammering and altering he got some semblance of order into the place. Every time he ran up the flight of stairs outside he felt a glow of satisfaction as he saw the new imposing sign-board which declared his business to the passing world, or such of the world as cared to take the short cut between Water Street and Chapel Walk.

He soon found out that one expense led to another, for with his possession of a store-room and office he realized that he must have some sort of odd-job man to be on the spot when he was down at the docks, otherwise he might miss some passing business. As he surveyed his dwindling cash reserves he realized that there was a limit to what he could afford, and that fact restricted his choice to an incapacitated elderly man or a young lad satisfied with a few shillings a week. In the end he decided on the former man and went down to the Seamen's Home to see if they had anybody to suit him. The superintendent opined that Silas Martin, an old sailor with a wooden leg, was the very man for the job; he was honest, at least he had never found him to be otherwise, and the only thing he knew against him was that he was fond of his liquor, and since the superintendent was anxious to get Silas out of the Home he looked belligerently at Stewart, remarking: "Who isn't, these days? But for five shillings a week what sort of a man could you expect?" So Silas packed his bag and took up his permanent abode in one of the outhouses in the yard bringing along with all his weaknesses, however, an unqualified loyalty.

Under this arrangement the business of 'James Stewart, Ship's husband', flourished more than its owner had anticipated and so encouraged him to work still harder. His enthusiasm even spread to Silas who, once he had settled in, started of his own free will to make fancy sennet mats to cover up the stone flagging, and when that was finished he embarked on the endless job of 'painting 'er down'. In spite of all the paint and other shipboard accessories which surrounded him and should have made him happy, there were certain misgivings at the back of the old sailor's mind. In a voice long since rendered husky by a too-liberal application of rum, he lost no time in letting his young employer know of them.

"We've got a tidy lot of sea stock aboard, skipper," he said one day with a calculating eye on all the bolts of canvas, coils of ratline and drums of Stockholm tar that spaced the shelves, "I 'opes as 'ow the freight money will pay for it all?"

"Pay for it?" queried Stewart, puzzled. "I'm hoping it'll more than pay for it."

The old sailor gave him a quizzical look. "Don't you think we've got a shade too many dry provisions? I ain't seen any kegs of rum around. When I signed on with you t'other morning I sez to myself, 'Silas, that's the end of salt 'orse and 'ard tack, but blimey, skipper, I ain't so sure. If we ain't careful we'll have the scurvy aboard afore we've cleared the Bar light-ship! You needs to stock a cask or two of rum, skipper, just to keep the old box on an even keel."

"Oh, I don't know why we should stock rum when there's any number of public-houses just around the corner?"

"Skipper," said the old sailor patiently, "I can see as 'ow you're new to this game else you'd know that 'ard tack without a dram of Nelson's blood to keep it pickled 'll cause a heap of trouble."

"Yes?"

"Yes," replied Silas solemnly, " 'ard tack without a drop of rum to soften it'll turn your blood blacker'n the London river."

"Oh! if it's only your blood you are worried about, Silas, that's easy, there is a sack of limes lying in the yard. Help yourself to them any time."

"Limes!" said the other disgustedly, "limes ain't no good; you'll never find 'em aboard a Yankee packet, and look 'ow they sails their ships. Look at me, 'ale and 'earty at sixty-three, and I've swallowed enough salt 'orse and Liverpool pantiles to kill an ordinary man. But see," he went on confidentially, "it's not limes, it's the poison from Jamaica that's kept all them weevils from breaking surface and kept me alive, wooden leg and all. If you'll take a tip from an old sailor you'll stow a couple of demijohns in the lazarette."

"Nothing doing, Silas," said Stewart pleasantly; "as far as you and I are concerned this is a dry ship. If any customer wants a couple of jars of rum sent aboard with their sea stock, well, there's time enough to slip round and get it from one of the publicans. But," he added ominously, "if you're worried about your future health, perhaps you'd better go back to the Home?"

"Now, captain," answered Silas, thoroughly alarmed as he thought of the welcome the superintendent of the Home might give him, "you do take on so. I'm not complaining about the wittels or the work. What suits you suits me," he went on ingratiatingly; "all I'm worried about is that I don't like to think of a fine young fellow like you getting taken up wi' weevils," and thinking discretion the better tactics at this stage in the conversation, retired to the courtyard.

Stewart chuckled at the old man's guile and then sat down to read the *Shipping Albion*. It was his first job of the day. In a little note-book he jotted down information as to the berthing of new arrivals and other items of information about them which that newspaper gave in detail. After a while he got up and with a parting word of advice to Silas set out on his daily routine of ship visiting. The little note-book served him well, and he soon began to amass an intimate knowledge of the history of each ship and the record of each captain. Through this knowledge he found himself welcomed aboard and in this way managed to make himself distinctive from the swarms of runners and crimps who waited on the quayside.

Until he got used to it those hours spent pacing up and down the quay, waiting for the ships to berth, seemed interminable. There was no alternative, for if he wanted the business it was no use sitting back in his office waiting for it to come to him. He had to go out and get it himself, and if the seamy side of the port elbowed and jostled around him he had to accept it. Even that experience was not without its value, for it let him see at first hand the chicanery which went on in the never-ending struggle of separating the sailors from their pay. The idlers crowding the quay never tired of telling of their professional astuteness. "Of course," they would confide to him with a hoarse chuckle, "it's easy getting money out of sailors; the difficult part is keeping ahead of others on the same tack."

Stewart got to know them all. A fog on the river might delay the dockings by some hours, but none of the runners dared to move away until the ebb was fiercely swirling past and it became evident that no more ships would berth that tide. Up and down, up and down those waiting runners would walk, in the manner of seamen pacing a ship's deck, but all the time keeping a wary eye on each other lest one of them slipped off to another picking. He came to know their faces like the back of his hand. Sharp, cunning features they were and he wondered how anyone could come to trust them. But sailors, he soon found, trusted everyone. They never learned either. Out at sea in the dog-watches, when all the glittering appeal of the port had been drowned in the hopeless eternity of the voyage which stretched ahead, they might curse all longshoremen, but everyone knew that back in port again they would rise to the bait of friendliness with never a struggle.

Amongst the 'idlers' themselves there was no love lost, and new-comers to the trade, especially, were harassed in every way in the hope that they would be discouraged and drop out of the race. But Stewart's water-clerking experience in India had hardened him to rebuffs, and all the animosity of the other runners waiting there with him could not dissuade him from competing for the masters' business, and success-fully competing at that. At the end of three months he was able to look back through his meticulously kept ledger and note with pride that not only was he paying his way but actually making a profit.

Silas, too, with one or two temporary lapses, was playing his part in laying the foundations of the firm. He had proudly triumphed over many of the difficulties that beset him, and not the least was the fact that he could neither read nor write. But, as he philosophically excused himself, come to that the skipper for his part couldn't turn a Flemish eye, and knew nothing about Carrick Bends and Matthew Walker's. The only unfair thing about that bosun's locker of theirs was that while the skipper's ignorance of sailor's knots and bends didn't matter, Silas' lack of writing and reading was a handicap; yet somehow he evolved a system of recording the orders that came into the office when Stewart was out. Then, later in the day, the two of them would sit down and Silas would interpret his rude, rough scrawls and between them they would piece together the sum total of the day's business.

In most cases, where the orders were of any length, they were already written down before they were handed in, and then Silas' task was easy, but requests for single items always came in verbally, and Silas, too proud to admit he could not write, would laboriously commit them to paper. If an order came in for ten casks of ships' biscuits to be delivered on board the ship *Lido*, the entry in the day ledger would be a rough drawing of the famous pantile and ten marks placed after it, and the order would be completed with a sketch of the ship *Lido* drawn from an imaginative memory and calculated to recall the ship's name to Silas—if no one else.

It was all very laborious and unsatisfying, for Stewart, by himself, could make no sense out of Silas' handwriting. At first he had endeavoured to teach him the alphabet in order that he might write the orders down in a more normal way, but Silas either would not or could not follow him, and in despair he had been left to his own devices.

"Why!" said Silas indignantly, "a nigger straight from Africa could understand what I writes. But try and get him to make 'ead or tail of that there fancy writing of yours, skipper!"

Silas' attitude was one of proud respect for his own ingenuity, and one of contemptuous indifference when Stewart, making up his ledger, sought an explanation of some particularly outlandish design.

"What the dickens is this?" the young man would say, sighing heavily, as he surveyed a new variation of Silas' ingenuity. "You know, Silas, your trouble is that you aren't consistent. Why a cask of beef should resemble something between a camel and a cow one day, and the next be a cross between a goat and a dog, baffles me."

Silas looked at him with disdain. "'Ave you ever tried to draw a cow, skipper? Then, if you ain't, you shouldn't get on to me. Anyway, cows, camels, dogs, goats, what difference does that make? they're all animals. And what's salt beef? It's meat of some kind, but even you with all your larning can't tell me what kind."

"All right, I'll grant you that," said Stewart wearily, "but that doesn't explain why dried fish should be a simple straightforward herring-bone one day and a Jew's nose the next!"

"Blimey, skipper, ain't you ever smelled salt fish? That's the idea, see; it smells something fit to knock a man down, so if I draws a Jew's nose why, even a baby could understand what that means."

Stewart gave him a long pitying look. "I'm not quite sure which it is, Silas, but you're either ahead or astern of your time. Perhaps in a hundred years from now someone will come across these drawings and give them the artistic appreciation that I cannot. I've no wish to cramp your style, but I do suggest you try to observe some consistency in your interpretation of the ships' store business."

The old sailor knuckled his head, puzzled. "Durned if I know what all them long words mean, skipper, but maybe you didn't know that in my time I've been ship's painter aboard a man-of-war!"

"It must have been in the Swiss Navy," said Stewart fervently, "for this is certainly not Englishmen's talk."

"What do you mean, captain?" asked Silas angrily. "I've a mind to pack my bag and let you see 'ow you gets on without me!"

"For goodness' sake calm down and come and explain what these hieroglyphics mean, otherwise I can see us delivering holystones instead of bread."

On that particular day it turned out that the emigrant ship *Sacramento* wanted thirty sheep (live), two cows (milkers), a couple of pigs and three dozen eggs. "You're going to have a nice time getting that livestock aboard anyway, Silas," jeered Stewart, but the old man was still smarting under the injustice of his employer's lack of appreciation and was not to be drawn. So Stewart turned to the next item. The barque *Ada Pearson* wanted paint; white lead and red lead, some gold leaf and some varnish.

"I don't know what ships and sailormen are coming to," growled Silas. "Who ever heard of varnish on a ship? Linseed oil's been good enough for seamen since Noah put to sea, but blimey, skipper, Samuel Plimsoll with 'is arguments and the Government with its new Act 'as made sailormen so proud that they've got to 'ave varnish for their spars now. It ain't seamanlike; all the same, skipper, we can supply 'em, and don't you forget to make 'em pay for it"; and having talked himself back into a good humour, he stumped off to the rum shop round the corner and left Stewart to get on with the business.

Such was the position at the end of three months, and on the night of Stewart's re-union with Captain Brady he was satisfied that he had got a firm foothold in the Liverpool ships' store trade.

THE 'PIG & WHISTLE'

The unfortunate termination of his meeting with Captain Brady could not be helped; he would go round and apologize and if he knew anything of seamen, all would be well. Meanwhile, business had to go on, and the following morning as usual he made his notes in his little pocket-book and then went off visiting the ships on his list. Too often, though, the captains were not aboard and so he learned that the business of canvassing for orders had to be carried on in those places which shipmasters frequented. The main resort of ships' captains ashore on business was the 'Pig and Whistle', a public-house just far enough away from the Dock Road to miss being a port of call for drunken seamen and yet near enough to the 'Shipping Mile' to be handy.

The landlord of the 'Pig and Whistle' was a man of rare cunning. A middle-aged shipmaster himself he had retired to make a far easier and more profitable living by tavern keeping. When he bought the 'Pig and Whistle' it was just one of the 208 public-houses which stood within a stone's throw of the Dock Road. He brought many novel ideas with him into his new trade, the chief of which was that women should not be served with liquor in his tavern. He aimed at making the 'Pig and Whistle' a place where gentlemen might meet and discuss business without interruption and diversion from trollops. All the same, he was sufficiently a man of business to know that nothing helps business so much as the sight of buxom wenches, red of lip and bold of eye, so he sacked his barmen and replaced them with four barmaids. He picked these girls carefully himself and because of them, rather than the quality of the liquor (though there was nothing wrong with that), the 'Pig and Whistle' became famous.

The captain's young ladies', as they were called, were dressed in fashions calculated to emphasize their physical charms and persuade men to stay beyond their intentions—but that was all. The girls gave themselves airs and plainly regarded their position as one of some importance in the world of taverns, and in this they were right, for in the 'Pig and Whistle' they were paid to be respectable, and the unusualness of this alone did more to establish the tavern's reputation and keep its customers constant than anything else. The captain's policy had paid and paid handsomely. At the end of a year he had found it necessary to increase his staff to seven, and he could look back with pleasure to the complete vindication of his policy.

They took a lot of managing, of course, always squabbling amongst themselves and for ever getting into trouble; for in spite of the landlord's watchful eye, temptation was very great and barmaids came and went fairly frequently. He paid them good wages and for the life of him he could not understand why they did not look after their jobs better. His friend, Dick Burt, landlord of the 'Red Lion', had warned him against the idea right at the start, saying that one Fanny would cause more trouble than a street of public-houses, and in a way Dick had been right. Still, they brought the custom, and as long as they did that he would forgive a lot.

From the girls' point of view, too, it was a good job. It was true the hours were long and the work was hard, but in scores of ways they were better off than if they had to work in the tap-rooms along the Piazza Gorree. There was only one nigger in their wood-pile and that was the public bar, a large, adjoining room much frequented by the riff-raff of the shipping world. None of the 'young ladies' liked serving there, though it meant nothing more than working the beer-engine and pushing the sloppily filled tankards across the counter. That was not their world, thought the barmaids as they prinked their hair and looked appraisingly over their shoulders at their reflection in the huge mirrors. The ignorant louts who patronized the public bar should take their custom to some place where it was welcomed, and with a disdainful sniff at the shabby unkempt individuals who hoarsely and indignantly demanded that they be given the full and proper measure, they contrasted their rough uncouth talk with the witty, daring conversation of the gents in the smoking-rooms and the snug. For all the unpleasantness of that public bar, none of the girls would ever leave the 'Pig and Whistle', they assured each other. They did, however, and as the captain contemplated each new face that he engaged he thought sardonically upon the frailty of human nature and the foolishness of women in particular.

Stewart found it politic to slip into the 'Pig and Whistle' on his way back from the docks, for then he would be sure to contact those captains on his list whom he had missed aboard their ships. He was in no position to spend his money freely and his visits soon taught him to count his change carefully, but for all that outward parsimony, he was an established favourite of the 'young ladies'. But unfortunately he was more interested in business than pleasure, and after a time they had given up sidling against him as they threaded their way through the crowded bar.

There was only one girl for whom he showed the slightest preference and that was Susy, a dark, vivacious young woman with twinkling brown eyes and happy, infectious laugh. She seemed to delight in saying audacious things to him, and after his early embarrassment he discovered that the only way to hold her in check was to be as equally facetious. That mutual kind of badinage made them friendly disposed towards each other, and already she had helped him by making a point of letting him know what shipmasters had been in, and once she had secured an order for him by judiciously mentioning his name to a customer. Yes, he decided, she was a good-hearted girl, but that was as far as his thoughts towards her went.

From the 'Pig and Whistle' he generally went back to Chapel Walk, and together with Silas sorted out the orders, and the old sailor made arrangements with outside porters for them to be shipped on board. Then Silas set about preparing the evening meal while Stewart scanned the *Shipping Albion* seeking for information which he might have missed, and so, one way and another, the days flew by and the business grew stronger.

CHAPTER 2

THE SHIPPING ALBION

IT was Susy who put him up to it. Why didn't he get something in the *Shipping Albion* about himself and the business? she asked, and it struck him that it was a good idea. He would call at the newspaper's office on his way down to the dock, and on the excuse of ordering a copy of the paper to be delivered daily at Chapel Walk he would let them know who he was and what he was.

As he walked briskly up Water Street he wondered why he had never thought of it before. Why, if he could get his name mentioned in the local shipping paper as having started a ships' store business, it would accomplish in a day what would probably take him months of footslogging round the docks. There was no doubt about it, publicity, advertisement was just the thing he needed.

The *Shipping Albion* was a newspaper peculiar to Merseyside alone. It had had a chequered career, and although for forty years it had eked out a precarious existence from its reports of ships' movements, it had lately taken on a new lease of life and was prospering under the proud ownership of Charlie Tomkins. Only a few years back Charlie had been a jobbing printer and then, one day, much to his angry dismay, he learned that his biggest customer, forgetful of his printing debts, had suddenly packed his bag and vanished from Liverpool—leaving a foundling, so to speak, the *Shipping Albion*, on Charlie's doorstep. It was such a poor, weak, ailing thing that its owner had certainly taken the best way out as far as his own pocket was concerned. Charlie went down and pessimistically looked around the deserted offices of the *Shipping Albion*, but there was little there to give him any hope of ever recovering the money they owed him. The only possible way was to go on printing and publishing the paper. And then Sam Sharp, journalist, had staggered across his path and slowly the *Shipping Albion* took a hold of Charlie Tomkins. It was something to own a newspaper and his chest swelled with pride every time he thought about it.

By printing it himself he found that he could just make a tiny profit, and then shipping started on one of its cyclical periods of prosperity, and for some queer reason beyond his understanding more people started to buy the paper, and, better still, more people found it expedient to advertise in its columns. That was what he liked, advertisements. He never quite knew how it all happened, for what with printing the reports of ship movements and making up the advertisements he had never paid much attention to the rest of the paper. He had left all that to Sam Sharp, and Charlie could hardly believe his eyes when people he did not know from Adam suddenly took to recognizing him

24

respectfully in the streets; real dressy people some of them were, too.

What, however, was far more important to his sharp Lancashire mentality was the fact that the *Shipping Albion* had developed into a money spinner, and he was making more hard cash now than he had ever dreamed possible. Though the money was rolling in he saw to it with real native caution that his mode of living did not change. His expenses remained at the same low, frugal level and he watched grudgingly every penny he had to spend. At times he lived in a state of alarm lest something should happen to this wonderful milch cow of his, and he was for ever dinning into Sam Sharp's unsympathetic ears that "we moant kill t'bird as lays golden eggs". People who advertised in the *Shipping Albion* were divinely right and so it came about that shipowners obtained a fiercely protective champion. The casual reader was never left long in doubt as to the newspaper's policy. It was lamentable but true, as Sam Sharp would confide with but little pressing, that in Charlie's eyes shipowners could do no wrong. But he as well as Charlie knew where the money came from, and knowing that, it was easy to fill their columns with lyrical praise for shipowning interests and sweeping invective for those who dared to oppose them. There were no half measures about the *Shipping Albion*.

The grandiloquent and even truculent tones which the paper sometimes adopted were sadly out of keeping with its miserable premises in Victoria Street. Nevertheless, mean looking and unpretentious as the building appeared outside, it might have been the Crystal Palace itself for the reverence which it inspired in the hearts and minds of the three people who earned their living within its shabby walls. Although each one of the three contributed a varying share to the paper's make-up, the wonder never quite left their faces when they saw the finished product of their combined labours.

There was Charlie Tomkins, the proprietor and printer, Lancashire born and bred. He had been a printer all his life and God help him, according to Sam Sharp, he'd never be anything else. Sam himself, was alternately editor, chief reporter, special correspondent, technical expert or any other learned authority which the event and the paper might call for. Sam made no bones about it, he could write anything, anywhere, any time. He worked best of all in his cups, and although this had proved to be his undoing on many another paper of far greater importance, his ability was never in doubt, and it seemed as though at last he had reached, in his little daily sheet of shipping reports and gossip, his true spiritual home. Sam wrote the copy, Charlie set the type, and that left only Harold, a white-faced, sharp-featured boy, whose job was to collect docking movements, advertisement proofs, and mind the premises when the other two were out. They were very strict about Harold and did not believe in putting temptation in his way, and he was not allowed to touch any money. If anyone came into the office to buy a paper or pay an account, Harold's orders were to run round the back and fetch the gaffer.

So, when Stewart got round to Victoria Street, and after a lot of poking about found the shabby little door that marked the entrance to this daily paper of the shipping world, he walked into an untidy disordered office in the midst of which sat a man and a boy in varying stages of idleness. The boy was perched on a high stool with his elbows on the counter and his inky hands cupping his face. He was whistling away shrilly, both cheeks fully distended, but the far-away look in his eyes plainly showed that his thoughts were miles away from that grubby little office. In the background, dark and obscure, seated, or rather lolling, in a chair with his feet raised off the ground by means of a three-legged stool, dozed a middle-aged man. His tall hat was tipped precariously forward, almost on to his nose, and his hands were clasped complacently together across his gently heaving stomach. "Today's *Albion*," ordered Stewart, deliberately placing himself across the boy's distant contemplation, and rattled the coins in his hand. The whistle ceased abruptly, so that for a second it seemed that an unearthly calm prevailed. Harold looked over his shoulder at the reclining figure, but at the very moment in which he was sliding Stewart's twopence into his pocket, a slow movement, like a ground swell disturbing the quiescent waters of a land-locked harbour, manifested itself in the dozing figure.

With a vast sigh Harold replaced the coppers and resumed his piercing whistle and vacant contemplation of the wall opposite. The lull in the eerie noise had been the boy's undoing and as the figure began to unfold, the first words that fell to Stewart's ears were, "Blast you, boy, stop that confounded noise," and the editor of the *Shipping Albion* came forward to greet him. Of course he'd heard of Sam Sharp before, who in Liverpool hadn't ? Sam was a byword in the town. His editorials were a continued source of delight and his flow of invective was such that many of his readers tried to formulate their conversation in the same style. Drunk or sober there was little doubt that Sam Sharp knew all that there was to be known about Liverpool's shipping. He gathered facts and information around him as a magnet attracts filings. It was only natural that Charlie Tomkins quailed at the thought of seeking another chief reporter and editor. There never could be such another as Sam, and so Sam continued to be the hope and torment of the *Shipping Albion's* proprietor, and beer continued to be the lubricant of the editor's journalistic inspirations.

On the morning when Stewart entered, the editor was sober. He advanced with dignity to the counter where the copies of the day's papers lay on sale.

"Pray excuse this urchin, sir," he said, "perhaps I can be of assistance ?" He fixed his watery, grey eyes on Stewart questioningly. "I regret I haven't the pleasure of your acquaintance, but as the humble. representative of this journal I am at your service."

"The fact is," explained Stewart, "I wish to become a subscriber My name is Stewart and I've just set up as a ship-chandler. I'd be obliged if you'd have the *Albion* delivered daily at my office in Chapel Walk."

"Delighted, my dear sir, delighted. What name did you say? Ah! Stewart, yes, any relation of the shipowner of that name? No, of course not. You'll pardon my curiosity, sir. I regret the *Albion* has not made your acquaintance before, but"—with a large expansive wave of his hand—"you'll appreciate the vastness of this great shipping metropolis of ours, and though it is our boast that the *Albion* is the eyes and the ears of the shipping world, we sometimes overlook the setting up in business of new arrivals. I'm glad you called, sir. We shall never forgive ourselves that we didn't call on you first. Still, it is not too late to make amends, and rest assured, sir, this journal will make honourable amends for its tardy recognition of your entry into the commerce of the port. You must favour me with the honour of an interview. Boy, bring me pencil and paper. No! never mind, on second thoughts you must accept a potion with me at the 'Red Lion'. No trouble at all, Mr. Stewart, our patrons' voracious appetite for news leaves me no alternative. Come, sir, the clarion presses are eager for information."

"The 'Red Lion' again!" said Harold with a derogatory sniff.

Sharp quelled him with a look. Half-way to the door he stopped, turned back to the counter and carefully counted the remaining copies of the *Albion* lying there on sale. Then, wagging an admonishing finger at the boy, he said, "Tell Mr. Tomkins when he comes in that I'm out to lunch with a client."

Seated in the back room of the 'Red Lion' the reporter briefly put himself in possession of Stewart's life history, and then he rapped out abruptly: "Now about the question of advertising. I would advise nothing large or pretentious as yet, but say a couple of daily lines at special weekly rates?"

"Here," broke in a startled but nevertheless resourceful Stewart, "have a drink!" and in a minute the conversation entered upon a less businesslike but more mutually pleasing phase.

As the time wore on Sharp became increasingly confiding. With but an appropriate word here and there supplied by Stewart, the journalist talked and talked, slowly and solemnly as though every word he uttered was to see the dignity of print. The more he drank the more voluble he became; the prophet behind the pen, the power behind the scenes, warning, encouraging, reminiscing; giving the impression of ponderous knowledge, of profound experience. To say the least of it Stewart was bewildered by such eloquence and sat on, half hypnotized.

Some hours later they were still there. Stewart had long since given up drinking as well as thoughts of business for the day. He sat there patiently, with the other's arm draped affectionately across his shoulders, a listener after Sam's own heart. But there came the noise of a commotion outside and then the next minute a burly, heavily bearded man of mature years swung into the room. He was hatless and coatless and an ink-stained apron was girded up around his middle.

"Nay, Sam," he said angrily, "wot abaht dammed paper ? Art never coming in to do a bit o' summat ? Wot's all this like ? On t'booze ?"

Sam rose with all the dignity that was left to him. "Mr. Stewart," he said, "meet my patron and fellow worker in the noble cause of shipping, Mr. Charles Tomkins." He turned, swaying, towards his employer. "Charlie," he said, "meet our latest client, Mr. James Stewart, ship's husband, who this very minute has begged me to take his advertisement in our columns."

"Eh ! 'asta, lad ? Then 'Ahm reet glad to meet thee. Sam 'ere mun write summat abaht thee. But nah, Sam, tha mun come back to th' office, else us'll miss t'blasted edition. Tha knows th' 'as a deal to do," and before Sam could voice any opinion he was bundled outside.

"They're a couple of cautions," chuckled the landlord; but Stewart was engaging in no further conversations that day, his routine would need revising and he opened out the *Shipping Albion* to see what ships he could still visit in the reduced time. But Sam Sharp with his talk had set the young man's mind wandering; he found it difficult to concentrate, and when, a few minutes later, a couple of customers came in he found himself unconsciously listening to their conversation.

It appeared they were a couple of Liverpool underwriters, but if their conversation was any guide one of them did not expect to be an underwriter much longer, for his talk indicated that he had been badly hit by a series of shipping casualties, and there he was, bitterly bemoaning his luck while his companion commiserated with him. If he couldn't reinsure his risk in the *Bangalore*, he was saying, he'd be finished, for another claim would break him.

At the mention of the ship's name Stewart pricked up his ears. That was the ship that Sam Sharp had been talking about. Six months overdue and only that morning young Martindale, the son of the owner, looking through his father's wastepaper basket for envelopes with foreign stamps on them, had come across a letter written in French. Such were the times that no letter that was not in good honest English ever received a second glance, and it had been thrown away. Young Martindale had been principally interested in the stamp on the envelope, but it so happened that in preparation for going into business he had been taught a little French and he picked up the letter and started to try and translate it. A word or two here and there he made out and then he sighted the word *Bangalore*. Just then Sam Sharp walked into the office. The boy showed him the letter, but Sam, for all his other accomplishments, did not know much French, yet he sensed there was a good story in it, and after ascertaining that no one else in the office knew about the letter, he swore the boy to secrecy and carried the letter away to have it properly translated, all ready, as he explained to the eager youth, for Mr. Martindale on his return from Manchester.

The letter when translated indicated that it was written in response to the master's request that his owners be informed of the safe arrival of the ship and cargo in a little harbour in the Marquesas away out in the Pacific. They had been in collision with a half-submerged derelict. The accident had brought all their masts down and had stove in the forefront almost to the collision bulkhead. Under jury rig and with the collision bulkhead shored up they had managed to fetch the shelter of the Marquesas. The captain had beached her on a sandy shore and temporary repairs were being carried out which would enable the ship to arrive home safely. The master reported that the cargo was undamaged, and he was sending this information by the master of a French schooner which had just called in at the islands.

Unfortunately, the master of the French schooner reported that the *Bangalore's* letter had been mislaid on the passage over to the South American mainland, but as he knew the contents he was sending them on himself and trusted that no inconvenience would be caused. "You see," said Sam Sharp to Stewart, "it's a first-class story, and once again the *Shipping Albion* will be the first to tell the world."

"But, surely," Stewart had said, "you're going to let Mr. Martindale know beforehand?" The journalist had looked at him pityingly. "What! and lose a good story?" No, the owner could wait till tomorrow, and it was only when Sam was half-way through his next drink that he suddenly remembered he shouldn't have told Stewart. "This, of course, sir, is in the strictest confidence between you and me."

"Of course, of course," Stewart had agreed, for it was no business of his. So that when the word *Bangalore* fell on his ears, almost within the hour of the reporter's story, he couldn't help but become interested.

Casually he joined in the conversation. "It's quite possible she may turn up, you know," he said sympathetically.

"Not a hope," said one of the underwriters gloomily.

"There's many another ship been six months overdue and still managed to make port."

"And there's far more that hasn't. Strikes me I'm finished."

"Oh, come, think of the *Marco Polo's* last trip, she was overdue long enough, but she turned up in the end. While there's life there's hope." Stewart went on to talk so optimistically that the two underwriters began to look at him appraisingly. No one but an idiot, they thought, would carry on talking like that. It was obvious he didn't know much about shipping or he wouldn't talk in that way of a ship whose reinsurance was quoted in the very paper in front of him at sixty per cent.

The two underwriters looked at each other significantly. They began to draw Stewart on; they found out about his business and learned that he was a new-comer to the port.

"Ever done any insurance?" one of them inquired.

"Heavens, no. Ships' stores are my particular worry. Each cobbler to his own last is what I say."

"Oh! I wouldn't say that. Look at Paddy McGee, the ragman, he's one of the richest men in Liverpool today through taking a little gamble now and then on marine insurance."

"I dare say he is, but everyone doesn't get his opportunities," returned Stewart.

"Well, if it's opportunity that you're looking for, why not have a little speculation on the *Bangalore*? you're so sure she'll turn up."

"I wasn't thinking about that," said Stewart hesitantly.

"Aye, it's just as I thought," said one of the underwriters, "talks cheap, but it takes a little courage to risk your cash. It doesn't look as though you've got much of either."

Stewart flushed angrily. "Why . . ." he began, and then stopped. These two fellows plainly took him for a fool. He knew as well as they did that on paper the *Bangalore* was beyond re-insurance, but he couldn't tell them that he knew the ship and cargo were safe, and after that last scathing remark he didn't think he would have told them even if he hadn't promised Sam Sharp to keep his mouth shut. The conversation suggested that there might be a bit of money to be made if he went about it carefully. It looked as though this was the thing called 'luck' over which he and Captain Brady had so nearly quarrelled.

He drew himself up as though offended. "I've got as much courage to risk my cash as anyone."

"Well, come on then, take a chance on the *Bangalore*."

"How much is she insured for?" asked Stewart doubtfully.

"£80,000 for the cargo and £20,000 for the hull."

"Phew!"

"I'll tell you what I'll do," said the underwriter who was carrying the risk, "I'll make you an offer. There's this ship that's overdue, but which you say will turn up; right? Well I got £1250 in premiums on her, £1000 on the cargo and £250 on the hull. Now I'm a sport I am, I'll give you a chance to make a bit of easy cash. I can't make over the policies to you, but if you want you can re-insure my risk and I'll pay you exactly the same premiums that were paid to me." He turned to his companion. "That's a fair enough offer, isn't it, Arthur?" Arthur marvelled for a moment and then hastily agreed. "Well, what do you say, young fellow?"

Stewart appeared to think for a minute and then, as though reluctant, said, "No, that's a bit too much for me; but," he continued diffidently, "I'm willing to take a chance on the cargo, provided we go straight round to the bank and put the deal through now before I've time to change my mind." But he needn't have worried, the underwriter was just as anxious to put the business through quickly, for it wasn't every day he met such a fool as Stewart appeared to be.

Half an hour later Stewart had as much as he could do to stop himself running all the way back from the bank to Chapel Walk. In his hand he clutched a banker's draft for £1000. So much for Captain Brady and his theory about luck, he was thinking, but after a while he began to grow a little uneasy. Just suppose the *Bangalore* didn't turn up and that the letter was a fake! He went hot all over, and put the thought away from him resolutely; there was time enough to meet trouble when it arrived. All the same, that night was the most unpleasant one that he could ever remember, and final relief did not come until the following day when, at the bottom of Sam Sharp's highly coloured account of this sea drama, he read a terse report which stated that the *Bangalore* had been spoken off the Scilly Isles, and a week later she was towed up the river and berthed in Sandon Dock, her cargo intact.

For a while Stewart scrupulously avoided the 'Red Lion' and abandoned his front office to Silas, with strict instructions to tell any caller who looked at all like an underwriter, that he was away on business. Then, after mature reflection, he realized that the underwriters were unlikely to trouble him, for if he had been guilty of sharp practice then so had the underwriter in urging him to take the re-insurance at par when the official rate was sixty per cent. After all, his initial intervention had been purely benevolent, he'd tried to tell the fellow the *Bangalore* would turn up and if he'd really been out for business he could have soaked him for a good deal more. Still, £1000 was very nice to be getting on with. That was the way to make money. There he'd been, flogging himself almost to death trying to sell stores to ships, and after three months of it all he'd got to show was a miserably fifty pounds; then, by way of contrast, a half-hour's conversation, and there he was the richer by a thousand pounds. Life was good, he thought, and on the strength of that reflection he put on his hat and set off for the 'Pig and Whistle'.

It was dark when he arrived and at the bottom of the few steps leading up to the Select Bar he bumped into a figure standing there. "Sorry," he muttered.

"Oh! it's Mr. Stewart," a girl's voice cried.

"Why, Susy," he exclaimed, recognizing her voice; "waiting for your young man?"

"No, I'm not!" she retorted somewhat sharply. "If you really want to know, it's my night off and I'm going up to Pitt Street to see my mother."

"Pitt Street! that's no place for a girl at night-time."

"Maybe not, but all the same I've got to go. It's over a month since I went, and she'll be wondering what's happened to me."

Stewart was feeling good-humoured, so he said on the spur of the moment, "Come along then, Susy, I'll see you safely there."

"You needn't bother, really, I'll be all right," but at the same time, lest he should take her words too seriously, she linked her arm in his and they set off.

"You know," Susy said when they were nicely embarked on the journey, "what you said just now about my waiting for my young man ? Why, you are a silly, I've got no one regular like. What made you think I had ?"

Of course it might have been Stewart's imagination, but he thought he felt a slight pressure on his arm. "Blessed if I know," he returned lightly. "I thought you young ladies at the 'Pig and Whistle' had any number of beaux ?"

"The other girls may have, but I like to keep to myself. You can't afford to be too friendly with the customers in a trade like ours. They're not all like you, Mr. Stewart. Why, you'd be surprised if I told you of some of the things that went on even in a respectable house like the 'Pig and Whistle'."

"I'm sure I should," Stewart said gravely.

"Some folks think that because a girl serves behind a bar that she can't be particular, and they're always trying to take liberties. Of course, mind you, if a young man happened to be serious it might be a different matter ; we girls are only human."

Stewart didn't know quite what he was expected to say so he kept silent.

"Take those captains that you come in to see, old as they are you'd be surprised at the way they carry on if a girl gives 'em half a chance. I do feel sorry for them at times, all alone in a strange port. But my ! look how many girls they've got into trouble."

"That's right, Susy, don't you pay any attention to what sailors say to you. After all, not seeing a woman for months on end makes 'em inclined to be a bit forward when they see a pretty girl around."

"Ooh ! Do you really think I'm pretty ?"

"Sure I do, the prettiest girl in the 'Shipping Mile'," said Stewart, full of good humour.

"Go on with you ; you're getting as bad as all the rest," and again Stewart could have sworn that he felt a slight pressure on his arm. "But I really am safe with you, aren't I, Mr. Stewart ?"

"Don't try me too far," he joked, and Susy laughed.

By that time they were taking the short cut that leads from Chapel Walk to Water Street, and Stewart, a little bit bored, was beginning to regret his earlier generous impulse.

"This is where you live, isn't it ?" asked Susy suddenly.

"Why yes, how did you know?"

"There's not much us girls don't know about our customers."

She was so plainly curious to see in what sort of place he lived that a few moments later he found he had agreed to let her have a peep inside.

At the top of the steps leading down to the basement she stopped. "You don't think I'm fast, Mr. Stewart?" she asked doubtfully.

He looked at her in the dark for a minute and then said slowly, "No, I don't think I would call you fast," and, somewhat reassured, Susy tripped down the flight of stairs and Stewart, as quietly as he could, opened the door. He earnestly hoped Silas was out.

"Ooh! It isn't half dark," she said, as she peered down the passage and Stewart struck a light. The flickering rays pierced the gloom and made the surroundings look more dismal. Susy gathered her skirts closely around her and fearfully asked if there were any mice about. A few steps down the passage they came to the living-room, and as Stewart turned to light the gas, the girl moved quickly over to the fire burning in the grate. The gaslight released her curiosity and critically she looked around.

"Why," she said, as though surprised, "it's quite cosy," and she went round the room trying out the chairs and looking inquisitively at the pictures Silas had tacked up on the wall. "Ships!" she said disgustedly, and turned towards the few books that lay forlornly on a shelf. He didn't expect that she would find much to interest her there, and he was surprised when she picked up a copy of *Adam Bede* and asked if she might borrow it. It appeared that she had overheard someone in the saloon bar saying it was a book he wouldn't allow his daughter to read and naturally Susy's interest had been stimulated.

Stewart, who valued his few books, tried to discourage her by saying it was written by a woman, anyway, but this fact intrigued Susy the more for, as she said, there must be something in it else the writer wouldn't have given herself a man's name. In the face of such reasoning Stewart could find no other excuse likely to put her off, and so he resigned himself to its loss.

It soon became obvious that all thoughts of going to her mother's had gone from Susy's head, and when, a few minutes later, she took off her hat and coat and settled down in a chair before the fire, he realized that Susy had other plans. With but little encouragement from him she began to talk about herself; about her childhood spent in the hovels off Scotland Road. It wasn't a nice story, but then, no story is which deals with poverty and destitution. She had never seen her father, she rather vaguely thought he had been drowned at sea but her mother never talked about him and to her daughter's enquiries had returned some vague noncommittal answer. Her mother was the daughter of a farmer up in Cumberland who, like a number of others, had given up farming in order to share in the high industrial wages that lured people into the towns from the country. Town life, with its slums and bad living conditions, hadn't suited him and he had died shortly after coming to Liverpool. Susy's mother had gone into service and while there she had married a sailor. He had gone away to sea again and her mother had never heard of him since. When Susy was born she had lost her position, and after that her mother had managed to eke out a precarious living for them both by cleaning in the city offices.

There was little money to spare, just sufficient, in fact, to pay the rent of a cellar and buy a few pounds of potatoes each week. In spite of these hardships Susy had been a sturdy child, thriving in the dark, sunless alleys. With scores of other children she spent most of that childhood in roaming the streets, often fighting with scavenger dogs for food. She was very proud of the fact that as far as she could remember she had never had a day's illness. Before she was ten she knew most of the things of life that were worth knowing. She knew all about men, for when she was barely in her teens she had had adventures which would have terrified anybody else but Susy. She took to standing outside taverns which sailors frequented in the hopes of picking up a copper or two, for already she had found that sailors were always generous. One red letter day a tipsy sailor was standing in the street throwing handfuls of shillings up in the air, and giving a wild cheer every time he did it. Hordes of children scrambled and fought at his feet like a lot of hens picking up corn. Susy was lucky and got one of the shillings, and she might have got more if a couple of dockside touts hadn't lugged the sailor back into the public.

When she was eleven she got taken up with the Band of Friends and lured on by specious promises had entered a charity school miles away in the country. That had been worse than living in Liverpool. They taught her to read and write and trained her up to be a domestic servant, but Susy had different ideas. When she was fourteen she was placed in a situation, but by that time her mind was made up, she was going to be rich, and the slavery of domestic service only confirmed her in this decision. The height of her ambition was to own a public-house in the Dock Road. She stayed on in domestic service until she was eighteen and had saved enough money to bring her back to Liverpool. She found her poor old mother still working away but by that time she had gone over to gin to comfort her over the vicissitudes of life in Liverpool. Her daughter's return had opened a rosy future in the old woman's eyes for here was a strong healthy young woman, fit to keep a body in her old age. With maudlin tears she sought to propitiate her daughter for her apparent neglect during the intervening years, and Susy, disgusted though she was, decided that she had a duty towards her own mother and had accordingly tried to do her best by working and living in the only place she knew as home.

Pitt Street, however, was no place for a girl of her looks and she was for ever being pestered by men, so that when her drunken old mother said that she was a fool for being so cool with them, Susy decided that it really was time she lived somewhere else. The opportunity came when she heard that the landlord of the 'Pig and Whistle' was on the look-out for superior girls.

Well, all that was getting on for two years ago now, and here she was approaching twenty and the least bit dissatisfied. The 'Pig and Whistle' was all right to start off with, but now she thought it was time to be getting on a bit faster. In spite of regular contributions to her old mother she had managed to put a little money by and was now keeping her eyes open for somewhere to start on her own.

Stewart listened to her story with growing interest. In their outlook on life they had much that was similar, but of course it would never do. He shook his head thoughtfully. Such ideas and ambitions in a young woman were all wrong. He argued that Susy's best plan would be to find herself a good steady husband and leave the getting rich to him. She was young and pretty, he advised her solemnly, and she could easily find herself a husband.

Susy laughed at his heavy, fatherly attempts at advice and embarrassed him considerably when she suddenly said, "Well, what about you, would you marry me?"

The young man looked at her reproachfully and he stammered and stuttered away, trying to say without offending her that he was in no position to marry and, anyway, he wasn't the marrying type. She cut his laboured explanations short by saying abruptly that she wouldn't marry him under any circumstances. Stewart, contrarily, did not like the manner in which she said this and, piqued, asked why not. "Oh! you're too stuffy," she replied impetuously, and refused to discuss it further.

"Look," she cried suddenly, "there's a mandolin. Can you play?" And excitedly she jumped up, seized hold of the instrument and pushed it into his unwilling hands. "Go on, play something," she urged, and she looked so animated that Stewart forgot his pique and began to strum a tune.

"Why, that's 'Champagne Charley'!" and she clapped her hands together gleefully. "Start all over again and I'll sing it."

This pretty duet was hardly under way when there was a noise in the distance of doors slamming and a voice raised in protest. The two, however, were so taken up with their own efforts that they failed to notice the ulterior disturbance. Then the door flew open and old Silas, rocking slightly, stood in the entrance looking at them sternly.

"What's all this?" he demanded truculently. "We ain't licensed for music and singing." He fixed his beady eyes indignantly upon Susy.

"Now you, young woman. What are you a doing of 'ere? This 'ere's a respectable ship-chandler's house."

Susy looked indignantly at Stewart.

"Be quiet, Silas," he said, "and get off to bed; you're drunk!"

It seemed as though an explosion might follow. Drunk, him, Silas Martin, the hardest case of them all. Never was such an insult uttered. For a minute the old sailor lost his breath, but when he recovered it he let them have it good and strong.

Stewart realized that with Silas in that condition it was no use arguing, so, irritably, he told Susy to put on her hat and coat and he'd take her back to the 'Pig and Whistle'.

"I should think so, too," boomed Silas. "Trying to turn the place into a bawdy 'ouse, that's what you are. Take 'er back, skipper and drop 'er in the river on your way."

This was altogether too much for Susy, and if Stewart hadn't forcibly bundled her through the door there was no knowing what she might have done, for she had completely lost those assiduously acquired manners of a lady, and had fallen back on the language she knew before the Band of Friends took her in hand.

The sharp night air cooled her anger a little, but she was in no frame of mind to accept Stewart's efforts at pacification. She accused him of not being man enough to prevent a lady, a guest in his own house, from being insulted by his servants, and, she added scornfully, "A one-legged sailor at that!"

When Stewart got back to Chapel Walk again he found Silas sitting in the one rocking-chair, drawn up to the fire. Tears of self-pity were coursing down the old man's weather-beaten cheeks. "To think I sh'd 'a sunk to this," he was muttering; "me, Silas Martin, bosun of the finest ships that ever put to sea, caretaker of a gay 'ouse."

"Silas, you idiot, pack your bag and get out."

"You're too late, skipper; I've signed off a'ready. I'm sort of particular in what ships I serves in," and with as much dignity as he could muster, he got up from the chair and stumped away with slow, hobbling, none-too-steady steps.

The following morning Stewart awoke with a start. Silas was standing by his bed; in his hand he held a mug of strong, black tea. "See, skipper," he said, "I've made you an extra drop o' special. I thought as 'ow you'd be needing it after the state you was in last night!"

"What the dickens . . ." began Stewart hazily, and then broke off as the events of the night before came crowding back. He glared angrily at the old seaman, "I thought I told you to clear out?"

"Now, skipper, don't let a little thing like last night upset you. 'Ere, take a cup o' this. Ah! that's better. I only interfered for your own good. I don't like to see you getting mixed up with dockside trollops. I reckon

I've got my duty to do and I was never a one for skulking down below when all 'ands is wanted on deck. You and me are shipmates and I don't intend letting anyone take advantage o' you like it was plain that young woman had a mind to. I knows you ain't been round the 'orn, skipper, but never you mind, you and me are shipmates and Silas Martin will see you comes to no 'arm.''

Stewart gave him a resigned look and got out of bed. It was plain to be seen that he had better accustom himself to the fact that Silas was an integral part of this ship-chandlery business.

St Nicholas' Church — the sailor's church

CHAPTER 3

GOING TO CHURCH

THE week-end habit was something that Liverpool took a long time in getting used to. But there was no doubt about it, the passing of the Factory Act in 1850 and the legal enforcement of Saturday half-holiday had established itself as a national institution, so that even the pressing claims of money-making had to take a rest between Saturday noon and early Monday morning. Consequently, the Sabbath descended heavily on the port of Liverpool, and an uneasy, gloomy quiet prevailed throughout the length of the docks. No ships sailed on Sunday and because of this, few ships took stores aboard on Saturday. The climax to each week of activity, as far as Stewart was concerned, arose on Thursdays and Fridays, when there was a last-minute rush to get the ships that were nearly ready away to sea before the week-end. It was bad business to leave ships in harbour over the week-end; just eating their heads off, so to speak, and doing nothing for their keep. At sea now, Saturdays and Sundays were like any other day of the week; once out of port ships had to keep going. Whilst it was all very well for shipowners to smile with satisfaction when their ships duly arrived, they were immediately concerned with doing everything possible to get them discharged and turned round and out to sea again.

Stewart probably resented this break in the week's activity as much as any shipowner with ships in the neighbouring docks to twit his conscience. The lucky deal he had pulled off over the *Bangalore's* insurance had done nothing to make him ease his efforts in getting business. If it were possible it but served to inspire him to further efforts, for although he was a firm believer in 'luck' he realized, in spite of what he had said to Captain Brady, that what was needed was hard work.

But there it was, on Saturdays and Sundays there was nothing he could do about it. Restlessly, over the week-end, he wandered about like a ship without a rudder. First in the courtyard and then in and out of the outhouses, then back again into the basement. His restless spirit urged him on. backwards and forwards, accomplishing little of purpose or of value. His movements, one Sunday, gradually intruded themselves on the attention of old Joe Eastwood, standing motionless as a sphinx at his window on the floor above.

The Eastwood brothers led very carefully regulated lives. At certain times, with clock-like regularity, they did certain things. Their lives were well ordered. In their early days they had scores of little coasting schooners to keep them busy, but they had not so many left now, and in their loneliness the two brothers spent a great deal of their time playing dominoes. If they weren't playing dominoes, it seemed to Stewart that they were standing at the window gazing at all the shipping on the river.

On Sundays, Fred stayed in bed all morning, though Joe, that tormented soul, got up as usual, but to mark the difference in the day he transferred his idle contemplation of the river as viewed from the front window, to the town as sighted from the back room. One hand in his pocket and the other for ever fiddling with his massive gold watch-chain, he stood there regularly every Sunday morning. No one could say if he saw anything or was just wrapped up in some vision of the past, as is the way of old men. On Sunday mornings even the town wore a somnambulant air and whatever activity there was to be seen was too far away to break in upon the serene regard of the old shipowner.

Stewart, however, that particular Sunday morning, was too near to avoid the old man's gaze and where for countless Sundays there had been undeviating tranquillity, there was now this figure of a young man, so symbolic of the go-ahead, unreliable times, aimlessly wandering to and fro in the yard below. At length it was more than the old man could stand; testily he flung open his window. "Mr. Stewart," he called in his high-pitched wavering voice, "don't you know that today is the sabbath? In these civilized parts no one works on the Lord's day. Take a rest, young man; keep your labours for the week-day. If you must do something then go across to St. Nicholas' church there and thank the Lord for His bounty." Stewart looked up in astonishment, but before he could reply old Joe had banged down his window and stumped off to another part of the house, his day ruined.

However, his purpose was achieved, for the young man, abashed, retired quietly to the obscurity of his basement and with righteous indignation on his part now noted that Silas was engaged on his normal Sunday morning routine. "Silas," he called out, "don't you know today is the sabbath, the day of rest?"

"That I do," returned the old sailor cheerfully; "can't you see, its dhoby day with me. I'm washing the sins out of my clothes. By the time I've finished they'll be whiter than any shipowner's soul. But what's come over you, skipper?" he asked anxiously. "I've never heard you worry about days of rest before? Mind you, I ain't saying it's not aforetime. You know what the Act says, 'On Sundays and Bank Holidays the 'ands shall engage in sanitary duties only.' "

" 'Or other duties which the master thinks necessary for the preservation of the ship,' " quickly supplemented Stewart.

"Aye! you're right there," growled Silas uneasily, "and I've allus thought it remarkable 'ow much preserving a ship needs on a Sunday. What with sluicing down, trimming lamps and the like, a sailor's lucky if he gets ten minutes to 'isself in the forenoon watch."

"I've been thinking things over, Silas. This work you're doing is wrong. In fact, we must both reform our ways. We must observe the sabbath, for it's the custom of the port. Our venerable landlord has just informed me that it is our bounden duty to go to church.''

"Beggin' your pardon, sir, church did you say? Gosh, skipper, you've taken me all aback. Now why in the name of Davy Jones should you get on about that?'' The old man stopped his rubbing and looked up apprehensively.

"Yes,'' said Stewart gravely, "church. It's our duty to go, and where duty is concerned the firm of James Stewart, ship-chandler, must not lag behind. A few steps away is the sailors' church of St. Nicholas and if we're to earn our bread by the labour of those who go down to the sea in ships then it's our duty to go and pray for their survival. I see it all now.''

Silas looked at the young man gloomily, and as the full implications of it all became apparent to him his face clouded over. After several attempts to speak, he finally said: "I tell you, skipper, I don't like it. No good ever came out of monkeying with such things. Them there sky-pilots as runs the 'ome drove me crazy a couple of voyages ago with their talk of salvation awaiting me inside their churches. Not me, though; I wasn't 'aving any. I've seen a fellow or two as made a 'abit of church-going and it taught me to give 'em a wide berth. No, skipper, I likes this craft; she suits me fine, but if it means I've got to go inside a church and bow and scrape along with a lot of other fellows in gaff tops'l 'ats then I'm asking to be paid off.''

Stewart looked at him sorrowfully. "You place me in an awkward position, Silas. You're too good a servant for the firm to lose and yet——''

The old man eyed him suspiciously and then somewhat reassured went on: "That doesn't mean to say I ain't a God-fearing man, skipper; it's just that I can't abide parsons. Say what you like, but they're no good for an honest sailorman. Look at my old shipmate, Sam Jenkins. Fifteen years we sailed together and not even a wench could part us. 'E was a good shipmate, was Sam . . . until 'e got took religious. And now look at 'im, a face as long as a fiddle. 'The devil's got ye,' 'e sez to me the other day outside the shipping office; 'come along and be saved.' 'But, Sam,' I sez, 'I ain't done no wrong.' 'That's what you think,' sez 'e, 'repent afore you go before your Maker.' I slipped me painter then, skipper, and tacked away, but 'e shouts after me, 'The writing's on the wall, Silas Martin, thou art weighed in the balance and found wanting.' But Lord, skipper, I've never 'armed a fly. A bit of fun ashore, a glass or two wi' old shipmates; there ain't no wrong in that as far as I can see. If there be, then I reckon I'm too old a sinner to change now.''

"Well,'' said Stewart with a heavy sigh, "if you won't go, Silas, then I must. I'm young enough to keep an open mind about it, and I'll have done my duty, and even in business you can't expect a greater profession of faith than that."

"That's right," said Silas eagerly. "You go and I'll look out for this place while you're away. There's the bell a ringing now."

St. Nicholas' was a handsome stately church, standing almost on the banks of the river. Its steeple towered up into the sky in conformity with the masts of the ships to whose service it was dedicated. The weather-vane at the top of the steeple was a fine model of a full-rigged ship ; it was positioned so that it had a perpetual following wind.

In those mid-Victorian days church-going was the great outward sign of respectability, and Sunday after Sunday St. Nicholas drew its full quota from the *élite* suburbs of Liverpool. Those who came were above the blandishments of chapel and rival forms of worship, for their main purpose in coming to St. Nicholas' was to see and to be seen. Carriages with finely attired ladies and prosperous-looking be-whiskered gentlemen were already beginning to arrive, and as the hour of the service approached the carriages followed one another in a constant procession.

Stewart, feeling out of place amidst all that display of wealth and finery, walked hesitantly across the flagged churchyard and lingered to watch the people enter. The ladies in their flowered crinolines and nest bonnets (no woman would dream of wearing a hat to church) made a pretty picture as they chattered and fluttered forward. But once inside the sombre porch the commotion ceased abruptly, and greetings, where still to be exchanged, were uttered in holy whispers or merely by a reverential inclination of the head.

The sidesman gave Stewart a swift, perfunctory glance and then frigidly conducted him to a pew at the back of the church. This pew differed from the others in that it had no doors, no footstools, and no carpet. There were a bare half-dozen pews of similar design, all clustered together like an isolation ward in a hospital. It was painfully clear that St. Nicholas' had little intention of encouraging those who did not subscribe to the respectability of a private pew. Feeling rather like a criminal he glanced at his immediate neighbours. They were a handful of poor, shabbily clad women. By way of contrast in the enclosed pews sat richly dressed ladies, casually, but none the less critically, eyeing each other's dresses, and close beside them their escorts lounged elegantly at ease.

The last hurried rush of late-comers was ended, and the service began with all the pomp and ceremony which St. Nicholas' affected. The morning sunlight slanted through the stained-glass windows, throwing slowly shifting beams of light across the chancel. The monotonous chant of the priest rose and fell in the theatrical cadence so carefully studied by the high churchmen of that time. To Stewart, accustomed to the dour severity of his Presbyterian childhood, it rang artificial and unreal. How far removed, he thought, from the simple austerity of the sea and ships and sailormen. Nowhere, as he took stock around him, could he see anyone even remotely resembling a sailor. True, many of those resplendent individuals lolling negligently in their pews were probably shipowners or shipbuilders ; indeed, he knew they were for he recognized some he had seen regularly pacing the 'Flags', but where were the seamen themselves ? It seemed as if Silas had been right when he hinted that the only connection between the church and the profession it sought to laud was the model of the ship on its steeple and the occasional lip service of a parson mumming through some reference to seafarers in the liturgy.

Taking his cue from his neighbours, he stood, knelt or sat as the occasion demanded. His prayer-book remained unopened ; even if he had been so minded he could never have found in time that part of the book which gave the words to the indistinguishable utterings of the priest and the vociferous choir, so he let his book lie idly on the shelf in front of him. Covertly, he watched the exaggerated devotions of the clergy and the imitative response of the congregation, and regretted ever having come.

After a time his thoughts began to wander and barrels of salt port, sacks of flour and various ships commenced to occupy his mind as he thought of the business he had to do on the following day. Orders were not coming in as fast as he would have liked, but, he thought philosophically, Rome was not built in a day, and in the long run it might pay to prosper slowly but steadily. Then there was that thousand pounds lying to his credit in the bank. He was almost afraid to think too much about it in case it should disappear so fortuitously as it had arrived. What was he going to do with it ? Should he put it into the ships' store business so that he could take on larger premises and employ runners of his own ? It was the obvious thing to do, and yet he had seen how hard it was to get business, and if it was difficult for him how much more so would it be for runners lacking his incentive ?

Suddenly his train of thoughts was interrupted by the sight of a small gloved hand, holding out towards him an opened prayer-book. For a moment he was nonplussed, and then he became aware of a delightful vision, smiling encouragement, leaning over from an adjacent pew. He took a deep breath, everything was forgotten, the church, the barrels of salt pork, the thousand pounds—everything but the entrancing creature so near to him. Mechanically he took hold of the prayer-book and then the directness of his gaze and the open admiration which he made no effort to conceal, proved disconcerting, even to a young woman who had so outraged decorum and courted scandal by her impulsive gesture, and she sought calmness and anonymity again in a demure concentration on the service.

At length Stewart realized his staring must be insufferable and with an effort he turned his eyes towards his newly acquired prayer-book. But his eyes were unseeing. His mind was filled with the picture of a fashionably dressed young woman, almost at his elbow. Surreptitiously he took another glance. More calmly now, he saw a tall slim girl about nineteen years of age with copper-coloured hair peeping out in gay curls beneath the bonnet which surmounted the delicate profile of her face. Even he, no connoisseur of womanly beauty, could see that she was remarkably beautiful. Never in his whole life had he seen anything so charming. It was not the classic features and the fine clothes so much as the air of calm dignity and assurance which attracted him.

The renewed intentness of his gaze did nothing to disturb her composure, and very unconcerned and correct now, she continued to follow the service, apparently unconscious of Stewart's existence. His early stupefaction was beginning to wear off and was slowly replaced with a curiosity, the strength of which astonished him. He speculated on her companion who, with visible signs of marked disapproval, had been witness to the little incident. By sharp contrast she was stout as the other was slim. Her voluminous black garments gave her the appearance of a fat, broody hen. With every movement she crinkled and rustled like some creaking gate, and her stiff unbending body reflected its distrust of the restricting bonds of her clothes in the unhappy, anxious expression of her face. He dismissed her as some sort of servant and returned to the delightful contemplation of her charge. Stewart wondered who she was and where she lived. Expectantly he turned to the flyleaf of her prayer-book and there read *Miss Elizabeth Mary Scripps*, written in a firm, bold, feminine hand. It was something, he thought, to know her name—he would never forget it.

As the psalm ended, he handed back the book; she acknowledged it smilingly, and for a brief second their glances met. He had time to notice a hesitant sparkle in her eyes before she turned away. Thereafter Stewart continued the rest of the service in a manner calculated to draw attention to his ignorance of the ritual, but all in vain, for not another glance did he get from Miss Elizabeth Mary Scripps. As he looked towards her and saw the tendrils of copper curls, shrouding a shell-like ear, and the soft rose-like bloom of her cheeks melting away into creamy whiteness, his brain gathered fire and his heart beat so loudly that he was sure others must hear. No one did apparently, for apart from the suspicious, uneasy looks of her stout companion, it seemed that the remainder of the congregation was unaware of the auspicious thing that had happened to Stewart.

Long after the service was over and he was back once more in Chapel Walk, his thoughts were exclusively centred on the young woman. He thought uneasily of that long homeward voyage from India and how he had promised himself that women should play no part in the life he had planned for himself. With the easy optimism of youth he had laid his plans, thinking that he could subjugate the passions of the body to the order of the mind. It seemed now that he had under-estimated the one or been over-confident of the other, for here he was, almost at the very outset of his career, with his thoughts dominated completely by a mere chit of a girl. The more he tried to turn his thoughts away from her the more insistent did his memory of her become. Swift visions of her delicate hands, her shapely feet (for he had been first in the churchyard to see her trip lightly away), or the way her bonnet was tied under her chin would creep upon him insidiously, at all manner of times and in a most disconcerting way. From that day onwards he became one of St. Nicholas' most devoted attendants.

No sooner had he returned from the docks on the following day, tired and discouraged through lack of orders, than in strolled Mr. Eastwood. "I see you took my advice on Sunday," he said affably.

"You mean about going to St. Nicholas', sir?"

"Aye, I didn't think church-going would be one of your habits."

"No, it has not been," said Stewart diffidently, "but I think I'll attend regularly in future."

The old shipowner looked surprised. "That's a quick conversion!" he said. "You know, if I'd thought it was going to take a hold of you like that I might have suggested a better place."

"I don't think you could have done that, sir. St. Nicholas' suits me down to the ground."

Mr. Eastwood appeared to pay no attention to that remark and he said: "Now if I were a young man setting up in business, I think I'd have gone along to Renshaw Street and listened to that great preacher John Hamilton Thom."

"But he's a Unitarian," said Stewart, aghast.

"What of it?" returned the other calmly. "His religion is as good as the next, and you only need to look at his congregation to see that. Some of the best and richest families in Liverpool."

"Unitarians?"

"Aye, the richest Liverpool merchants are mostly Unitarians; fine upstanding families like the Rathbones, Tates, Gaskells, Jevons, Mellys and scores of others. I think they're realists in religion like they are in commerce. I've seen hundred pound notes in the collection plate up there. You'd do more for your business if you made a habit of going to Renshaw Street chapel than ever you will by going to St. Nicholas'."

"Surely more people go to St. Nicholas'?"

"Perhaps so, but the size of a congregation means nothing, it's the quality of the individual in it that counts."

The old man went on to talk more generally of religion, and from that he wandered off on to memories of Liverpool's commerce, and after a while Stewart began to realize that Mr. Eastwood was a friendly old man, genuinely interested in the progress of his ship-chandlery business. The young man warmed towards him, and almost before he was aware of it he found himself expounding upon his business hopes and ambitions.

Mr. Eastwood listened attentively and then, when Stewart had got to the end, he said with a twinkle in his eye, "I heard on the 'Flags' last Friday that you'd turned speculator as well as ship-chandler?"

Stewart looked at him doubtfully and thought it wiser to say nothing. "Yes," the old shipowner went on, "I heard you had milked Harrison the underwriter to the tune of a thousand pounds."

The young man laughed rather self-consciously. "Of course, it was sheer luck, you know, sir. I can't claim much credit for that. Harrison practically forced the business on me. I did all I could to tell him the ship was safe without betraying another's confidence."

"I'm not blaming you," interposed the shipowner, "it's each man for himself these days, and from all accounts Harrison got his deserts. I'm surprised, though, that you should stick to this sort of business," and he inclined his head towards the ship-chandlery in the other room. "Selling goods to ships that nobody else will buy is a poor way of making a living. There's nothing grand in making a fortune out of sailors' bellies. No, I'd have thought a young man with your imagination would have had higher aspirations than that."

"Oh, I don't know, sir," replied Stewart defensively, "it's a service."

"Umph!" growled the other. "And a mighty poor one judging by the company it attracts. Have you never thought of going in for merchandise, or even shipowning?"

"That's a bit too ambitious even for me, sir."

"There's more of the thrill and adventure of life in that. Besides, you'd be doing some good in the world, opening up commerce, carrying the necessities of life from the producer to the consumer. That's the sort of business you should be engaged in, my boy. There's romance in that, and what is more, fortune, if you've got the vision and the right sort of enterprise."

"I've never really thought about it like that," admitted Stewart, wondering. "I started out ship's husbanding because it seemed the easiest thing to do without much capital."

"Yes," said Mr. Eastwood, looking sadly into the fire, "I'm afraid that is what decides so many of us . . . the easiest way of doing. Fred and I as well; and now all we're good for is looking back on the past and regretting the opportunities we didn't take. Where we made our biggest mistake was in hanging on to our little coasting schooners when the steamers came. But twenty years ago we were doing very nicely so why should we change? Well, here we are, sitting in a fusty out-of-the-way office, seeing all we've built knocked down by folks who had more imagination and courage."

"Shipowning requires capital, and far more than I've got," said Stewart, stirring to the idea.

"You've got a thousand pounds, haven't you?"

"Yes, but——"

"There's your opportunity," interrupted Mr. Eastwood, and then added cuttingly, "unless you prefer to go on shipping rank meat, and short weight at that, to foreign-going vessels!"

"I wouldn't get much of a ship for a thousand pounds," argued Stewart, "and even if I did there's always the running expenses on top of that to be considered."

"You're only putting obstacles in your own path," said the ship-owner scathingly. "If everyone approached business in that frame of mind there'd be no trading anywhere. A young man's got no right to think that way, it's only when you get old, like Fred and myself, that you can afford to let discretion govern your actions. If you were willing to take on an insurance risk of £80,000 with no capital at all, I should have thought the matter of running expenses would have been child's play to a man with your imagination."

"That was different, sir. I knew the *Bangalore* was going to turn up and that her cargo was intact."

"No, you didn't, my boy. All you knew was that she was safe in harbour some thousands of miles away and several months ago."

Stewart couldn't help thinking that if Harrison had put it like that he would never have had the courage to take him up on the offer.

"It was still a great risk her ever getting to Liverpool," went on Mr. Eastwood earnestly, "and, don't you see, all business is a risk, and if you want to get on you must seek and take risks. It's the way we established our trading supremacy. There's an opportunity offering now that you will never see again. The whole world is waking up to commerce, and by that I don't mean the plundering of uncivilized countries for the benefit of a few rich people, but a vast, mutually beneficial exchange of commodities. If you want an indication of the way trade is developing, look at the export figures quoted in this morning's *Shipping Albion*. In the last ten years they've more than doubled themselves. There's your opportunity, young man. Ships! shipping ventures! They'll give you more satisfaction than skimping sailors' rations. There! I've talked too much, but all the same, you think over what I've said," and with that he got up and shambled off to his dominoes.

He had succeeded in firing Stewart's imagination. There was no doubt about it, Mr. Eastwood was right, shipowning was the thing. The young man scratched his head ruefully; how was he going to get sufficient capital to start? It meant getting hold of someone to go into partnership; but the only possible people he knew were shipmasters. There was Tom Cairns of the *Magento*. Tom must be worth a mint of money judging by his prodigality on shore, but on the other hand, good shipmaster though he was reputed to be, he was too fond of the bottle to make a comfortable business partner. There was Elijah Thompson, who a short while back had arrived with a consignment of cotton from the Southern States. Captain Thompson must have made a fortune on that one trip alone, but there again he would hardly be suitable, for it was common knowledge that he was an irascible old chap. Pleasant enough to do an hour's business with, but far too settled in his ways to think of working with a man not half his age. What about Captain Brady of the *Bellerophon*? He knew him better than any of the others, and in spite of their little difference of opinion of the other night, he was the most likely of them all.

The more Stewart thought about it the stronger grew his belief that the two of them together would form an ideal partnership. He felt that with Brady on the poop and a smart young fellow like himself looking out for the shore-end of the business, things just couldn't go wrong. He began to wonder how he might approach Captain Brady. The *Bellerophon* was a long way from being the smartest vessel in Liverpool, but she was a sound ship and a secure command, and old Brady might not be inclined to sacrifice that job for a venturesome, will-o'-th'-wisp scheme proposed by a young, inexperienced man. It would be no use either trying to interest him in the scheme by talk of rich profits ready for the taking, for on his own admission he wasn't very interested in money for money's sake. There was only one way in which to capture his interest, and that was by putting before him the prospect of becoming master of his own vessel. That was the talk. Brady would fall for that. All these years at sea, and master in name only. . . .

Stewart sat on in the dark, absorbed in the future, forgetful of the present, while the night drew on and the flickering fire cast quaint, giant shapes on the wall at his back.

Water Street

CHAPTER 4

A NIGHT ON THE TOWN

"How's things?" said Stewart pertly, walking into the 'Pig and Whistle' for the first time for nearly a week.

"Don't you dare to speak to me," said Susy with a haughty toss of her head. "I wonder you've nerve to show your face in here after the way you insulted me the other night."

"Oh, come, Susy, let bygones be bygones. See, I've brought you a present," and he held up an Indian shawl a seaman had just given him for bringing his baggage ashore.

Susy clapped her hands in excitement. "Why, Mr. Stewart, that's too kind of you. You shouldn't have done it. I wasn't really angry with you, it was just that one-legged drunken creature of yours, I wonder you put up with him."

"Well, Susy, you know how it is; he's only got one leg and I feel sorry for him. Not, mind you, that he had any right to speak to a respectable girl like you the way he did; but as you say, I'm too easy-going with him and I came to apologize."

"Now, Mr. Stewart, that's real nice of you, but you needn't have gone and bought me a present," and she looked at him archly and then continued: "I hope you don't think I'm a girl to be bought with such things?"

"Good heavens, no!" laughed Stewart carelessly. "I've no designs on you, Susy; I leave that to the other customers."

"Oh! you do, do you?" exclaimed Susy wrathfully. "Then let me tell you that I'm a good girl, I am, and there's nobody here can say I'm not," and she glanced round challengingly at the deserted bar.

"There, there," said Stewart soothingly, "the customers are all agreed, and I wouldn't for the life of me suggest anything else. I only want to declare that my intentions are strictly honourable."

"Oh! Mr. Stewart," whispered Susy coyly, leaning towards him, "you put me all of a flutter. That's the second offer you've made me almost within a week. One of these days you'll wear me down and I'll say yes!"

"Behave yourself, Susy," said Stewart uneasily, "or I'll tell the landlord where you really were the night you went off to your mother's!"

"You wouldn't dare," said Susy confidently.

"Wouldn't I just? Another chirp out of you and your reputation's ruined."

Susy smiled, and when she did that Stewart had to admit that she was good to look at.

"You know there's no one but you, Mr. Stewart," she said, her eyes twinkling.

"Really?" fenced Stewart, not knowing whether she was serious or not.

"Really!" said Susy, bending still further forward towards him, and her face came so close to his that the embarrassed young man stepped back a pace.

"Look," she went on, "I've got another evening off soon. How would you like to take me to the Amphitheatre?"

"But——" protested Stewart mildly.

"No buts, please," she interrupted, "you can hardly expect me to come round to Chapel Walk again after what happened last time."

"I wasn't thinking of asking you to come there," expostulated Stewart.

"Well, then, I can't accept your presents without being nice to you in return, can I now? And you're too shy to ask me out, aren't you?"

"All right, Susy, you win," laughed Stewart; "but don't make this into a regular habit."

She looked at him, annoyed, but said sweetly, "You do flatter a poor girl so."

All the same, Stewart reflected as he came out, it was good to know they were friends again. She'd done him many a good turn in the past and it might not be a bad plan to show his appreciation by taking her out.

Walking down the street he couldn't help wishing he were on equally good terms with Miss Scripps. That was the girl for him, but how was he ever going to make her acquaintance? How was he to know that she was even the slightest bit interested in him? He caught a glimpse of his reflection in a shop window, so he stopped to see what manner of a man he was, anyway. The sight was far from encouraging. It was the first time in years that he had ever examined his appearance at all closely, and it gave him a shock. Was that shabby, unkempt figure really his own? He looked around to see if someone else stood at his elbow. No, it was himself alone, and he looked at his reflection with some distaste. He really must smarten up, get some better clothes and a hair-cut. Right before him was a barber's shop, so in he went to put into effect the first of these good resolutions.

Twenty minutes later he came out carrying a small bottle of hair-dressing. The little barber had devoted eighteen of those twenty minutes to a dissertation on the diseases and infections of the scalp and the need for the frequent application of a tonic; and in the frame of mind which Stewart was in he found a ready listener.

By the time he reached home his interest in his appearance had vanished and he was wrapped once more in his new, fascinating vision of becoming a shipowner. He sat down in the arm-chair, picked up the

Shipping Albion and read Netlocks' notices. Iron vessels, wooden vessels, ships, brigs, screw steamers, paddle steamers, craft of all kind were advertised for sale by auction. There were scantlings and specifications for the knowledgeable reader, and trades and reputations for those others who might be interested. Judging by the names of the ships on offer, he thought the secondhand market was not very brisk. It was the time to buy all right.

It seemed that for £2000 you could get any shape of vessel ranging from a soft wood clipper built in the '40's to a spanking new, applebowed, coasting schooner straight off the stocks. Having regard to the limited capital he and his partner (whoever that might be) could put up, there was only one kind of vessel to start shipowning with and that was a nice little brig, say about ninety feet long and drawing ten feet of water and capable of lifting 200 tons of cargo. Such a vessel would experience no delays in finding shipments or in waiting for water to cross a bar or dock sill. She'd be fast enough and yet require only a small crew to man her. He'd seen several such vessels like that down in Salthouse Dock, but none, so far as he knew, were likely to be up for sale

With his mind busy on these details he scanned the list of ships that Netlocks advertised as shortly coming up for auction. There appeared to be any number of brigs for sale, but none were of the handy size he had in mind. Perhaps he had better slip round and see Netlocks themselves, they'd be better able to advise him of what was likely to come along, and so he slipped on his hat and went round to that office in the Tower Building.

It seemed as though the fates were with him, for on his return Silas told him that Captain Brady had just been in and left his sea-stock order.

"Good," said Stewart, rubbing his hands; the captain was not the sort of man to let a silly argument come between friends.

"Oh, yes," said Silas, wrinkling up his brow in an effort to recapture his memory, "and 'e 'ad a Yankee skipper with 'im; said 'e was the master of that there blockade-runner which docked on this morning's tide."

"That's right, I saw her come in."

"And Captain Brady sez 'e 'opes to see you in the 'Pig and Whistle' and you'd better not forget."

"What do you mean?" began Stewart haughtily—Silas was getting altogether too impertinent.

"Captain Brady, skipper, not me, sez as 'ow you'd better not forget."

"Ah! that looks as though he's got something for us." He looked at his watch. "I think we've just got enough time to fix up the *Bellerophon's* list, so come on, Silas, off with that jacket and let's get down to work."

By seven o'clock the order was completed and all stacked up ready to be taken down first thing in the morning.

"All right, Silas, that'll do for today."

The old sailor wiped the sweat off his brow, slipped his coat on and stumped off towards the door, making dry noises in his throat. At the doorway, he stopped speculatively. "There ain't a chance of a sub, I suppose, skipper?" he asked wheedingly.

"Why, I gave you one last night, and now I come to think of it, the night before as well!"

"Not the night before," protested Silas, and then, seeing the frosty look in Stewart's eye, added hastily: "Well, maybe you did, skipper, but all the same it'll come off on pay day."

"You're right there," said Stewart, pulling out a shilling and flicking it across the room. "Now mind you behave yourself and—keep away from the 'Pig and Whistle'," he added as an afterthought, "I don't want to see your evil face leering at me out of a tankard."

"Leave it to me, skipper," said Silas with a wink, and caught the shilling deftly. Just before he closed the door he said, "I 'opes as 'ow that young lady's language 'as improved," and with a hoarse chuckle he pulled the door to just in time for its frame to receive the heavy ledger which Stewart hurled at him.

The clock was just striking eight when Stewart pushed through the little door of the tavern. It opened into a passage off which the various parlours were spaced. It was a narrow passage, feebly lit by a single gas-jet. At the end was yet another door and that led into the main saloon, with its famous half-secluded nooks. It was a much bigger room than the others, and although less snug and cosy, it was nevertheless one of the most popular meeting places in Liverpool, and he knew he would find Captain Brady there.

Sure enough, as he opened the door he saw the captain and his Yankee friend engaged in some pleasantry with Susy.

"Good evening, gentlemen," he said, and Captain Brady, turning, greeted him cheerfully.

"Hullo, my boy, take a stool. What'll you have? A sherry for the young gent, me gel, and look alive."

Susy departed haughtily; she wasn't accustomed to being spoken to in that manner.

"I want you to meet a friend of mine, Joshua Creesy, master of the American ship *Uriah B. Heap*. Captain, meet one of the straightest men in Liverpool and, believe me, a ship-chandler at that."

"I can't believe it, Tobias. I never knew a ship-chandler yet who wasn't as crooked as a bed-spring. Still, I guess we've all got to earn our living somehow, and who are we to criticize, eh!" And he poked his elbow jocularly into Brady's ribs.

Stewart joined in the laugh.

"You're not the famous Captain Creesy of the *Flying Cloud*?" he asked—"the clipper that made the record passage from New York to 'Frisco."

The American looked up in surprise.

"No!" interrupted Captain Brady proudly. "Joshua's only claim to fame is that he has just diddled the whole of the Federal Navy and brought a cargo of cotton into Sandon Dock. The first for six months."

"I saw you docking, Captain," said Stewart politely. "I heard you'd had a good trip."

"Well, as for it being a good trip," said the American, "it depends which way you look at it. If you're talking about speed I should say no, but if you're alluding to dollars I should say yes. I reckon the cargo lumpers are breaking out the most expensive cargo of cotton ever shipped into Liverpool."

"And if I know you, Joshua, you'll have pocketed a good deal of it, eh?" chuckled Captain Brady, delighted at his friend's success.

"I ain't aiming to complain; that one trip's made me more money than I've earned in these past six years."

"Jingo!" said Stewart enviously, "I suppose you'll be anxious to get turned round, Captain, so as you can pick up a second cargo."

"No. Enough's as good as a feast, and I'm not risking my neck again, at least not yet awhile."

"Give America a miss until it's all over," advised Captain Brady. "Take a cargo to Australia. Young Stewart here will fit you out."

"You know," said the American thoughtfully, "I guess wars are bad things, and civil wars worse than most, but whichever way you look at them you've got to admit they're good for business. My trouble is that I can't make up my mind as to which side is right, and there's no room in America just now for a man with ideas like that." ·

"It's all a sad business," said Brady sympathetically.

"How long did your trip take?" questioned Stewart thoughtfully. He wasn't particularly interested in the ethics of wars.

"Fifty-four days from Galveston to the Bar Lightship."

"Aye, that's a poor passage," agreed Captain Brady.

"Mind you, there was incidents enough on that one passage to satisfy even my liking for excitement," said Captain Creesy.

"I'm sure there was, Captain," a voice broke in, and looking up Stewart saw the ubiquitous reporter of the *Shipping Albion*.

"Bring up your chair, Sam," Stewart invited resignedly. "You know Captain Brady? And this is Captain Creesy, master of the *Uriah B. Heap*."

"The very gent I'm looking for," said Sharp. "Allow me to shake you by the hand, sir, and congratulate you on the most memorable passage of the century."

"Take the weight off your legs," advised the American drily, pushing a stool forward.

"I've been down aboard your ship, sir, and the mate told me that you were ashore on business. Now all business in Liverpool sooner or later gets round to the 'Pig and Whistle', so I hove to in the lee of the saloon bar here, if you'll excuse the nautical parlance. And now may I say again, sir, on behalf of my paper and as a humble representative of this great port, we are proud to make your acquaintance. In the taverns throughout the city tonight you'll hear the name of the *Uriah B. Heap* on every man's tongue. They have the facts but the details are lacking. Captain, the *Shipping Albion* would be honoured to report verbatim the account of your passage."

"Say, what is all this?" drawled the American. "The freedom of the city?"

"Go on, Joshua," encouraged Captain Brady, "spin 'em the yarn. After all, yours is the first ship to run the blockade these six months past."

"Gentlemen," said Sharp, feeling himself on the verge of securing a world-shaking story that even Topliff's agents hadn't got, "this auspicious occasion calls for refreshment. I beg of you all to accept the hospitality of the *Shipping Albion*. Wench! charge the gentlemen's glasses."

"Good God!" murmured Stewart, this was an event. He was right, it was an outstanding occasion; whatever expense the *Shipping Albion* might be put to that night, Sam Sharp's conscience was clear; it was legitimate expense, the price a newspaper of standing must be prepared to pay for its information. So Susy filled their glasses and they listened attentively while Captain Creesy gave an account of his passage.

Other than the short, sharp run in cutting free of the blockading gun-boats, Stewart didn't think there was much in it. It was the thought of all that freight money that stirred his imagination. When the captain had finished, the young man said, "Your owners must be pleased, Captain."

"Owners!" ejaculated Captain Creesy. "Why, I am the owner of the *Uriah B. Heap*. You don't think I'd risk my neck to get that cotton out of Galveston in anybody else's ship, do you?" he asked, surprised.

Stewart looked at him with increased respect. "Shipowning must be a profitable venture as far as you are concerned then, Captain," he said.

"As far as anybody's concerned," broke in Sharp, "you don't need to run a newspaper to find out that it's the easiest way of getting a living from the sea; Dr. Johnson spoke the truth when he said only fools go to sea. Present company always excepted, of course, gentlemen. As soon as a shipmaster realizes that, he steps ashore and becomes his own owner."

"I don't agree with that," said Captain Brady hotly. "I like the sea, and I wouldn't stop ashore amongst all you landsharks for double the wages I'm getting now."

The reporter looked at him loftily. "All the same, sir, with due deference to your good self I still maintain that going to sea is worse than going to gaol. Nine times out of ten your bed's dry in gaol, which is more than you can say it is at sea. No, Captain, I am firmly of the opinion that the wisest thing a shipmaster can do is to get a ship of his own. Go to sea if you must, but at least make certain that no one else profits from your misfortune, and you'll only do that by owning your own ship. The wise shipmasters always do, and how many times do you hear of such a one failing? They've got a bit of money, they've got the knowledge of the sea and they've always got business ability. I'll grant them that, and the combination is bound to succeed."

"Hear, hear," chipped in Stewart enthusiastically. Sam Sharp certainly knew what he was talking about. The least he could do was to buy drinks all round and keep the ball rolling.

Captain Brady gave him a disgusted look, but Sharp pushed his empty glass forward with alacrity, and finding his talk appreciated, returned to the attack.

"I'm surprised you've never gone in for shipowning, Captain Brady. A smart man like you. If you really like going to sea then get yourself a partner." His head searched round for his replenished glass and his watery eyes fell on Stewart's eager face. "Yes, get yourself a shore partner, a young man like Stewart here."

The young man gazed hopefully at Captain Brady, but it was Captain Creesy who spoke.

"That's certainly the way to look at it. I'm darned if I'd sail another's ship for him. All you're doing, Tobias, is putting money into some fellow's pockets who never budges from the stool in his counting-house, never stirring a hand to help you."

Stewart decided the moment was propitious. "It would suit me fine, Captain Brady. How about it? I've got sufficient capital to go half shares."

The old captain's face had been a study of changing emotions. At first he'd been angry at the journalist's suggestion, and then, when his American friend spoke on the same lines, his expression changed to one of perplexed bewilderment, and the final shattering blow had come when young Stewart, a mere whippersnapper of a boy, calmly proposed going half shares with him. That last concrete suggestion had definitely startled him, and alarmed, he said, "Not so fast, young man." Indecision was still plainly visible in his face when, a few moments later, he went on, "It's true I have thought of shipowning—but not from a money-making point of view," he added sharply, with a glance towards Stewart, "but just for the sake of owning the ship I was master of."

"Exactly," said the young man; "then here's the opportunity."

"Nay," the old shipmaster said slowly, "it's not a decision to be lightly undertaken in a tavern. There's a lot more to it than just saying,

'Right, we'll form a partnership.' I must have time to think it all out clearly and without the aid of a couple of glasses."

"Wisely spoken, Captain," said Sharp, holding his empty glass up to the light for the purpose of inspection; but no one took notice of his hint.

"I'll tell you what, young man, I'll think it over on this next voyage. When I get back in three or four months' time we'll discuss it seriously, then."

"All right, Captain," said Stewart, disappointed; it was no use trying to hurry the old man.

Captain Brady got to his feet; it was nearing nine o'clock and all this talk of shipowning had unsettled him; he wanted to get back to the familiar surroundings of his own ship. So he bade Stewart look after Captain Creesy and excused himself abruptly.

After he had gone Sam Sharp said: "Captain Brady's right. Liverpool's not worth staying up for, though I remember the times when it was. Take this public, for instance, in another hour's time the place will be empty and the landlord will be putting up the shutters."

"Yes," put in Stewart, "but don't forget that Paradise Street and Whitechapel will just be starting to open up. Your dance halls, music halls, brothels, and drinking and gambling dens down there are just as prevalent as ever they've been."

"But why should this place be closing down then?" asked Captain Creesy wonderingly.

"It's been like that ever since this present landlord took over," said Stewart quickly, determined to do his duty as host and rather proud of the knowledge that he had acquired from Susy. "It's just that little bit out of the way to cause sailors and others making the rounds after ten o'clock, to let it slip from their befuddled memories, and it never was much of a night-house. When this landlord took it over he started to open and close at different hours to the other pubs. If a fellow stays up later than ten o'clock, he reckons that it's not liquor he's looking for, and since he never aspired to be a brothel-keeper or pimp he simply puts up his shutters."

"You seem to know a lot about it," grumbled the reporter, unused to having others usurp his position as distributor of Liverpool information and gossip.

"Well, it's true enough, isn't it?" challenged Stewart.

"I guess the landlord must have his head screwed on the right way," said Captain Creesy.

"You know," said Sharp, looking at the other two sadly, "here am I sitting gossiping in a bar, when I ought to be across the road helping Charlie put the edition to press; but good company is hard to leave, gentlemen."

"We don't mind your going, Sam," said Stewart, thinking of his pocket.

"I allow myself certain liberties of conduct," went on the reporter, ignoring the interruption, "which in weaker men might be regarded as indulgence. However, on this particular occasion I have no compunctions; my services to shipping are never governed by my personal inclinations, so at times, when business is not pressing, I permit myself to relax in the mellow companionship of gentlemen like yourselves."

"I suppose that means you're staying?" said Captain Creesy humorously; he was getting to understand the reporter.

"But what about Captain Creesy's blockade-running account?" asked Stewart. "I thought it was a matter of life and death the way you bludgeoned it out of him?"

"My boy," said Sharp tolerantly, wiping his moist moustache clear of the froth of the slightly fresh beer, "news in a paper of repute like the *Shipping Albion* is never a matter of time but one of presentation. How long did Captain Creesy take to cross the Atlantic?"

"Fifty-four days," replied Stewart, wonderingly.

"Well then, another day's delay in publishing this epic event won't matter. You see, it's all a question of perspective. Mind you, I've an idea that Charlie Tomkins often gets thoughts like yours. It's a great pity, for there is a man who has failed to keep abreast of his paper, the greatest crime in journalism. I regret to say that he cannot appreciate the standard of the *Albion's* columns. Everything for speed, as though it mattered! I'm for ever telling him that his paper has got a reputation, and news is news whether we publish it today, tomorrow or next week. Poor Charlie! he can't see it. If only he'd take a glass now and again he'd be more human, but no, he's got a printer's soul! God help him."

"Then where do we go from here?" queried the American visibly, growing restless and pointing out that he was anxious to celebrate his first night ashore since leaving Galveston.

The journalist protested that he was past celebrating anything. When people got to his age they no longer looked for an excuse to drink, but drank as much and as often as they could; it helped to straighten out life's many difficulties. At least, that was Sam's belief. He warned Captain Creesy against expecting to find much fun in Liverpool in spite of what young Stewart had said.

Captain Creesy, however, would have it that the place must be pretty lively, for wherever he had met British seamen the talk had always been of Liverpool. Paradise Street and Whitechapel. Why! the chanties alone were living testimony to the place. The captain suddenly began to sing 'Oh! Nancy Dawson—she robbed the bosun'. "Now," he said, breaking off abruptly, "I heard the sailormen say that Nancy Dawson lived in Liverpool. You're a journalist, you should know, was there ever such a girl?"

Sure there was, Sharp told him. In fact, she still worked a beer engine up in Kelly's tavern. She was no longer the lively young woman sailors wanted to spend their money on. But old age and lack of beauty notwithstanding, she was still capable of filling Kelly's every night. She was still the most famous barmaid in Liverpool, though she must be well on the way to sixty. To listen to her chiveying the young men and old lechers was one of the best bits of sport in town. At one time the crowd round her bar in Paradise Street was made up entirely of sailors and their hangers on, that was how she came to figure in the sailors' chanties. You wouldn't find many sailors near her now though, for after they took to singing about her she became popular with landsmen, and sailors couldn't get near her bar for the strangers that came down just to have a look-see. A big brewer heard of her and he offered her a job in a public at the top end of Lime Street, and that was the last Paradise Street saw of Nancy Dawson. Occasionally, a few old timers who remembered her in the good old days would go up to see her, but to most other seaman she was only a name in the capstan chanty.

Yes, Liverpool was changing so fast that when he looked back it made him feel really old. When he first came to Liverpool thirty years ago, sailortown was the main district, lying close to the river. But now the town stretched miles into the country, and, in sympathy at any rate, it was drawing farther and farther away from the sailors and ships who'd made it. Every year, in his opinion, the gap between the town and the port grew wider. Liverpool had become commercialized, rows of fine mansions had sprung up in Parliament Street and Canning Street, but the people who lived in them didn't spare much thought for the ships and the seamen who made their wealth possible. It was a pity, for it never did anybody any harm to recognize where their money came from.

Still, the reporter wound up, if they were going to have a night out they'd better make a start. The places that were left wouldn't last much longer, and it would be something for young Stewart there to remember in the years to come just what sort of a place Liverpool was in the 'sixties. They'd better start off at the 'Oriel'. It wasn't a place where you'd meet many seamen such as the term meant then, but they'd meet the sailors of the future—the engineers from the steamers. It was the only tavern in which you'd find them in any number; they mostly came from Sam Cunard's vessels. So the three of them got up from their stools and went out into the passage with its one gas-jet hoarsely burning in the gloom.

The 'Oriel' wasn't far away and after a few minutes' walk they turned down Water Street, by that time quiet and deserted. Half-way down was a narrow forbidding archway with an oil-lamp feebly flickering on the words: 'Oriel Bar. Beers and Spirits'. They turned into the dark alleyway, and suddenly, like a host of wraiths rising from the dead, they felt rather than saw hordes of little children scrambling up from the warmth of the groups in which they had been lying. They swarmed around them, begging for coppers. Captain Creesy flung them a handful and in the ensuing scramble the three managed to push on. Occasionally, as they pressed on in the dark they tripped over the drunken forms of men and women, incapable of progressing farther. At last they passed out of this furtive alley and entered a small courtyard off which opened several doors leading into the many bars of the 'Oriel'. One of these doors flew open and a bundle of humanity came hurtling out to finish up disastrously in the mud at their feet. Shrill cries of both male and female voices punctuated the air and coarse laughter echoed dimly from the bright interior. Silhouetted in the doorway a potman wiped his hands on his apron and, looking out into the gloom, bawled, "Don't show yer ugly mugs around 'ere again," and disappeared inside again, kicking the door closed after him.

"Come along, gentlemen," Sharp said calmly, "that's the public bar—not our destination."

They passed two more doors before the reporter deemed they were sufficiently far enough up to venture inside. It was a large room, the two ends were brightly lit and the lighting there had to suffice for the rest of the hall. A great gilded bar with huge ornamental mirrors and a profusion of brass rails and marble slabs dominated one end, while at the other a raised stage, draped with heavy crimson curtains, formed the platform on which sat the musicians, a band of some half-dozen performers in shirt-sleeves and waistcoats; some with low-crowned beaver hats on, and others without hats plainly preferred the adornment of their own well-greased black hair and fastidious quiff. There were a couple of fiddles, a piano, a cornet, concertina and a false-nosed funny man making great play with a drum and a variety of noise-making instruments attached to it. At a little table, to one side, resplendent in tall hat, white shirt front and evening coat, sat the chairman, smoking a cigar.

It seemed as though the band and the customers were competing against each other in producing noise. Barmen, sweating profusely even without their jackets, added their own strident voices to the din, bawling and shouting their rhythmic orders across the full length of the room. In between the two brightly lit ends were scores of little round-topped marble tables and at one of these the three revellers from the 'Pig and Whistle' sat down.

They were no sooner seated than a woman merged up to them from the gloom of the smoke-laden atmosphere and said, "Are you looking for company tonight, gents?"

Sam Sharp turned to the other two. "I'm not so young as I used to be, but how about you two?" he said quizzically, then, observing their expressions, he turned and said kindly, "Some other time, lass," and without further importuning the wretched female receded into the gloom out of which she had emerged.

The chairman rapped loudly on his table with a gavel and the cry went up from the well-drilled potmen, "Order, gents. Order please," scarcely stopping from their business of sliding the mugs expertly off their trays on to the tables. Few paid any attention, but the chairman was picked to over-ride such little obstacles as noise and inattention, and in a sharp high-pitched voice set out to make himself heard above the uproar. "Gentlemen and ladies," he cried, "the masters of music 'ere 'ave given us 'igh-class hentertainment tonight. If there's anybody present who would like to show his appreciation by buying them a little refreshment, now's the time. Two bob will buy 'em a drink apiece. Fiddling or blowing, squeezing the music-box or banging the drums; it's thirsty business. Where are those sailors? Come along, Jack. Stand the boys a treat!" The sailors, however, were missing and only the silent taciturn group of engineers, leaning on the brass rail of the bar, sucking at stubby black pipes, were there to listen unmoved to the appeal.

"Do you see Cunard's engineers, Captain?" asked Sharp, leaning forward and indicating the men at the bar. Stewart, interested, turned round; there they were, each dressed in an identical navy blue serge suit, a black silk muffler round each neck, and each with a low-crowned Derby hat on his head. "There's the writing on the wall," said Sharp. "Call 'em two-by-fours if you like, but they're the fellows who are going to matter at sea!"

"Nonsense," said Captain Creesy irritably, "don't you believe it! The only thing that keeps those fellows afloat is your Government's subsidy. Thank goodness we don't have any truck with them on the other side of the Atlantic."

"All right, Captain," said Sharp placidly, "have it your own way, but you mark my words, the time's not so far distant when all your beautiful sailing ships will disappear like the winds that drive 'em along. There will be no call for sailors; in fact all we will need will be machine minders, engine drivers, mechanics, to see that the wheels go round. It is the beginning of the industrial age, gentlemen," and he shook his head sadly. "Look at Manchester, Birmingham, Liverpool and a dozen other industrial overcrowded towns, opening up and spreading over the countryside like a black plague. I remember the times when things were different. Barbarous, they call 'em now—but I wouldn't. In those days there was no mass herding of people into the slums that have grown up around the factories. Gold didn't lure men to desert the fields. A man's wealth lay in the skill of his hands; craftsmen, native ability, that's what England stood for. No one starved who could and would work, and no one lacked shelter who could seek it, for no matter what others may say of those days, no one can deny that the labourer was worthy of his hire. Nature regulated things in her own way; seasons came, seasons went; first the sowing, then the reaping. Folks got out of the

land just as much as they put in . . . and there was always the harvest.
But now, with these great whirling machines, fashioned by man,
governed by no such strength as Nature, who can tell what will happen?
Cycles of prosperity and depression—whoever heard of such talk before
the start of these modern industries? The lean years and the fat years
of Nature's bounty, that was the nearest we ever got to it before, and
even in the leanest years there was nothing like the misery you'll find
skulking in the darkest corners of our so wonderful modern cities."

"Say! what is this?" asked Captain Creesy in amazement. "I
thought we were all out to enjoy ourselves?"

"Cut it short, Sam, for goodness' sake," said Stewart; "you'll have
us both in tears in a minute. I feel as though I've been listening to one
of the *Albion's* editorials!"

"Not on your life, you haven't," said Sharp more cheerfully. "Why,
if I wrote stuff like that you'd see our advertisements drop away like
gold from a sailor's pocket. But listen, there's the chairman announcing
the programme."

"Gentlemen and ladies, for your hentertainment tonight the
management 'ave a special surprise. At great expense they have decided
to revive the grand old English sport of Purring, and two gradely
fighters 'ave been matched 'ere tonight for the championship of
Lancashire. With the championship goes a purse of ten golden sovereigns which I 'old in my 'and 'ere. Mr. Landlord, are those doors bolted
and barred?"

"Aye, hall correct, Mr. Chairman."

"Then, gentlemen, I introduce to you Eliza Spraggs, the present
champion of Lancashire, and Bella Watts, the challenger from Lilley's
cotton mills at Oldham."

The heavy velvet curtains went up behind him and there stood
two massive women grinning uneasily as they bobbed up and down
in response to the stamping and whistling which greeted their appearance. They were both dressed in much the same fashion. Their hair
piled high on the top of their heads was securely fastened by a tight-
fitting bonnet. Both wore seamen's jerseys, one red and the other blue.
From the jerseys downwards hung a stout, voluminous skirt, rimmed
like a crinoline and ending about six inches from the floor. Their feet
were encased in wooden clogs.

"Now, ladies," said the chairman, "this fight is to be fought with
the feet, no hitting with the hands, no scratching, biting or pulling of
hair, and no kicking above the knee. In all other respects the match
will be fought under prize-fighting rules. Submission will be the only
gauge of victory." He turned towards the audience. "Now before the
fight begins I want the backers of these two ladies to step up 'ere and
lay the side stakes in accordance with the 'Oriel's' rules."

"Get on wi' t'match," somebody yelled from the back of the hall.

The chairman merely raised his voice a little higher. "If I think the fighters are not trying, then the side stakes will be confiscated and drinks served on the 'ouse."

At the conclusion of these remarks two men, clad in loose-fitting check suits, stepped on to the stage and were introduced in their turn as the well-known sportsmen Jem Slade and Spider Mayne. At the chairman's invitation they sat down at his table. Their runners stood about the hall, shouting the odds they were offering and taking. The 'Oriel's' patrons were in good humour. It was a long time since they had seen a purring match and bets passed freely amongst the sportsmen in the hall inclined to back their fancy.

The reigning champion was the smaller of the two in height but she was more stockily built; she had the face of a backward child, but legs and body were witness to where her strength lay. The challenger, Bella Watts, much younger, towered above her opponent, and although her ankles were twice as thick as a man's wrist the knowing ones pointed out that she was top-heavy.

The chairman rapped on his table. "Order, please, order," the cry went up from the waiters in the body of the hall. "If you are ready, ladies," the chairman said, "the fight will begin." Potmen whisked the stools away from the stage and the two women, picking up the front of their looped skirts sufficiently to give their legs the necessary freedom of action, advanced cautiously towards each other. The turmoil in the room suddenly quietened down. The barmen and waiters gathered along the walls at the side, glad of the respite from their labours. From crevices and nooks they produced huge tankards of beer surreptitiously hidden beforehand for just that moment. They brought little clay pipes from out of their pockets and settled down for a brief rest. The atmosphere in the centre of the room, already thick with the smoke of a hundred pipes, became even darker as the gas-jets over the bar were lowered to a dim, sibilant flame, the only noise to be heard save that of the hesitant clogs of the women on the stage.

Round and round the two women circled, each waiting for the other to make an attacking move. Suddenly a guttural roar rose from those in the hall, for Bella, bent on kicking the champion off her feet, lunged her right leg forward with all the weight of her thirteen stone behind it. The other was too quick and with a swift movement dropped her skirt and let the folds take the blow. The fierce sweep carried Bella forward and deftly the champion stepped aside, and as the momentum carried her opponent past shot out a sharp side flick at the other's ankle. It produced a gasp of pain from Bella and a roar of applause from the audience. Bella withdrew a little to regain time and her breath, but the champion, roused by the shouts of the crowd, leapt to the attack with a speed which belied her appearance. Blow after blow she directed towards Bella's ever-withdrawing legs; not great lunges, such as Bella had essayed, but sharp, wicked jabs which, if they had once found their mark, might have cracked the shin-bone. But Bella, for all her great size, was nimble on her feet and by side-stepping and withdrawing, avoided the direct blow with a defensive dexterity which drew forth the vocal admiration of the onlookers.

The clogs beat an almost incessant tattoo on the wooden staging, but it seemed that the champion's attack was being conducted at too fast a pace to continue. Both women were showing signs of fatigue, and Bella's face, particularly, revealed her desperation. The champion's impetuous attack in the end proved to be its own undoing even before exhaustion brought it to a halt. The savage jabs became slower as the excitement led to lack of control and gave the younger woman a respite. Seizing her opportunity she now hopped forward and slightly sideways, and as the champion's clogs travelled aimlessly past her, summoned up all her remaining strength to deliver a hard blow at the back of the one leg that supported her opponent. With a heavy crash Eliza fell to the ground. The house was in an uproar and shouts of encouragement and advice filled the air. Jem Slade, Eliza's backer, slipped on to the stage and unceremoniously hauled her across to a chair handed up to him. Roughly he began to inspect the ankle. With a grunt of relief he saw it was undamaged. Seeing the blow coming she had voluntarily lifted her foot off the ground and Bella's sweep had encountered little resistance and caused no harm save the champion's undignified fall to the ground.

"Ye're all right, Liza lass," he assured her; "don't rush things, there's plenty of time."

"I 'ad the bitch there, Jem, but she's not so daft as she looks. I'll tak' it easy for a bit."

She got to her feet and, lifting her skirt just the least bit higher, went out to meet Bella, waiting with a smirk on her brutish face. Once again they started to perambulate around each other. Bella, now confident, advancing, and Eliza, more cautious, retreating, the while the crowd whistled and cat-called their displeasure in their desire for more excitement. For all her backer's advice and her own declared intentions, the older woman knew that her opponent's endurance was greater than her own. If she was to win again, it would hardly be through biding her time. Of a sudden she decided to stop retreating, and by a skilful feint and a quick forward movement turned her defensive retreat into an attack which quickly got Bella hopping from one foot to the other, and the crowd roared its approval at this change of tactics.

In spite of her previous lesson, however, the champion was still too eager. Swinging her foot back just a little too carelessly she caught it in the fold of her skirt and for one horrid second stood poised on one foot, vainly trying to free her other clog. Bella Watts wanted no other opportunity and, grinning triumphantly, rushed forward to sweep the champion off her feet. Eliza coolly kept her head, and as she saw the other's clog travelling towards her, quickly dropped one side of her hooped skirt and in so doing, not only foiled the blow, but released her entangled clog. In her turn she saw Bella's defenceless shin and shot out her freed foot, travelling no more than six inches. With a howl of pain Bella hopped on to her sound leg, but the champion was not to be denied and in swift, short taps, her clogs found their mark, first on one leg and then the other. Poor Bella hopped about in noisy misery, striving to avoid those painful blows, but her movements were gettng slower and slower. Eliza felt that it was in her power now to finish off the match any time she liked, but first of all there was the ignominy of her first fall to be wiped out, and viciously she pressed on harassing the other, but purposely withholding the final blow which would end it all. The crowd were on their feet now, stamping and shouting excitedly, and no one paid any attention to the sound of hammering that came from the main door.

The hammering on the door grew louder and those nearest turned angrily towards it and then, as their apprehension communicated itself to their immediate neighbours in the hall, the clamouring and shouting of the audience died ominously away.

"Open, in the name of the law," a strong voice cried outside.

"The police!" A whisper ran round the hall and in a flash the purring match was forgotten, and there was one huge scramble towards the small emergency exit at the other side. At the foot of the stage the chairman and the two backers had mysteriously disappeared, but the two Amazons, unconscious of the diversion, were still at it when a potman rushed in between them.

"Chuck it, you silly bitches! T'police are outside. If you don't look slippy it'll be Australia for you both, and wi'out a return ticket!"

The howling Bella stopped her whimpering and both, with an alacrity that said much for their stamina, ran after the potman, who, seeing there was little hope of getting through the milling crowd around the small door, made for the cellars. Closely followed by the two women, now trembling with fear, he slipped around the back of the bar, kicked aside an empty sack and there, flush with the floor, lay a trap door. He seized hold of the ring-bolt, opened the trap and the three of them disappeared from sight.

Captain Creesy and Stewart at first found it all highly amusing and a welcome change from the spectacle of purring, but Sam Sharp speedily disillusioned them. The penalty for these illegal sports, he said, was transportation. There'd be wholesale convictions for those who were caught, and the sooner they got out of it the happier he'd feel. While he was speaking Stewart caught a glimpse of the barman and the two causes of all the trouble disappearing behind the bar.

"There's someone who knows another way out," he said, and wasting no further time the three made for the bar.

The trap-door was quickly sighted and they descended into the blackness of the cellar. At the bottom of the steps they came upon the barman. "What do you want?" he asked threateningly.

"Quit talking," said the American, "and get us out of here."

"There goes the main door," said Stewart, as a splintering crash echoed dully, and was followed by a renewed outbreak of cries and shrieks, indicating that a number of people still remained in the hall. That settled the barman, he needed no further urging, and lighting the stub of a candle he led them over the loose earth of the newly hewn floor, past barrels of beer and cases of spirits which stood out eerily in the feeble yellow light. The cellar was cavernous, and though the stock of liquor was large it occupied only a small area directly under the bar above. Rats scuttled across their path, startled by footsteps and the increasing noise above. The rough rock walls glistened with sweat which shone in the gloom like miniature rivers of silver.

A minute or so later they came to the other end and there confronting them they found some small narrow stone steps cut in between the two half-rounded gutterways which reached to the main service hatch in Water Street. The barman drew the bolts quietly and then stood listening before attempting to raise the hatch itself. A sudden shaft of light at the other end of the cellar put an end to his indecision; the police were about to search the cellar. The barman flung back the hatch with his shoulders and they all clambered out into the street. It was deserted, and they gave a sigh of relief as the fresh air struck their brows, cool and clean after the filthy atmosphere of the cellar. The barman and the two women took to their heels and disappeared down the labyrinth of alleys.

"This place is not healthy," said Sharp, and they, too, set off to put as much distance between themselves and the 'Oriel' as they could.

They went on down to the Pier Head and into Mother Simpson's coffee-rooms. "I wish we had something to lace this coffee with," said the reporter, who felt the need of some stimulus, but neither of the other two paid any attention. Stewart sat with his head in his hands and even the American looked a bit pale. "Well," he said, "so that's purring! I'm not squeamish, but after that show I'll admit that you Britishers have stronger stomachs than most. I've had enough for one night."

"Why, Captain," protested Sharp, "the evening's just beginning. I thought you wanted to see Nancy Dawson's?"

"I feel as though I'm going to be sick," moaned Stewart. "I'm going home," and forgot all about his resolution to stick close to Captain Creesy until he'd got his order out of him. His obvious misery set the two older men laughing, but he was beyond caring what they thought, so he trudged the short distance to Chapel Walk and went to bed.

CHAPTER 5

WARNED OFF BY 'IRISH' HIGGINS

STEWART dowsed his head in a bucket of cold water that Silas, knowingly, had placed in the yard, and after a while his head became a little clearer, his burning forehead a little cooler. His mouth still tasted horribly and his body had a weary, languid feeling as though he were recovering from a severe beating. Even his very finger-tips seemed to be burning dully, and the veins on the back of his hands stood out thickly. Never again, he thought, even for the sake of getting an order, would he be persuaded into drinking as much as he drank last night.

"What's the matter, skipper?" asked Silas slyly. "Been eating something that don't agree with you? Now take them oysters they're selling off the barrows down at the Pier Head. They taste fine and dandy when you're eating 'em, but my oath, once they settle in the bilges they raise 'ell."

"It's all right, Silas," grinned Stewart feebly, "I haven't been eating any shell-fish."

"Then you must have been drinking Scott's beer! If you've got to go inside a Scott's 'ouse, for mercy's sake drink something else than their beer. Why you wants to drink beer at. all ain't for me to ask, although my mate Tom Briggs always 'ad it that with liquor it was quantity that counted. 'E liked to feel full and then 'e knew 'e 'ad 'is money's worth. But even Tom would never touch Scott's beer. I never 'ave 'eard a good word said of it and yet look at the number of publics that sell nothing else! Danged if I know any other line of business where you sell stuff to folks that don't like it and yet'll always buy it. It's not as though there weren't other beer in Liverpool, and good beer, too."

"Silas, for the love of Mike, if you must talk, talk about pirates, farmers, icebergs—anything, even your old ships, but for God's sake leave beer out of it."

"All right, cap'n," said Silas in a huff. "If you don't want my advice it suits me, though I could name you a dozen cap'ns who'd be glad to 'ave Silas Martin around when they get into shoal water," and in high dudgeon he walked off.

Ill though Stewart felt, there was still work to be done; the *Bellerophon* had to be stored and several other jobs as well, so with a self-pitying groan he set about the day's business.

Two days later Stewart was down at the lock-gates to see the *Bellerophon* sail. Captain Creesy was there, and they laughed over the affair at the 'Oriel'. They climbed aboard to bid farewell to Captain Brady, and as they came ashore again the American promised to let Stewart know when he would be storing. Things were looking up and

Stewart felt distinctly cheerful as he made his way back to the office. The sight of St. Nicholas' church as he came along the Dock Road sent his mind racing back towards the girl he had encountered there. Only last Sunday morning she had recognized him and smiled, but like a stupid fool he had stood there awkwardly, not even having the manners to bow in return.

Late that afternoon he was sitting mooning at his desk in Chapel Walk when he heard the sounds of footsteps coming down from the street, and with a heavy sigh tore himself away from that auburn-haired vision and prepared to come down to the sordid realities of ship-chandlery. Without any preliminary knock the door swung open and in stepped a remarkably dressed man. On his head at a fashionable angle sat a light-coloured top hat. A deep, white collar kept his head singularly erect, and an extravagantly made cravat flowed in generous proportions over his white shirt front. Beneath his dark morning coat a large expanse of canary-coloured waistcoat was visible. Brightly checked trousers were looped under his highly-polished peg-topped boots. To complete the picture he carried a silver-mounted cane in his yellow gloved hands.

Stewart gaped in astonishment at this dandified figure.

"Is your employer in?" the stranger asked in a rich, Irish voice.

"Yes, he's in," said Stewart, not quite grasping the question.

"Then kindly ask him to step out here a minute."

"But I am here, I mean I am my own employer."

The other gave him a sharp, appraising glare and then with a sniff of disdain said, "I've called about an advertisement that has appeared in this morning's *Shipping Albion*.

"Yes?" said Stewart hopefully.

"The advertisement concerns a person calling himself James Stewart, Ship-chandler."

"That's me," the young man said, perplexed, and then recalled dimly some vague allusion Sam Sharp had made about advertising.

"In that case I'll come to the point of my visit," said the other boldly. "My name is Higgins—Daniel Higgins—and as the head of the Liverpool Association of Ship-chandlers I have to advise you that there is no opportunity for you in this port, and that you will have to close down this business of yours."

Stewart was startled and disturbed. "For what reason?" he managed to ask quietly.

"For the good enough reason that ship-chandlery in Liverpool is a matter of arrangement between the members of our association."

"I never knew there was a law against anyone supplying ships, provided he could get the orders?" Stewart said sarcastically.

"You are right," said Higgins smoothly, "there is no law, but at the same time you should know that established ship-chandlers in the port are prepared to control the rights of entry into their trade, and since we deem the port to be already properly serviced by the existing firms of ship-chandlers, we are not prepared to encourage newcomers.

"Oh," said Stewart truculently, "and how do you intend to stop me ? This is a free country, isn't it ?"

"I don't see that I'm called upon to explain the matter to you, young man, but if you'll allow yourself to think of your suppliers, you'll realize that those same wholesalers are also suppliers to the members of our association. Stretch your mind a little more and I'm sure you'll appreciate whose orders they value most highly."

"You mean that you'll stop me from getting my supplies ?" asked Stewart, really beginning to get anxious.

The Irishman inclined his head.

"But this is unfair !" Stewart began angrily, but a look at Higgins' imperturbable countenance soon revealed that it was useless to lose his temper. He was in a dilemma and common prudence urged him to keep calm until he found out exactly how he stood. He thought of all the unpaid stocks which he had packed into the courtyard buildings ; if he wasn't careful he was going to be caught with bills for more than he could pay out of the business. He determined to be conciliatory.

"This is a great surprise to me, Mr. Higgins. I had no idea I was trading in a reserved market."

"Well, you know it now," said the other noncommittally.

"What would you advise me to do ? I've got all this stock on my hands and the wholesalers will never take it back."

"That's your look-out," the Irishman said tersely and unsympathetically, then, after a deliberate pause, he continued : "As it happens one of my water clerks has just left me and if you want his job you can have it. I've heard you're an energetic young fellow."

So there it was, Stewart thought bitterly, back to the old grind of water clerking again, and this time amongst the riff-raff of the shipping world. "Thank you for your offer," he said with a gratitude he was far from feeling, "but what about my stock ?" and he glanced despairingly at the extravagant stores he'd taken delivery of.

"I don't see that they're any concern of mine, but later on I may be willing to give you a price for them, and of course you will realize that it will be much lower than that at which you bought."

Stewart's little world seemed to have collapsed upon him and desperately he tried to think of how he might save something from the ruins of all his high ambitious hopes. He must have time to think it all out. "Can't we come to some mutual arrangement, Mr. Higgins, whereby I'm still allowed to keep on my business ? I haven't been established long, but already it's on its feet and prospering."

"I didn't come here to bargain, young man. I came here to close down your business. However, I have offered you the opportunity of working for me, take it or leave it. Here's my card, let me know by noon tomorrow what you have decided, but meanwhile—keep off those ships in the docks. I bid you good day."

Long after he had gone, Stewart sat there with the card between his fingers, irresolutely weighing up all that Higgins' visit implied. Whichever way he looked at it he could see no way out. If the remaining shipchandlers in the port were in league to put him out of business, he was in no position to fight them. Bitterly he thought of that advertisement in the *Albion*; it had brought him publicity all right! What was it Sam Sharp had said? "Quick results!" The old soak had been right there, he thought grimly, and he searched round for the offending copy of the newspaper before he remembered he had given it to a visiting captain.

On the spur of the moment he decided to go up to Victoria Street and find out what the advertisement was, and if Higgins was as powerful as he sounded.

Sam Sharp was sitting all alone in the main office. Harold and his penetrating whistle had been packed off home for the day, and in the back printing room, Charlie Tomkins was laboriously putting the edition to bed. Sam was taking his ease with the air of a man well satisfied with his day's work. The editorials were completed and he was newly back from reading them out to Charlie. He sniffed at the memory. Charlie was all right—damn' good printer, in fact—but he knew nothing about writing. The finer pieces of composition, the higher flights of airy persiflage, were all lost on Charlie. Look at the leader he'd written about that Yankee's scheme to lay a telegraph cable across the Atlantic with the *Great Eastern*; the biggest ship in the world to lay the biggest cable in the world. It had been as witty a piece of satire as ever Swift or Pope wrote. What was that phrase he'd used? "White elephants rushing in where angels feared to tread." That was a good one; but Charlie never got it. He just wasn't sensitive to the finer writings. It was all a waste really; Sam thought he should be back in London turning out his masterpieces of prose for the *Daily Thunderer*. A writer could be sure of being appreciated there; but in these uncivilized parts the only things people read were ship arrivals and sailings and Lloyd's casualty returns. They were mercenary barbarians in the provinces, their souls never rose above money.

At this point in his ruminations, Stewart walked in.

"Hullo, young fellow, you're just in time to restore my faith in humanity. Lend me your arm as far as the 'Red Lion' vineyard," and almost before he was aware of it the young man found Sam's arm linked in his and the office door banging to behind them.

"Sam," he said, "what did you put in the *Albion* about me this morning?"

"Eh! What's that? Oh, your advertisement. Didn't you get the proof? Then it must be that young scamp Harold. That boy's more trouble than the rest of the paper put together. Make no mistake about it, Mr. Stewart, if the details are wrong we'll publish a correction free of charge. Like all papers proud of their reputation, we're particular about little things like that."

"I don't care particularly whether it's right or wrong," said Stewart grimly, "I only know it's put me out of business. A fellow named Higgins called this afternoon and warned me off."

"Irish Higgins! Phew, that's bad, lad!"

"Who is he, Sam? Is he as powerful as he says he is?"

"I should say that he and the *Shipping Albion* are the two most potent forces in Liverpool today," the reporter said pompously.

"Now, that's very instructive," said Stewart bitterly, "it tells me a lot."

But Sam Sharp was not to be hurried, and after his glass had been refilled, he went on to tell what he knew of Higgins.

"He first came to Liverpool in 1830, just one of the thousands of Irish emigrants who were pouring into the country. As you see him now, he's a rich man. He owns a score of public-houses stretching alongside the docks. You can't mistake which are his, they're more pretentious, more gaudy than any of the others. They're dressed up outside like himself, but I can't say I recommend them inside."

"But I thought he was a ship-chandler," said Stewart, puzzled.

"Now who's telling the story?" asked Sharp indignantly. "Here, fill up this glass and let me get on with it. Well, shortly after he landed he got a job as potman in Mike Donovan's place and before long he was the tenant in Draper's house facing the slipway, and the next time he moved it was into his own public, and he's never looked back since. From one tavern to another he's gone, all within the 'Shipping Mile', of course, and now he must have close on twenty public-houses raking in the shekels for him. Money was pretty free about the time he started pub-keeping, and it came his way so fast that he began to look for other things to invest it in. Yes! the sun's always shone on Irish Higgins —though, give him his due, he's worked hard.

"After that his calculating eyes settled on seamen's boarding-houses, and up to the time the Government put a stop to it, I reckon he must have made a cool thousand a year on crimpage alone. Then he got a hankering after respectability and put some money into the ships' store business. 'Daniel Higgins, Ship's husband' looked and sounded better than 'Daniel Higgins, Publican and Boarding-house Keeper' and I don't blame him either."

"Has he ever gone in for shipowning?" asked Stewart meditatively.

"What! Irish Higgins? Not likely; there's far too much risk in that. All he's interested in is 'certs', and business which other men won't touch."

"Surely he's got some sort of scruples?" protested Stewart.

"Scruples?" scoffed the journalist. "He's never heard of the word, and that's why he's so successful—that and a natural instinct for showmanship. There's many a man in Liverpool who remembers his first tavern, 'Higgins Hotel' they'll tell you was written right across the front in large gold letters. Oh! he's a business man all right. He does quite a nice little side-line now in sailors' advance notes. His runners boast that no destitute sailor ever appealed to him in vain. No, sir! once a sailor went to Higgins, he didn't remain destitute long, but next morning he'd be sure to wake up aboard some ship outward bound which no sober man would join. He couldn't be destitute either for he would find a parish-rigged sea-chest alongside him, a proof of Higgins' thoughtfulness.

"He's been more ambitious lately, and it was said a year or two back that he was going to put up for the new Dock Board. That rumour put the cat amongst the pigeons all right, for the thought of having to serve alongside a publican upset the shipowners more than if they'd woken up one morning and found the river dry. However, it turned out to be no more than a rumour, for on nomination day his name was missing. Somehow, I don't think even Irish Higgins with all his money could get on the Dock Board. Of course, he's on the City Council; he had no trouble in finding a seat there. On polling night he scattered the hospitality of his pubs far and wide and went in by a mile, and he's been there ever since."

"It surprises me why a man with so many interests should bother himself about my tinpot business," complained Stewart bitterly.

"It may surprise you," said Sharp, "but I can't say it surprises me. It's typical of the man that if he sees the slightest threat to any portion of his business, off he goes with silver-mounted cane and top hat and sets about removing that threat personally. That's what makes him so outstanding."

"His clothes alone do that," said Stewart sourly.

"Aye, they're all part and parcel of his showmanship, my boy, though he wasn't always dressed like that. There's Joe Skinner of the *Mercury*, who remembers seeing him at an Irish political meeting dressed in rough corduroys, as Irish an emigrant as ever paid his twopence to get into this land flowing with milk and honey. No! you'll never find another man dressed like him. Higgins is all for the glitter of diamonds, the dull gleam of gold, the solid chink of silver, bright lights and noisy music—that's Irish Higgins. Everything he does is done to draw attention. Everything must be bigger and better. The dance hall at the back of the 'Duke of Wellington' has a bigger steam-organ than any dance hall within two hundred miles of Merseyside. The side-shows, the vaudeville he puts on at his various hotels, as he insists on calling them, are all bigger and better than those put on in rival publics. And as regards himself—'Look as though you're worth a lot of money and you'll never lack for it' he says. That's his motto and that explains his massive, diamond tie-pin and all the rest of his fancy rig-out. It's not that he's clever or even educated—why, it's well known that he can barely write his own name—but by jove he can count."

"It looks as though I'm up against a pretty tough customer," said Stewart dolefully.

"I'll say you are," said the reporter discouragingly, "and from what I know of Irish Higgins I don't think we'll be troubling you for a renewal subscription for that advertisement of yours."

"You're bright and cheerful," said Stewart balefully; "after all, I never asked you to put that advertisement in."

"There's gratitude for you," said the reporter reproachfully, and he looked surprised when Stewart angrily stood up and stamped out of the bar.

Stewart had learned all he wanted to know about Higgins but he was still without advice as to what he should do, and acting on an impulse he decided to seek his landlord's opinion.

"Come in," called out Mr. Eastwood in response to Stewart's hesitant knock, and since it was night-time Stewart found him sitting in an old arm-chair in a dressing-gown and with a long taselled smoking-cap on his head. His feet were immersed in a bowl of warm water and a large book lay on his knee. He looked at the young man in surprise and then, becoming aware of his diffidence, bade him take a chair.

"You find me in rather a domestic habit, Mr. Stewart, but I must confess I was hardly expecting callers at this hour. Fred's in bed, but, no matter, pull your seat up and we'll have a game."

"I'm afraid, sir, that I haven't come to play dominoes," said Stewart, "the fact is, I've come for your advice," and in a sudden burst of volubility he unburdened himself of the dilemma in which Higgins had placed him.

The old coasting shipowner heard him through patiently, and then he sat silent for a while. At last he said: "It looks very much as though your ship's husbanding days are over, young man. I can't see any way out of it for you. Personally, I can't help thinking it's a good thing, for you know my views on that trade, but the thing, of course, is to extricate you from that position without losing too much money on your stock," and he lapsed into another long silence. "How much is your stock valued at?" he asked eventually.

"I was able to get credit for £1500," said Stewart anxiously, "and of course I accepted the goods, thinking I should be able to get rid of them."

Mr. Eastwood looked at him gravely. "If the wholesalers demand their accounts you'll be bankrupt?"

"It was an ordinary business risk, sir," said Stewart defensively.

"Did Higgins say how much he was prepared to give you for the stock on your hands?"

"No, but from the tone of his voice I gathered it wouldn't be much, certainly nothing like the price I bought the stock for."

"There are, of course, other ship-chandlers in Liverpool," said the old man musingly.

"They're all in the association though," Stewart said, seeing little hope there.

"That is so, but the association, if I know anything of Liverpool, is not so united as all that. While they may band themselves together to keep others from entering the trade, they'll still be competing pretty freely amongst themselves."

"Yes, they do that," said Stewart, thinking of the many tricks he'd seen ship-chandlers' runners play upon one another.

"Then, there's your chance. You must play off one ship-chandler against the other. You're not going with empty hands. Your record proves that you can get orders, and in addition to that you have stock valued at £1500. You should get reasonable terms, but it looks as if you'll have to become another man's water clerk, at least, for a time."

Stewart looked at him hopefully. "Then you really think I might be able to sell my stock for a fair price?"

"You'll be a fool if you don't," Mr. Eastwood replied shortly; "use a bit of guile when you see Higgins tomorrow. Let him know that if his terms aren't suitable you'll take your services, including the goodwill and stock, over to McGregors, and mark my words he'll come round to your way of thinking. Well," he went on, "I am afraid that is the best advice I can give you. It looks as though this is the end of the firm of James Stewart, Ship-chandler. Don't be downhearted, my boy, this life is full of reverses and you'll get over them."

So taking what comfort he could from these words, Stewart returned to the basement. Back in his parlour he took out his ledger once again and decided to rule it off and see how he stood. His bills with the bakers and other suppliers had better be totalled up; he must know the worst. Sadly he surveyed the book; even if Mr. Eastwood's scheme worked, that ledger would no longer hold out its former fascination. In the future, as somebody else's runner, it would be a case of just coldly recording the goods in and out. A record of ships visited. A purely impersonal document with none of the entries warming his heart and fanning his ambition as they had done in the past. Mr. Eastwood was right, it was a poor sort of business and the sooner he was out of it the better. All the same, there was a sense of frustration upon him. "Oh, hell!" he said, shutting the ledger angrily, and decided to go to the 'Pig and Whistle' for a drink.

"My, you are late," said Susy, looking at the clock. Most of the habituées had already departed and a bare half-hour remained before the shutters went up for the night.

"Give me a drink," he demanded miserably, "and for God's sake cheer me up."

Susy looked at him in astonishment. "Goodness," she cried, "you haven't half got the willies. You must have been working too hard. Here, drink this," and she handed him a glass of whisky. "You know," she went on, "a young man of your age doesn't want to spend all his time with men old enough to be his father. Why don't you get hold of a nice girl now and take her out sometimes? The change would do you good. Those friends of yours are making you as old as themselves."

"By jingo, Susy, you're right," said Stewart, slapping the bar-counter hard. "how about you and me going to the Amphitheatre some night?"

"Oh dear," she said regretfully, "I've just promised to let Mr. Taylor take me to the 'Star' on my next night off."

"Never mind, then," said Stewart, suddenly diffident, "I dare say I can get someone else."

Susy looked up in alarm, "Of course I could put Mr. Taylor off till another night."

"No, don't do that; you've made your promise, you must stick to it."

"I know he wouldn't mind really."

"No, a promise is a promise," said the young man determinedly.

"I love horses and circuses," she said.

"There'll probably be some good vaudeville turns at the 'Star'."

"I don't think you really want me to go with you?"

"It's a pity Mr. Taylor asked you first; still, it can't be helped."

"I could put him off if you really wanted to take me?"

"Mr. Cooke's putting on Mazeppo with Wallett and others, and there's a new riding act called Paddy Kelly, the hero of the Russian War," said Stewart casually.

Susy's eyes sparkled with excitement. "That settles it," she said gaily. "Mr. Taylor will have to wait," and then the landlord came out to put up the shutters and Susy had to dash away to carry out some last minute orders. So Stewart strolled back home, feeling a little more cheerful as the whisky warmed his stomach.

Meanwhile, the man who had brought about this swift change of circumstances was carrying out his nightly tour of inspection. Every night at six o'clock he set off on his rounds, but that particular night he had so far departed from his custom as to leave half an hour earlier in order to deal with the firm of James Stewart, ship's husband, en route. Afterwards, he had continued his journey. His first call was invariably at the 'Man at the Wheel', his biggest house. The manager followed him round obsequiously, endeavouring to anticipate criticism by moving stools and tables this way and that, giving a kick or two to the saw-dust on the floor, and fussing needlessly with the gas-jets.

Higgins believed in the personal touch, and that was why every night he made a point of visiting each one of his taverns. He couldn't manage each bar himself, but the deputies he appointed could be sure that hail, rain, snow or disaster, the boss would be round at some period during the night to eye speculatively the state of the customers, and mentally jot it down for comparison with the receipts brought to his office the next day. The district was rough, and vice and foul play lurked threaten-ingly in every shadow, for there was no attempt made to enforce law and order in that dockside area, at least not at night-time. So Higgins took no chances and two ex-pugilists followed a few paces in his rear, his personal bodyguard.

It was a long business, but then, so was the night, and with no clos-ing hour to speak of there was time enough to walk from one end of the Dock Road to the other. That nightly walk, too, gave Higgins incom-parable opportunities of observing what was happening in taverns other than his own, but above all, it satisfied him that business was brisk in his own houses.

His routine was fairly rigid. From the stately house which he maintained at the lower end of Duke Street amongst the wealthy city merchants, he rarely ventured until evening. That house, he imagined, gave him the standing of a highly respected member of Liverpool society.

It was to this house that Stewart went on the following day, and the nearby Custom House clock was just striking twelve when he arrived outside. It was a plain, dignified building, no different from its neigh-bours, but for all its lack of trimmings it gave the impression of solid prosperity, so representative of the age. The massive carved door was surmounted by a delicately panelled, semi-circular, glass fanlight, and on either side were two smallish pseudo-Greek columns supporting the lintel.

Stewart seized the highly polished brass figure that did duty as a knocker, but long before the echo of the brief thunderings had died away the door swung silently open and a great negro, dressed extrava-gantly in white knee breeches, ushered him inside. He found himself in a large, airy, well-lit hall, from whose finely moulded ceiling hung an imposing chandelier, with hundreds of small twinkling glass pendants reflecting the light. On the tiled floor were spaced costly rugs and skins, which made footsteps sound harsh and staccato one minute, then soft and muffled the next. The furniture, arranged decorously, was the work of skilled foreign craftsmen.

As he followed the negro, Stewart surveyed his surroundings appreciatively. It was the first time he had ever been inside a house designed originally for some merchant prince, and he was awed at the wealth displayed by the costly fittings and paintings. They carried on down the hall, past the wide staircase with its beautifully carved balustrade flighting up to other floors, and eventually reached the back of the house and that part which served as Higgins' office. By contrast, the room into which he was shown was plainly and sparsely furnished, but it served to emphasize the grandeur of the rest. It looks, thought Stewart, as though there's plenty of money to be made somewhere and Higgins seems to know where. His reflections were cut short by the sound of footsteps outside and then Higgins entered.

"Well," he asked curtly, "have you made up your mind ?"

"Yes and no," began Stewart.

"What do you mean ?" barked the other angrily.

"There's one or two things to be discussed first," said the young man coolly ; "the principal one is the question of my stock."

"I told you I'd take it from you at my price."

"That's just it. Your price may not be my price, and unless I'm guaranteed the same price that I paid for it, then I'll take my business elsewhere. I may as well tell you I have already been in touch with other ship-chandlers in the port.

"Why come to me then ?"

"I promised you that I would, and I'm still prepared to come to you provided you give me fair treatment."

Higgins looked at him scathingly. "Give me your ledger," he demanded, and as the other handed it over he pretended to examine it closely. "These orders you've got are only for single ships. Why," he scoffed, "my runners contract for whole fleets. There's not much good-will about your business."

"Even your runners couldn't get those orders," said Stewart calmly, "and what is more, I can guarantee that when those ships come back to Liverpool again they'll give me their orders."

Higgins handed back the ledger, he knew that other ship-chandlers would certainly take this young fellow on if they sighted the transactions he had negotiated in four months. "I'll pay you three quarters of the cost of your old stock and employ you at one per cent commission," he said.

"No," the young man said firmly, "take my stock at cost price or I offer it to someone else."

The Irishman looked angrily across at him. It was a new experience to be challenged like this, and it looked as though his temper might get out of hand. Stewart's calm assurance, however, showed him that here was someone of different metal and he'd have to treat him in different fashion. Cunningly the Irishman lapsed into a broad Irish brogue, "Sure now, Mr. Stewart, I admires your spirit, but ye don't happen to be one o' th' Sons of Orange now, do ye ?"

"Why, no !" exclaimed Stewart, surprised. "Who are they ?"

"Never ye mind, me lad. I'll take your stock and you'll come and work for me. When it's all sold I'll see about putting you on to a proper wage and commission. But mind you, not a day before."

It seemed that the interview was over, but half-way to the door, Higgins turned round and said, "You may be a smart young fellow, but no funny tricks with me. If you understand that, it may save us both a deal of trouble later on. You'd better bring that ledger of yours over here every Saturday, so that I can see what you're up to."

The next minute he'd gone, and the negro was there to show Stewart the way out.

He walked across the hall with mixed feelings. The only good thing about it all was that he was managing to scrape out of his ship-chandlery business without burning his fingers, yet the unfairness of practically having to work for nothing until he'd sold all his stock was galling.

Nearing the door he heard a girl's high-pitched voice calling out excitedly, and the next instant there was a commotion on the stairs and a dog came bounding down with a slipper in his mouth. Hard on the dog's heels came a breathless, red-haired young woman. Only when she was at the bottom of the stairs did she catch sight of Stewart, and she stopped suddenly.

"I'm sorry," she said, "I had no idea there was anyone else in the house."

The young man, hardly believing his eyes, started forward, murmuring to himself, "The girl in the church!" Miss Scripps, too, judging by her heightened colour, appeared to have recognized him. But of course it was no time for formal introductions, for there stood the young lady precariously balancing on one foot, the other being modestly withdrawn out of sight. When he at last realized her embarrassing position he hastened to retrieve the cause of her dilemma.

The dog thought it was all part of the game, and with slithering, scratching feet darted from refuge to refuge, while the negro servant and Stewart both vainly tried to coax it near. What with the girl's laughter and Stewart's hopeful, enticing calls, they were making quite a disturbance, and when at last, bright-eyed and panting, the dog allowed itself to be cornered, the young man, considerably dishevelled, deemed it best to approach the animal cautiously on all fours. He was in the act of picking up the slipper when a heavy voice rang out coldly, "What the devil are you doing there?"

Stewart stopped as though he had been shot, and peering over his shoulder he saw the critical figure of Higgins approaching from the back of the hall. There was a flurry of skirts, and, unseen, Miss Scripps darted hastily up the stair, the dog flying after her, still with the slipper in its mouth. The negro servant looked dumbly on as though he had just noticed Stewart crawling about the floor. The young man rose self-consciously to his feet. The Irishman was glowering at him suspiciously;

there was no sign of the girl or the dog—but there was the open door and the street. Stewart decided it was no time for explanation and precipitately fled.

Once outside, his self-possession returned slowly, but he was still experiencing a feeling of elation when he found himself back in Chapel Walk. He was mystified to find that Miss Scripps lived in Duke Street, but that fact didn't worry him unduly; what pleased him was the knowledge that now he did know where she lived and henceforward there was nothing to stop him from getting to know her properly, or so he thought.

The following week he went to see Higgins several times on pretext of business. The Irishman thought it was keenness, but very shortly he grew tired of these uninvited visits, and at last put an end to them by declaring sourly that any problems Stewart might have in connection with his work would keep till the Saturday when he brought his ledger along. If he wanted anything else he had better apply to Higgins' foreman at the Salthouse Dock warehouse.

Stewart, in his new frame of mind, was not the sort of man to accept that state of things indefinitely, and after the rebuff from Higgins his mind was constantly preoccupied with plans and schemes for getting better acquainted with Miss Scripps. He got little encouragement, for on Sunday the young woman had looked right through him as if he hadn't been there and, perplexed, he wondered why.

Meanwhile, Susy's free evening came and went, but Stewart those days seemed to have forgotten all about the 'Pig and Whistle', and his promise to take Susy to the Amphitheatre. Discouraged at the way things were progressing, he returned one day from the docks, realizing that in his present state of mind he could make nothing of this business of selling ships' stores for his new employer. He sat wearily at his desk, his face cupped in his hands and, as always, when he sat down with nothing particular to do, the vision of Miss Scripps rose up to disturb him.

He sat there mooning for a while and then resolutely picked up his pen and started scribbling away furiously. When he had finished he folded the paper carefully, placed it in an envelope and addressed it to Miss E. M. Scripps, Duke Street. Then, his courage faltering, he sat back irresolutely, waiting for the ink to dry.

By discreet inquiry he had ascertained that Higgins left home regularly at six o'clock each evening. Stewart thought that if he wished to meet the girl without being interrupted, the time to do it was in Higgins' absence. The scheme which he had just worked out required a good deal of courage, but in the end his feelings for Miss Scripps overcame his nervousness.

That evening, a few minutes before six o'clock, he stood idling in-conspicuously outside a little nautical optician's shop at the bottom end of Duke Street. His plan was to wait there until he saw Higgins sally forth and then, after a reasonable interval, present himself at the door. He would tell the negro that he had a letter to be delivered personally to Miss Scripps.

Standing there somewhat apprehensively before a disorderly array of compass cards, blue-back charts, telescopes and a whole heap of navigational instruments and books, doubts began to assail him. His throat dried up mysteriously and he felt so nervous that for two pins he would have given up the idea, but somehow his boots seemed glued to the pavement and he knew even while he was standing there, gazing anxiously at the dusty contents of the optician's window, that there was something impelling him forward.

Promptly at six o'clock the door of No. 7 swung open, and the familiar, strikingly dressed figure of Irish Higgins appeared. Stewart, in the feeble gaslight of the street lamps, dimly made him out as he descended into the street; the Irishman passed close to Stewart's back, and turning the corner leading to the Custom House was lost to sight.

The next quarter of an hour seemed interminable. Each minute suggested another obstacle, to his imagination. This would never do, he told himself, and delaying no longer, walked quickly over to the house, ran boldly up the steps, and, as though to defy his failing spirits, rapped loudly on the door. For some unknown reason there was a pause before the door opened and he realized that he still had time to rush down the steps again and be lost amongst the passers-by. But before this final urge could be put into execution, the imposing door swung open and the opportunity to withdraw was gone.

He produced the letter from his pocket and told the negro servant that he had orders to give it to Miss Scripps herself. The servant showed him into a large adjoining room and then padded away into another part of the quiet house. During his absence, Stewart was at liberty to review his next course of action. So far, it had all been too easy, but what was he to say when the girl appeared? He stared round anxiously, searching for some excuse that would explain away his presence and permit him to wander into the Elysian fields of her friendship. There was nothing in that over-furnished room to give him inspiration or guide him as to how he might overcome those first few, rapidly approaching critical moments. There was a hint of grandeur in the lofty room with its small paned windows, but he missed it, his attention noticed, instead, the cramping confines of the heavily brocaded lace curtains and the wallpaper violently patterned with coloured flowers. His gaze wandered over the chairs and sofas upholstered with rich red plush, past the round table covered with a crimson cloth and decorated with an incongruous basket of waxed fruit. He noted the bronze athletes on the mantelpiece, and his glance came to rest on a large gilded mirror disfigured with numerous fly spots. As he surveyed this tawdry piece of work his spirits rose. Why, he reflected, he'd seen many a similar mirror in the interiors of the dockside public-houses. The thought gave him confidence, he felt he was in a familiar atmosphere and his customary buoyancy of mind began to reassert itself.

Before his confidence, however, could be restored, the door opened, and there confronting him was Miss Scripps. Now that she was standing in front of him, his self-assurance, so recently summoned, ebbed swiftly away. For what seemed a long time neither of them spoke; Stewart, because his wits had deserted him entirely, and the young woman because it was deemed unladylike to speak to a man first.

What on earth could he say? Feverishly he cast about him, but to no purpose. At length, when the silence was becoming unbearable, Miss Scripps said, "I understand you have a letter for me?"

"Yes! . . . No! . . . that is . . ." he began, now feeling thoroughly alarmed lest the contents of that letter be ever disclosed, "there was a letter, but there's no need for me to deliver it now." His eye desperately sought the mantelpiece and on it he saw the bronze figure of an oil-skinned sailor throwing a rope. It was a lifeline in more than one sense, for it suggested an idea.

"You see," he began, "I'm trying to organize a concert in aid of seamen's charities, and having seen you in church I thought—I wondered—if you would care to support us? Of course," he gabbled on recklessly, "I don't know whether you sing, or play or have any other accomplishments, but I thought you might be interested enough to help us in some way."

The young woman looked at him in bewilderment, and Stewart, thankful for her silence, launched into a torrent of explanation. Each step took him deeper and deeper into the mire, and he floundered on, feeling safe only so long as he kept talking. Eventually, even his inspiration dried up and he stood there uneasily, considerably disturbed by the vision of this cool, slim young woman.

"This is all so very strange, Mr.—er—— Why," she laughed, "I don't even know your name."

"Stewart," he hastily apologized.

"Well," she went on, looking puzzled, "I was only talking to the rector this afternoon and he never mentioned a word about this concert."

"I'm afraid I've misled you, ma'am," stammered Stewart, "it has nothing to do with the church really; in fact it is just the idea of a few of us who, through the connections of our business, are interested in seafarers."

"In that case I must speak to my uncle, Mr. Higgins . . ."

"Oh, no," interposed the young man hastily, "I don't think that is at all necessary. You see we are not looking for financial support; all we need are voluntary helpers."

"Is it a bazaar you're holding?" she asked, more puzzled than ever.

"Hardly that, ma'am," he faltered, "though we may have a few exhibits of seamen's work on show."

"Well, why do you want me to assist?"

Stewart was nearing the end of his endurance and he looked anxiously at the marble clock above the fireplace. He edged towards the door, his courage fast giving way. But further questions were forming on the young woman's lips, and he thought he detected a determined gleam in her eyes. It was time he was off, the ice had been broken; his intention had been achieved; he backed into the hall with almost indecent haste. The negro was standing ready with his hat, and hurriedly seizing it, Stewart uttered a few indistinguishable words and left Miss Scripps without further formalities.

Out in the night air, with the door of No. 7 closed behind him, Stewart wiped his brow and ran a finger round the edge of his collar. Of course he'd get out of it all right by telling her the next time they met that the scheme had been dropped by the sponsors. His mind was quite easy on that point.

View of the Mersey

CHAPTER 6

PLANNING THE SHIPPING EXHIBITION

LIFE after that incident took on a more pleasant aspect. Stewart set to work with renewed zeal and even Higgins was impressed by the amount of business he secured. That pleasant state of mind wasn't to continue for long, for two or three days after his visit to Duke Street, and in the late forenoon, he happened to be busy in the outhouses checking through an order, when Silas came up with an offensive leer and said that a couple of Judies wanted to see him.

"What?" exclaimed Stewart, astonished. "Who are they and what do they want?"

"Search me, skipper, 'ow should I know? Maybe they're just curious and want to see what a ship's husband looks like; or maybe they've heard we stock a nice line of ear-rings and thimbles! But whatever they want, skipper, they've made up their minds to stay awhile, for they've backed their tops'ls and dropped their anchors in the parlour."

Stewart hurriedly went inside. It was probably a couple of captains' wives looking for their husbands. He pushed open the door and then stopped, confused. "Why, ma'am . . ." he said.

"You do look surprised," said Miss Scripps, a trifle aggressively. "I hope Martha and I haven't done wrong by bearding the lion in his den, but the fact is, Mr. Stewart, I was so interested in the scheme you proposed the other evening that I've been around the parish getting other ladies interested."

"Good heavens!" cried Stewart, aghast.

"You did say you wanted a few lady helpers," she said reproachfully, disappointed at Stewart's lack of enthusiasm.

"Of course, of course," he hastened to assure her; striving to make his voice sound grateful.

"Here is a list of their names."

Stewart took the piece of paper mechanically, and wondered apprehensively what was to follow.

"The rector, too, was extremely interested," continued Miss Scripps, "and I took the liberty of promising that you would come down to the Church Hall next Friday at half past four so that you could explain it all more fully to them."

Stewart made a half-hearted excuse. "That really is my most busy time," and then, noting the gathering signs of disapproval, lost no time in adding that of course nothing would stop him from being there.

After his visitors had been carefully conducted off the premises, he returned to his desk. Why hadn't he told her there and then that the scheme had been dropped? The truth was that Miss Scripps had taken him unawares, and it was only after she had gone that he realized he had let his opportunity slip. His troubled eyes rested on the slip of paper naming the ladies she had approached in regard to the scheme, and as he scanned down the list his face grew longer and longer; it appeared that the wives of many of the most important citizens had indicated their willingness to help. He put his head in his hands and groaned deeply. The affair had suddenly become much more than a joke, and unless he was very careful he would be hopelessly committed to it. The only person who might be equal to the occasion was Sam Sharp. Like a drowning man clutching at a straw, Stewart set out to find him.

It was nearly one o'clock and at that hour he knew that the reporter would be at Nicholson's 'Slaughter House'.

He found Sharp leaning up against the bar, nibbling the biscuits and cheese which the landlord thought fit to provide for his before-lunch customers. The young man went straight to the point.

"Sam," he said, "I'm in the dickens of a mess." Then, seeing the older man's tankard was empty, tactfully had it replenished.

Sharp listened gravely to Stewart's story, and when he had finished said sagely:

"You've let yourself in for something there, young man. *Cherchez la femme*," he added knowingly, "and I'll solve half the world's troubles. Still, here you are in the devil of a hole and we've got to get you out of it. Sam Sharp never deserted a friend yet and . . . make it a pint, miss . . . he isn't going to now. Let me get this straight; you've got yourself entangled with this young woman . . ." He broke off suspiciously. "You haven't got her into trouble?"

"No," said Stewart impatiently, "it's not a sordid intrigue."

"Who is she then?"

"Irish Higgins' niece."

"Holy smoke, no! Nay, even for the sake of friendship I'm not getting mixed up with Irish Higgins. I know my limitations. You'll have to work out your own salvation."

"But Higgins doesn't know anything about it," pleaded Stewart.

The reporter looked at him doubtfully. Catching sight of the barmaid he said, "Give me a double-rum quick, Elsie." Then turning to Stewart he said, "Let's have something to drink first, maybe it sounds worse than it really is."

Sharp drank the rum and then continued thoughtfully, "You say all these interested folks are churchgoers?"

"Yes," said Stewart wearily.

"Well, listen carefully, young man, I've got an idea. They'll be thinking that it's some sort of concert-cum-bazaar, and you've got to convince them that it's nothing of the kind. Tell them that you're inviting artistes from the local theatres to supply the entertainment. They'll never stomach professional troupers. In fact, to make doubly certain,

I'll get a couple of mummers from the 'Star' to go down with you on Friday. They'll do anything for a glass of beer."

"It's a good idea," said Stewart hopefully, "and you really will get hold of these fellows for me ?"

"Rest assured, boy, Sam Sharp's word is his bond ; you should know that by now. I'll have them in the 'Pig and Whistle' for you half an hour before your meeting. That should fix it."

For the rest of the week Stewart had to pacify his fears that this arrangement would extricate him from the mess into which he had fallen, and to keep his mind off less pleasant things he worked doubly hard in soliciting orders from the ships in the docks, and the extra business he secured kept him engaged every evening. His continued absence from the 'Pig and Whistle', however, did not go unnoticed by Susy. She put it down to the fact that Stewart had failed to take her to the Amphitheatre, and his guilty conscience was keeping him away. But if he thought that time might heal the wound he had inflicted on Susy's pride then, she assured herself, he was going to be very much mistaken.

On Friday afternoon, just before four o'clock, Stewart calmly strolled into the 'Pig and Whistle'. Except for Susy, the place was deserted. She greeted him frigidly.

"I've had a couple of nights off since the last time you were in," she said nonchalantly.

"Have you now ?" he replied, looking anxiously round for signs of the reporter and his friends.

His off-handedness was a little too much for Susy, and angrily she demanded, "I thought you were going to take me to the Amphitheatre ?"

"Bless my soul, now I come to think of it, so I was. Clean slipped my memory. Still, another time will do, Susy ? You haven't seen anything of friend Sharp ?"

Susy's attitude changed. "Now you come to mention it, he was in here with a couple of actors from the 'Star'," she said a shade too innocently. "My, they were having a beano, but you'll see for yourself, they said they'd be back to meet you !" and she gave him an enigmatical look that made him uneasy.

He hung on ; half past four came and still there was no sign. He couldn't wait much longer, and at five o'clock he decided to give them up, and looking darkly at the triumphant Susy he made towards the door.

As he hurried down Chapel Walk he vainly thought of what he should say. Perhaps they would all have gone, but as he opened the door of the Church Hall, that hope faded. He was quick to sense the unsympathetic atmosphere as Miss Scripps introduced him to the rector, and all too soon he found himself launched into an address to an extremely critical audience. Before he had got far, there was a disturbance outside

and a considerably agitated young curate came hurrying over to the
table at which the rector sat with Stewart.

"There are three men outside, very much the worse for drink," he
whispered in horrified tones. "They insist they have been hired by Mr.
Stewart to address the ladies."

The rector tugged at Stewart's coat, and thankful for the interruption
the young man stopped to listen to what the rector had to say. He simu-
lated surprise and shook his head deprecatingly; there must be some
mistake. All the same, he thought it would be best if he went outside and
dealt with them. The rector was never a man to shirk his duties and he
insisted on going too, leaving the young curate to calm the ladies.

Outside the hall the door was barely shut on them when Sam Sharp,
with an unsteady gait, reeled alongside Stewart and threw his arms
affectionately round the young man's neck. "They won't let'sh in,
m'boy," he hiccupped.

Stewart unhooked the arms from his neck and said as firmly as
he could, "Stand back, my man, I don't even know you."

"Wha'sh that y' say?" said Sharp stupidly. "It'sh me, your ol'
frien' Sam."

Stewart looked apologetically across at the churchman. "I think
I'd better call the police," he said.

"Police! Who says police?" and there rose up from the background
a tall, cadaverous-looking individual whose floppy hat and flowing
cravat proclaimed him to Stewart as one of the actors from the 'Star'.
The fellow strolled theatrically over to Sam Sharp and linked his arm
in the reporter's, then, with a histrionic gesture, said, "Come, let's away
to prison; we two alone will sing like birds i' the cage."

"King Lear, three eight," triumphantly called another voice, and
the third member of the trio came into view.

"Quite right, quite right," said the tall actor, and then, catching
sight of the rector, stalked malevolently towards him.

"I know thee not, old man; fall to thy prayers.
How ill white hairs become a fool and a jestor!
I have long dreamed of such a kind of man, so surfeit swelled.
so old and so profane."

The startled clergyman jumped back a pace.

"There'sh gra'tude," mumbled Sam Sharp, tears welling up in his
eyes; "it seems we're no' wanted. C'm on, le'sh find more 'spectable
company," and arm in arm they staggered away, tags from Shakespeare
floating dimly over their shoulders.

"Bless my soul," said the astounded parson, "never in all my twenty
years in this parish have I ever known anything like that," and he
glanced suspiciously at Stewart.

Back in the hall Miss Scripps came across to tell him that the ladies had agreed to form a committee amongst themselves, and they had appointed her as chairman. "Excellent," said Stewart, his spirits rising at the sight of the meeting now in process of breaking up. "Then if it's all over I trust you will permit me to escort you home. This is an unpleasant neighbourhood." So for five wonderful minutes he walked by her side.

His heady excitement didn't forsake him until some time after he had left Miss Scripps at the bottom of Duke Street, but at last his woolly dreams disintegrated and he realized that his last opportunity of withdrawing was gone, and he was irrevocably committed to this wild scheme. The only consolation he could gather was that it meant seeing Miss Scripps frequently, but even this, his sub-conscious mind warned him, judging by past experience, might prove a sugar-coated pill.

Still, if he made a success of the whole affair, Miss Scripps would undoubtedly think highly of him, and determined to do his best he went upstairs to seek Mr. Eastwood's advice.

The old shipowner, after listening carefully, looked at him admiringly. It was a first-rate idea, but what had made him think of it? The old man became mildly enthusiastic, and when they started to discuss where it should be held, Mr. Eastwood said right away, there was only one place and that was St. George's Hall.

"But," gasped Stewart, "that's far too big. It's only going to be a church bazaar sort of thing."

Mr. Eastwood pooh-poohed the idea. Ten years previously he had visited the great Crystal Palace Exhibition, and it had left such an impression on him that he thought Stewart's modest plan, involving some shabby little parochial hall, not worth considering. "You must think largely, Mr. Stewart," he admonished surprisingly, and under this stimulating advice the young man began to hold more ambitious views.

"But just a minute, sir," he said doubtfully, "wasn't the Great Exhibition a financial failure?"

Mr. Eastwood admitted that it was, but went on to reassure him that the reason lay in bad administration. The people had come to see it. That was the point. People always would go to see an exhibition, and all that was wanted was a little careful scrutiny of the expenses beforehand.

Stewart went happily down to his basement again and sat down to elucidate some of the many ideas which Mr. Eastwood and he had debated between them.

The very next day he set about initiating some of the schemes which called for outside assistance, and on his way back from several visits to other influential shipowners whom Mr. Eastwood had recommended, he decided to slip into the 'Pig and Whistle'. He found Sam Sharp there looking the picture of misery. The old reporter began to apologize for the unfortunate misunderstanding, as he called it, of the day before, but just then Susy came up and Sam, with a reproachful look at the girl, lapsed into a morbid silence.

"My," said Susy perkily to Stewart, "you aren't half looking pleased with yourself."

"Who wouldn't be with you around?" he asked ironically. She gave a sniff wnich all too plainly indicated what she thought of him, and moved away again.

Sharp leaned towards him, placatingly. "That young woman mixed my liquor yesterday," he said with a belief born of long cogitation.

"I suspected it," said Stewart, "but don't you worry, Sam, I handled that meeting all right. The date is fixed and the show comes off in two months' time. I'm only sorry I can't stop to explain, but you'll realize how busy I am!" and feeling very important he left the reporter sitting there.

What he had said about being busy turned out to be more true than even he had suspected, and every day now his time was fully occupied in contacting interested persons and generally getting under way the whole machinery of organization.

At the end of ten days, the Ladies' Committee began to get restless. Except for that fleeting visit to the Church Hall they'd heard nothing further. They searched in the Press for some report of the part the Ladies' Committee was supposed to play, but in vain.

As a result a determined young lady, accompanied by Martha, waited on Stewart one bleak February afternoon. He, all unknowing, was seeking brief respite from his crowded busy days by making himself pleasant to Susy at the bar of the 'Pig and Whistle'. With an eye to his business future he had gone there purposely to make up their earlier quarrel, and he found Susy quite amenable since she felt she had paid him back for the slight he had imposed upon her.

It was very pleasant dallying there in the warmth of the bar; chatting idly away and listening to the girl's quips, he felt it was just the relaxation a busy man needed.

"Come along, Susy," he was saying, "just to show we're friends again have another glass of port," and because he'd had a couple of drinks on an empty stomach put his arm in friendly fashion around her slim waist.

"Now, now, Mr. Stewart," she said, feebly attempting to remove his arm, "I'm a good girl I am, and I don't want any of your nonsense!" And then, obeying some sudden impulse, she stopped struggling, put her head forward and lightly kissed him on the cheek.

As though he had been stung, Stewart's arm dropped to his side, and with an awkward laugh he said : "Good lord, you mustn't do that, Susy! Suppose the landlord saw you!"

"Well, we've got to keep the customers satisfied somehow," she replied perkily, "and, anyway, what about you putting your arm round a respectable girl's waist ?"

He was humming happily to himself when he arrived back at Chapel Walk, in fact he was in such high spirits that he gave Silas a slap on the back and without listening to him flung open the door cheerfully. He stopped abruptly, half-way in the entrance. "Why! Miss Scripps," he said nervously.

"Yes," replied that young lady frigidly, "we've been waiting half an hour, but of course, Mr. Stewart, we realize you are a very busy man, and it is only right that we of the Ladies' Committee should be the ones to be inconvenienced."

"I assure you, ma'am," said Stewart placatingly, "if I'd known you were going to call I would never have ventured a foot across the door-step."

Miss Scripps relented a little in the face of such earnestness, and Stewart went on to talk with increasing confidence of all the work he had done since their last meeting. Then he noted her cold, critical gaze, and it put him completely off his stride.

"You've got some red paint on your left cheek!" she informed him startlingly.

"Why . . . I . . . er . . ." stammered Stewart, now completely confused, and to recover time he strode over to the mirror. He saw the marks made by Susy's painted lips. Embarrassed, he attempted to rub the tell-tale marks away. "That's the worst of being a ships' store dealer. Red paint . . . ! One's apt to get covered with all sorts of things," he finished lamely.

"It appears to be a dirty sort of business," she said enigmatically, and then turned to the reason for her visit. The Ladies' Committee were getting anxious. There had been all those advertisements in the newspapers and not a word about the activities of their committee. Where did they fit into the general scheme ?

Of course. It struck him like a flash. Give them the platform entertainments. Would they care to make themselves responsible for that side ? He produced sketchy suggestions for her guidance. Play-acting would fill the bill nicely. The plays should have a strong Christian theme yet be applicable to the principle of the Exhibition. Any amount of ideas suggested themselves to him, but doubtless the Ladies' Committee would prefer to choose their own.

For fully a minute Miss Scripps sat there without saying a word. Stewart took her silence for admiration, but of course, he was mistaken there.

At last Miss Scripps said, "All this is going to take a lot of money."

Stewart, carried away with the impression he thought he was making, said recklessly: "Don't worry about that, ma'am ; just sign the bills and send them in to me."

So the young woman duly reported back to her committee, determined in her own mind that the entertainment side of the Exhibition would be the most outstanding.

For the next few weeks, Stewart's life was fuller than it had ever been. His poor ship-chandlery business went unnoticed, except by Higgins. The young man still took his ledger along every Saturday, and Higgins' smile of derision as he examined the scant number of entries was disconcerting. However, Stewart assured himself that he could put up with that; his main concern at the moment was the Exhibition. After that was over, there would be time enough to worry about ships' stores, and actually, as the opening date of the Exhibition drew nearer, he lost sight altogether of the fact that his principal means to a livelihood was selling stores to ships.

Problems to solve and decisions to take kept him tied more than ever to his stool in Chapel Walk, and he even had no time to worry or think about Miss Scripps and her Ladies' Committee.

Eventually, with a host of arrangements and details still to be completed, there was only another week to go. The proprietor of the *Shipping Albion*, who had magnanimously agreed to co-operate with the publicity, set out to warm the advertising pace to its climax. Liverpool's Maritime Exhibition formed a topic of conversation for everyone, and there could be no doubt that Charlie Tomkins had done his job well.

The only thing that seemed to hang fire was the Shipping Pageant, for although Stewart had advertised prizes, entries were painfully slow in coming in, and he sat puzzling over this last detail one evening when the door opened and Susy, of all persons, walked boldly in.

"Good evening," she said cheerfully, "I hope you don't mind me dropping in ? But I was passing this way so I thought I'd return the book I borrowed. You never seem to come to the 'Pig and Whistle' these days, or I'd have given it you there."

Stewart placed the book back on the shelf. "You're sure you've read it ?" he queried. "You've only had it five or six months !"

"It's nothing like so long," she said coolly. "Anyway, even if it is, I've brought it back, haven't I ?"

"I suppose you're on your way to your mother's again ?" he said resignedly.

"Now how did you guess that ?" she asked brightly. "Ooh ! you do look tired. Why don't you take a night off from all this work and come along with me to the 'Star' ? They're playing *The Murder in the Red Barn*; one of our girls said it was ever so good."

"Can't be done, Susy. I'm much too busy. The Exhibition is due to open in four days' time and there's still lots of work to be done. But look," he added generously, "here's two tickets for the greatest exhibition Liverpool has ever had. You'll be able to tell your grandchildren about it in the years to come !"

Susy took the two tickets and looked at them curiously, "Do you think it's going to be a success?" she asked.

"Nothing can stop it," he replied confidently.

"Isn't there something I can do?" she asked.

"I'm afraid there isn't, Susy. You see, we're not licensed for drink, and you'd be lost without your beer-engine."

"I'm a good enough dancer to appear in those theatricals that folks say you are putting on, and I've got a good pair of legs, too!"

Before Stewart could say a word she had hitched up her skirts a little and was about to demonstrate a few steps. The young man dragged his hypnotized gaze away and looked fearfully at the door. If old Mr. Eastwood was to come down now as he had promised! . . . "Susy," he said, scandalized, "behave yourself."

"Well, they're all right, aren't they?" she asked, looking down admiringly, and not until he reluctantly admitted that they were did she permit decorum to return.

Stewart mopped his perspiring brow with one hand while the fingers of the other drummed nervously on the desk. "I'd willingly give you something to do but . . . perhaps if you went and saw Miss Scripps she might find a place for you in one of the tableaux."

Susy tossed her head indignantly. "No, thank you," she said, "I'd sooner stick to my beer-engine, as you call it."

"Unless you've got some idea that might be useful for the pageant?" he asked hopefully.

"How about Lady Godiva and a white horse?" she asked cheerfully.

"Be sensible," he said irritably. "So far I've only got five entries."

He looked so worried that Susy shed her light-hearted manner and thought seriously for a minute. "Why don't you get the brewers to help you," she asked suddenly. "They'd like the idea of putting their drays into a procession, especially if it would help people to notice their publics. If you can get Captain Evan Rees to let us girls off for an hour we'd jump at the chance of a ride on a dray—all decked out in our Sunday best."

Stewart looked up hopefully; it seemed a good idea. "But I don't know any brewers," he said dejectedly.

"You know Irish Higgins, don't you?" she said sharply.

"Yes, but——"

"He's the man to see. He'll fix it up for you. All you have to do is to make him understand that it's a good advertisement, and he'll put all twenty of his wagons in the show."

Stewart stood up and started pacing about the room. There was a lot in the idea, and if it had been anybody else but Higgins! . . .

Susy regarded him with scorn. "If he's all that's worrying you, I'll go and fix it up myself."

"You!" said Stewart, astonished. "Why, what could you do with a man like that?"

Susy told him that Higgins had been pestering her for a long time to take over one of his public-houses; he knew who was responsible for the 'Pig and Whistle's popularity.

"What I like about you, Susy," said Stewart, "is that you're so modest and retiring!"

"Oh! very well then, if you don't want me to help you——"

"Now, Susy," said Stewart hurriedly, "don't take me up wrong. You know I think a lot of you, but I'm just a poor youug man struggling for a living."

"And what do you think I am?" asked Susy indignantly.

"A good girl, I hope," said Stewart, raising his eyes piously to the ceiling.

She looked at him, exasperated, and before going out she said, "Believe me, Mr. Stewart, you've got to be a good girl to get along in my business."

He sat there for quite a white after she had gone, thinking about her and trying to analyse his emotions. She never set his pulses racing as Miss Scripps did, and yet he liked her company, liked the amusing things she said and did.

ST. GEORGE'S HALL

That last week seemed to flash by, and with scores of things still to be done, the opening day of the Exhibition arrived. At three o'clock in the afternoon the mayor performed the opening ceremony before a crowded audience. Shortly afterwards, Charlie Tomkins came up rubbing his hands and beaming all over his face. He slapped Stewart enthusiastically on the back and said gleefully, "Nah, lad, wot did Ah tell thee?" and looking round him, all Stewart's fears of failure disappeared. Judging by the crowd, the Exhibition was a success. Silas came up to report that the queue of folks waiting to get in stretched round the building and disappeared out of sight beyond Clayton Square. Tomkins looked at the crowd in the main hall. "I reckon there's a good seventy-five punds there," he said calculatingly, and hurried away to congratulate his advertising patrons on the publicity he had secured them.

But Stewart could not afford to stand there idling, there was plenty of work for him to do in seeing that the administration worked smoothly and darting here and there he encouraged and reprimanded and generally saw to it that the paid staff were earning their wages. Towards nine o'clock he began to think that now he might take a little respite from his labours and have a look how the various entertainments were going. He decided to go and see the second performance of 'The Mutiny of the Bounty', which the Ladies' Committee were putting on.

He made a special point of sitting beside Mr. Cooke, the manager of the Amphitheatre.

"It's very good of you to allow your artistes to appear in this show," he said gratefully.

"Nay, sir, I'll make no bones about it, I've closed down for spring cleaning this week. It's these actors as should be grateful to you. They'd be getting nowt otherwise."

"You mean we're paying them?" asked Stewart in surprise.

"That's what I understood from the young woman who engaged 'em. If there's a mistake you'd better let me know quick and I'll get 'em off the stage. I never was a man for seeing an artiste bilked!"

"No, no, Mr. Cooke, it's quite all right. Of course I remember now," and after further re-assurances he slipped away and went in search of Miss Scripps.

He found her at the back of the stage in company with the rest of the Ladies' Committee. "Miss Scripps, can I see you for a moment?" and when she came up to him he said anxiously: "Is it true that you've agreed to pay these actors?"

"Of course," she said, astonished at the question.

"But I . . . er . . . thought, I mean I understood . . . I hadn't thought of expenses in that direction. I naturally believed that the plays would be put on by the Ladies' Committee themselves!"

Miss Scripps looked at him coldly, "Surely, Mr. Stewart, you told me not to worry about expenses when we first discussed the matter? After all, what is a nominal payment of £100 when I've got the best actors in the North putting on a different play each night for a week?"

"£100!" echoed Stewart weakly. "It's nothing, of course. There aren't any more bills, are there?"

"Oh, yes," she replied calmly. "I've been meaning to let you have them earlier, but I never seem to have seen you!" and out of a satchel she produced a handful of crumpled accounts.

He took them in awed silence. "You're sure this is all?" he said, barely above a whisper. Miss Scripps nodded frigidly; she didn't like his manner at all.

Stewart took the bills into the little office that was at his disposal, and carefully he straightened them out on the table and surveyed them with gloomy foreboding. Then he got another piece of paper and started to tot up the figures. In a few moments his fears were realized. The Ladies' Committee had taken him too literally. The fault was undoubtedly his. Hadn't Mr. Eastwood warned him at the start to watch the expenses carefully? But then, there had been so much to do, so many people to be spurred on. There'd been no time to check on the expenditure; his main anxiety had been to get things moving.

Ten o'clock came, and slowly the great hall emptied. Shortly afterwards the cashier came in, burbling with satisfaction.

"A very successful opening, Mr. Stewart, 10,253 persons have paid for admission, and the gross takings are £256 6s. 6d.; a very fine sum if I may say so."

It was better than Stewart had expected, and he cheered up a little until he remembered it was Saturday and the daily attendance for the rest of the week would be nothing like so large.

As the week drew on it became apparent that he was going to be badly out of pocket. The ironical thing was that everyone else thought it was a great success, for the crowds did appear to come. But he needed crowds twice that size at sixpence a head to make the thing pay, and they only materialized on Saturdays.

At last, on Thursday, he realized there was nothing else for it but to tell Mr. Eastwood. The old shipowner listened in silence, but his face was expressive enough.

When Stewart had finally completed his dismal tale, he waited for the reproaches which he knew he deserved. But Mr. Eastwood sat quietly for a while, and at last he said, "We need something more than the Exhibition now," and again he relapsed into silence.

The young man looked at him anxiously. The thought of that thousand pounds of his own lying in the bank was merely depressing. He'd never forgive himself if he had to take that to clear up the debts of the Exhibition.

Slowly, Mr. Eastwood said that there was of course the *Great Eastern*, due in Liverpool on Sunday morning, but Stewart, uncomprehending, didn't see how that could help.

"Now if you could get the Cable Company to throw her open to the public for the benefit of charity——"

"Why," began Stewart breathlessly, enlightenment beginning to creep upon him, "if only we could——"

"She's the wonder ship of this century, and perhaps the next," said Mr. Eastwood gravely, "and I think I know who are the agents. Mind you, I'm not promising anything, but you never know, it might be the means of turning the scales in your favour."

Stewart could hardly control his excitement.

"Give me an hour," said Mr. Eastwood, "and I'll let you know one way or the other."

Sure enough Mr. Eastwood was as good as his word, and a little later he walked into Stewart's office and told him that the necessary permission had been obtained. "But charge a shilling a head," he said; "don't make the same mistake twice!"

Stewart hardly waited to hear him; he was already half-way through the door on his way to the offices of the *Shipping Albion*.

"Charlie," he called out excitedly, waving away the boy Harold. "I want the whole of your front page!"

"What for?" asked the astonished printer.

"The *Great Eastern*! 700 feet long, 80 feet beam, 50,000 tons displacement. Phew! Charlie, put it all down in that front page," and the young man, as though overcome with the thought, sat down in the *Albion's* one rickety chair. The printer was looking at him as though he'd gone mad, so Stewart, more calmly now, carefully explained his scheme for placing the *Great Eastern* on view on Sunday.

"Alreet, lad," said Charley doubtfully, "tha can 'ave t'front page, but ee by gum it'll cost thee summat."

So on Friday morning the *Shipping Albion* spread the news that the largest ship the world was ever likely to see would be on view to the citizens of Liverpool all day Sunday. The cost of that single advertisement was all of £50, but Stewart was an ambitious promoter; he reckoned he was going to get 20,000 people down to see her, and he was never the man to spoil the ship for a penn'orth o' tar! At a shilling a head he should take a thousand pounds. His business now was to make the public aware of the great opportunity that awaited them, and what better way was there than getting John Nicolson to knock up a rough model of the ship, bolt it on one of the flat drays and parade it through the town?

It was with all his hopes centred on the *Great Eastern* that he sat in the little office in St. George's Hall late on Saturday evening, waiting for the cashier to come in with the final list of the Exhibition's receipts. The show was over, the hall was cleared, and already the workmen were pulling down the various stands, for the agreement called for everything to be cleared by midnight.

Very shortly he had the final figures. Altogether, the income from all sources came to £869 14s. 11d. He thanked the various officials for all they'd done and set off for the greater privacy of Chapel Walk to make his final reckoning. Anxiously he totted up his expenses; they came to £1305 5s. 7d.! and there'd probably be another £100 on top of that. He looked at his amateurish balance sheet balefully; there must be no mistake tomorrow.

It was after midnight when he finally put down his pencil and went off to bed. All his arrangements for the *Great Eastern* had been completed. One hundred sandwich-board men, sabbath or no sabbath, would parade the town from dawn till dusk. A relay of drivers had been detailed to keep the model of the ship in progress from suburb to suburb. A score of clerks had been hired to take their turn collecting at the top of the gangways, and to facilitate their work he'd had big signs painted stating boldly "No change given". In all consciousness he didn't see what else he could have done. The Dock Board had

promised him four gangways—"three for going up and one for coming
down" the landing-stage master had told him. No! as he went to bed
he didn't honestly see what more he could have done to guarantee
success, and, in any case, it was too late now. The fact that Miss
Scripps and the Ladies' Committee did not approve of his latest scheme
disturbed him not at all, but there he underestimated them.

Castle Street

CHAPTER 7

THE 'GREAT EASTERN' TIES UP

His head had barely touched the pillow, or so it seemed, when Silas rushed into his room excitedly.

"She's coming up the river now, skipper," he cried as though the end of the world were at hand.

Stewart looked at his watch. "Good heavens," he cried, "nine o'clock!" He jumped out of bed, and flung his clothes on hastily.

Already on the landing-stage was a vast crush of people watching the arrival of this leviathan of the deep, and a murmur of surprise went up from them when it was seen that the pilot was going to put her alongside while the ebb was still making. It still wanted an hour and a half to slack water; old-timers on the river-front shook their heads disapprovingly. It was a very risky thing to do with a ship that size, and the pilot had no right to do it with the landing-stage crammed full of people. One mistake, and that monster would smash the floating timbers of the stage to matchwood and there'd be hundreds of people thrown into the river. No! the pilot had no right to take such a risk. He was only trying to show off!

But there she was when Stewart got down, nosing slowly shorewards, the pilot's intentions plain to be seen. Eight threshing steam-paddle tugs ahead and another eight astern, besides four others lashed alongside amidships out of sight of the folks on the landing-stage; all endeavouring to control the giant vessel. She appeared to have too much way on her; if the tide caught her now she'd sweep down bodily on to the stage and all the tugs in the world would never hold her up. Broader and broader she canted across the stream, presenting an ever increasing surface of hull to the fast flowing tide. There was no doubt about it now, the tide had definitely got her, and with apprehension the professional onlookers saw her gather momentum as she swung inshore towards the stage.

A hoarse, unintelligible shout rang out from the pilot, a tiny figure standing on the inshore sponson; there was a dull thud, then a rattle which rose to a terrifying roar as the starboard anchor cable went thundering out after the anchor.

"Slack away, slack away!" yelled the pilot frantically, gesticulating fiercely with his arms and jumping up and down in his excitement.

"Oh! Mr. Stewart," a girl's voice cried at his shoulder, "do you think it's going to run into us?" He turned quickly round.

"You here, too, Susy?" he asked in surprise.

"It's far too big for the little stage, isn't it?" she asked breathlessly.

"Not 'er, miss," interposed a calm but knowledgeable neighbour; "the stage's nearly half a mile long, whilst that ship there is only 679 feet. I reckon you could put four of 'er alongside comfortably."

Susy was not the only one on the stage to get excited, and already a murmur of apprehension was rising from the crowd as the great hull sheered down upon them, seemingly out of control.

"Look!" someone cried hysterically, pointing at one of the little forward tugs which at that moment parted its tow rope and darted unexpectedly forward, to be brought up just as abruptly on the shallow mud banks of the river.

"They can't stop her now," several people said, and glanced anxiously over their shoulders; but they were so tightly wedged together that few could have got off the stage had they been so minded.

All this time the chain had been thundering out through the hawse pipe, and though the paddle wheels still churned slowly ahead, they appeared to be dipping ineffectually into the water. Even the informative stranger at Susy's elbow was getting a little perturbed.

"It's about time he went full ahead on 'is port paddle and full astern on t'other," he said.

"Why doesn't the pilot hold on to the anchor," asked Stewart anxiously, thinking that if the *Great Eastern* crashed into the stage it would cost him £500.

"If 'e checks 'er too soon," returned the stranger, " 'e 'll just drag 'is anchor 'ome, that's why. All the same, I reckon 'e's got enough chain out now to 'old 'er with."

Their further fears were halted, for suddenly the pilot, who by now seemed to be towering up in the skies above the folks on the landing-stage, bellowed out, "Hold her, Mr. Mate," and a quieter, unheard order sent the inshore paddle racing ahead, throwing off great swirls of water. Almost instantly the anchor cable grew taut and the bow started to veer outstream again, then calmly and peacefully the great ship dropped alongside and ropes were out securing her fore and aft before those on the stage itself were even aware that she was safely in position.

"A nice bit of work," said the stranger approvingly; "you've got to give the Liverpool pilot 'is due. Wouldn't have cracked an eggshell coming alongside like that."

"Where are you going?" called out Susy, catching sight of Stewart elbowing his way towards the gangway. "Can I come too?"

"Sorry," said Stewart over his shoulder, and then, softening his heart, added, "but if you're at the bottom of James Street at three o'clock this afternoon I'll take you aboard and introduce you to the captain."

There was no time for further explanations for already Mr.

Eastwood and the agents were going up the gangway, and brushing off the restraining hands of dock officials, he ran after them. The arrangements were quickly made, two collectors placed at the top of each gangway, and the signal given to the policemen to let the crowd come. Stewart went to the ship's rail and watched the people on the stage struggling and pushing to get on the narrow gangway. The weather was fine, the crowd he had hoped for was there; thankfully he paused for breath, took off his beaver hat and wiped his perspiring brow. At the end of an hour the crush on the stage was as thick as ever, yet such was the size of the ship that only a few score of people were visible about her decks, the remainder of those on board were climbing purposefully up and down ladders, exploring the inner workings of this modern wonder of the world.

Later on, Stewart accepted the captain's invitation to have lunch with him in the palatial after cabin. He was confident of the success of the enterprise and over the coffee and cigars he was expanding companionably when he suddenly remembered his promise to bring Susy on board. Regretfully, he got to his feet; it was a nuisance, but he felt he owed her something for having got Higgins to take part in Saturday's procession.

Susy was a little late in arriving but so was Stewart, and he had just got there when she came breathlessly along, apologizing. She was dressed in the very height of fashion and there was a high colour in her cheeks from her last-minute exertions, but Stewart wasn't thinking how pretty she was, he was disgustedly looking at her dress, and his newly acquired displeasure with all women was strong upon him.

"You've certainly picked the dress for the occasion," he said sarcastically. "How on earth do you think you're going to get up and down a ship's narrow gangway in a crinoline ? And, anyway, you know it's always blowing half a gale down at the pier-head. If you go down there in that dress, what with the wind and all, you'll have the whole crowd following us."

"I don't mind," said Susy spiritedly, "I'm not ashamed of my legs, and I don't see that you should be."

"Look," said the young man patiently, "we'll forget there's half a gale blowing down on the river front, but we can't forget there's ladders to climb—and you'll never climb them with all those bedclothes wrapped round you!"

"Bedclothes, indeed!" said Susy indignantly, and was going on to tell Stewart what she thought of his opinions, when she stopped and a malicious look came into her eyes. "Perhaps you're right," she said meekly; "if you can give me twenty minutes I'll go and put on something more manageable ?"

The thought of what the wind might do to that crinoline was

sufficient to make Stewart wait an hour if necessary, so the girl slipped away and in half an hour came back changed.

"Good God!" said Stewart, stricken, looking at her in bewilderment. This time she wore what she told him was a crinolette. To his stunned eyes it appeared to have shrunk considerably in front, but as though to make up for that, billowy masses of material were heaped in the rear, and as she slowly and impudently turned round for his inspection, his petrified gaze fell on the enormous bustle.

"This is the very latest fashion, Mr. Stewart," she informed him coolly, but he was too dazed to speak. As they set off, she placed her hand companionably on his arm, and like that they joined the stream of people making their way down to the landing-stage.

Stewart felt uncomfortably conscious of that great protuberance in her rear and prayed fervently that he would see nobody he knew; but Susy, on the contrary, delighted in the attention and stir she created as they went along. Occasionally, out of sheer devilment and to annoy Stewart, she gave a little wriggle to her rump, which caused the amused pedestrians to burst into peals of ribald laughter. Stewart went deep red as he heard their guffaws, but he hadn't the courage to look round.

"Walk a bit faster," he hissed, anxious to be lost in the obscurity of the crowd on the landing-stage, but Susy, keeping a tight hold on his arm, refused to be hurried.

As they approached nearer to the stage he saw, above the heads of the people in front of him, several large placards which had certainly never been there an hour ago. He forgot about Susy's awful bustle and pushed forward curiously into the agitated crowd. His curiosity changed to suspicion, and then to anger as he realized that there was something afoot to keep the people from boarding the ship.

After much elbowing he got near enough to read the placards. "Remember thou keep holy the Sabbath Day", one baldly announced; another stated simply, "The seventh day is the Sabbath of the Lord thy God"; and several others all testified to the same motive and, to Stewart's mind, organized opposition. But the crowd on the landing-stage was in no mood for sermons and they intended spending the day as they wished. Stewart noted with satisfaction the jocular resentment and thinly veiled hostility of a section of the seething crowd around the notices. They had been cheerful, good-humoured all morning, enjoying the thrill of seeing and visiting the ship that men said was a hundred years ahead of her time. It was an exhilarating contact with the sea and the mystery of foreign lands; what right had these psalm-singers to try to interfere with the poor man's pleasure? Let them stick to their churches and Bibles, and leave simple folk alone. These were plainly the thoughts of the crowd, but the little band of Sabbatarians were not easily dismayed and, clustered closely together for moral support, they sang hymns, impervious to the mockery of those around them.

Then suddenly, as Stewart continued to thrust his way forward, he caught sight of Miss Scripps bravely holding aloft one of those flimsy banners; near her stood the pale-faced young curate looking far from happy, and close at hand were all the rest of that Ladies' Committee of hers.

"What fools!" he muttered to himself angrily, and noting their lack of success would have been content to leave it at that. It was only when he glanced at the faces of the crowd around them that he began to grow uneasy. Making up his mind quickly he pushed his way through to Miss Scripps, hoping to make her aware of the shifting temper of the crowd. She looked indignantly at him for a moment and then turned away.

"Miss Scripps," he called urgently, "you're only irritating the people here, can't you stop all this? You're simply asking for trouble."

The young woman paid no attention and Susy tugged anxiously at his arm. "Leave the silly bitches to get what they deserve," she said angrily, and already cat-calls and jeers were drowning the sound of the hymn the Sabbatarians were endeavouring to sing.

Desperate, Stewart turned to the curate: "I suppose you and your precious vicar put them up to this," he said.

"Indeed, you are mistaken, sir, it is Miss Scripps' idea. She persisted in it, and I only came along to give them what protection I could," and Mr. Puddicombe glanced around nervously at the sea of unfriendly faces that hemmed them in.

"Have you no authority with them?" asked Stewart.

Mr. Puddicombe made an agitated gesture. "Look at them yourself. Is there any man living who could do anything with them now?" he said, and as Stewart looked at the determined faces of the ladies, strengthened by the opposition they were encountering, he realized the futility of trying to dissuade them from their purpose.

The crowd meanwhile was getting more restive and more incensed. Their earlier good humour was giving way to a more unpleasant mood, as those in the rear pressed them closer round the valiant singers. Shouts of "Go home", "Look after your kids, missus!" and previous cheerful advice had died away and was replaced by a new, dangerous tone.

The shouts now were "Tear their banners down", "Throw them in the river". The surging, angry crowd hustled them this way and that and always nearer to the river's edge. Gradually the banners disappeared from sight, all save one, to which Miss Scripps foolishly clung.

"Give it up, Miss Scripps," implored Stewart, "and I'll close the ship down," but she wouldn't even look at him. He turned to the curate, bent on impressing the seriousness of the situation upon him, but that worthy individual was missing, he had been engulfed in the crowd; only Susy stood close beside Stewart. "Susy," he said, "we've got to get these women aboard that ship before they come to any harm."

"You're a fool to worry about them," she said, but all the same she moved towards the Ladies' Committee and started to persuade them to go with her. After the banners had been torn from their hands they began to waver, and the threat of being pitched into the river penetrated even their exalted minds. Susy, with her broadest and coarest Lancashire repartee, gradually cleared a way for them and steadily but surely edged them towards the nearest gangway. All followed her except Miss Scripps; one glance at Susy and she became more determined than ever, though every second saw her pushed just a little nearer to the edge of the landing-stage. There was no time for further pleading; something had to be done quickly, so Stewart grabbed hold of her wrist, intent upon dragging her after him through the crowd and away from the river—but he was too late; those nearest thought he, too, was one of the evangelists and they closed round him. He struck out blindly with his one free hand but without avail, and the next minute over went the two of them into the river.

Stewart held determinedly on to Miss Scripps, for the thought was at the back of his mind that if he once let go he'd never find her again in those dark, turgid waters. It was only a drop of five or six feet, but even so it seemed an eternity before they hit the water, sank and reached the surface again. Fortunately it was the peak of slack water, and the ebb had not yet started to run, otherwise they might never have come to the surface again. Miss Scripps lay limp in his grasp and he struggled with her to a ring bolt in the side of the stage some ten feet away and there, holding on grimly, he gasped for breath. The crowd near the spot, as though suddenly conscious of what it had done, melted away. Their place had miraculously been taken by a dock policeman and a stage attendant, who stood staring stupidly down at Stewart and Miss Scripps, the attendant poised in the act of throwing a heavy lifebuoy to them.

"For God's sake don't throw that thing!" gasped Stewart, fearing that he was about to be brained. The attendant, disappointed, laid the lifebuoy down and grasping the girl by her arms hauled her to safety. Busily tending her they left Stewart to find his own way out as best as he could.

They carried Miss Scripps away into one of the shelters, but no one gave Stewart a thought except Susy, who at that moment hurried up rather dishevelled.

"Why, you do look funny," she giggled in surprise; "you're all wet! Have you been in the river?"

"No," he said bitterly. "I got caught in a passing shower! Didn't you notice it?" but his shaft of barbed venom went clean over her empty little head.

"Where's that girl?" demanded Susy next.

"In there." Stewart nodded briefly towards the shelters, but just then a loutish young man came up to them, grinning all over his face.

"Excuse me, miss, but you've dropped your bustle!" and he held out to her the latest aid to feminine beauty.

Susy, without blinking an eye-lid, looked at him coolly. "Young man," she said, "I would have you know that I've never worn such a thing in my life!" and she swept off with her head held high in the air towards the shelter.

"Well! would you believe it?" asked the flabbergasted young bellow. "I saw it drop off her clean as a whistle!"

"All right," said Stewart wearily, "give it to me; I'll see she gets it back," and with the bustle in his hand and a trail of water behind him he squelched his way homewards.

By the time he had returned in dry clothes to the landing-stage, both girls had gone home; Miss Scripps apparently being none the worse for her experience. Much relieved, he went aboard the *Great Eastern*.

Only half an hour remained to go before she pulled off into the stream to anchor for the night. Already the twenty little tugs were nosing alongside her again, whistling shrilly, and the mate was prowling angrily round the decks chasing ashore the last of the visitors. If Miss Scripps had only known, her demonstration was just six hours too late. Even if the crowd had been sympathetic, her interference at that late hour would have made little difference.

He went into the cabin in which the two old clerks were busily engaged counting out shillings, and stacking them in neat rows. "What's the verdict, Tom?" he asked genially.

"One thousand one hundred and nine pounds, twelve shillings," came the laboured reply.

Stewart felt like doing a little dance, it was better than he had expected.

"Stop a minute, gentlemen," he called, "this calls for a little celebration; we must drink to our success."

The other two looked at him cautiously, and one of them said: "I don't mind if I do. What about you, Alf?" The other slowly nodded his head. "Aye, it's been a right thirsty day." So Stewart went off in search of a bottle of champagne. He felt the Seamen's Charities owed them that much.

Much later in the night, and when the ship was safely lying at anchor out in stream, the three of them got a tug to put them ashore, and as they walked happily off the landing-stage the silver clinked encouragingly in the bags they carried.

Nothing else would satisfy Stewart when he arrived in Chapel Walk but to find out as near as possible the financial results of the past hectic nine days. He sketched out a rough balance-sheet.

	£	s.	d.	
Receipts from the Exhibition, etc. ..	869	14	11	⎫
From the *Great Eastern*	1,109	12	0	⎬ CREDITS
Total receipts	£1,979	6	11	⎭
Expenses on and for the Exhibition ..	1,405	5	7	⎫
For the *Great Eastern*	156	10	6	⎬ DEBITS
Total expenditure	£1,561	16	1	⎭
Final Credit Balance	£417	10	10	BALANCE

As he sat back and looked at these few brief calculations he sighed heavily; if that was all the profit he could show after two months hard work such as he could never have believed possible, and enough anxiety to last him a lifetime, then he decided he'd never make a fortune. How did fellows like Leyland and Baines manage it? Of course there was the reputation he had gained and, he supposed, the experience, but that was scant consolation.

Speculatively, he looked at the figures again; they showed a net profit of £417 10s. 10d. Cross off the odd pounds, shillings and pence, and that left a nice round sum of £400. Was he only going to get reputation and experience out of the whole business? What about the thousand pounds of his own that he had stood to lose? Ten per cent on a thousand pounds was a hundred pounds! . . . Surely he had earned that . . . so he crossed out the £400 and substituted £300, and feeling better for that little bit of financial astuteness, he retired to bed and for the first time in two months really felt like going to sleep.

On Monday morning Stewart went along to see Charlie Tomkins. He was amazed at the welcome that the printer gave him; admittedly he'd become a figure of increased importance by reason of the Exhibition . . . but all this sudden effusiveness! . . . all this backslapping! . . . it left him nonplussed.

"Liverpool's reet proud of thee, lad," said Charlie, pumping the young man's hand up and down, "an' so am I."

"Oh, I don't know," said Stewart modestly, "we ought to have made a great deal more."

"A fine bit of publicity, me lad. I thought I were a smart 'un, but tha's got me beat," and the printer gave him a prodigious wink.

Stewart's forehead wrinkled in bewilderment.

"Nay!" chuckled the printer, "I wouldn't 'a' thowt on it meself."

"What on earth are you talking about, Charlie?" asked Stewart perplexed.

"Eeeh, lad, cum off it! Tha's knows what I'm driving at. Divin' in t'Mersey to rescue that lass of Irish 'Iggins."

"Diving in! Why, I was pushed in," began Stewart indignantly.

"Tha'rt a card alreet," said Charlie admiringly, "but tha' moant say we didn't do thee justice in t'*Albion*."

"Here, let me have a look at a copy," said Stewart fearfully, and taking one off the counter opened it at the main news page. His eye first encountered the description of the *Great Eastern's* visit, and then skipped across to the next two columns. In amazement he read in type almost as big as that alluding to the *Great Eastern*, an account of how Mr. James Stewart, the gallant and capable organizer of Liverpool's Maritime Exhibition, had saved from certain drowning a young woman who had been borne over the edge of the stage by the dense crowd of sightseers.

He flung the *Albion* down disgustedly on the counter. "Who ever wrote that, Charlie, wrote a lot of tripe."

The printer looked annoyed. "Doan't thee believe it. If it's in t'*Albion* it can't be tripe. It's truth all reet. But tha'rt a one for getting into t'news; damned if I'd 'a' risked me neck to get me name into t'papers."

Nothing that Stewart could say would make the printer believe that it hadn't been carefully thought out beforehand, so the young man gave up arguing. "Anyway," he said, "I'm here to settle up my advertising bill, and I may as well tell you that I want ten per cent discount for cash."

"'Ere, 'alf a mo'," blustered Charlie, "'ow can tha' say tha'rt paying me cash, when some of th' advertisements went in two month ago?"

"Your first bill only arrived this morning, and here I am, prompt on the nail to settle it."

"Nay, lad," the printer protested, hurt, "that was only to suit thy convenience like."

"Ten per cent off £420," said Stewart firmly, "is £42. Here's £378, that's all I'm going to pay!"

The printer looked at him sorrowfully. "Tha' drives a 'ard bargain, lad; still, tha'rt a brave young chap, so I'll let thee off wi' it."

"Nonsense," said Stewart, exasperated, "discount for cash is business and don't you forget it. Now I must find that drunken reporter of yours. . . . I'll make his ears tingle."

The *Albion* had done its work well, and everywhere he went that morning he heard people talking of his brave deed, almost as much as the visit of the *Great Eastern*.

In the 'Pig and Whistle' Susy hurried over to him all smiles. "You aren't half a hero," she said admiringly. "I was just telling the customers all about it, same as I told Mr. Sharp on the landing-stage yesterday."

The young man looked at her stonily. "So you're the source of all this blather?"

"Now, Mr. Stewart," she said hastily, seeing his face cloud over, "you'd better be nice to me or I'll tell them all what really did happen. Miss Scripps told me the whole story and it was really you who pushed her into the river!"

This latest piece of infamy left him speechless, and then at last the funny side of it all dawned upon him and he began to laugh.

"That's better," said Susy impudently.

"Did that precious Ladies' Committee come to any harm?" he asked.

"Not them," she replied with a sniff. "When they realized that they might get a ducking in the river, they couldn't get up that gangway fast enough, and would you believe it, that clerk of yours actually had the cheek to ask me to pay!"

"Here's a sovereign," he said magnanimously. "I don't suppose he got anything out of you."

"I bet it's a bad one," said Susy, looking at it mistrustfully.

Lime Street and St George's Hall steps

CHAPTER 8

PARTNERSHIP WITH CAPTAIN BRADY

THINGS went on peacefully in Chapel Walk for the next few weeks and then one morning, Silas, still disgruntled with life in general, picked up his telescope and walked down to the Pier Head to see what flags were flying on Bidston Hill. Shortly afterwards he came stumping back. "The *Bellerophon's* semaphored, skipper," he called out and Stewart, startled, jumped out of his chair. Here was Captain Brady back again and he'd done nothing about getting hold of a brig. He slipped on his jacket, left his breakfast half finished, and set out for the ship auctioneers. Only when he was in the street did he realize that it was not yet nine o'clock, and Netlocks would not be open ; so he decided to take a walk round the block until the time came.

He sauntered into Water Street, just by the Tower, and turned up towards Castle Street. Then he crossed Drury Lane, with its low-roofed dwelling-houses mixing oddly with the newly constructed, towering warehouses. The street was steadily becoming more and more crowded with scores of sombrely clad individuals all purposefully bent forward, hurrying to work. They carried umbrellas loosely folded, and the majority wore boots that buttoned underneath trousers tight to the leg. Some wore the popular stove-pipe hat and others the low-crowned plebeian bowler. The elder men were encased in frock coats, but the younger ones satisfied themselves with dark heavy jackets, buttoned high on the chest. Flowing whiskers and moustaches of all styles graced both youthful and elderly faces, and these hirsute decorations were the sole outward expression of their individuality.

In all other respects those mildly hurrying figures were identical ; even their purpose was the same, for prompt at nine o'clock they would be engaged in opening huge ledgers preparatory to making entries in fine, delicate, copper-plate handwriting, or they would be opening letters and laboriously concocting replies in mellifluous language. Within that district surrounding Water Street, every man's business was in some way or other connected with shipping, for this was the very centre of the 'Shipping Mile'. Not a woman was to be seen. The few taverns which dotted the street were boarded up ; they had the desolate, neglected air of an abandoned ship. Whatever the district might be by night, there was no doubt that by day the business of commerce was the only thing that mattered.

As yet it was too early for the shipowners and principals to put in an appearance, for those gentlemen were under no obligation to work from nine till six, with a mere half-hour for lunch. But presently, round about ten o'clock, a carriage or two might be expected to roll up with the more diligent and progressive of these aristocratic merchants. By that time the slave-like routine would have swallowed up the earlier scurrying figures on the streets, and the dour forbidding buildings would be crammed full of bent shapes, poring over the details of invoices, mates' receipts, bills of lading, manifests, clearances and the score of items that went to the business of shipping.

At nine o'clock the crowded streets suddenly emptied—save for a few fearful late-comers, anxiously wondering whether they might sneak indoors and escape the eagle eye of the head clerk. That worthy sat at his raised desk, with his minions all neatly arrayed in front of him. He was always on the look-out for those who hoped to creep in unobserved. A clerk was never late twice; the first time, he incurred an acid look and a withering comment, the second time . . . well, there never was a second time.

After the doors of the counting-houses had closed on the office staffs, the streets in the 'Shipping Mile' contained only a sprinkling of people: messengers, agents, perhaps a master mariner or two. Then, later on, pale-faced men in shabby blue serge suits would begin to converge on the taverns; a few tawdrily dressed, buxom females would make their appearance and join the pale-faced men standing in humble little groups outside the taverns' private doors. When they were all there, and not a minute before, the doors would be opened mysteriously and the little groups would vanish inside, and the street would again be almost deserted.

But those industrious clerks in the offices opposite could tell you that it wasn't quite the same, and as their interest in advice notes and bills of lading waned, they sought temporary diversion and relaxation in looking down from their windows on to the streets. They were supreme artists in deceit. When the head clerk looked up, everything was as usual, bent backs, laboriously scratching pens, a hive of industry calculated to deceive anyone. But the industry was superficial, for every one of those black-coated workers was aware of what was happening over the way in the street. With the re-opening of the tavern doors, and the appearance of a pot-man in shirt-sleeves, intent on taking down the wooden shutters, the clerks covertly checked their time-pieces—it was half past ten o'clock. From then onwards the taverns showed increasing signs of activity. Buckets of water were produced and the fronts were swilled down with as faithful a routine as ever characterized a ship at sea. The outsides of the taverns were easily the cleanest buildings in the street. With the shutters down, a good view could be had of the interior—barmaids scrubbing away, dusting tables, or polishing glasses. In half an hour's time the doors would be officially opened to the public and everything must be in readiness for the first thirsty customer and the business of the day.

The public-houses in Water Street catered for the business gentleman during the day-time, but of course they didn't neglect the sailors at night-time. While other taverns might open at five and six o'clock in the morning to catch the early dock labourers, the city taverns opened sedately at eleven o'clock. At that hour precisely, 'the old codger', or more respectfully the senior clerk, would with a nice sense of timing pull out his watch, exhibit mild astonishment, then murmur reprovingly to himself but loud enough for all to hear, "Umph! time I was at the Customs House". Then, having changed his threadbare, alpaca office jacket for the more dignified morning coat, he would, with a last admonishing glance at the slaving juniors, sally forth, the time-honoured and recognized first customer of Water Street's saloon bars.

His departure was the signal for work to cease; pens clattered on the desks, pipes came out and the repressed sporting instincts found outlet in solemn discussions and an exchange of opinions on the respective merits of Tom Sayers, the British champion, and Heenan, the American, and of the incredible fight they had fought. But the still younger clerks were too immature to enter into such weighty discussions, and they all clustered round the windows, first of all to watch gleefully and irreverently 'the old codgers' assembling in their favourite taverns, and then to watch the never-ending, changing scenes in the now busy street below. The principals had been and gone; some of them to make a few business calls, but most to join acquaintances in the morning perambulation on 'The Flags'. Afterwards they would adjourn to their clubs and the daily papers. There they would remain in obscurity until late in the afternoon when they might again reappear at their offices, walk slowly down like some deity between the desks of their toiling minions, and disappear behind the door of their holy sanctum. After a few minutes of reverent waiting, 'the old codger would humbly knock at the door, be admitted, and after explaining the progress of the day's work, would emerge, his face reflecting his master's mood.

Stewart, as he idled up Water Street, was conscious of all these things happening in the background, and it made him speculate on his own prospects. Even touting for ships' stores was better than being a poor devil of a clerk, chained to a desk for the whole of his life. In a sense he was his own master and that, with all its ups and downs, was something precious to cling to. If he was industrious he would reap the profit himself; if he was idle ... but then, he wasn't, so why worry about that?

Of a sudden his spirits rose; it was grand to be alive, to have opportunities lying ahead, to pit your wits against those of other men. More cheerful, he turned along Fenwick Street, past the Underwriters' rooms, where gross, opulent men looked unseeingly from out of the library windows at the passers-by, the envy of countless poverty-stricken clerks. He sauntered past the numerous banks and offices, the outward symbol of the increasing prosperity of the age. Perhaps he would open his own bank some day, he mused, just as so many other merchants had done, and men would come to him with their money. Such thoughts were intoxicating.

He continued on past Nicholson's tavern, its dignified front giving it the appearance of a rich merchant's city house. Then he turned down into James Street, where the chill wind from the river cleared his head like a pinch of snuff and sent the blood coursing swiftly through his veins. He rammed his hat firmly on his head and forced himself forward against the strong invigorating gusts, and not until he had cleared Pilkington and Wilson's corner and gained the protective shelter of the arches of the Piazza Goree did the force die out of the wind. He found himself thinking of the slaves who, so legend claimed, had lain chained to the walls of the vaults over which he was now walking. What a history Liverpool had ! Folks were wrong when they dismissed the town as a mere cancerous growth of industrialism. True, there were no ancient buildings such as many another town could boast, but in Liverpool every yard of that area facing the river was linked up with the romance of commerce. What opportunities there had been in the past, and what opportunities there still remained. He believed that the port had only touched the bare fringe of its potential prosperity, and he determined that he would be at hand to take advantage of what the port offered.

It was in this buoyant frame of mind that he came to Netlocks' shabby, tumble-down auction rooms. The door was standing open so he slipped inside and introduced himself to the two brothers who had but recently stepped into their father's shoes. Briefly he explained what he was looking for, something about ninety feet long, drawing ten foot of water, and lifting up to 200 tons.

There were not many brigs about answering to those conditions they informed him, pessimistically shaking their heads.

"Just a minute," said one of the brothers thoughtfully, "there is this letter from the executors of the late Captain Robertson, asking us to go over to Chester and value his coasters before they come up for auction. You never know, there might be a brig amongst them."

"I must know today," Stewart said anxiously.

"That's all right," one of the brothers said, "I'm slipping over to Chester on the next train. If you care to call back here about seven tonight, I'll let you know if there is anything suitable for you." And with that Stewart had to be content.

Back in his office he called out for Silas and said, "Slip down to the lock gates, and tell Captain Brady when they bring the *Bellerophon* in, that I'm sorry I can't get down, and ask him if he would mind looking in here on his way to the Custom House in the morning."

After those brief instructions he went round to his bank to get a proper statement of his account. It was just as well to have all his facts

and assets nicely marshalled, it would enable him to present his arguments more forcibly with Captain Brady. Here was a chance to get
clear of ship-chandlery, and he meant to talk so convincingly that any
fears or scruples the old captain might have about shipowning would
be swept clean away.

Captain Brady duly appeared at Chapel Walk first thing the next
morning.

"My, but you're early, Captain," Stewart said, pleased.

"Aye, lad, I was never one for stewing in my bunk when there's
a course to be set."

"What sort of a trip?" the young man said pleasantly.

"Fairish. Can't complain, I suppose."

"I'd have been down to meet you, only I had to go round to
Netlocks about that ship of ours," Stewart said boldly, thinking it
best to delay no longer.

"A ship?"

"Well, a brig then, to be exact." It was no use the old man looking
surprised like that. Then a horrid thought flashed through his mind
that perhaps the captain had forgotten all about their earlier talk of a
partnership.

"You've thought about that question, Captain?" he asked.

"That's what I'm here for," replied the other shortly.

"That's splendid, Captain. I've got everything——"

The other cut him short. "I don't mind telling you, young man,
that I've lain awake many a night thinking about it. I've come to
the conclusion that there's nothing like a bit of money for giving a
man grey hairs. I know there's some folks'd say, never mind the
worry, let's have the money, but if it's going to stop me sleeping at
nights I reckon I'd be happier without the worry and the money."

"Goodness, Captain, those are strange words for a shipmaster.
I always thought you fellows could never have enough?"

"Don't take me up wrong. The making of money's one thing, but
the spending of it is another. If you earn it the hard way, you aren't
going to stand up and roll it down the gutter. What are you to do
with it, then, when you have got it? That's been my trouble for these
past twenty years. If you put it in the bank there's always the worry
that one day you'll come back to port and find the place with the
shutters up, like I've seen before now."

"Oh, come, Captain, surely you're looking on the black side.
But if it is the way you feel there's only two things you may do. One
is to buy a licensed house, and the other is to take a part share in
the ship you sail. In either case, you will at least have your money or
its equivalent in stock around you."

"I don't fancy buying a licensed house because I'm a sailor and
I aim to stay at sea. As for a ship, well, I would have bought a sixty-

fourth share here and there, but I never knew the masters well enough to risk splitting my money, and I've never had a chance to buy a share in the ship I was master of."

"Then here's the very opportunity, Captain. If you're interested we can buy a ship between us and you can sail as master!"

"Of course I'm interested, or I wouldn't be here, but"—he looked at the young man searchingly—"I'm not interested for the same reason that you are. You're one of these ambitious young men, just like Baines was, but I'm not. All I want is some place safe and sound to keep what little cash I have got. All my life I have been a careful man and I'm not denying but what I haven't got a tidy sum put by, sufficient to take up a share or two, and that's why I'm tempted to do what you say, for the thought of that there money lying underneath my bunkboard is a powerful worry at times."

"You mean you take all your money to sea with you?" questioned Stewart, astonished.

"What else is there for me to do?" returned the captain defensively.

"But that's madness, Captain. Why, if you lost your ship you'd lose all your savings as well! You'd do far better to come in with me. I know it's a venture, but it's no greater risk than you're already taking, sailing around with all that cash under your bunk. Besides, think, Captain, with you in command of your own ship at sea, and me looking out for cargoes at this end, it should be a profitable partnership."

"Aye, there's something in what you say. Right, then," said the old man, suddenly making up his mind, "I'll do it."

"You mean you'll come into partnership?" demanded Stewart, now hardly believing his ears.

"I mean I may as well put this cash of mine in a place where I can keep an eye on it and maybe help it along. If I'm on my own vessel I'll know for certain that 'Acts of God' will be the only serious hazard the ship will have to face."

"That's true enough, Captain," said Stewart soberly, "but you'll know better than me how powerful they can be at times."

"Look here," began Captain Brady, dashed at the other's changed demeanour, "do you want me to come in or don't you?"

"Of course I do, Captain," Stewart said hastily, "but I don't want you to under-estimate the risks attached to the business of shipowning. We won't make our fortunes right away!"

"I'm not interested in making a fortune, but tell me your plans and let's get it all straight."

"I suggest, Captain, that we each put in a similar amount of money, and I'm willing, since you're to be the master, that the ship should be registered in your name. That should safeguard your savings and satisfy my conscience."

Brady looked at him suspiciously, but said nothing.

"I shall be your manager and agent," Stewart went on persuasively, "and we'll get the partnership deed legally drawn up—not that we need any such document, but it's orderly and we'll know definitely our obligations towards each other. The agreement we'll run on will give the sole charter rights to the firm of 'Stewart and Brady', who alone will be empowered to hire the ship out or run her themselves."

"What's this firm of 'Stewart and Brady' you're talking about?"

"Purely nominal, Captain, it's me really; you have the ship, I have the company, that's fair enough?"

"All right, go on," said the captain, doubtful about the complexities of business.

"For a period of one year the profits will be put into the company to provide further capital for development. The position will then be reviewed, and if the firm of Stewart and Brady deems it expedient, then the profit shall be distributed equally. Should there be no profit, then the loss will be borne out of funds provided by me," said Stewart glibly, fully convinced that the contingency would never arise.

"Where's the catch in all this?" asked Brady, rather surprisingly.

The young man looked hurt. "There's no catch in it, Captain. I think the terms are generous."

"Aye, that's just it, they're too generous."

"I'll be perfectly honest with you, Captain, for I don't want you to have any regrets afterwards. The main thing is I need your money to buy the brig. As for the losses mentioned in the agreement, I have no intention of there ever being any, or I wouldn't be putting this scheme before you now. The only thing we have to settle is the question of capital. Can you raise a thousand pounds?"

Brady knitted his brows and appeared lost in thought. He was uneasy now that the actual question of money had arisen. Stewart watched him calculatingly. Why hadn't he suggested two thousand pounds. The old boy had got that and more besides.

"It's a lot of money. Practically everything I've got," said Brady, peering over the top of his spectacles. It would never do to let this young fellow know how much money he had got, for in spite of all that generous talk a few moments ago, he was still suspicious. Stewart was a nice enough young fellow, but he was a landsman, and where money was concerned, he'd never yet met one who was to be trusted, though they were full of high-faluting talk.

"Yes," agreed Stewart diplomatically, "it is a lot of money, but I'm going to put up the same amount, you know, and whereas you have got a good cover, I've none at all." That should fetch the old man. "Two thousand pounds," he continued, "is little enough capital, and by the time we have bought a ship there won't be much left. Still, freights are high and merchants just can't get bottoms. The Peninsular and Mediterranean trades are showing up so well that if I'd known of ships seeking I could have filled at least a dozen, there's so many cargoes on offer. That's why we must get in now, Captain, while the trade's good. As an investment you'll get no better return anywhere, and shipping is going to be the trade of the future. Why," he went on convincingly, "this Liberal Government is seeking to encourage men like us. There's Gladstone, a Liverpool man, all out for free trade for he knows what it means to shipping, and now they've introduced this limited liability of shareholders . . . the country's trade is bound to forge ahead, and we must be in it."

"Limited liability," said the old man, suddenly grown weary, "I know naught and care naught about it. I do know about ships though, and whether there's money to be made or not doesn't interest me like it does you. There's only one thing attracting me towards this scheme of yours, in spite of what I've said earlier, and that is to be master of my own vessel. Ships have been good friends to me and I reckon they are the truest things I've come across. Maybe to you they're just baulks of timber and bolts of canvas, but not to me or any other sailor that's worthy of the name. For forty-two years, man and boy, a ship has been my home. Sometimes I've had to do things with them that I've been ashamed of, but I always swore that some day I'd try and make up for some of the unseamanlike things I've been compelled to do. Many's the time I've said that I'd get a ship of my own, just for the sake of running her properly, with neither too much nor too little cargo. I swore, too, that she'd have proper sails and good rigging. I promised myself that I'd keep her bottom clean and sound, and that I'd ease her instead of driving her in heavy weather . . . and a whole lot of other things that anyone would like to do for those things in life which they think the most of. But until you happened across my path, it was only a dream at the back of my mind. As you grow older, opportunity somehow grows less and it seems to me that this'll be the last chance I'll ever get to turn those dreams into something real."

"I'm glad you feel like that," said Stewart quietly.

"And as for this legal agreement of partnership which you talked about, well, I don't want it. If we can't rely on each other's word at the beginning, then there's no point in going further. Let's shake hands on it. The feel of a man's hand means more to me than all the high-sounding words which lawyers put into agreements! There now, that's settled. Sink or swim, we're in it together to the tune of a thousand golden sovereigns."

Stewart was pleased, and he went on to explain in detail his plans about the ship and the trades he had in mind. He explained that through Mr. Eastwood he'd got to know a number of merchants

interested in the Continental and Mediterranean trades. He'd culti-
vated their acquaintance especially, for the short seas trades were a
much safer prospect than the Colonies or America, and besides, the
demand for tonnage on those short trades was greater than the supply.
With their limited capital they could not expect to buy anything
sizeable, so it looked as though circumstances would have to govern
their actions.

The idea of short frequent voyages appealed to the young man
because it meant that they'd be turning money over much sooner
than if they chanced a long passage westwards. Then as regards
cargoes, that was easy. There were tons of Birmingham goods already
lying in the sheds on the quays, just simply waiting for bottoms. And
if the worst came to the worst there was always coal.

Stewart said that what he had in mind was a regular service,
sailing on specified dates advertised months beforehand.

That couldn't be done, maintained Captain Brady, not with one ship
and that ship a wind ship. He said they'd need to have several ships
before they could embark upon a scheme like that.

Nevertheless, Stewart persisted that the only way to build up a
shipowning business was to provide something constant and regular
that shippers could rely upon, and although Captain Brady shook his
head pessimistically, the young man urged that on a short trade such
regularity was possible. He was forgetting the delays there were
bound to be in getting homeward cargoes, the old captain told him,
though he admitted that regularity was the thing which shippers
desired most of all.

In the end the young man managed to convince him that it would
be better to return homewards with half a cargo than to waste time
abroad seeking consignments. If it got to be known that every six
weeks, regular as clockwork, they'd be on the loading berth, there'd
be no difficulty in filling their holds, and those outward cargoes were
the ones which produced the best freights. Of course there would be
wine and wheat parcels available in certain seasons which they could
obtain abroad with but little difficulty and no delays, and for that
reason it would be a wise plan to make Oporto a port of call whether
or no they had anything to discharge.

Captain Brady began to absorb a little of the younger man's
enthusiasm. With average winds, he estimated that the round trip to
Spain and back could be accomplished in just under a month. Stewart
seized upon this to say that a regular sailing every sixth week allowed
them sufficient margin to offset undue contingencies such as contrary
winds, and permit them to establish a reputation for regularity. Even
Captain Brady had to admit that this was a safe allowance.

"But here we are," he grumbled, "counting our chickens before
they're hatched. We haven't got a ship yet!"

All the same, the young man's enthusiasm was infectious, and the captain went on to enumerate the qualities which he thought a ship should have to compete successfully in the trade they had in mind.

"For the Spanish trade," he said, as though that point was already settled, "we need something smallish. You mentioned a brig earlier on?—that's just the right craft. A nice, handy seaworthy vessel with a shallow draught and a small wages bill. The trouble is there's never many vessels like that up for sale."

"Ah, Captain," said Stewart triumphantly, "now you'll see the advantages of having a shore partner. While you've been away I've kept my eyes and my ears open, and what is more, I've had Netlocks looking out for me. Only last night Bob Netlock told me he knows of the very thing we're looking for. Here's the scantlings. A wooden brig with two decks, ninety feet long, twenty feet beam, and drawing a loaded draught of eleven feet. Said to lift one hundred and eighty tons."

"That's about the size of cargo we could lift without too much seeking," said Brady reflectively.

"She's coming up for auction next Friday."

"What's her name?"

"The *Mary Jane*."

The old man shook his head doubtfully. "I don't know of any Liverpool brig of that name."

"It's a long time since she was in the Mersey. In fact she's been sailing out of Chester for the past few years. She's not old as wooden brigs go, built by Landers of Whitehaven in 1820. I wondered, Captain, if you could slip over to the Dee and have a look at her? If you're satisfied we'll make a bid."

"If she's in anything like good fettle she'll cost £1500," said Brady warningly.

"Well, that still leaves us £500 for insurance, dues, stores and wages. More than ample I should say. It should be enough to keep us afloat until we get our first freight money."

"There'll be other expenses," said Brady determinedly, thinking of all those things he had promised himself if he should ever become an owner.

Stewart dismissed the suggestion lightly. "We'll cut our shore expenses to the bone. There'll be no agent's fees nor commission. No office expenses, for I'll register the company of Stewart and Brady at 3 Chapel Walk."

Captain Brady was impressed with all this efficiency. "But what about your ship-chandlery business?" he asked.

Stewart gave him a quick look. "I'm letting it go, Captain. It's served its purpose. It's got you and me into shipowning and it's shown

me that there's a nice little business in the Spanish trade. You know,"
he went on, anxious to keep the conversation away from ship's husbandry, "it surprises me that none of the big shipowners have bothered
with that trade."

"I can't say it does me," said Brady; "these short-seas trades are
all very well, but no deep-water shipowner will bother with them.
Why should they, when ships like Beazley's *Star of the East* can bring
'em in a matter of £9,000 net profit in a single voyage that lasted only
nine months?"

"Is that what she made?" asked Stewart in an awed voice.

"Would you bother with chicken feed, even though it is on your
own doorstep, when you can make a fortune on a single deep-sea
voyage?"

The talk of so much money depressed Stewart, and rather deflated
he started to ask questions about the running costs of a brig.

"Now for a handy little craft," said Brady, highly pleased at
being able to put a damper on this too effervescent young man, "I
reckon we'll need one mate at two pound ten a month, a carpenter
at two pound——"

"Just a minute, Captain, I'll get a pencil and jot the figures down."

Then, as Captain Brady listed the crew, the young man neatly
tabulated them.

CREW EXPENSES PER MONTH:				£	s.	d.
1 mate at £2 10s. per month	..	..	..	2	10	0
1 carpenter at £2 per month	..	..	..	2	0	0
5 seamen at 30s. per month	..	..	..	7	10	0
4 ordinary seamen at 10s. per month	..	..	..	2	0	0
1 steward and cook at £2 per month	..	..	..	2	0	0
then						
Food for 13 people at 6d. per day per head	..		..	12	0	0
Total	..	..	..	£28	0	0

Stewart looked at the figures calculatingly. "Now that gives us
a minimum wage and victualling bill of approximately £30 per month,
without the master's pay. What have you in mind, Captain?" he asked
delicately.

"The Liverpool rate for master is one pound a day," said Brady
stolidly.

"But the *Mary Jane*'s only a small brig," said Stewart hesitantly.

"Never mind the size, that's the rate."

"Don't you think it would be better if we made our two salaries
debit entries in the voyage accounts?" pleaded the young man.

"No, I don't. And let me tell you this, I think you're harping too much on the saving and skimping. Before we know where we are we'll be thinking of saving at the expense of safety. We'll be taking on deck boys instead of sailors, or perhaps apprentices instead of either. Then we'll be letting worn sails and strained rigging make do for just another trip. Then it'll be the turn of the men's victuals and the ship's stores! Nay, I've had too much of that at sea. It's always been a case of making do for just another trip."

"But surely, Captain," protested Stewart, "it's the ordinary practice of shipowning to cut down expenses?"

"You're right there, my boy, and that is why the calling is in such bad shape. Only a little while back you were trying to tell me that it was the masters who were at fault. I remember that argument even though you make out you've forgotten!"

"No, Captain, I admit you were right then," the young man said placatingly. "You explained how it was all due to 'Acts of God'."

"Well, maybe I did," said the old man, rather confused, "but that doesn't relieve shipowners of the duty of seeing that their ships are properly found, and that's just what most of them don't do. If money is tight, it's much easier t~ make their ships go short of something, and the next thing you find is that your ship's undermanned, under-rigged and making slower passages, and some of them never get back to port. Shipowners are mostly alike, and I can see we have got to set ourselves certain standards or we'll be as bad as the rest of them. It's all a question of principle, and the way you're setting about the whole thing makes it stink of cheap-jack shipowning. I'll be no partner to that!"

Stewart felt like flinging his pencil down. If this was the way they were going to start their business, it was going to be hopeless. "Look, Captain," he said patiently, "if we both take out of the company the money to which we're entitled, we won't be able to run a rowing boat let alone a brig the size of the *Mary Jane*."

"Well, if we can't make the business pay with reasonable expenses, then we'd better call the partnership off and save our money," said Brady uncompromisingly.

"We've got to compete with other established shipowners, you know."

"I know what you mean, and I'm warning you from my experience. You start off by cheese-paring, and then, before you know where you are, it's become a habit, and from habit it becomes a custom, and then, as far as a shipowner's concerned, things have always been like that, and there's no point in changing them. No!" he continued, his voice gathering conviction, "the rate for master, a master mariner, is £30 per month. That's the wage you'd have to pay another man, so put that down on your bit of paper, Mr. Stewart, and let's have no more of this nonsense."

Stewart shrugged his shoulders despairingly; the whole thing was impossible, but what was there he could say? The captain was by now thoroughly aroused, and stood glaring at the young man critically, in a most unusual fashion.

"And while I'm on the subject," the captain continued, "take a word of advice from me and watch yourself closely, or you'll turn out to be as grasping as many of the other shipowners. Making a lot of money is not everything, as you'll find out before you're much older. To my way of thinking a shipowner holds a trust for both ships and seamen. Those are strange sentiments for this age, but so long as I have anything to do with the business, those will be my sentiments. My first consideration will be the ship, then the seamen, then the firm of Stewart and Brady—in that order. Don't you worry, there'll be plenty of profit left over for you."

"It's your money as well as mine, Captain," Stewart said pointedly, "but after all that, if you want £30 a month, £30 a month you shall have, and that brings our total wages and victualling account up to £60 a month. Add another £30 for insurance and depreciation and we get up to £90 before we've even started to earn a penny!" His voice showed how hopeless he thought it all was. "Furthermore, there are the light and dock dues, which on short voyages, frequently calling at ports, are likely to be nearer £20 than £10. So now we're up to £110 a month!" Grimly he went on, "And I suppose if you're to be paid, I must be paid, too."

"You paid!" growled the old shipmaster, astonished. "What for? Will you be pacing the poop alongside me? No! get that out of your head. We cannot afford to pay you. You'll have to be satisfied with the commission you get from the shippers. That's business, so don't try to catch an old hand like me."

Stewart's sense of humour came to his aid, and he laughed. "If you put it like that, Captain . . . well then, we need £110 a month to pay off our charges. Liverpool to Lisbon freights for Birmingham goods are steady at 17s., so that in freight money on the outward cargo we should pick up £150. Suppose we managed half a cargo homewards at the same freights, then that would bring our total receipts up to £225. Working on an average voyage of six weeks that gives us an expenditure of £170, leaving a fine balance of £55."

"There you are, then," said Brady knowingly, "I told you there would be enough left over," and as though to mitigate the harshness of his earlier plain speaking, he went on to discuss amiably the technicalities of the trade they were purposing to enter.

"There are a number of advantages," he volunteered, "in these short trades. For instance we'll sail on monthly articles . . . there's a lot to be said for that, especially when it comes to getting a crew and, oh! before I forget, there's another thing I ought to mention," and his voice took on a critical note again.

"Go on, Captain, let me hear it." Stewart was resigned to anything now.

The old shipmaster looked at him shrewdly and said : "You're as smart as they make 'em, I know, but don't try to be too smart. You know what I mean. Business will come without any sharp practice so long as I'm master of the brig. I've never had any shady dealings in my life, and God help me, I'm not going to start now. In shipowning there's plenty of chances for doing those things which may be inside the law and yet against a man's conscience."

Stewart smiled uneasily. "I think you've got the wrong impression of me, Captain," he said.

"Perhaps I have, but at this stage it is as well that we agree as to the fashion in which we do business. If it is known that we have certain trading principles I'll guarantee we'll never lack for trade, though I admit we may not make so much money at the beginning. Let the smart ones boast of their quick deals, they'll burn their fingers in the end. Honest dealings are what we want, whether it is with rich city merchants or with the hands for'd of the mast. Let's build up goodwill before we worry about building up cash reserves. That's all I've got to say, and so long as you remember those are my sentiments I reckon we'll knock along together."

Stewart heaved a great big sigh. "I think I know your point of view now, Captain."

"Good! Well that's settled, then," said Brady in a cheerful voice. "Tomorrow I'll slip over to Chester and take a look at the brig. You know, young man," he went on confidingly, "the idea's beginning to get a hold on me. I think we'll make good partners. You've got more brains than me, I'm not denying, but," he added defensively, "brains aren't everything. All the same, with your brains and my money and honesty, the firm of Stewart and Brady, shipowners, should come to no harm!" and he sat back and beamed.

"There's my money in it as well, Captain."

The old shipmaster chuckled and got to his feet. "No offence meant in what I've been saying now!"

"Of course not," said Stewart a trifle ruefully, and even managed to smile.

Well, that was that he said to himself when the other had gone. At any rate the partnership had been agreed upon, and though it looked like being anything but the one-sided affair he had imagined, the scene was set for the next move forward, and he fervently hoped that it would be more successful than his short career as a ship's husband.

Meanwhile, there was all that wretched stock in the outhouses to be disposed of before he could finally say he was finished with ship-chandlery. The thought of Irish Higgins rose displeasingly, but from there it was easy to pass on to thoughts of Miss Scripps, though even they were hardly as pleasant as he would have liked. He could not deny that he received little or no encouragement from her these days. Ever since that affair on the stage she had been particularly remote. Susy had told him with a laugh that Miss Scripps thought he had organized the crowd against her,

"You'd better stick to me, Mr. Stewart," Susy had said; "that young woman thinks you're the devil himself!" Perhaps Susy was right. Anyway, after that exhausting interview with old Brady he felt he deserved a drink, so he got up and went across to the 'Pig and Whistle'.

Susy wasn't there, the landlord told him shortly. She'd got another job.

"Sudden, isn't it?" asked Stewart in surprise.

"Yes it is!" Captain Evans Rees sounded angry, and he went on to talk about ingratitude. He'd taken the girl on when she knew nothing about the business. He'd taught her everything that he knew, and now, when it was reasonable to expect a little return for all his teaching, she'd calmly up and told him that she was leaving to become manageress of one of Higgins' houses!

Stewart started guiltily, but the landlord was too disgruntled to notice the other's uneasiness. The landlord said that he expected the girls to get into trouble and leave him for that reason, but not for this . . . to go into another public! After all he'd done for her it was downright dishonest.

"You're right there," Stewart sympathized. "Women are all the same, they've got no sense of right or wrong," and he thought bitterly about Miss Scripps, and the way she had treated him since he pulled her out of the river. "All the same, Susy brought you a lot of trade, landlord."

"Aye," the publican growled, "and she'll take it with her. If I'd only known she was thinking of moving I'd have increased her money and made her manageress here, if that was all she was worried about. The trouble with her is that she's not normal like the other girls."

"You mean——?" Stewart lifted his eyebrows significantly.

The landlord nodded his head gravely. It was too much for Stewart, he laughed outright. "Well, she certainly happens to have her head screwed on the right way."

"I tell you she's got no feelings for men," went on the landlord angrily. "No heart; she'll lead 'em on till they're fair daffy, and then she'll tell 'em to go and cool off in the river!"

"Well, you should know, landlord, but where's she gone?"

"Nay, I'm not advertising her place," and he moved testily away. It didn't matter, though, for the other girls soon told him that she'd gone to the 'Unicorn' in Hackins Hey. It was only a short distance away, so after a little while he set out to see what sort of a place she had moved to.

"So you've done it?" he greeted her rather self-consciously.

"Of course I have. A girl like me's got to get on or get down," she said perkily, "and I'm on my way towards getting a tavern of my own soon."

"You're so young and defenceless," Stewart remarked, not quite knowing why he said it.

"Get on with you," she returned brightly; "if you'd had my experience you'd be twice the man you are!"

He looked round at the opulent bar. The place was quite new and the smell of fresh paint still lingered in the air.

"Yes," he said, "you're getting on in the world. I hope you're still a good girl?"

"I'm too good for the 'Pig and Whistle'," she replied flippantly.

"Poor old Captain Evans Rees, he's very upset." Stewart looked at her searchingly, and then sorrowfully shook his head. "I don't believe it," he said mysteriously.

"Believe what?" she asked curiously.

"He insinuated that you were——" He broke off significantly and tapped his head.

"Why, the nasty——" she began indignantly.

Stewart covered his ears in mock horror. "Spare my innocent youth, please, Susy," he protested.

"If Captain Evans Rees has started to blacken my character, I'll blacken his eyes for him," she said pugnaciously.

"Now, Susy, no one's said anything about your character," the young man said, endeavouring to soothe her indignation. "In fact we're all agreed you're a model of virtue so far as we're concerned."

"I should think so, too," she said angrily, "and if you or anyone else comes around here casting aspersions on my reputation I'll get you put out."

"Peace, peace," said Stewart placatingly, alarmed at her belligerent attitude. "I never knew you were so touchy."

"It's all very well you saying 'peace, peace', but I'll have you know that I'm not going to have any man dominating me! . . . not for a few minutes' pleasure at any rate."

"You sound as though you know a lot about it!"

"And why shouldn't I?" she asked more calmly. And then her mood, changing as it so often did, she went on coyly, "Passion hasn't left me untouched, sir!"

It was Stewart's turn to become angry now. "You talk too glibly of these delicate subjects," he reproved.

"Hark at him!" said Susy ungrammatically.

"In my opinion, Susy, you are a very forward, impudent young woman. I agree with Captain Evans Rees, I don't know how you've managed to keep out of trouble."

"It's easy," she said blithely. "Put yourself in my hands and I'll teach you more in five minutes than you'd learn in a lifetime from that fancy woman of yours."

"Please keep my friends out of this," he said frigidly.

"You're a cool one and no mistake. You come in here trying to take a rise out of a poor, hard-working girl, and you don't like it when the boot gets on the other foot. But I'm busy. Mr. Higgins will be round in about half an hour, why not stay and have a chat with him? I'm sure he would look forward to it!"

That was enough for Stewart, he gulped down his drink and made for the door, followed by Susy's derisive laughter.

Dale Street (the south side)

CHAPTER 9

BUYING THE 'MARY JANE'

CAPTAIN BRADY had a wonderful day at Chester. He'd gone over in the early morning train and it was with pleasurable anticipation that he had sought out the brig. He clambered aboard and went round her critically. He found her as tight as a drum in spite of her age. In a riverside tavern he had chanced on a fellow who had sailed in her. She was a bit wet for'd he'd been told, but that was only to be expected of a fast sailer.

All day he had remained aboard, examining this, surveying that, his only companion being the watchman, an old sailor who, no longer able to find employment at sea, was reduced to watching over ships in port. He was a typical old salt and claimed to know the brig well, and certainly he was eloquent in her praise. She'd been a regular trader out of Chester, mainly because her owner lived there, though actually she was a shade too big to use the port comfortably. Now the owner had died, and only last week all Chester had turned out to give him a funeral that the town was not likely to forget. The brig, the watchman had heard, was to be sold by some foreigner with the name of Netlock. He'd been over her a couple of days ago, but he was only a landsman, he didn't know much about ships!

In the watchman's eyes there was no doubt that whoever bought her would get as sound a little craft as ever sailed out of the Dee. She'd been on the Continental trades for the past few years and done very well by her owner.

Old Brady left the galley to the garrulous watchman, and stood surveying the rigging. The temptation was too great, he began to labour aloft, but before he had gone very far he realized how long it was since he'd last ventured above decks. Still he persevered and didn't rest until he had seen with his own eyes that alow and aloft, both standard and running rigging were in good order. That was an important point with him, for it meant the brig had been well cared for.

From the extremities of the yards he next went down to the depths of the holds. The bilges were proof that she was tight enough. He stuck the blade of his knife in the fissure between the side planking, and as he pulled it out he gave a grunt of satisfaction at sight of the salt on the blade. Double skinned and salted between! You couldn't ask for a better hull than that. No wonder there were no signs of weeping timbers.

Satisfied, he climbed up to the main deck again. There were the sails to be looked at, but he found them all neatly stowed in the sail locker and he couldn't do much about inspecting them then and there, at least not by himself. Time enough for that when he had got the brig round to

Liverpool. And as for getting her there, why, he'd tow her round and then get a couple of idlers off the quayside to set the canvas while the ship lay in dock. It was hardly likely, with the rest of the hull in such good condition, that her sails would be rotten. He looked at the spars again; it was a pity she had the single topsail. Ever since he'd seen Captain Howes' rig in the *Great Republic* he had longed to have a ship with double topsail yards, but it seemed it was not to be yet. Still, it was no use wasting time wishing, for there were still the peaks and lockers and other out-of-the-way spaces to be looked at, and busily he set off for'd.

The captain hummed happily to himself; he couldn't remember the time when he'd been so happy. This was a job after his own heart, in fact, he told himself disdainfully, he was more of a mate than a master, but even that didn't prevent him from receiving the maximum pleasure from poking around with his knife, swinging on ropes and halyards, and easing their lay so that he might test their age. As master, he'd left the maintenance of his ship to the mate, and many a time he had chafed at this irksome custom of his profession, but he'd always observed it. On the *Mary Jane* at that particular moment, however, there was no mate to eye him with resentful looks as he pulled on braces, topping lifts, and fingered the rigging.

He said to himself that he would re-arrange the shackles and guys so as to get the smartest effect with the least effort. In his mind's eye he saw the hands scraping the detestable paint off the masts and yards. It was incredible how some men—good seamen at that—would persist in painting their spars. He saw the grimy deck holystoned until it was as white as snow. In the bosun's locker he ran his fingers through the mass of thimbles and earrings, marlin spikes and serving boards, while his professional eye assessed the remaining stores.

The saloon and after quarters were small, but there was no harm in that, and at least the lazarette looked dry enough for any stores. At last, with a sigh of regret, he noticed that it was becoming too dark to carry on further. He pulled out his watch and with an exclamation of surprise saw that it was nearing his train time, so, tipping the shipkeeper sixpence, he walked down the gang-plank, and with many a backward look wound his way to the station, his thoughts completely occupied with sails and rigging, pumps and limber holes, snatch-block leads and braces and hosts of other, to him, fascinating details. Whatever doubts there had been in his mind, that visit to the *Mary Jane* had dispelled them all.

It was late when he got back to Birkenhead and crossed over in the cheap ferry to Liverpool, nevertheless, he made straight for Chapel Walk. He was barely inside the doorway when he launched out into an eulogy of the *Mary Jane*. Stewart persuaded him to sit down, and marvelled at the change from the old man's usual caution, but wisely he made no comment. That single visit had converted Brady from being a rather hesitant supporter to an eager, enthusiastic partner.

As the day of the sale approached, Stewart found himself with plenty to do. First of all he had to persuade Captain Brady to take his hoard of gold from underneath his bunkboards and deposit it in a bank. This was as difficult a job as any, for the old shipmaster was far from being a trusting soul. For instance, he'd always made a point of collecting his freight money in gold, for he didn't like those scraps of paper which some merchants expected him to take. And so far as his own savings were concerned he believed in keeping them nice and handy under his bunk. You could see your money better there ; you could feel it, you could count it over and over again if you had a mind. Gold was currency in any man's country from Hong Kong to Pernambuco. But as for that piece of paper, which was all he'd got for a thousand sovereigns, what would it be worth on the West Coast ? Or up the Yellow River ? He held the paper contemptuously in his hand.

Stewart patiently pointed out the many advantages of bankers' drafts and bills. Look how difficult it was to carry a thousand sovereigns around. Think of the risk of it being stolen. Now with that scrap of paper, as he called it, it didn't matter whether his ship was thieved, fired or lost, his thousand pounds would still be lying in Mr. Martin's counting-house. Besides, for business reasons they would need to have a banking account. The captain could say what he liked about South America and China, but that didn't alter the fact that here in Liverpool, merchants would give them short shrift if they were so old-fashioned as to demand their freight money in gold. Then their possession of a banking account would, later on, when they had bought their ship, make it possible to arrange an overdraft for running expenses.

"A lot of moneylenders," said Brady unconvinced. "Why, they never even counted my money, but just threw it on to a set of scales, as though a thousand sovereigns were a sack of potatoes !"

"The modern banking system," said Stewart, determined to do his best, "is one of the wonders of England. Without it we'd still be talking of the marvellous inventions of this century, instead of enjoying their practical application. Look at the railways, Captain, people wouldn't be travelling all over the country at speeds up to forty miles an hour if the banks hadn't advanced the money to lay the iron tracks. Look at anything you've a mind to, that in this age we call progress—none of it could have happened without the banks to provide the capital and facilitate the exchange of money."

"You sound like Sam Sharp," said Brady sourly, still grieving for his thousand sovereigns.

"After all, Captain," persisted Stewart, "look at it in a sensible fashion. Your thousand pounds and mine too, they're only minute drops in the pool of finance. There's always safety in numbers and if the iron-masters, and the cotton-masters, to say nothing of shipping companies like McIvers'—if they're willing to entrust their money to the banks, then I don't think you and I need worry. By establishing our account at Mr. Martin's house, the firm of Stewart and Brady has acquired something concrete. We have something in common with like-minded progressive men engaged in commerce."

"It may be all you say," said Brady doubtfully, "but all my life I've been accustomed to seeing and feeling my money around me, and what's been good enough for forty-two years still seems pretty good to me. What's the point in having money if you're going to let somebody else keep it ? And this overdraft you talk about, whose money is it that they're going to lend us ? If they'll lend other people's money to you and me, what's to stop them lending your money and my money to other people ? There's a lot of things about this modern business that I don't understand". He shook his head pessimistically, sorrowfully. "If I hadn't set my mind on that little brig lying over at Chester, I tell you straight I wouldn't have gone on with all this jiggery-pokery." The perplexed wrinkles bunched deeper on his forehead, and the weather-beaten face expressed concern as he viewed with increasing alarm the complex pattern of modern commerce. It was asking too much of a man, especially at his time of life, to throw overboard all the rough and ready economic precepts which he had laboriously acquired. He didn't want to substitute them with these glib, new-fangled methods which young Stewart was forever talking about. They might be modern, but that didn't mean to say that they were necessarily better than the system which had served him and his father before him. His old father would turn in his grave if he knew that a son of his had deliberately and knowingly surrendered the savings of a lifetime to the custody of a man he had never seen before. Perhaps he'd been too long away from Yorkshire. Harking back, he dimly recalled that song his father had taught him to sing long before he'd ever thought of going away to sea

> "Tha mun see all, and tha mun say nowt,
> Tha mun tak all, and tha mun pay nowt,
>   and if ever tha does owt for nowt
> Tha mun do it ... but do it for thi sen."

The lively air ran through his head. It was a long time, a very long time, since he'd thought of that song. Nostalgic memories glazed his eyes. In a way he'd tried to live up to his father's teachings. Goodness only knew where he was now though. That young fellow Stewart with his plausible tongue had made him do something which he would never have done if he had had all his Yorkshire wits about him. Stewart was a smart young fellow, everyone said so ; but he himself, at his time of life, had got no business getting mixed up in these get-rich-quick schemes. Everybody talked about money these days. Money, money, money—wherever you went on shore it seemed to be the only thing that folks talked about. He reflected sadly, In spite of his old father's advice he saw that money for its own sake had never really appealed to him. He'd worked hard and he'd saved hard, and now he'd got a tidy sum put by, but what was he to do with it? Ships were what he really cared about, and going to sea suited him fine. The life might be hard, but at least you knew where you were most times. There was none of that eternal worrying about money, wondering who was trying to diddle you! At sea you did your job honestly and patiently, there was nothing much that could happen to you outside of what the underwriters in their fancy language called "Acts of God and Restraint of Princes". You didn't want fairer than that. But once you stepped off a ship's deck, it was like going into a thieves' kitchen, with every man's hand against his neighbours. You needed to be as sharp as a cargo of monkeys to keep what you'd got. Look at young Stewart there, the boy was all right really, but he'd got bitten with this money bug and as a result there was he, an experienced shipmaster, minus a thousand pounds. He could hardly realize it, but as he looked at that slip of paper in his hand, it was borne in upon him.

He'd listened to Stewart, and then soberly and calmly he'd gone back on board, prized up his wooden bunkboards, and with a thousand clinking, gleaming sovereigns in his leather bag he'd taken the horse omnibus to Water Street, and handed over his cash to a little fellow at the back of a mahogany counter. Afterwards they had gone to the town clerk's office and registered themselves as shipowners, with a capital of £2000. It seemed strange to have done that before they'd even bought a ship! but that apparently was the modern way. It was what you said you were, rather than what you really were that counted. Well, the deed was done now, and in the eyes of the law they were ship-owners, and he'd gone back to the *Bellerophon* and spent the night quietly, thinking over these amazing things.

Such was the state of affairs when the day of Netlocks' sale dawned bright and clear. The two embryo shipowners—the one old the other young, like conspirators seeking mutual encouragement—kept close together from early morning onwards. Of the two, Captain Brady's nervousness was the more plainly evident. He fiddled about unnecessarily, his self-confidence replaced by a general diffidence. He sought assurance from Stewart by every word and gesture. As always happened to him indoors, tiny beads of sweat formed on his brow and his fine silk bandanna was working unceasingly. He ambled about the store-room at Chapel Walk, uneasily picking up and fingering serving boards, rolls of lamp-wick and any other article that his gazed chanced upon. He examined them all with detailed care, as though they were objects of the greatest importance; but in truth he hardly saw them, for his eyes had a faraway lack-lustre look. In Captain Brady's mind there was only the thought that at last he was on the eve of realizing the thing he had dreamed about. In a few more hours, God willing, he'd be entitled to pace his own poop deck—literally his own.

There'd be no disturbing vision of some shipowner sitting back in his office judging him. It was the thought of that figure sitting stern and implacable that had helped to make up his mind to go in with young Stewart. The shadowy figure of that shipowner had always shaken his confidence in himself. He'd never been good at explaining away his actions, and his attempt to justify them, months later, had always been feeble. I haven't this gift of the gab, he would tell himself miserably as he strove to forget his halting, futile attempts to explain why he'd bought this, or why he'd gone a few extra miles in seeking another cargo, or why he'd done something else. To a man accustomed to being master in every sense of the word, it was a humiliating position. He liked to be responsible to no one but himself—Captain Brady, master mariner. He had no doubts about his own ability, the doubts only came when he had to meet his owner in the smug quietness of some fusty office.

Well, here was the opportunity to rid himself forever of that smouldering flame of doubt. His thoughts turned more directly to the brig herself. Thinking things over he thought that he might break a lifelong rule and try out that new gadget there'd been so much talk about, the 'Patent Reefing Gear'. If it meant being able to do the job more quickly and efficiently it would be well worth while, particularly so since the *Mary Jane* only had the single cumbersome topsail. Somehow, though, none of these patents seemed to be any good on a ship, the old ways were the best.

Stewart, too, found difficulty in settling down to work. Here they were, on the verge of becoming shipowners, a momentous period in both their lives, yet somehow he couldn't get excited about it, and his visions were quite different from old Brady's. The brig was not so predominantly in his mind for one thing, the real object of his pre-occupation being the auburn-haired young woman in Duke Street.

"Ever been to a ships' auction before?" abruptly interrupted Captain Brady.

"Lots," said Stewart nonchalantly, and turned once more to the sheaf of papers lying on his desk.

Not many streets away, Harry Glover, the old clerk at Netlocks, was going slowly through the auction list for the day. His eyes chanced upon the name of the brig *Mary Jane*, built 1820. Not old, as ships went; he remembered vessels that had been up for auction over a hundred years old, and they'd fetched a good price even so. You wouldn't get one of these iron vessels to last anywhere near so long. Thirty years was as much as you could expect from an iron bottom. The *Great Britain*, the first iron ship ever built, was barely twenty years old, and they said that already she was a mass of rust inside ! No, he hoped they wouldn't get too many iron hulls to knock down. Netlocks had a reputation, they liked to handle good, sound ships. They didn't want Tom, Dick or Harry, or whoever bought a ship there, to be able to come back and say he'd bought an old junk.

Glover was more jealous of their reputation than the family of Netlocks themselves, and he'd shake his head gloomily at the increasing proportion of iron, screw and paddleships which were creeping into their lists. He'd been in Netlocks' employ since the business first began, and as the sole survivor of those dim and distant days he often presumed to urge his conservative, foreboding views upon the sons of the founder.

But the firm had to advance with the times and after listening respectfully to what the old clerk had to say, one of the present principals would try to explain why they couldn't accept his advice.

"You know, Harry, we are living in the age of progress. We can't afford to lag behind and deal only with wooden wind-ships !"

Old Harry would refuse to be convinced, and he'd mutter in reply, "No good'll come of it, you mark my words," and away he'd shuffle to his shining padded stool to resume his morbid hobby of reading through the casualty reports and the *Albion's* obituary notices.

His warnings bore some fruit, however, for when they got a doubtful lot, Master Bob didn't do much to encourage the bidding, and old Harry entered the sale up with glee when the price of such lots fell below what the seller had thought to obtain. It meant less commission, but the satisfaction of knowing that Netlocks had not been a willing party to a doubtful venture more than compensated for the reduced fee.

Netlocks weekly sale of ships was an event of importance in Liverpool maritime circles. Whether they were in the market or not, most shipowners found it expedient to attend. For all their daily companionable walks up and down 'The Flags' and their jovial exchange of jokes, they kept a shrewd eye upon each other's business activities. If it was a question of new tonnage, they revealed the fact casually whilst pacing the well-worn flags. But for secondhand tonnage and secondhand information they had to go along to Joe Netlocks Ship Mart. Old Joe himself was dead now, and with him Liverpool had lost a remarkable character ; still, his sons continued to do their best, ably assisted by their father's clerk, Harry Glover.

Neither of the two sons was the man their father had been, that much went without saying, but they were conscientious, hard-working 'boys', and of course the atmosphere had not changed very much. The same type of people came, the same sort of gossip was tossed around. Some new shipowner was setting up office in Water Street—he was going into the South American trade, tramping if freights held good, otherwise coal out and grain home. Certain Liverpool merchants were getting capital together to start an Atlantic service in opposition to Cunard and Inman. They had already registered themselves as the National Steam Navigation Company, and their first three ships were now on the stocks. As a favour to American opinion they were going to call them *Louisiana, Virginia* and *Pennsylvania*. They were going all out for strength in construction, rather than speed—an original idea for those go-ahead times. Another shipowner, gossip said, was going out of business. His ships might be expected to put up at Netlocks any time now, unless they were sold by private treaty. Not worth much though! Sam King, who started them off, died three years ago, and his son Geoffrey had played ducks and drakes with them. Couldn't last another six months—too fond of women and the bottle. And so the gossip went the rounds in that famous long room of Netlocks.

An hour before the sales were advertised to start, people began to assemble in that long room. It still bore the traces of the dividing wall which had been knocked down some years previously to make the room capable of accommodating all those who wished to attend. And there the crowd would gather, and speculatively watch who was buying. Long after the last lot was sold, they would linger on in little gossiping groups, providing information for anyone with a finger in the shipping pie.

Charlie Tomkins, printer and proprietor of the *Shipping Albion*, always attended those sales himself. You learned more about shipping in old Joe's room in one afternoon than you could pick up in twelve months hanging round the docks or idling on 'The Flags', straining your ears to catch at a passing sentence. Sam Sharp could look out for the ships in the docks; he could even go and have a good blow-out at the shipbuilders' expense whenever there was a launch! but an important event like Netlocks' weekly sale—that required his own personal attention. Besides, he liked meeting all these rich nobs of shipowners, they made him feel important, and he'd go up and ask them if they had any shipping questions they would like him to ventilate in the Press. Some of them were a bit short, but he'd put up with that so long as they gave him their advertisements.

He reflected with pleasure that the *Shipping Albion* was a proper little gold mine. All he'd got to do was to be affable to the advertisers, and make out times were hard when Sam Sharp tried to pin him down for an extra guinea. It was lucky that Sam was such a beggar for the booze, the *Albion* would never have kept him otherwise. Funny thing was that the more drunk he got the better he wrote. It was a bit worrying at times, wondering if Sam would turn up with his copy. But they'd always managed to produce a paper even that night Sam had got rotten drunk in some rum shop off the Dock Road and had been shanghaied aboard a ship waiting in the river. If Charlie hadn't gone personally to Irish Higgins, Sam might still be sailing round the world. He chuckled at the memory; it was just the experience Sam had needed. Sam only got drunk in those publics now in which he was known, and where he knew he could be found if he hadn't turned up in Victoria Street by a certain time.

When Tomkins started coming to those weekly auctions, Joe Netlock had had his desk right up at the top of the room, alongside the window overlooking the river. His clerk, Harry Glover, used to sit close beside him, and as Joe knocked 'em down, Glover would enter them up in the massive, great ledgers that practically covered the whole of the table. The two sons used to stand respectfully in the background, playing no part other than to turn up *Lloyd's Register of Ships* if further particulars were needed to liven up the bidding. Well, old Joe was gone now and the two 'boys' had the business between them. Really, except for the sight of old Joe sitting behind that desk, things were much the same. . . .

The two 'boys' were men about forty years of age, but none of those frequenting the rooms ever alluded or thought of them other than as 'Netlocks' boys'. The habit had persisted since Joe had brought them to their first sale, and made them stand deferentially on one side so that, he said, they might grow up in the business properly. Making them stand kept them awake, too, and they hadn't missed much. Now, however, they had taken over the management themselves, but it made no difference to Harry Glover, he still called them Master Bob and Master William. It was a great condescension on his part when, a few years back, he had responded to their hesitant use of his Christian name, Harry, instead of the formal Mr. Glover their father had insisted upon. It was typical of them, he thought, all for progress and little or no respect for their elders. Goodness knows what the guv'nor would have said if he had been alive and seen all this carrying on with iron hulls and the like. Many's the time he'd heard him say, "We moan't bite off more'n we can chew, 'Arry!"; but these young boys now—calling him 'Harry' indeed.

The old clerk shuffled in and about the room, his aged, bleary eyes for ever clouding over, his snuffling nose for ever leaking. Around the walls hung pictures and half models of ships whose fortunes had led them through Netlocks' hands. Ships whose names were known in every port hung silently there. There were a great many others, whose names few could recall, but they all made a fine galaxy, a sort of illustrated guide to the progress of the firm of Netlock and Sons, Ship Auctioneers.

Old Harry in his shufflings to and fro would sometimes stop and peer closely at some of these prints. His face would wreath up in a toothless grin as the dim outline of one of his favourites pierced the haze of his vision, and for a while he would be wrapped up in happy memories of the past. A past studded with wonderful sailing ships, and peopled with captains and seamen the like of which these youngsters would never see. Then, as his gaze followed lovingly the whole pageant of sail, it would come across an ugly stump of a funnel, not quite hidden by sails, belching out dense volumes of smoke. The toothless grin would fade and a grim, forbidding expression take its place. They'd had no right to put that horrible picture of the brig-rigged steamer *Sea Lion* up there. Yet young Master Bob had insisted in spite of his protests. It was history, he had been told ; a milestone in the march of progress. Bah ! if that was progress he was glad he wouldn't live to see much more of it.

Sixty years he'd been at Netlocks ; it wasn't a bad record he supposed. Liverpool wasn't much of a place when he and Joe had started knocking 'em down. In fact Chester was supposed to be the coming port, and he might have gone there for his living if by chance Joe Netlock hadn't mentioned to his father that he wanted a boy to help him. Yes, Joe Netlock had been a good employer ; he'd like to have left the business when Joe died, but he'd promised that he'd stay on and look after the 'boys'. Perhaps it had been a mistake, for they cared for nought he might say. Oh, aye, they listened to him all right—after all, hadn't he been selling ships long before they were born ? They'd been good years when Joe was alive. It had been Harry and Joe then. Now it was 'Master Bob' and 'Master William'. He could tell they didn't even like that, but they could go hang as far as he was concerned, that was as far as he was prepared to go.

How Joe and he had laughed when the boys complained of being called Bobby and Billy. They weren't bad boys really, not a patch on their old dad, of course, but that seemed to be the way nowadays. Maybe Netlocks was no worse off than other family businesses.

The management of Netlocks was not the only thing that had changed for the worse in Glover's opinion. Look at all those bits of paper that were handed over to him at the desk, instead of good hard cash. Some of the people that bought ships didn't even bother to bring bits of paper with them ! You had to send round at the end of the month and remind them that they'd bought a ship, and hadn't paid for it ! . . . as though anyone could forget a thing like that. It wouldn't have done for Joe. "No brass, no ship," is what he would have said, and folks would have known he meant it. They'd been good, stirring days when Joe was alive, and somehow Harry couldn't help thinking that the best had all gone with him.

The old man looked round him distastefully ; all this bustle and noise ; everybody clamouring, shouting, knocking each other over if they thought they could make a couple of shillings. How different it was to the days when principles counted for something. Like a pack of hungry vultures the customers were now ; a man was barely warm in his coffin and there they were, asking when his ships were coming under the hammer. Joe would have put them in their places.

Joe had been a stickler for correctness. There had never been anything shady or mean in his actions. If he didn't like the look of a ship, or heard there was some dubious reason for her being put up for sale, he would refuse the business. "I reckon we 'aven't come to that yet, 'Arry," he'd say.

Yes, life in those days was good, quiet, simple, orderly. Gentlemen pressed one another to take business. There was none of this uncivilized, cut-throat competition. Honour, principles, obligations, they didn't play much part where money was concerned these days. Yet Joe had believed the 19th century to be full of promise; things like the railways, the penny post, the abolition of slavery, even the coming of the steamers. Joe had said they promised well for the future . . . but he'd forgotten about the men. How else could they explain that somehow all these wonderful inventions and developments had not made much difference, in fact there was more poverty and unhappiness than ever before.

Well, it was getting on for sale-time; he'd better be getting out the ledgers from the safe. He could hear dimly the scraping of chairs, the hearty greetings, the old familiar noises which were part of his very life. He opened the massive iron safe that stood in the corner, as it had done since the time Joe had brought it back from a junk shop in Sea Brow, years ago. Breathing heavily, with the ledgers clasped tight in his arms, he moved slowly across the intervening passage into the long room. Familiar faces appeared before him.

"Good afternoon, Harry, a nice day," one after the other greeted him.

There was Mr. Thompson of the Thames and Mersey Line, Mr. Iredale, Mr. Jones, Mr. Westcott, Mr. Booth, young Mr. Beazley, Paddy McGee, the one-time marine store dealer, Henry Fox, the Fernie Brothers, all of them good sailing-ship owners. There was Ernest Royden, and Laird the shipbuilders, all there as usual, just as they or their fathers had been for the past sixty years.

Others were coming in. He recognized Charles MacIver of the Cunard, energetic and forceful; he had brought his engineer, Robert Thomson, along with him. Old Glover sniffed his disapproval, he didn't hold with engineers. Following them was young Ismay, someone was saying that he had just got back from South America; Imrie, his bosom friend and companion, was with him. Then along came William Inman, another youngster who had successfully challenged Cunard's Atlantic trade, and behind him there was tall, gaunt Stephen Guion, the American who had made his home in Liverpool.

As might be expected, all the latecomers were steamboat-men, and they gravitated to that side of the room where steamship interests predominated. Old Glover compared the rugged, honest faces of the sailing shipowners with those other newcomers . . . even if their clothes had not proclaimed it, they were poles apart. They had nothing in common, and as though each knew it they kept to their own sides of the room, steam and sail never mixed.

The ship's clock, a souvenir of the memorable sale of the *Corinne Griffiths*, struck one bell. It was half past four. The room was full, the 'boys' were at their desks; the doors were closed. Glover opened his ledger, the signal for the commencement of the business. In a weak, feeble voice he read out the specifications, which he held shakily in his hands close to his nose, of the first lot on offer.

"Old Harry's getting worse than ever," whispered potential buyers, vainly striving to catch what he said. The old man's indistinguishable drone went on and on, detailing scantlings, orlop decks, deadweight, fast passages, favourite employment, the reasons for selling, anything in fact that would stimulate the interest. Glover no longer drafted out the advertisement of the sale—too old, not modern enough, he thought bitterly, but no one should ever stop him reading them out as he had done with Joe! Mumble, mumble, mumble, the voice trailed on. Bob looked across at William; it was too ridiculous, how much longer in the name of sentiment would they have to put up with this sort of thing. Mumble, mumble, mumble. The two partners sighed in despair. A phrase, or a word here and there, filtered through . . ."good cargo carrier" . . . "eighty days Liverpool to Melbourne" . . . It was a good thing, thought Bob, that it was the firm's custom to send copies of the advertisement to likely buyers as well as pasting the information on the boards outside the office. Those who were likely to buy would have found out all the details of the ships before hand. Harry's laboured mumblings didn't matter so much, he supposed, the only thing was that they annoyed his sense of progress. He liked to think that the firm of Netlock and Sons, Ship Auctioneers and Valuers, was a modern efficient business concern. The sound of the old clerk's voice was like putting the clock back to the easy-come, easy-go business methods of his father. Of course the guv'nor had been a fine fellow, hadn't he started the business? But he'd never had to handle the work which William and he were conducting. Between them they'd put the business in another class altogether. Times had changed with a vengeance. If they kept on as they were doing they'd have to open permanent rooms in London, and one of them stay down there instead of rushing backwards and forwards by train. Thank goodness there were at any rate no stage-coaches to be endured.

Sitting back in the chair his father had always occupied, he reflected with pride that William and he were a couple of live wires. It was a pity that old Harry was there to remind them constantly of the sleepy past . . . but they'd got to put up with him for the sake of their father's memory. Old Harry had kicked up the deuce of a shindy when they had suggested that he take a well deserved pension. Funny old beggar;

never married, seemed to have no interests outside his casualty reports and the picture gallery. Had he stopped talking? No, his jaws were still moving, but then, that might be the quid of tobacco that he was always chewing? Yes! he was sitting down, thank goodness; now to get on with the business.

Bob needed to do very little talking, all he needed was an eager eye, roving here, there and everywhere, searching for a nod, a wink, or perhaps an upraised finger. No time was wasted, the business was conducted quickly. He knew where the bids would come from, but there was an art in it all the same. He knew just when to mention a shipowner by name. It had often tipped the scales another couple of hundred.

At that particular sale business was fairly brisk. Those interested knew what they wanted, and what they were prepared to pay. There wasn't a face that he didn't recognize. They were a queer hard-looking lot with their Dundreary whiskers and stove-pipe hats. It was a perpetual pin-prick with him that clients all kept their hats on during the sale. Affable to him as they always were, the mere fact of their keeping their hats on plainly indicated that they had no intention of letting him forget his position. They were a conservative, self-satisfied lot, yet if it came to real cash, he wouldn't mind betting that he could show them a sovereign or two. Nevertheless, he was pleased to think that their sales attracted such a company. They were influential all right, but he knew how to handle them. Just the proper amount of respect at the right time. Whatever happened, no potential customer would be upset for lack of deference on the auctioneer's part, and that applied whether they had scores of ships or were just contemplating buying their first hull like young Stewart there, the youngest of them all. What was it he was after? Ah, yes, the Chester brig. Should do well with her. Smart youngster, had been making money out of ships' stores they said. Well, it seemed as though they all started that way, though to look at them now you'd think they'd never known the time when they hadn't two coppers to rub together. Not many of them started as young as Stewart; wonder if there's anyone backing him? Said he was prepared to go to fifteen hundred pounds. He'll be lucky if he gets her for that. Give him a chance though, he looks the sort of fellow who'll come back to us.

Gradually the sale wore on, and at length lot 3006 came up. It was the last on the list. Old Harry got up and spoke her name lovingly, built forty years ago, about the time when Joe and he were in their prime. If he knew anything about ships, she'd be a damned sight sounder in wind and limb than he was. Ships had more to them than men, built to last, that's what they were; solid timbers of British oak, you couldn't beat that. Forty years ago . . . what fleeting memories crossed the old man's mind. No one seemed to be much interested in the brig except young Stewart. She was too old for the rest, but what did they know of age ? sitting there with their minds full of everything new, worshipping the future.

It was the end of the sale. The day which old Glover loved best was drawing to a close. To spin it out a little longer, he unconsciously went slower than usual. The brig seemed to symbolize much that was his life. He lingered on, as though fearful of bringing it to an end. The restless stirring of feet and the scraping of chairs left him untroubled, but eventually the faltering voice could no longer protract the sale of this final item. There was nothing further that might be said. With unseeing eyes he backed slowly down into his chair.

"Old Harry won't last the year out," whispered someone in the back of the hall, but no one else had much time to think about it for progress and efficiency was on its feet, talking.

"The last lot, gentlemen. This stout brig, good for many another year of faithful service. Can I ask £800 ? . . . Will anyone give me a start, then ? I don't need to remind you, gentlemen, that her oak timbers and fittings alone will bring in more than £800. £500 then ? Thank you, sir, £500 from the shipbreakers. Six. Seven. Seven hundred from Mr. Stewart." At the mention of his name, many heads turned round to look at this new entry into the auction mart. Flagging interest revived slightly. The brig was no earthly use to a ship-chandler . . . unless he knew something about her stores and stock which the advertisement didn't.

A couple of owners employing brigs pricked up their ears. They'd agreed beforehand that she wasn't worth buying. They looked across at each other suspiciously. Had the other fellow put Stewart up as a blind ? It looked a bit fishy somewhere.

"£800," said one.

"£900," nodded the other.

"£1000," indicated Stewart calmly.

"£1100 from the shipbreakers," said the auctioneer.

"£1500," said Stewart desperately.

This was bidding. The two brig owners looked across at each other and uneasily shook their heads. Unless Stewart knew something he must be a fool to risk £1,500 on a forty-year-old-brig.

And for once in his progressive life, Bob Netlock, as though anxious to finish for the day, pressed no further.

With his hammer poised in the air he repeated : "£1500 I am bid for this lot 3006, the brig, *Mary Jane.*" He wasted no further time. Once, twice, three times, he rapped the desk and the sale was completed. And that was the way in which the firm of Stewart and Brady acquired their first vessel.

St George's Basin and St Nicholas', the sailor's church

CHAPTER 10

NINE DAYS TO CROSS THE ATLANTIC

THEY walked back to Stewart's office, the young man bubbling over with relief, but Captain Brady's mental state could best be judged from the activity of his silk bandanna.

Outside the entrance to No. 3 Chapel Walk, Stewart's eyes rested upon the wooden sign, 'James Stewart, Ship's Husband'.

"Ahoy, Silas," he called, and as the old sailor came stumping out he said : "Take that signboard down and slip round to the Vauxhall Foundry and get them to cast me a brass plate. I want 'Stewart and Brady, Shipowners, nicely printed on it. Can you remember that ?" and jauntily he followed Brady down the steps and into the room.

"Well, Captain, we've done it now," he said gleefully. But poor old Brady was no longer excited, reaction had set in, Stewart felt the other's pessimism reaching out towards him. "Here," he said quickly, "we need to celebrate. It's not every day we become shipowners," and waving aside the old man's protests he carefully piloted him out again, and they carried on to the 'Unicorn' in Hackins Hey.

After a few glasses of rum the captain's depression was routed, and he began to take a more healthier view of things. Susy had been there to welcome them as soon as they arrived, for earlier on she had made it clear to her assistants that no one but herself was ever to serve Mr. Stewart.

"He's her fancy man, see !" said one of the barmaids in an undertone.

"If Irish Higgins finds that she's playing that game, she won't last long," retorted the other.

Meanwhile, the two new shipowners and Susy were having a convivial party. They drank to the firm of Stewart and Brady. Then to the brig *Mary Jane*. Then, on Brady's proposing, to Susy and the 'Unicorn'.

"Who's going to make their fortunes first, Susy ?" bantered Stewart, but that young woman was busy making up to Captain Brady, and they were getting on famously together.

"I hope you'll always bring your custom here, Captain," she was saying, looking at him with ingenuous eyes. "I can promise you and any other sailor a fair deal."

"That's more than any sailor has a right to expect," said Stewart. "Don't you be taken in with this young woman, Captain ; she's out for the shekels !"

"Not Susy," said Brady admiringly, "everyone knows that she's the only barmaid in town who'll give a sailor the right change."

"I'm not a barmaid, I'm the manageress here," said Susy proudly, as though to show Stewart that he was not the only one who could get on.

"Don't you worry, lassie, you can rely on Tobias Brady to send you custom. I don't mind wagering that as soon as the folks get to know that you've taken over the 'Unicorn', the place'll be so crowded that an old-timer like me will never be able to get his foot across the doorstep !"

"That's what Susy thinks," scoffed Stewart, "but she'd have to be a hundred per cent. smarter to get folks to come into a Higgins' house . . . at least when they're sober."

Susy looked at him cheerfully. "Thank goodness, then, there's not many sober folks around these days."

"You'll have a fine time with a bar full of drunks," said Stewart, who appeared to have some sort of grievance against her being there at all. "Who's going to keep order for you ?"

"Susy can handle a drunk better than you or me, my boy," Brady chuckled, now firmly of the opinion that she was the most admirable female that he had ever known.

"Phooh !" said Susy light-heartedly. "If drunken men were all I had to worry about they'd be the least trouble. Thank you for nothing, Mr. Stewart. You'd be of greater assistance if you told me how I can stop my cellar-man and the two barmaids from diddling me on the till !"

"There's only one way to do that," said Stewart, confident of his ability to solve any problem, "and that is to have someone behind the bar responsible for the stock and the till."

"How do you mean ?"

He looked at her pityingly, it was plain to be seen that the girl had no business ability.

"It's like this," he explained, "if you let all three of them go behind the bar and help themselves they're sure to swindle you. But if you make one person responsible for measuring out, then the serving can be left to the others. And all you have to do is to measure up the stock before you open, and do the same when you close down. The difference will be the cash that whoever you put behind the bar will hand over to you from the till. It's quite simple," he concluded smugly.

"That means I shall have to take on another girl," said Susy thoughtfully.

"Better that than finding yourself five or six pounds out of pocket at the end of the week. Though why you can't do it yourself beats me."

"I want to move about among the customers," said Susy defensively. "I want to make them welcome, so that they'll come again and help me build up the trade. You can see for yourself the 'Unicorn's' got plenty of room for more people, small though the place is."

"If you want to get trade by sitting on your customer's knees," said Stewart cuttingly, "go ahead, I don't doubt the customers will come, but you'll still be short in the till at the end of the week !"

"Who said anything about sitting on the customer's knees?" Susy said, angry at last.

"Of course the girl's right," interposed Brady tactfully; "it's personal attention that counts in the hotel business. Make your customers feel that you'll be disappointed if they don't drop in again soon."

"Hotel business!" sneered Stewart. "Giving it fancy names won't disguise it from what it is!"

"You've got some need to talk," Susy replied with spirit, "at least it's honest, and that's more than you can say about your ships' store business!"

"Oh, and what do you mean by that, my pretty maid?" asked Stewart smoothly.

"Don't call me your pretty maid," said Susy angrily, "and don't forget that I've got ears. Perhaps you don't remember the holystones they found in the barrels of salt pork which you shipped on board the *Antiope* in the Salthouse dock? I can tell you a good many of my customers haven't forgotten it!"

Captain Brady cocked his ears incredulously. To his way of thinking the greatest crime of all was any jiggery-pokery with a ship's stores. "Is this true?" he asked.

Stewart was confused and his face reddened. "Of course it isn't, Captain. There was some complaint about the *Antiope's* salt pork, but it had nothing to do with me, I only shipped it on board for Irish Higgins. You see, Captain, I happen to be one of his water clerks. The whole affair was arranged between Higgins and the ship's master. Nobody would have been any the wiser if the sling hadn't given way while they were hoisting the sea-stock on board."

Brady looked at him suspiciously. "I never knew you were a runner for Irish Higgins," he said slowly, "and if I had, you would certainly never have got my order. I always understood you were in business for yourself?"

"So I was, Captain, the last time we met, but I've had a bit of bad luck and Higgins put me out of business, and until I can get rid of my present stock I'm compelled to keep in with him."

Susy walked triumphantly away, and Stewart laboured and sweated to allay the captain's misgivings. The whole business took a lot of explaining, for the old man was inclined to think the worst of the complicated nature of shore-based commerce.

At last Brady said hesitantly, "Well, I suppose it's all right, but it is certainly the queerest log that I've ever come across."

Susy, humming happily to herself, came over to them again. "Won't you have a drink on the house?" she asked Stewart impudently. "You must be dry after all that talking!"

The young man glared at her. "No, thanks," he said curtly, and in a wave of anger got up and left them both.

"He seems to be properly annoyed," said Brady, puzzled.

"He'll get over it," she replied calmly. "I knew there was nothing in that story really, but he thinks such a lot of himself that I couldn't help taking him down a peg."

"You like him, eh?" quizzed the old man, beginning to see light.

"No, not specially," denied the girl with a shade too much conviction; "to me, he's just one of the customers."

"But I thought you didn't believe in offending your customers?" Brady said, a trifle maliciously.

"Oh! Mr. Stewart's not one to bear malice, I'll say that for him. He'll be in again tomorrow when he gets over it."

"He's right about you taking on someone else to look after the bar and the till," said the captain thoughtfully.

"Do you really think so?" asked Susy, looking at him as though it was only his opinion that counted with her.

"It's the common-sense thing to do," he replied sympathetically, and went on to inquire how the business was progressing. But Susy had not been there more than a few days, and could only explain her scheme for making the place a success. She was the first tenant, and she did not expect the 'Unicorn' to become famous in a night or so. Then there was the fact that it belonged to Irish Higgins. Stewart was right about that. Higgins' name would stop a lot of people from coming into the place. Her brow clouded over anxiously; she had not particularly wanted to come there, in fact if she had not gone to Higgins to ask him to put his drays in the Exhibition procession, she might still have been at the 'Pig and Whistle'. Not that she was sorry she had taken it on; after all, she was only twenty-one, and it was an opportunity to get on . . . she did not want to remain a barmaid all her life.

Captain Brady thought for a while, then he said, "Do you really think you'll be able to manage this tavern on your own, lass?"

"Certainly I do," she replied, the doubt apparently never having crossed her mind.

He shook his head dubiously, then suddenly he asked, "How much money would it cost to buy a place like this?"

"Far more money than I've got," she said with a rueful laugh, "but all the same I intend to have a place of my own someday."

"Yes, but how much would it cost?" persisted Brady.

"Why, you could get a beer-house for as little as £50, but a proper public, with wines and spirits," she said professionally, "would cost you anything from a hundred to five hundred pounds. But you aren't thinking of going into the trade, are you, Captain?" she asked curiously. "If you are I'll give up this place and come and work for you. How about that?"

The old man laughed. "Now, Susy," he said, "none of your little tricks on me, I'm not Mr. Stewart. But listen," he said, becoming serious. "I'm willing to lend you £200 to set you up on your own."

"If only you meant it!" she sighed longingly.

"Of course I mean it. You find a nice little public-house which you can buy for £200 and I'll see you get the cash!"

Susy's eyes shone excitedly; but she had not been in business without learning a thing or two. "There'd be no funny business, Captain," she said shrewdly, looking him squarely in the eye.

"Susy," he chided her, shocked, "I'm much too old for anything else."

"I don't know so much about that, the older some men get the sillier they become," but she said it in such a way that Captain Brady had to laugh.

"Well, there it is," he said amiably, and stood up. "I'll be in Liverpool another three or four weeks, so you'd better make up your mind before I sail."

But Susy's mind was already made up. "I'll start looking round right away," she said happily.

"Hurry up, then, and get clear of this fellow Higgins, I never did like the sound of him . . . and mind, not a word of this to Mr. Stewart."

"Why?" she asked, puzzled.

"If he thought I had another couple of hundred pounds he'd pester the life out of me until I'd agreed to put it into this shipowning firm of ours," and with a kindly smile he left Susy, for the first time in her life, at a loss for words. Her mind was a riot of ambitious, excited thoughts. For £200 she could find a better place than the 'Unicorn'. The thing was to decide which district to set up in. There was the Dock Road with its sailors and longshoremen, or the commercial end of the town where money was nothing like so free but the company much more select.

Ever since Susy was a young girl the summit of her ambition had been to own a public-house in the Dock Road. She had spent a lot of time dreaming about it. An honest public-house in the Dock Road would be something so unusual that it could not help but be popular. The only thing against it was the women. Sailors would not come unless the place was filled with trollops—but she was not going to have them all the same. Captain Evans Rees had the right idea; no women were ever served in his house. That policy paid in the 'Pig and Whistle' even though the landlord did not know how to manage his barmaids. That ignorance cost him a lot of money, but it would not cost Susy much in the house that she ran. At any rate, the idea would be worth trying.

She would have regular closing hours, and treat the barmaids like human beings. For the customers there would be food as well as liquor, and a good professional show at night that would keep them happy and amused as long as they remained there. They would want women, sailors always did, but they could seek them elsewhere after she had closed. She decided that her public-house would be something unusual, something different from the other places with which she would have to compete.

Captain Brady was feeling in a benevolent mood; he was sorry Stewart had dashed off like that, after all, they were partners, and to Captain Brady, with his old-fashioned ideas, that meant much. He found Stewart, eventually, in the 'Pig and Whistle', expanding discursively to Sam Sharp and a certain Mr. Douglas Hebson, who was importantly introduced to him as the consulting engineer of the Inman Line. The old sea-captain's face clouded over; the young fool had got into bad company! he would have to stay and see him out of it.

At the sight of Brady, Stewart's loquacity suddenly deserted him and the conversation became more general. As was the custom in any place in Liverpool where progressive shipping men gathered together, the talk was of steamships and what Mr. Hebson called "The Fleet Messengers of the Mersey", meaning the big trans-Atlantic passenger steamships. It was a subject that was distasteful to Brady and he lost no time in expressing his opinion. Stewart, out of humour with his partner, said, "Come, Captain, just because your father sailed a ship a certain way, and your father's father sailed her the same way too, it still doesn't mean to say that's the best way."

"Well, I reckon the old ways are good enough for me, young man. These steamers and other new-fangled notions are not for the likes of seamen!"

"There's much to be said on both sides," said Sam Sharp with the air of a Solomon. "Fill 'em up again, Miss Elsie . . . wooden ships and iron men, or iron ships and wooden men, whether they're driven by God's bounty or by the mechanical genius of mankind, what does it matter so long as they fulfil a service?"

"We want no blaspheming here," Brady said sternly.

"The steamer," went on the reporter, impervious to the interruption, "is here to stay. A proof of that I saw with my own eyes at the Custom House this morning, when the master of a steamer produced two newly indentured apprentices for the Shipping Master to look at!"

Captain Brady nearly had apoplexy. Apprentices in a steamer! What did they think they were going to learn there? How to rig a funnel maybe—or splice a broken paddle-wheel perhaps? Pshaw! it was sheer nonsense!

"It is not so ridiculous as you imagine, sir," said Mr. Hebson stiffly. "After all, there's no point in learning to drive a stage-coach if you want to be a locomotive driver."

"Who wants to be a locomotive driver?" asked Brady with all the scorn his simple soul was capable of. "A real seaman would be ashamed to set foot across a steamer's gangway!"

"It's only a matter of time," said Stewart, nodding across at the engineer.

"Time nothing, young man!" barked Brady. "Look at the *James Baines*, sixty-three days from Liverpool to Melbourne. Where's the steamer that's going to beat her record, eh? Look at Captain Samuel's ship the *Dreadnought*—nine days to cross the Atlantic!"

"The old, old argument," sighed Mr. Hebson wearily.

"But surely, Captain," ridiculed Stewart, "you don't seriously believe the *Dreadnought's* story? It's all hearsay. It's never been officially accepted in the Press, has it, Sam?"

"The Press!" snorted Brady contemptuously. "What's the Press, anyway? There's a lot of things that go on in this world that the Press never hears about."

"Not in Liverpool, though——" began the reporter defensively, when Mr. Hebson interrupted him.

"The *Dreadnought's* passage lacks confirmation, sir," he said to Captain Brady. "My interest, as these other gentlemen are aware, lies in the Atlantic crossings, but the only ship I've ever heard of who did the passage in nine days was the ill-fated Collins' liner, the *Pacific*, in 1851."

"There was the Cunard flyer *Persia*, you know, Mr. Hebson," corrected Stewart, proud of his knowledge of shipping records, "she crossed the Atlantic in nine days in 'fifty-six and again in 'fifty-seven."

"So she did," acknowledged the engineer graciously, "but of course she was a steamer like the *Pacific*."

"I'm telling you," said Captain Brady doggedly, "that the sailing ship *Dreadnought* crossed from New York to Queenstown in nine days seventeen hours. It was in 'fifty-eight, and I had it direct from the pilot cutter off the Bar. It's common enough knowledge amongst sailing-ship men."

"Speaking as a humble representative of the much maligned Press," said Sharp pompously, "I wouldn't go so far as to say the story's true or untrue. Braver men than I tackled Captain Samuels when he arrived. but he ran them off the ship as soon as ever he learned that they doubted his word. The mate was too cowed to speak, and as for the rest of the crew they'd spin a different yarn every time you'd stand them a glass of beer. And there the matter stands, gentlemen."

"If it were true," said Stewart dubiously, "I can't see MacIvers, Inman and all the rest persevering with steamships, can you, Mr. Hebson?"

"Our steamers are making good profits," said the engineer cautiously.

"So they may be," said Brady, undeterred, "but so are a great many other shipowners who never soiled their fingers or their reputations with coal-burning boxes. And as for all your opinions I'll only say that I was reading in the *Albion* this morning, that it was fifty years since the first steamer was launched, yet it went on to say that only one ship in ten today is a steamer! So it doesn't look as though many shipowners agree with any of you."

"All the same," said Mr. Hebson with a smile, "I'll stick to my view that all ships will be steamships some day."

"Look at the British mercantile marine today," said Brady, now thoroughly roused, "it's never had so many, or such fine sailing ships."

"Yes, you're right there," conceded Mr. Hebson

"You know, though," said Stewart maliciously, "I've heard it said that American ships and seamen are better than ours!"

"I think even Captain Brady will admit that was the case before the Civil War," remarked Mr. Hebson good-humouredly, "but of course it was due to the fact that they studied this shipping business from a scientific point of view. It wasn't a case of man-made ships but God-made sailors, with them; they looked deeper into the matter. They looked at their ships, they looked at their gear. As a result, they built ships with finer lines, and then they produced improved blocks and introduced mechanical appliances to help work the sails, and so you got American ships sailing faster with twenty hands than a British ship of the same size with thirty hands. But Captain Brady will be able to tell you more about that than I can," he ended tactfully.

A little sympathetic consideration always brought a response from Captain Brady, and when he saw that they were all looking towards him with the proper respect due to a shipmaster, he became more friendly disposed.

"I'd be the last to deny that we owe the Americans a lot as regards sailing a ship, but then, they've been more fortunate than we have, especially in regard to their officers. They've got a better type of man following the sea, and they've encouraged their seamen more. In American ships their apprentices are all boys with Grammar School education, whereas many of our ships are manned with poor-law apprentices unable to read or write. Then, in American ships, those boys rise to command at an early age and with it they get a financial interest in their ship. No wonder they nearly drove us off the sea."

"I think we've got the Civil War to thank for the fact that they didn't," said Mr. Hebson thoughtfully, and added with a provoking smile, "that and the American dislike of steamships."

"At any rate," Captain Brady remarked, ignoring the opening, "it's different now. Ever since the 'fifties we've had as good a mercantile marine as the Americans. Ships like the *Marco Polo, Donald Mackay, Lightning, Champion of the Seas,* all of them every bit as good as, if not better than, the Yankee ships."

"Let me see," said Mr. Hebson gravely, "weren't they all built on the other side of the Atlantic?"

"Perhaps they were, but that doesn't alter the fact that at this moment British shipping leads the world."

"She certainly does in the casualty returns," remarked Sam Sharp, and Stewart, with vivid memories of his own dispute with Brady on this matter, hastened to change the subject.

"What do you make of this fellow Plimsoll?" he asked.

"Frankly, I don't know," returned Mr. Hebson; "he seems sincere enough, but he obviously hasn't the slightest technical knowledge of what he's talking about. Yet look at the fuss he's creating."

"Don't tell me," groaned the reporter, his head bowed in his hands, "don't I have to report his speeches? Pure bunkum, sir, but that doesn't mean to say they're bad politics, especially in his case, when he's hoping to stand for Parliament."

"If he's going into Parliament, it is to thrash the matter out properly," defended Captain Brady. "I've heard him speak, and there's a lot in what he says."

"I'm not so sure that I can agree with you there," said Mr. Hebson, smiling faintly, "and to illustrate my point, I invite you to look at American ships again. They load every bit as deep as British ships, yet they have nothing like the same casualty lists."

"But then," said Stewart, belatedly coming to Captain Brady's assistance, "there's nothing like so many American ships afloat as there are British."

"We own just double the tonnage of the Americans," Mr. Hebson replied, "but for every Yankee ship you see in the casualty lists, you'll see four British!"

"Of all the many reasons which may place a ship in the casualty returns, I would venture to suggest that overloading is by no means the most important," remarked Sam Sharp, feeling it incumbent upon himself to earn some of all this refreshing hospitality. He took a long drink, smacked his lips and went on: "Of course there may be one or two owners who specialize in 'coffin-ships', but then, there's black sheep in every trade. Look at it in a sensible light," he invited; "if a shipowner wishes to cast away his ship, as Plimsoll would have you believe they all do, would he fill her full of cargo to do it? There's plenty of ways of doing it without that."

"There may be something in what you say," Captain Brady remarked slowly. "As a seaman I know there's as much danger in a ship without cargo, as ever there is in one with too much."

"Exactly," joined in Mr. Hebson. "Well, then, who is to decide when a ship is overloaded? Certainly not Plimsoll, nor any one else standing on the quay arguing about it. With all due respect to you, Captain, I don't think that even you can decide in port——"

"Why——" began Brady indignantly, but Mr. Hebson would not be interrupted and he continued :

"It happens like this. At certain stages a ship is what you call seaworthy, and the next . . . she's unseaworthy. But who knows when one stage is reached and the other left behind ? How are you going to tell, Captain ? By figures and calculations ? I don't believe it. Freeboard is all very well, but it is handiness that counts. You can't tell in port how a ship will behave out at sea."

Captain Brady did not like to admit that this was so, and to an engineer least of all, and since he felt his professional reputation was at stake, he made up his mind to talk about seamanship and leave all this dangerous theory alone. "So long as a ship will sail and steer," he said profoundly, "a good seaman can keep any ship afloat."

Mr. Hebson was unimpressed and refused to be side-tracked. "It's not a question for Plimsoll at all—or for the Government. After all, it's the underwriters who pay, and the matter should be left in their hands. If I know anything about them they'll jib soon enough if they think ships are being lost through overloading."

"I don't see how you can possibly say how a ship was lost if she never turns up again," said Stewart.

Mr. Hebson's hobby-horse, however, was Plimsoll, and he refused to be turned away. "Mind you," he proceeded, "I am sure the fellow means well, but he's got his facts wrong. If he wants to help sailors, let him get Parliament to pass a Bill to stop under-manning. Or let him get the examinations stiffened in regard to those who have to take command at sea. Let him start about getting them better food and wages and less working hours. Sailors would have something to thank him for then."

Sam Sharp looked up in alarm. "Do you want to kill the industry ?" he asked.

"Is it a fact that the Cunard have never lost a life at sea, in spite of what Plimsoll is saying ?" Stewart asked.

"It is," said the reporter, determined not to be excluded from the conversation, and looking as solemn and wise as his liquor would let him. "And I hope you see the inference, Mr. Stewart. Landsmen don't know much about ships and seamen, and if you tell them that scoundrels of shipowners are so greedy for profits that they overload their ships, they'll believe you. They can just about understand that if you go on and on piling cargo into a ship she will eventually sink."

"Why don't shipowners defend themselves against these accusations ?" asked Stewart, puzzled.

"For the simple reason that they know it would be a waste of time. Plimsoll says it's shipowners' profits or men's lives, and it would take a brave man to stand up against that argument. When such a fellow as Plimsoll starts stumping the country with a platform like that, he'll rouse the people more than Moody and Sankey could with their hymn-singing. These are unsettled times all right, and what with Government interference, the shipping industry is not the business it was." After that informative speech, the reporter, mollified, sat back in his chair and took a long drink.

"Well, I don't know," said Stewart innocently, "in spite of what you say about Plimsoll and Government interference, shipowning still seems to be a profitable venture. At least Captain Brady and I think so, for today we too have joined the hallowed ranks of Liverpool shipowners!"

"Steamships, I hope?" said Mr. Hebson gravely.

"No, sir," growled Brady, "just a little, plain, honest sailing brig."

"We might go in for steam later," Stewart added apologetically.

Captain Brady pricked up his ears. "That's the first I've heard of it, young man," he said warmly.

"This news calls for something special," Sam Sharp remarked hopefully, a pleasant look of anticipation lighting up his face. "I shall be proud to drink to the success of your enterprise. The country needs more men like you."

"All right," said Stewart cheerfully, ordering more refreshment, "but mind you, Sam, we want no more friendly notices in the *Albion*," and a little later they all separated.

Early Saturday morning Captain Brady left Liverpool for Chester. Stewart had suggested he take a Liverpool tug and tow the brig round, but the captain said that was unnecessary expense. If he couldn't sail her round with a crew of runners then he was no seaman. The runners would want a sovereign apiece for the passage, and he worked it out that he could easily get the brig round for seven pounds, including the tips to the lock-gatemen. A tug would cost ten pounds alone, without the other expenses. It was on little things like that that young Stewart revealed his inexperience. He might be a progressive young fellow, yes. But all the same, he needed someone like Tobias Brady to steady him up.

Meanwhile, his young partner was resolutely making up his mind to round off his business arrangement with Irish Higgins and find out where he stood with Miss Scripps. He was finished with shipchandlery and the sooner he squared up with Higgins the better. It wasn't going to be so easy, for there was the thought of Miss Scripps to hold him back from a too hasty conclusion of the only opportunity left to him for re-establishing himself in her good graces. If what Susy said was true, and that she did really believe he was responsible for her fall into the river, it was going to be uphill work. But did she really believe that? If she did, why had she not denied that ridiculous story in the *Albion*? or why had she not told her uncle? Perhaps she thought more of him than her actions had indicated? Hopefully, he picked up his ledger and set out for Duke Street.

At twelve o'clock prompt he was shown straight into the back room where Higgins sat waiting. The ledger was inspected quickly and a caustic comment passed about the scant entries. The truth was that Stewart had had no time in which to seek new business, but he could hardly offer that as an explanation. Instead, he ventured to say, with a faint attempt at jocularity, that by the time Higgins' runners were finished there was not much business left for him. Higgins' curt rejoinder soon made it clear that he, on his part, was not inspired by the conciliatory spirit of the younger man.

Contemptuously, the publican flicked back the pages of the ledger, tracing the ever-declining business that Stewart had done. If these were the best results he could show, then there was little point in maintaining their connection, and sarcastically he suggested that the young man should seek some other form of employment . . . if he could?

Stewart amiably said that he thought that might be best too, as he had just lately gone in for shipowning, and did not think he could find the time to serve the two interests.

Higgins was not impressed, and his derisive expression as he looked at the ledger showed plainly that if ship's husbandry was any guide, Stewart would not do much with shipowning. With a snort of disgust he pushed the ledger into the drawer and turned his attention to other documents lying on his desk. That was the usual signal that the interview was at an end, but this time Stewart continued to stand there, awkwardly shifting his weight from one foot to the other. Higgins looked up again.

"Well," he snapped, "what are you waiting for?"

"Wh . . . what about my commission?" the young man stammered, his courage not yet equal to broaching the subject to Miss Scripps.

"That will be sent round to you."

"But what about all the stock I've still got on my hands?"

"That's your concern. You had the opportunity of getting rid of it when you worked for me."

There was a longish pause, and then the young man suddenly burst out, "Mr. Higgins, there's something else I want to talk to you about."

The other showed his irritation. "My time is precious. Anything else you want to say had best be said to my storekeeper at Salthouse Dock. Good day!" and he turned deliberately to his desk again.

"It's about your niece. I want to marry her!"

For a second Higgins' face remained uncomprehending, and then, as the purport of the young man's statement dawned upon him, his face became as red as Stewart's, but it was from anger rather than embarrassment.

"Are you mad?" he exclaimed, and he got up and pulled violently on the bell-rope. When the negro appeared he sent him for Miss Scripps.

A few minutes later Stewart's ordeal of silent waiting was ended, and the girl came breathlessly tripping in. Apparently unconscious of Stewart's presence, she went straight over to Higgins and linking her arm affectionately in his asked, with a false note in her voice, what he wanted.

"This fellow," said the publican, unable to keep his voice firm, "has just had the impertinence to tell me he wants to marry you! Have you ever given him any encouragement?"

Stewart's spirits dropped as he encountered Miss Scripps' cold, unfriendly eyes.

"None whatever," she said serenely. "You don't think I would encourage anyone you don't like, do you, Uncle?"

The young man looked at her in despair, but after that first fleeting, impersonal glance she disregarded him entirely.

"It's just what I thought," said Higgins. "Has he been pestering you with his attentions?" and in a daze, Stewart continued to look and listen while the young woman went on to say that of course she had seen a lot of Mr. Stewart through her work for the Exhibition, and now that she thought back, he had been rather forward at times, but then, there had always been Mr. Puddicombe, the curate, near at hand to save her from any unpleasantness.

"But, but——" stuttered Stewart.

"Hold your tongue!" cried Higgins, very angry.

Miss Scripps' eyes took on that soulful look that Stewart knew so well. "I think he is an extremely impudent young man," she said calmly.

That was enough for Higgins; he was as much the dupe of his niece as Stewart.

"If I were a younger man I'd give you the thrashing you deserve," he said, and advanced threateningly, while Stewart, alarmed, retreated ignominiously. He cast a reproachful, imploring look at Miss Scripps, but there was no encouragement there, and anxiously deciding that discretion was the better part of valour at that stage, wasted no time in leaving uncle and niece alone.

A veil had perhaps better be drawn over Stewart's immediate thoughts as he walked down Duke Street. His earlier optimism had given way to disillusionment. This complete rebuff was beyond him, and he would have been still more puzzled if he could have seen Miss Scripps just then, giving Martha a highly coloured account of all that had taken place. His discomfiture turned to anger. His whole being craved for sympathy and, hardly knowing, his steps led him in the direction of the 'Unicorn'.

Susy greeted him with surprise. "We aren't half honoured," she said. "It's not every day you condescend to pay us a visit at this time of day!"

"Oh! lay off, Susy," he said miserably, and seated himself down at a stool near the bar.

The 'Unicorn' was almost deserted, the busy lunch-time trade which she had hoped for had not yet materialized, and it would be later in the day before the customary trippers and the sailors started to come in.

"Lost all your money, dearie?" she asked cheerfully, surveying his mournful face, and went on to prattle blithely, for she herself was in excellent spirits as a result of a night and morning spent in thinking over Captain Brady's offer. There was no reciprocal liveliness about Stewart though, and her verbal sallies went unchallenged.

When she realized the depths of his depression, she became curiously sympathetic, and under her skilful questioning the whole story of Miss Scripps' infamy was laid bare.

"It strikes me that there's something going on between her and that curate," said Susy darkly. "You know, Mr. Stewart, that young woman's church is her public-house, and she's not for the likes of you. You ought to think yourself lucky that you've found her out so early."

The combination of Susy's healing sympathy, and the warming effects of a couple of glasses of rum, made Stewart begin to feel less sorry for himself. Here, at any rate, Susy's tender solicitude led him to believe his advances would not be spurned. Suddenly an idea occurred to him.

"Could you get the rest of the day off?" he asked eagerly.

"What for?"

"There's an excursion to Blackpool. Leaves at two o'clock. What about it?"

She shook her head regretfully. "I wish I could."

"Come on," urged Stewart, "you can trust your barmaids for half a day, surely?"

"What time does it get back?" she asked, torn between her wish to go and the knowledge that she ought not to leave the 'Unicorn'.

"Round about midnight," he said. "Come on, Susy, it'll do us both a power of good."

"All right, then!" she cried excitedly, her mind made up. "I'll meet you at the top of Moorfields at ten minutes to two," and she dashed away to make her arrangements, and under the heady prospect of this outing, the vision of Irish Higgins and Miss Scripps receded from his mind.

CHAPTER 11

AN EXCURSION TO BLACKPOOL

THE half-day excursions which enterprising railway companies had instituted, were still too new an innovation for a thoroughly train-conscious public to resist. Railways were the fashion, and even to those who did not remember the hardship of the stage-coach, they were an irresistible attraction. It was an adventure to get into a locomotive coach and be hauled through the countryside at thirty miles an hour. It was a thrill to go to towns and places which previously had been as remote as London, or even America. But you could not spend all your days flying about the country, even if your pocket could afford it. Once you had had the initial experience of a ride in a steam train, there was no further reason why you should go for another, unless you had to get somewhere. And very few people had cause to venture outside the boundaries imposed by the limitation of walking, or horse-drawn vehicles, for both towns and villages in the 1860s were still parochially-minded in business and private affairs.

It was with the purpose of breaking up this ancient custom of insularity that the railways had hit upon the idea of special excursions. The idea had caught on, and the question "What excursions are running over the week-end?" was as often on men's tongues as what was on at the theatre. The prosperity of the age put gold in men's pockets, and in the congested, industrial areas of Lancashire the hundreds of thousands engaged in coal hewing, cotton spinning, and shipping, all showed a willing desire to spend the money the new industrialism gave them.

Wakes and local festivals no longer kept the people in their home towns; they moved from the dirty, smoke-laden atmosphere of mills, pit-heads and hovels, to the clean, invigorating areas of Blackpool, New Brighton and Southport. All three resorts were being developed to attract the holiday-maker. Southport was sedate and respectable, but while New Brighton, seeking to emulate the reputation of its namesake on the south coast, only managed to progress slowly, Black-pool became a name that conjured up visions of heaven to tired, dirty employees, whose daily horizons were towering chimneys and gaunt grey factories.

Few were so poor that they could not afford to put by their spare coppers. Saving clubs and tontines sprang up by the score, and at cheap rates the railways put excursion trains on to carry them to the paradise of Blackpool or elsewhere. Most of these excursion trains ran on Saturdays, with just a few on Sundays, and although they were hailed with delight by thousands of poor working-class people, the residents of Blackpool were hardly so pleased. Their opposition to this week-end intrusion was misguided but understandable, but there was nothing they could do about it, for the week-end habit and the Wakes were firmly established, and thousands poured forth from the grim, forbidding industrial areas to seek the tonic to body and mind which Blackpool gave.

When Stewart arrived at Exchange Station he found a milling mob surging round the ticket-office. There was an air of happy excitement about. Artisans in cloth caps and check suits elbowed and pushed their way forward. Scores of women, with seeming hosts of children hanging tightly on to little tin buckets and wooden spades, hovered anxiously on the outskirts.

Children crying, women shouting shrill instructions, and men swearing profusely, all combined to make the station a miniature Bedlam ; and in the background was the muffled shriek of steam whistles and the noisy shunting of trains.

The big clock relentlessly showed the advancing hour, and the crowd was growing rather than lessening as Stewart resolutely followed the fashion and elbowed his way to the ticket-office. Men stood on his toes, dug him in the ribs with their elbows, gathered round behind him and pressed forward. Eventually he came within sight of the ticket-window and saw the sweating clerks counting change, stamping tickets and keeping up a running fire of backchat with the anxious trippers. Then it was his turn ; he planked the exact money down, got his two tickets, and after a sharp but shorter struggle, fought his way out from the dense pack of people.

Punctuality was not one of Susy's virtues, and as the big finger of the clock crawled slowly up past the quarter hour, to ten minutes, and then to five minutes to the hour, Stewart began to pace impatiently up and down. When the clock showed two minutes to two o'clock he saw her hurrying up Moorfields. He'd have known it must be Susy even if he had not sighted her face, for a great white feather curled upright from the back of her hat and danced gaily over her forehead.

There was no time for comment or explanation, and he seized her hand and hurried her across the street and up the station steps. The barrier to the platform was just being lowered ; they ducked under it.

"Hey," yelled the ticket collector, "you're too late, she's just off!"

The guard was already waving his huge green flag and blowing his whistle, and heads were crowding out of every carriage window.

"We've got to run," said Stewart, and together they sprinted up the last twenty yards, the feather on Susy's hat beating a mad tattoo, while the onlookers cheered. The train was starting forward in a series of sharp jerks when they got abreast of the guard's van.

"This'll do," panted Stewart, and dodging behind the girl he heaved and pushed, and as she tumbled inside he jumped in after her. When, a few seconds later, he had recovered his breath, he stared at the drooping feather and said in a resigned voice, "Well, thank goodness you aren't wearing that damned bustle!"

Susy had collapsed on a big leather trunk. "My," she gasped, "if this is how you go to Blackpool, once in a lifetime's enough for me!"

The guard swung inboard, and saw them with astonishment. "Yer must 'a' got on 'er when she wor moving!" he said accusingly.

"True," said Stewart nonchalantly.

"It's a h'offence. Ain't you read the Company's Byelaws?"

"Actually, we had got to article 29, paragraph 3, subsection D, when your whistle blew. That's why we're late, see!" said Stewart facetiously.

"Oh! Mr. Smartey, eh? Well, I've a good mind to stop t'train and put you off!"

"Ooh!" thrilled Susy tactfully, "can you stop the engine as easily as that?"

"'Course I can. I can either pull that chain there and tell the driver to stop 'er, or I can put the brakes on mesel' with this 'ere lever!"

Susy, openly admiring, gazed wide-eyed at him.

"You've no right to be in this wagon," he said, weakening.

"Here's a shilling. We're sorry we got in here, but we hadn't time to look for seats," said Stewart, thinking it better to be more conciliatory.

"Well, sir, if you puts it like that, it's different. Between you and me, you're better off in 'ere than packed like they are up int' coaches."

"You'll let us stay, then?" pleaded Susy.

"It's agin orders, luv, but seein' as 'ow it's you, I'll say nowt about it." He gave her a ponderous wink and Susy giggled provokingly.

"'Ere, luv, tek this cushion o' mine, it'll mek things a bit easier for yer like."

The train gathered speed, it creaked and groaned and rattled, but Susy had fully recovered her breath now, and in her lively fashion she was entertaining both Stewart and the guard. It was only forty miles to Blackpool and they were due there at four o'clock. But as the journey progressed, Susy's high spirits began to falter, and the colour began to fade from her cheeks.

Stewart noticed that she was holding her middle tightly, and he grinned maliciously and said, "You're very quiet all of a sudden!"

"I've got a pain in my . . . er . . . I've got a pain," she concluded weakly.

"Stand up to the window, luv, and get a breath o' fresh air," advised the guard kindly.

"For heaven's sake don't be sick in here," warned Stewart.

She looked at him with indignation, the white feather bobbing despairingly. "Who said I felt sick?" she said, staggering across to the window.

"Far better put your fingers down your throat and get it over," said Stewart unkindly.

"Aye, lassy, that's the best thing to do," agreed the guard wisely, nodding his head.

"I tell you I'm all right," she said desperately, longing for the solid comfort of the firm earth beneath her feet.

"It's alreet, luv," persisted the well-meaning guard, "they're allus sick on this 'ere excursion. You should see the mess the cleaners 'ave to deal with at t'other end."

Susy looked at him miserably.

"In fact it might be called a sickening excursion," said Stewart brightly.

"Oh! leave me alone," moaned Susy, hanging grimly on to the window.

"Only 'alf an hour more," encouraged the guard, and although to Susy it seemed like years, the train eventually whistled and rattled into Central Station, Blackpool. The wheels had no sooner stopped turning than Susy became her bright perky self. Her feathered hat was once more settled in its proper position; the colour returned slowly to her cheeks, and with a happy laugh she jumped on to the platform ahead of Stewart and together they surged out with the crowd into the street.

Spirits were prematurely high and many showed signs of having already taken ample liquid refreshment on the journey. Harassed mothers vainly tried to control their exuberant children, as they sought, at the same time, to keep their erring husbands from slipping into the first public-house. The crowd from the station surged on to the sea-front. Shouts and laughter filled the air, the joyous atmosphere was infectious, and good humour spread from one to the other and made even harassed mothers smile now and again. Hawkers in the gutter shrilly offered a variety of false noses, comic paper hats and noisy wooden rattles; the spirit of carnival was abroad, there was no time for depression.

It was the first time that either Stewart or Susy had been to Blackpool and they set out to enjoy themselves. Susy, in her element, exchanged jokes and quips with all and sundry.

"Tha'r't a bit o' alreet!" shouted a passing young man, admiringly.

Susy uttered a little shriek and turned round abruptly.

"What on earth's the matter?" Stewart asked, puzzled.

"He pinched my behind," she said angrily.

"Is that all? Well, don't stick it out so much!"

"How dare you?" she demanded indignantly.

"Oh! come off it, Susy; if you go around ogling men all over the place, what do you expect?"

Susy was speechless.

"Never mind," said Stewart calmly, "we're here to enjoy ourselves, so come along."

Indignant words formed on Susy's lips, and then she thought better of them, and after swallowing once or twice, she said imperiously, "Get me a bag of winkles."

"Please yourself," he said, "but I'm having a bag of mussels," and after he had bought them from a barrow-hawker on the side of the road, they proceeded along in more contented fashion, Stewart, with his pocket knife, prizing open the shells, and Susy, with a pin he had given her, extracting the winkles and gobbling them up enthusiastically. It was great fun, and they laughed at each other's comical efforts.

In a short while they came to the pier where a brass band was doing its best to make itself heard above the noise of the crowd. Round and round the band the merry couples gyrated and strutted in an abandoned polka. Many of them were drunk, and their ridiculous antics kept the onlookers shrieking with delight. Faster and faster went the music, round and round raced the dancers, the women's feet barely touching the planks of the pier as their partners boisterously essayed to swing them in the air. Susy, holding Stewart firmly by the hand, pushed her way to the front, and there, with parted lips and shining eyes, she stood, aching to be in amongst it all. But Stewart boggled at the last few yards separating them from the arena itself.

Then the music came to an end and off they went in search of other entertainment. All sorts of side-shows were ranged along the road, competing with the public-houses for the visitors' patronage.

"Go and get your bumps read," urged Susy, as they stood outside a phrenologist's booth, looking at the queer collection of human skulls.

"Not me!" scoffed Stewart self-consciously. "I don't believe in that sort of thing."

"What! and don't you believe in fortune-telling neither?" Susy asked, incredulous.

"Of course not. I only believe in things I can hear or see or smell. Look there's a placard about Charles Leybourne; that's more in my line now." Susy looked more closely at the poster; it stated that Charles Leybourne, the celebrated comedian, was appearing at the Briarbanks Hotel, and singing his popular songs. "I vote we go and listen to him," said Stewart enthusiastically.

"Oh dear," sighed Susy, "I didn't want to go into a public-house. I thought we might have kept out of them just for today," but Stewart was so eager and so sure that they would never have another opportunity of hearing this wonderful man that she weakly gave in.

Without much difficulty they found the Briarbanks and went inside. The concert-room was thick with smoke and heavy with the smell of alcohol. Once inside, Susy's professional instincts got the better of her, and she took charge of the expedition and elbowed and pushed her way to the front. The sawdust was thick upon the floor, and the long, low benches around the tables were filled with men and women shouting and singing the popular choruses of the day. The room was packed, but like everywhere else, good humour prevailed, and the discomfort was accepted as part of Blackpool. On the stage vaudeville turns succeeded one another in swift succession with the crowd applauding generously.

The only drink they could get was champagne. Susy's cheeks blenched when she heard that—Blackpool had at last succeeded in impressing her. The champagne was sold in shilling bottles and when it was poured out it barely filled a wine glass! All the same, she had never before heard of a public-house that only sold champagne. Her respect for Blackpool increased enormously.

"Oysters as well?" asked the potman, and seeing Susy's eager face, Stewart nodded in agreement.

Oysters and champagne! That was Blackpool; they both felt they were sampling the real gilded life. 'Champagne Charley' and 'Piccadilly Lil', you could appreciate those two songs in Blackpool for the trippers themselves were the Charleys and the Lils. Then at seven o'clock Charles Leybourne himself stepped out on to the stage and sang the song of the year. Stamp, shout and whistle as the crowd might, he would give them no encore. His contract called for one song and that was all Charles intended to sing. They would have to come in again if they wanted more.

As he stood bowing in acknowledgment of the applause, he could not help recollecting that a bare three years before he, too, had been one of the crowd down there; a common artisan who, for half a day, acted and spent like a lord. Now he was an artiste, making so much money with his songs that he could live like that every day of his life if he so minded. But he was not a north-countryman for nothing; shrewdly he knew that his popularity might vanish as quickly as it had come, and meanwhile he was hanging on to his brass, singing only the one song his contract called for. It was better to do that and leave the crowd whistling for more than it was to sing encore after encore and have some of them leaving before he had finished. Besides, it was not the proper Blackpool season and, adamant, he left the stage.

Susy was disappointed with him; she thought he ought to have been a whole lot funnier than that . . . with everyone drinking champagne, too!

From the Briarbanks they wandered on to the Palatine Gardens, the town's latest attraction. Susy's tireless energy was wearing Stewart out, and he suggested that they stay and watch Christie's Nigger Minstrels, but she said they had not seen half the place yet, and on they went to the fairground. There they rode on roundabouts, traversed helter-skelters, and went soaring heavenwards in gorgeous swing-boats. He put his foot down about going on the joy-wheel, and forcibly restrained Susy from making a public exhibition of herself. The joy-wheel was a massive, horizontal wooden platform, almost level with the ground; it started revolving slowly, gradually gathering momentum until there were none of its original passengers left on board. Stewart thought it was far better fun to watch the shrieking women and men come hurtling off in a welter of skirts and flurry of clothing.

"Such sights!" he said, pretending to be shocked. "I'd never be able to look you in the eye again, Susy, if you went on there."

"I've got my pantalettes on," she said, unashamed, and showed such an inclination to try her luck that Stewart said hurriedly:

"Come along, we've had too much of this noise, let's take a walk up the North Shore." So, leisurely, they set off along the sea-front again.

"How much time have we got?" she asked presently.

"The train leaves at ten," he assured her, but his mind was that instant made up that they were not going to be on it.

It was dark now, and the gas-lamps competed feebly with the hoarse, roaring naphtha flares that illuminated the various attractions. They took a horse-tram and drove out to Cleveleys, and then walked along the quiet, romantic sand dunes. Susy chattered happily away, and in the dark Stewart slipped his arm around her waist in a friendly fashion, and she leaned her head contentedly on his shoulder. As if by accident his arm slowly worked upwards and he found his hand encountering the soft swelling of her breast. His hand stayed there nervously, and then, gaining courage he drew a deep breath and allowed his fingers to exert a slight pressure.

Susy never stopped talking, but calmly moved his hand down to her waist again.

"Let's sit down for a while," said Stewart naively, and Susy said she did not mind if they did, so they found a sheltered sand dune, and Stewart spread his jacket face downwards on the sand. They sat there, Susy talking and Stewart listening, and the lights of Blackpool shining dimly in the distance. But Stewart's thoughts were miles away from what Susy was saying, and his mind was occupied with his strategy for the coming hours. Perhaps there would be no need for his scheming; nevertheless, there was that thrill of expectancy, of doubt as to what was going to happen that night.

He stretched himself out, and as he lay there, looking at the stars, he interrupted her guilelessly by saying, "Susy, are you happy?"

She leaned on one arm and looked down at him. "I don't believe you've heard a word I've been saying," she accused. He reached up and pulled her roughly down to him and kissed her fiercely.

"Oh!" she gasped, when at length he let her go, "you've fair knocked the wind out of me," but with an exultant thrill he noticed that she was content to lay where she was. His lips sought hers again, this time more gently, and he felt her slightly parted lips respond to his own. His hands once again, seemingly by accident, encountered her breasts, firm and alluring, but although Susy's lips were soft and responsive, she yet casually and calmly found time to remove his hands to some less sensitive part of her body. Stewart felt mildly irritated, baffled by this prudery, and changing his tactics he sought, with soft, tender caresses, to lure her into a state of blind, implicit trust. Then, deeming the moment ripe, his hands moved purposefully and lightly cupped her breast. There was no suspicion of an accident this time, and as Susy lay quiescent under this bold move, Stewart's passion gathered fire.

Suddenly the girl whispered, "You've forgotten her now?"

Nothing else that she could have said could have proved so devastating. The flame went out of him and he made no reply, but his thoughts turned to Miss Scripps and a great bitterness against himself came over him. They both lay there after that, not speaking a word, and then he noticed that Susy was shaking violently.

"Why, you're crying," he said, abashed, and as though to make amends, clumsily tried to kiss the salty tears on her cheeks. She pushed him roughly away, and turning her back on him began to cry unrestrainedly. This was terrible. He had no idea what to do, what to say, so man-like he left it to time to provide the solution. At length it seemed there were no more tears left in her, and mournfully, still with her slender back towards him, she said, "At least you might have pretended you loved me."

Anything, he thought, was better than those disturbing sobs, making him feel so despicable, so he seized hold of her hand and said, "But surely, Susy, you know I do like you."

"That's not the same as loving me," she said sorrowfully, and made an effort to get up.

"Sit down," he told her harshly, "let's get this thing settled."

"But it's time to go, isn't it?" she asked tremulously.

Without replying he got to his knees and placed his arms about her waist, and in the struggle they both fell back, giggling, in the sand.

"That's better," he said, "there's only you and me here now, Susy, so don't let's worry about anyone else."

"Well, you behave yourself then," said the girl, more cheerfully, and not wishing to start those distressing tears again, he became more decorous. He lay there with his arms about her, and as the warmth of the embrace dispelled his earlier bitter emotions he almost fancied he did love Susy.

Later on they got up and wandered slowly back to the horse-drawn trams. Stewart looked at his watch, it was an hour slow, but Susy didn't know, and when he showed her the time she sighed happily and said she'd never forget this trip to Blackpool.

"I don't want to go back a bit," she confessed.

"It would never do to spend the night here together," he said, hoping that his voice sounded as though he might be shocked.

"Don't you worry, we're not doing," she said coolly; and as they walked slowly from the tram to the station she said, puzzled, "It's funny there's so few people about, isn't it?"

Only one or two drunkards staggered across the street or reeled out of doorways, and the sight of them stirred her professional instincts, and she asked Stewart if he'd ever seen so much liquor served in such a short time as they'd seen at the Briarbanks. "I think I'll come and take a house at Blackpool," she said; "there must be a fortune in the trade."

"It's seasonal," he reminded her, striving to make his voice sound normal, and just then a neighbouring clock chimed out the hour.

"Good heavens!" said Stewart, simulating consternation. "Did you hear that? It's eleven o'clock. My watch must have stopped."

Without another word they dashed up the street, but when they arrived at the station the gates were closed and the place was in darkness.

Susy became agitated. "We've missed the train," she began accusingly, and Stewart thought the moment opportune to hammer on the iron gates to drown her upbraiding. Eventually a railway man—the night porter—came out. Holding his lantern high up in the air he surveyed them caustically.

"Don't tell me you've missed the train as well, Mister! Never mind, you're in good company, there must be a couple of thousand like yourself. You'll find them all dossing down on the beach. You'd best go and join them, for there's nothing leaves this station before ten tomorrow morning," and turning his back on them he disappeared into the gloomy, cavernous station.

Stewart held up his hands defensively as Susy angrily turned towards him. "It's no use getting excited. I admit it's all my fault. But we've missed the train and the thing is what are we going to do now?"

The logic of this reasoning impressed her and she sensibly realized the futility of saying the things she had in her mind, so with a withering look she finally said: "You've got me into this mess and it's up to you to get me out. But one thing you may as well know, and that is that I'm not sleeping out on the sands!"

"Of course not," said Stewart placatingly, "we'll go and get rooms," but it was easier said than done, for all the vacant lodgings had by that time of night been taken. After an hour of weary tramping from boarding-house to boarding-house they were still unsuccessful, and as they rested for a while on a bench on the sea-front, Stewart said uneasily that it looked as though they might have to stay out all night.

"Not me," said Susy, a determined glint in her eye. "I know how to get a room, even if you don't."

"No," said Stewart, all melodramatic, "not that !"

"What do you mean, 'not that' ?"

"Why—er—not what you were meaning to do !"

With an abrupt exclamation of anger Susy restrained herself and said cuttingly : "Well, you get off and find me somewhere to sleep then. I'll wait here."

Stewart pretended to be upset, but it gave him the opportunity he wanted. Although it had been impossible to get two single rooms, he did know that he could get one room, and that one room he planned to share with Susy.

After a decent interval he returned in what he hoped was a dejected frame of mind. "I've got a room," he began, when Susy cut him short.

"Thank goodness," she said, and jumped up from the bench and in her relief failed to hear him say that it was a double room.

By the time they got to the place they had both brightened up considerably ; Susy, because she was going to sleep in a bed after all, and Stewart, because he thought she had tacitly accepted the implications of a double bed.

A slatternly woman met them at the door, but before she would allow them in she demanded the ten shillings in cash.

"Why, that's sheer robbery !" said Susy indignantly, but Stewart merely shrugged his shoulders. What else could they do ? And after he had handed over the money, the landlady gave him a candle and indicated the bedroom door. The room was no palace chamber, to be sure, but it had a bed, and the linen looked clean, and after all, it might have been a good deal worse. Stewart set the candle down carefully on the dilapidated washstand, and when he turned round he saw that Susy had stretched herself luxuriously on the bed. "Thank heavens for this, anyway," she said, and in the dim, shadowy light of the candle he thought he had never seen her looking so desirable. With a nervous artificial kind of a laugh he came over and sat down beside her.

"Jove ! you're pretty," he said, taking hold of her hands.

"It's taken you a long time to find that out," she replied, yawning wearily.

"I may not have said it in so many words but I've always thought so. Susy, you're lovely !" He lay down on the bed and attempted to embrace her. She sat up with a laugh. "Here, here, Casanova, you're too rough."

"Let me take your clothes off," he begged eagerly.

"What!" exclaimed the startled young woman, coming to her feet in a bound. "Are you drunk?"

"They've got to come off sometime."

"How dare you insult me like that?" said Susy wrathfully.

"Oh! if you're going to carry on like that I'm going to get into bed," said Stewart sulkily, and started to peel off his jacket.

Susy was scandalized, and with both hands on her hips she advanced menacingly towards him.

"Who's sleeping in this room?" she asked ominously.

"Why, we both are," said Stewart, surprised; "I told you it was a double room."

"Double nothing," retorted the young woman, and the next thing he knew was that, handicapped by his half-divested jacket, he was being bundled unceremoniously out of the room with a brusqueness that shattered all his tender dreams. The door slammed behind him and he heard the sound of a bolt being driven home. He started to hammer angrily on the door, and then he noticed a great giant of a fellow, clad only in shirt and trousers, surveying him caustically.

"What's all this 'ere row? Either go in or stay out; this is a respectable 'ouse.'"

Susy's laughter echoed softly through the door, but there was no answering sign of merriment in the forbidding eyes of the landlady's husband. So Stewart despairingly turned and groped his way down the creaking stairs and out into the street. It was well after midnight, the wind was cold and there was no chance now of finding another room. It looked like the beach after all. Dejectedly he turned up his coat-collar and went down on to the sands, and even there he had difficulty in finding a sheltered place, for in the dark it appeared as though the whole of Lancashire was spending the night there.

After a while he found a space and sleep came, and in unconsciousness his misfortunes for a time left him. When dawn broke he got up, feeling as stiff and weary as if he had walked about the whole night long. Ruefully he shook the sand out of his hair, tried to dislodge it from between his collar and neck, and then he bitterly recalled the events of only a few hours earlier. So that was the fate of his ill-starred excursion to Blackpool. There was only one thing to do, now that it had started to drizzle, and that was to find a tavern and repair the ravages of the night. At least he ought to be able to get a good wash and a sound breakfast, which was more than Susy would get in that third-rate boarding-house. He took what satisfaction he could from that thought. Jove! he was unlucky with his women.

Susy was at the station when he arrived a few minutes before ten o'clock, and in addition to looking clean and tidy, her expression was as sweet and innocent as if she knew nothing about the dark incidents of the previous night. Even the ridiculous white feather had taken on a new lease of life, and was bowing and swaying with all the animation of its owner.

Did he have a good night's rest? she enquired brightly, but he was not to be outdone, and although anger was in his heart his pride made him answer in a nonchalant and carefree tone.

The journey back was accomplished drearily. He didn't have the satisfaction of seeing her ill from the train's motion. They had a carriage to themselves, but there was something lacking for all their formal politeness, and soon the conversation languished and died.

At Liverpool, Stewart had so far recovered as to say that he hoped her absence from the 'Unicorn' would not lead to trouble, but that eventuality didn't seem to worry Susy, and as they parted she thanked him prettily for the outing.

"We must go again sometime," she said, "but you won't forget, will you, that I'm a good girl, like you've always told me to be," and laughing lightly to herself at some obscure joke of her own she went on her way.

The Goree Warehouses, George's Dock

CHAPTER 12

OUR FLAG'S UP ON BIDSTON HILL

"HAD a good time, skipper?" Silas greeted him, with an understanding wink, a broad smile on his face.

"What on earth are you talking about?" said Stewart irritably.

Silas continued to beam and stood there rubbing his hands affably.

His employer looked at him suspiciously. "For two months now, Silas," he said, "you've been going about with a face as long as a fiddle, and now you suddenly look as though you've swallowed the ship's cat. What the devil have you been up to?"

Instantly the smug grin disappeared from Silas' face. "Nothing, skipper, nothing. Everything's shipshape and Bristol fashion, just as you left it," he said, a shade too hastily, but Stewart was too tired to worry about Silas, and he tumbled into bed, anxious to make up for his night on Blackpool sands.

Later on in the evening he awoke and jumped out of bed; there had been far too much idling around, it was time he was seeing to the *Mary Jane's* first cargo, or at least getting his plans ready as to where he was going to get that cargo. He took heart from the fact that business never rebuffed him as did women; perhaps it was all an omen, a hint that he should stick to business. But he was too unsettled, his thoughts kept straying and at last he flung his pencil down in disgust. He would go and have a game of dominoes with Mr. Eastwood, and perhaps the old gentleman would volunteer some information as to potential shippers and save him all this worry.

"You look depressed, my boy," said the old shipowner; "sit down, and I'll give you three games."

Stewart got the dominoes out and shuffled them on the little table at which they always played. As he drew a chair up, the old man chaffed him lightly that it was no time for depression, had he not just become a shipowner? He ought to be feeling on top of the world.

Stewart gave a forced laugh and said sheepishly: "I'm happy enough, sir. I suppose one's not meant to have everything."

Mr. Eastwood eyed him shrewdly. "You sound to me like a man with domestic troubles?"

The young man needed no encouraging, and he so far forgot himself as to describe the way he felt about Miss Scripps. He spoke rapidly and feelingly, and at the end he apologized half-heartedly for worrying the old shipowner with his private affairs. Mr. Eastwood waved the apology aside; far from being bored with Stewart's personal problems he was glad to hear them, and being a much older man he might be able to advise him. If he had had someone to confide in, he went on reminiscently, he might have made a better life of it. We all needed advice some time or other, and since there had been no one to warn him against stubbornness and pride he had made a pretty mess of things.

The old man got up from the little table and walked over to the window and gazed out into the night, lost in thoughts of the past. "If my son had lived," he went on, without turning round, "he'd have been forty-three years old today."

Stewart looked up in wonder, for he had never known that Mr. Eastwood was married.

"He was a young man about your own age, the last time I ever saw him and, God forgive me, it was my stubbornness and pride that drove him to his death along with his wife and daughter." He paused again, and Stewart felt uncomfortable, as though he were trespassing on painful private memories. After a time Mr. Eastwood went on with his story. His wife had died in childbirth, and Fred and he had been left with the double task of developing a newly established coasting trade and the far more complicated business of nurturing a motherless child through the various stages of infancy.

When the boy was fourteen years old he had been brought to the office and painstakingly instructed in the details of the business that would one day be his. Looking back it was easy to see that they had been foolish in trying to absorb him into the business so completely. Nevertheless, he had grown into a fine, upstanding young fellow, well-liked by everyone, and they ought to have realized that some time or other he would seek the companionship of younger people than themselves. But they never gave that a thought and their sole concern was that he should learn the business properly.

Just after his twenty-first birthday he came and told them that he wanted to get married. It was about the time when there was talk of repealing the Navigation Acts and shipping was unsettled, and things were not going well with the firm of Eastwood Bros. So they told him to put such nonsense out of his head; he was too young to know his own mind. All in good time; when the business was ready for it, they would pick a wife for him. It was that very protectiveness that had goaded the boy beyond the limit of his endurance. He said he wanted to marry the daughter of a ship's captain who had recently been lost at sea.

It was the first time that he had opposed his father, and his earlier implicit obedience made Mr. Eastwood think that he would readily accept his decision. But this time he had not, and they had both been so obstinate that before they realized it things had gone too far. Threats, rather than reasoning, took over the argument, and in the end the boy had gone away and married the girl and started out to try to making a living on his own. It must have been a terribly hard struggle, but he had his pride and never gave any indication of how things were faring. Indeed, he had never again set foot over his father's doorstep, and they had never passed another word together.

Old Eastwood paused in his story, memories more than twenty years old were surging upon him bitterly, bowing him down. Yet Stewart realized that there was much that night be said for him, though the shipowner never attempted to defend his actions. It was the custom for parents to be stern and demand unquestioning obedience from their children, and Mr. Eastwood had acted no differently from the average father.

For two years the boy had tried to make a living on his own, and then his wife had had a daughter. The quarrel between them, ridiculous and childish as it was, might have been made up, but there was no chance of a reconciliation, for the young couple had decided to emigrate and sailed almost immediately for America. They had sailed in the Blackball liner *Savana*, along with 500 other emigrants. On the way over the ship collided with an iceberg and only a handful of survivors had reached America.

The news did not reach Liverpool until many months later, but Fred had suggested that he should go over and see if there was any trace of them. There was none, of course, and Fred and he had never mentioned the incident since.

That had happened in 1843 and the pain was as strong today as ever it had been, a permanent reminder of the folly of pride and obstinacy.

Stewart sat quietly at the little table, the dominoes lying forgotten in front of him. What were his own wretched misunderstandings in face of the old man's sad story? He could see now why Mr. Eastwood was so sympathetic and tolerant to everyone, even to the extent of watching his own coastal shipping business being filched away by less scrupulous competitors. It made Stewart feel insignificant and petty, as he compared his own dreams of aggrandisement with the elder man's attitude towards life.

"Never let pride dictate your actions," Mr. Eastwood was saying; "never be ashamed to admit you were wrong, and, above all, never be hasty in condemning others. If someone had given me that piece of advice forty years ago I should be a happier man today."

He turned at last from the window, sat down at the table and started to stack up his dominoes.

"But there, I've no right to bore you with an old man's mumblings."

"Not at all, sir," said Stewart humbly, "I know I shall profit from this advice of yours."

The old man clapped him affectionately on the shoulder and smilingly said: "Of course, if you want some real advice, here it is. Don't take too much to heart what that young lady of yours does.

Women are queer creatures. They like to think they're bright and elusive; they hate to be accepted as a settled institution in a man's life, though that is what they all aim for. They're the cause of most of the world's unhappiness I'm afraid . . . but then, they're responsible for all the real happiness. A good woman's love is one of the blessings of this earth, but it is not to be won lightly. It's a long time since I did any courting, and I'm not sure I know what these modern young women are like, but in spite of all you hear I don't think they've changed much."

"You think, then," said Stewart hopefully, "that I stand a chance?"

"Of course you do! It's like fishing, only she's the angler and you're the poor fish. At this stage she's just playing you before she lands you high and dry."

"Oh!" said Stewart thoughtfully, "two can play at that game."

"Not with women you can't," said the old man, with a chuckle, "for if you think that, along may come a bigger fish and swallow the bait, hook, line and sinker."

"Yes, I suppose that's true, too," said Stewart, thinking of Mr. Puddicombe.

"Let me see, what is it we're playing?"

"Threes and Fives, sir?"

"No, let's have a change, what about Matador? Have you got a double six?" And so the game progressed, and shortly Mr. Eastwood found that he had won easily. After all, he and Fred had been playing dominoes for years, whereas Stewart was still a beginner.

At the end of the third game, as Stewart was shuffling the 'bones' for yet another hand, Mr. Eastwood said casually: "I suppose you're busy collecting your first cargo? Are you having much luck?"

"I'm just starting to think about it, sir," said Stewart cautiously.

"Been round to any of the shipping agents?"

"Not yet, because until the brig gets round here I'm not quite sure when we'll be ready for sailing."

"Double six? No? Double five, then? No? Right, I'll start her off with a double four. You're not likely to get anything under three weeks, seeing you've not advertised her in the *Albion*."

"I hardly expect we'll be ready before then," said Stewart, anxiously seeking his hand for something else beside a double three. "Captain Brady has very strict ideas about fitting-out first," and he planked down a three and a five.

"Keep an eye on him there, my boy," said Mr. Eastwood, playing a six and a two. "It's not much use spending a lot of money on second-hand tonnage. You'll never make a new ship out of her, don't forget. What you want to do is to run her as hard as you can; she can't have many more years service left in her. Don't start playing your doubles yet!"

"It's the only three I've got."

"Tut, tut, don't tell me that, boy," and smiling he laid down a lone and a four. "Still can't go, eh? There! I'll give you a chance," and Stewart gratefully took the opportunity.

"Captain Brady's all right, sir, he's just keen on her being seaworthy."

"That's all very well so long as you don't forget you're shipowners and must live in competition with others. If you've got new ships it's all right to keep them in good condition, but secondhand ships are always a bit of a gamble. What! knocking again? You must be playing badly; see what you can draw. You know you should get around to those agents and merchants soon. You'll find that the most successful shipowners in Liverpool always make a point of visiting their shippers every day."

Stewart, drawing steadily from the unused dominoes, said politely, "That's a point I shall remember, sir," and then swore under his breath as he drew the double six; there wasn't a hope of getting rid of it.

"You're bound to make mistakes at first," said Mr. Eastwood, playing calmly and confidently, "but so long as you watch what the successful fellows are doing and try to follow their example you'll keep your head above water. Dear me, I've got to draw myself now—most unusual! I've been doing too much talking, I must keep my eyes on the 'bones'."

"I do know most of the shippers in town," said Stewart.

"Then keep after them, my boy. If you merely advertise and sit in your office, a few parcels may come along, but they won't come anything like so fast as if you make a habit of going the rounds of shippers every day. It's the personal touch that counts. There! I'm out. Why, you've got a handful of bones left," he said delightedly, his one vice apparently being that he liked to win.

"I'm afraid you're much too good for me, sir," said Stewart modestly, then tactfully he added: "You don't know of any cargo offering for the peninsular trade in the near future, do you, sir?"

Mr. Eastwood relaxed happily in his chair and thought for a moment. "Off-hand I don't, but if it will help you on this maiden voyage, I think I can safely promise you a hundred tons."

"That's very good of you, indeed, sir," said Stewart, delighted. "Would you like another hand?"

"No, that's enough for tonight. You owe me five pence 'alfpenny. Let me have your sailing date as soon as possible, and meanwhile don't forget about those agents."

Stewart descended the stairs well pleased with his visit, and in a much better frame of mind he went to bed.

He was rudely awakened the next morning by Silas shouting excitedly, "Our flag's up on Bidston 'ill, skipper!"

"Our flag?" puzzled Stewart, pulling on some clothes, but the old sailor with his telescope was up on the walk again. When Stewart arrived there he took the telescope from Silas and training it on the telegraph station on Bidston Hill, he saw fluttering in the breeze a flag with a St. George's Cross and a ball in the middle; he couldn't distinguish the colours.

"It's me own flag," said Silas, capering gleefully, and went on to explain that the piece of bunting flying there was the newly designed, distinctive house flag that he had stitched together and delivered to the signalman on the tower.

"It's as good as any," said Stewart, vainly trying to conceal his excitement.

"You could pick it out at twice this distance," affirmed Silas proudly.

"All right," the young man laughed. "Come on, Silas, this is an occasion, we must drink a toast!"

"My oath!" said Silas, astonished. "Do you really mean it?" And although it was barely eight o'clock they trudged down to the Dock Road, and inside the first open tavern they solemnly toasted the auspicious event.

Some few hours later, from the landing-stage this time, they sighted the brig coming up the river in the wake of a steam tug. Stewart hardly knew what he had expected, but his first reaction was one of disappointment as she swept past the stage and dropped anchor off Rock Point. She was barely larger than the tug that towed her. Was that all they got for £1500? He got hold of a waterman and bargained to be taken off to the *Mary Jane*. The tide was running too strong for a rowing boat, he was told, for although the boatman could get him out there all right he wasn't prepared to pull his heart out trying to get back to the landing-stage again.

Stewart offered him double fare but it was no use, the boatman refused to consider the journey till within an hour of high water. When they did set off the last of the flood was making about three knots, and as they neared the brig the waterman turned his boat round to stem the tide. He stood facing forward and with a few deft strokes piloted her expertly alongside. His oars were shipped and his boathook out almost in the same movement. He flung his boathook at one of the brig's for'd washports, and as it caught hold he more leisurely dropped the boat astern to a rope ladder hanging loosely over the side.

"Come up and have a glass of rum," Stewart invited, and he climbed laboriously up the ladder and sprawled awkwardly over the gunwale on to the deck.

"Welcome aboard," Captain Brady said heartily, and somehow to Stewart he seemed to be a different man as he stood there on his poop, bellowing his greeting. The captain's diffidence of manner on shore was

The busy Mersey

gone, and was replaced by an air of complete confidence. Here on his own poop Brady was in his element. It was only when that first mooring-rope went out that he felt his assurance disappearing, for he knew that when he set foot on shore he would be in a hostile world, where the dearly learned lessons of the sea were of little value. The people were different, the bustle and rush of shore life held something disconcerting to a seaman. But for the moment he was not worried with such thoughts. Here he was, master of his own ship, entertaining his partner on board for the first time. It was a serious occasion, and young Stewart had to be properly impressed with a shipmaster's position.

The stately procession proceeded slowly along the poop to the companionway leading down to the main saloon. The stairway was heavily decorated with finely carved scrollwork. Quaint figures of dolphins, ships and mariners, carved in different coloured woods, were let into the panelling that enclosed the way down from the upper deck. The stairway wound down in a half-spiral and finally debouched with a flourish into the spacious saloon.

The saloon was a low but handsome cabin running the entire width of the ship. It was panelled out in dark mahogany and massive carved pillars were spaced about, supporting the head beams. In the centre stood a beautifully kept stove, surrounded by a network of fine brass rails, fenders and cinder pits, all elaborately polished to the colour of gleaming gold. From a stove a bright brass chimney was curved and angled several times before it reached the deck above. From the heavy, slightly arched beams of the deckhead hung a couple of equally ornate brass lamps, suspended in gymbals. The deck was holystoned white and smooth, fancy sennet mats and well-scrubbed canvas runners covered the main treadways.

On the forward side of the stove was a table covered with American cloth, and bolted along one side were the swivel chairs peculiar to ships. Large glass ports pierced the for'd bulkhead and looked out on to the main deck. Underneath the ports a thickly cushioned settee ran from side to side serving as a bench for the table. Standing back a little from the stove was a sideboard dresser with marble top and brass rail, surmounted by a large gilded mirror dulled beyond use by the damp sea air.

The starboard side of this dresser gave off into the captain's sleeping cabin, while on the port side the steward had his pantry and cubby-hole. Farther aft, beyond the saloon, there was accommodation for two mates with a little messroom attached, for they were not allowed to enter this holy-of-holies, the captain's saloon.

"What do you think of her?" Brady asked proudly.

Stewart was at a loss for words. The magnificence of the saloon had dispersed his disappointment at the brig's size, and he was obsessed with the thought that he owned a half share in all this.

"A nice 'andy craft, sir," said Silas, touching his hat respectfully to the master.

"You're right there, my man," said Captain Brady; "she'll suit us fine. Don't you think so, Mr. Stewart?"

At the captain's bidding Stewart took a seat and Brady went on to give an account of the passage round from Chester.

"I took a tug after all," he said, "you see there was no knowing what state her canvas might have been in, and I'd have had to get tugs to get her out of Chester as well as to bring her up the Mersey, so I changed my mind and kept the same fellow right through."

"Good," said Stewart. "I've arranged for a berth in Salthouse Dock, right at the top, and it's out of the way. The Dock Board told me that it wouldn't be wanted for a fortnight, so you can lay there in comfort, Captain. I hope you won't be too long, though, and as soon as you give me an idea of when you'll be ready to sail I'll get after the cargo."

"By this time tomorrow I'll be better able to tell you," Captain Brady promised.

They went up on deck again and Stewart was ceremoniously shown round the ship. With but little persuasion he agreed to stay on board all night so that he might sail into dock with the *Mary Jane* on the next tide. Silas had to stay, too, and he went for'd singing happily, and introduced himself to the three runners in the foc's'le as the company's marine superintendent. Captain Brady, in a sudden burst of generosity, gave Silas a bottle of rum, and the old sailor spent one of the best evenings he could remember before he finally became unconscious and was tossed by the runners into a spare bunk.

The old sailor was up long before they were due to move, and when the time did come to weigh anchor he hobbled round the capstan, hindering rather than helping, but so obviously pleased to be on a ship's deck again that they put up with him.

The *Mary Jane* was warped through Canning half-tide dock and finally secured fore and aft in Salthouse Dock. Shortly after the tug had cast off, Stewart went ashore, for Captain Brady had no time to spend gossiping.

Lying on the mat of No. 3 Chapel Walk was a letter. With a quickening heart he recognized Miss Scripps' handwriting and eagerly tore the letter open.

Dear Mr. Stewart,

I have a particularly urgent matter to discuss with you. I called yesterday but you were out, and since the matter in question is of the gravest importance, I do most earnestly beg of you to be at home this afternoon at four o'clock.

Very sincerely,
Eliz. Mary Scripps.

He read it through several times. She was calling round to see him at four. All would be explained. He pictured their touching meeting. He looked at the letter again and doubt began to grow. It wasn't very friendly, no matter how you read it—but then, no young woman of quality would dare to reveal her true feelings in a letter. Really he had no cause to be alarmed, there was nothing strange about that polite, cold tone. It needed only such thoughts as these to boost him up to the very pinnacle of happiness. Life was wonderful, he felt, and for the remainder of the afternoon he paid little attention to business and concentrated solely on how he should speak and act when Miss Scripps arrived.

The time went very slowly and his restless eyes turned frequently to the big clock on St. Nicholas', which he could just see from his window.

Silas cleaned the parlour out till it shone spick and span, enough to satisfy even the mate of a Western Ocean Packet. The skipper's nerves were on edge, thought Silas, as Stewart followed him closely round to see that he missed nothing. At last even Stewart's eagle eye could find no fault, and the old sailor retired to the courtyard, wondering why they were 'cleaning ship' like that.

At a few minutes to four Stewart heard her light steps on the stones outside. He wanted to get off his stool and rush to the door, and it was only with difficulty that he restrained himself. It wouldn't do to appear too eager. Unfortunately for his plans there was a limit to his endurance, and before she could lift the knocker he swung open the door and held out both hands to her. It seemed to Stewart that he had never seen her looking so beautiful.

Miss Scripps was very self-possessed and there was an aloof air about her that made her the more attractive; the colour in her cheeks, and her figure so erect and supple, embodied all that Stewart thought was beautiful. His adoring eyes beamed on her fatuously, but Miss Scripps, to his dismay, avoided his outstretched hands, in fact it almost seemed as if she pushed past him as she swept into the parlour.

It was when she spoke that all Stewart's fond hopes and illusions melted away, for it was a cold, metallic voice that addressed him, bereft even of friendliness, let alone affection. The young woman gave him little time for further speculation, for she was talking rapidly about Martha. At first Stewart couldn't make head or tail of it. Something about Martha and Silas she was saying, but he wasn't very interested; all he was concerned with was their two selves. His eyes rested on those delicately moulded lips, watching the way they moved when she spoke; the delicate lines of her nose, the bewitching combination of her eyebrows and eyelashes.

The colour in her face was increasing, as Stewart's apparent inability to understand what she was talking about made her launch into ever more direct explanations. She said, with a flash of temper, that he was the most stupid person that she'd ever met. The young man looked at her in a bewildered fashion.

"But I thought you were coming here to explain about the misunderstanding at your uncle's?"

"I'm sure I don't know why you should think anything of the sort."

"But, your letter——" began Stewart helplessly.

"I'm here to talk about Martha and that horrible old sailor of yours," she interrupted impatiently.

"What about them?" asked Stewart, more puzzled than ever.

"Martha never came home on Saturday night!" she said, as though that explained everything.

"Well, what of it? Surely Martha's old enough to know her own mind," said Stewart, attempting to be humorous.

"It's not that at all. Martha was detained in this house last Saturday against her will."

"What?"

"Must I repeat everything I say?" she asked angrily.

Suddenly Stewart began to laugh, he couldn't stop, for the thought of sixteen-stone, middle-aged Martha being detained by frail, one-legged Silas was too much for him. "I'm sorry," he said at last, "I just can't believe it. Why Martha must be forty if she's a day."

"The question of her age doesn't enter into it," said Miss Scripps, now scarlet with anger; "the fact is that she was held in this house against her wishes."

"How could Silas, who's only half her size, detain a woman like Martha? It just doesn't make sense."

"I have reason to believe that he plied her with intoxicating liquor," said Miss Scripps, gazing frigidly through the window.

"Good heavens!" Stewart gasped, and in spite of the other's angry countenance, began to laugh all over again at the thought of Martha and Silas tippling away together.

"It's no laughing matter," said Miss Scripps furiously. "I think uncle was right when he said that your whole establishment was unsavoury."

"If this story is true," said Stewart gravely, "Silas, at any rate, deserves that reputation."

"See if he denies it!" she cried.

So Stewart called the old sailor in from the courtyard. When the old man caught sight of Miss Scripps he retreated a step. "Good afternoon, miss," he said ingratiatingly; "it's nice to see you again."

Miss Scripps did not deign to reply.

"Silas," said Stewart sternly, "what's all this nonsense about you and Martha?"

"Search me, skipper," said the old sailor uneasily.

"Is it true?" Stewart demanded.

Silas hedged nervously. "It just depends what you're talking about, skipper."

"Miss Scripps says that you kept Martha here against her wishes on Saturday night."

"What! Me keep Martha Braggs!" He looked hurt. "It was the other way round. She's been after me ever since we started working up for the Exhibition. Given me a real dog's life she 'as. I asks you, skipper, do you think a little feller like me could keep Martha in 'ere if she made up 'er mind to get out? Struth, it was me that was the one as tried to get out. I thought you'd be back from Blackpool any minute."

The reference to Blackpool upset Stewart, and, confused, he turned to the girl. "You see," he said weakly, "it's Martha's fault every bit as much as his."

"Nonsense!" retorted the young lady with spirit. "Martha's not a loose woman, and I want to know what you're going to do about it."

"What can I do? The thing's over and done with now."

"They must marry," said Miss Scripps with determination.

"Holy Mother!" pleaded Silas, terrified. "Honest, skipper, there was no 'arm done that way."

"He can't support himself, let alone a wife," said Stewart to Miss Scripps.

"But what if there should be . . . er . . ." Miss Scripps broke off in confusion.

"At Martha's age?" he asked incredulously. "Anyhow, according to Silas, Martha is as pure as ever she was."

"Martha tells a different story."

"She's probably suffering from drunken hallucinations," suggested Stewart, striving hard to make her see the humorous side of it all.

But Miss Scripps was not that way inclined. "It's all your fault," she flashed at him illogically.

"My fault?" Stewart fell back a step. "Why, I have never even spoken to Martha alone."

"If you'd been here to look after your house instead of spending the week-end at Blackpool with a barmaid, this would never have happened."

"Why . . . er . . . er . . ." stammered Stewart aghast, shocked to think that she knew all about his excursion. It was going to take a lot of explaining away. He looked at Silas ferociously; it was plain that he'd been talking on Saturday night, choose what else he might have been doing. "Get out!" he hissed, and Silas, scared for the second time that day, left hurriedly.

Stewart turned towards the young woman. The tears were welling up in her eyes. Whatever was there wrong with an innocent excursion to Blackpool ? But above all, why was she so concerned about it ? He began to look at her with hope again in his eyes.

The young man called forth all his powers of persuasion. How could he possibly look at another woman when Miss Scripps knew that he was head over heels in love with her ? It was sheer misfortune that they had missed the train, and, anyway, he had only taken the girl there because he felt sorry for her. As he went on with his story he became bolder by reason of Miss Scripps' quietness. Her tears were still hovering, but at least they were not flowing, and the business of Martha and Silas appeared to have slipped into the background.

Stewart thought that all this was very significant, and his eloquence going to his head suddenly caused him to turn from the defensive to the attack, and he vehemently accused her of leading him on and then denying him in front of her uncle. It was too much. The tears rose and fell this time, and the sight of them immediately put an end to Stewart's composure. Then, before he knew how it had happened, she was in his arms, crying to her heart's content. It was heaven to Stewart, and he prayed that time might stand still. He took advantage of the girl's silence to tell her of all the things he and his shipowning firm would be doing in the future. If he was successful he would be in a different position to approach Mr. Higgins.

Nothing further was said about the unfortunate expedition to Blackpool, and after much useless self-recriminations they came to an understanding as to themselves. Miss Scripps' tears dried up as if by magic, and she said, "You will make Silas marry Martha ?"

"Most certainly," he said emphatically. The old sailor must not be allowed to continue preying upon innocent women. Then, as happy as a few minutes before she had been miserable, Miss Scripps got up and left him without even attempting to explain her own behaviour on the previous Saturday.

CHAPTER 13

THEIR MAIDEN VOYAGE

FOR the next few days Stewart thought he must be the happiest man in Liverpool. Captain Brady had given him a date for sailing, and on the strength of that the younger partner went from shipping agent to shipping agent, searching for odd lots of cargo to make up his dead-weight. No rebuffs—and he got plenty of those—could keep his spirits down, and gradually he contracted the whole of the brig's cargo space.

Captain Brady was equally happy, and the only cloud on his horizon was young Stewart's natural tendency to try to skimp him on the stores he ordered.

On the advertised date the brig was on her loading berth, and the cargo began to come down on to the quay to be shipped aboard. Every morning, while she lay there with the freight going steadily into her holds, Captain Brady and Stewart spent half an hour pacing up and down 'The Flags'. They rubbed shoulders with the cream of Liverpool shipowners, but though Leyland and McIver, Porter and Iredale, Guion and Inman, Brocklebank and Beazley walked up and down companionably, they walked past the firm of Stewart and Brady as though unaware of their existence.

Captain Brady was uneasy at the sight of so many shipowners, but Stewart insisted that they continue to promenade for half an hour. "We've got as much right here as anyone, and though they may not recognize us now, the day will come when it will be different," he said darkly.

Even the Greek shipowners, and there were any number of those gentlemen, passed them by without recognition, and Stewart looked in vain for the friendly nod which would mean that the firm of Stewart and Brady was acknowledged by the coterie of 'The Flags'.

'The Flags', however, was an institution that demanded a long apprenticeship or an outstanding commercial success. Those were the only means of introduction. Until you had acquired the one or the other, there was no possible chance of being recognized by those who had arrived. Mr. Eastwood said that there was any amount of information to be picked up there, and as Stewart and Brady ambled up and down, the younger man said, "Keep your ears open, Captain, we may pick up something."

"Pick up, indeed!" said Captain Brady scornfully. "If it's only to eavesdrop that we're parading up and down here, then you can do it without me," and he would have walked indignantly away if Stewart hadn't said that he was only joking.

Sailing day approached at last, and Captain Brady was secretly relieved to see Stewart taking on automatically many of the shipping formalities that normally he would have been required to do. The conducting of business on shore had something disconcerting to those who had spent a lifetime at sea. Ships and seamen he knew like the back of his hand—even the sea, treated with respect, held no misery comparable to the complicated shipping business which a shipmaster was now expected to handle. Only a few years earlier it had been so much easier. No stringent regulations to be observed, a master took his ship to sea, he brought her back again; it was nobody's business save those who held ownership shares, and of course the underwriters. But now the Government was stepping in and imposing any number of restrictions, and threatening penalties for their non-performance. It was not as though the new laws were couched in phrases which an ordinary man might understand. Devised by lawyers and drafted in tortuous sentences, they were beyond the understanding of most shipmasters. If they looked at the regulations one way they might do this; if they looked at them another way they might do that; but whatever course they took one thing would be certain, their interpretation would not be the interpretation of the Government's runner, newly installed in the Custom House to administer the Merchant Shipping Act.

Captain Brady was better off than many of his fellow master mariners, for he could read and write, and had had a fair education, but for the majority it was, indeed, a mystery how they managed to get from one part of the world to another. No wonder there were so many shipping casualties—although Captain Brady would never dream of admitting such reasons to Stewart or any other longshoreman. Examinations for Certificates of Competency, as they called them, had been introduced way back in 1850, and it was a good job they'd given Certificates of Service to those who were already masters, for they would never have passed those examinations, simple though they were.

Well, here it was 1862, and now they were introducing certificates of competency for seagoing engineers! . . . That was going a bit too far. That was the weak part about the Government, they did not understand moderation. Let them get a 'bee in their bonnet' about examinations and they were examining everybody—as though it mattered whether marine engineers could read or write!

Stewart came aboard with the brig's clearance and put an end to Captain Brady's pessimistic ruminations. Everything was fixed, the younger man said, the crew would be aboard five minutes after midnight and all the papers and documents were in order. There was nothing else to be done except for the captain to go along to the Custom House and put his signature to one or two things.

"You've saved me a deal of trouble," said Brady gratefully.

"Think nothing of it, Captain, I like that sort of trouble; all you've got to do is to make a good passage. Get what cargo you can abroad, but don't waste any time looking for it. I'm advertising you to sail from Liverpool again in six weeks' time."

"You can rely on me to have her back in time," said Captain Brady, confidence in his voice. Then, in a rather different manner, he continued: "I'm giving a small supper on board tonight. In a way it will be a bit of a send-off for our first voyage, but really it's by way of thanking you for all you've done."

"A first-rate idea, Captain," said Stewart; "I'll ask some of the shippers down."

"You'll do nothing of the sort," said Brady emphatically, "this is going to be a little family party with none of your advertising about it!"

The young man shrugged his shoulders. "All right, Captain, have it your own way, but I think you're missing an opportunity. Who's coming?"

But his remarks had upset the old man and he refused to say who he had invited. "All that concerns you," he said, "is for you to get yourself aboard prompt at seven."

"Aye, aye, Captain." Stewart grinned, and away he went ashore to arrange for the steam tug to tow them out into the river the following morning.

Captain Brady's guests were Mr. Eastwood, Mr. Smithson, his former owner, and Susy. During the past three weeks, busy though he had been, he had nevertheless found time to see a lot of the girl since she had decided to accept his offer of help. In a fatherly way he had grown strongly attached to her. Only the day before she had told him that there was a public-house up for sale which would suit her very well, and they'd both gone to have a look at it. If she thought it was all right, he said, it was good enough for him, and he had handed £200 over to her and waved aside her offer of a receipt or other formal bond.

"Don't worry if you lose it," he had said kindly, and that was all there was to it.

If his friends got to hear about it they would probably think he had gone completely out of his head, but he was a pretty shrewd judge of character, and if he knew Susy she wasn't likely to give him away or, for that matter, lose his money. That gift of his and Susy's obvious pleasure had made him a very happy man. He didn't care whether he ever saw the £200 again, it had been worth that much just to see the girl's face light up when he had suggested it. Well, she'd bought a place of her own now, and according to her, he was a publican as well as a shipowner. Mildly he reflected that he, too, was getting on in the world.

So it was really as a gesture of goodwill towards Susy's new venture that he had invited her on board for supper. Mr. Smithson he had asked because he had been a very fair owner of the *Bellerophon*, and it would be a nice change to offer him hospitality as a brother shipowner. As for Mr. Eastwood, he had secured them the major part of the *Mary Jane's* first cargo and he was in honour bound to ask him. And then, finally, the little party was to be made up with Stewart. He paused for a moment while he thought of that young man. It would have been all the same, he supposed, if he hadn't invited him, he'd have turned up and taken a seat. There was no way of keeping him down. He'd been a trying customer these past few weeks, a regular jack-in-the-box, popping on and off the brig at all hours of the day. His energy was exhausting to others. Thank goodness, anyway, he did not have to take him to sea with the brig. In fact it would be a blessed relief to get to sea again after these last few hectic weeks. The only person he would miss would be Susy. It was a shame that a girl like her had to earn a living by keeping a public-house. However, he had moved her out of range of a good many evils of the trade. Next time he was ashore he must try to persuade her to go in for another line of business; she was too fine a girl to be working a beer-engine.

Susy was the first guest to come aboard. Dressed simply and neatly in a way she knew the old man liked, she curtsied demurely before him. He greeted her fondly and they sat talking together of their joint venture into the licensing trade, until they were interrupted by the arrival of Mr. Smithson and Mr. Eastwood. The two shipowners knew each other already, and when they saw a pretty young woman standing there beside the captain they livened up and became quite jovial.

"Your face is vaguely familiar, ma'am," said Mr. Eastwood in a puzzled sort way. Susy smiled uneasily; she didn't want to explain before these fine gents that she worked in a bar along the Dock Road.

Captain Brady came to her rescue. "She's my ward," he explained proudly.

Then Stewart arrived full of good humour. "Why, Susy," he said, stopping suddenly at the foot of the stairway, "I didn't know you were going to be here."

"Ha! Ha! my boy," laughed Mr. Eastwood roguishly, a look of understanding coming on his face. So this was the young woman who was the cause of Stewart's unhappiness the other evening. He dug the young man slyly in the ribs. "You've got an eye for a pretty girl, eh?"

Stewart became confused. It was the first time he had sighted Susy since their excursion to Blackpool. The older men all laughed at his embarrassment, and then they sat down at the table with Captain Brady at the head, Stewart and Mr. Smithson on one side, and Susy and Mr. Eastwood on the other.

They were still making jokes at Stewart's expense when heavy, ponderous footsteps were heard labouring down the companionway, and the next instant the unsteady figure of Sam Sharp stood before them. Stewart rose to his feet apologetically. "I took the liberty of inviting the Press along, Captain," he said nervously.

"And rightly too," boomed the reporter, looking slowly around. "Don't get up, Captain," he continued, waving to the perturbed ship-master to keep his seat, "and good evening, gentlemen," he said to the others. His swaying figure showed plainly that he had already wined. Just then his watery eyes caught sight of the shrinking figure of Susy. "Ah! Hebe herself!" he exclaimed, and unable to retain his balance any longer, collapsed into the one vacant seat at the end of the table.

"Steward," called Captain Brady, an ominous frown on his fore-head. "Lay another place for Mr. Sharp."

"Where do you keep the things?" asked young Stewart, jumping anxiously to his feet.

"Not you," growled the captain; "the steward I said."

"Sorry, I thought you called my name."

The other guests smiled, and under the influence of wine, liberally supplied by the steward, the supper-party started to progress favourably.

"I give you a toast, gentlemen," cried Captain Brady gravely. "The wind that blows, the ship that goes and the lass that loves a sailor."

"All this," said Sam Sharp, trying to live down his cool reception, "reminds me of the great days of Liverpool sailings, when every ship that mattered gave a banquet before leaving. Plenty of wine and plenty of copy. Ah!" he sighed enviously, "those were the days."

"There was just a shade too much wine about them if I remember rightly," said Mr. Smithson. "Do you recall, Mr. Eastwood, those bombastic speeches of Captain Forbes, especially that one he made before the *Schomburg* set out on her maiden voyage?"

"Baines, his owner, was every bit as bad," put in Captain Brady.

"And look where it led them," said Mr. Eastwood, "the *Schomburg* thrown away on that first voyage and the rest of the company in not much better fettle either."

"Yes," remarked Mr. Smithson, "Baines got his success too cheaply. I think he appreciates now that creating fleets and husbanding ships is not a business that can be learned easily."

"What happened to Forbes?" asked Stewart curiously.

It was the reporter who answered him. "He's set up for himself as a ship's agent. I saw him the other day clearing the Glasgow ship *Highland Pride*."

"So that's what he's doing," said Brady, interested; "last I heard of him was in 1859 when he commanded the *Hastings*."

"He lost her towards the end of the year," said Mr. Smithson laconically. "Dammed if I know—begging your pardon, ma'am—why the underwriters put up with him."

"The underwriters seem content to put up with anything these days," said Mr. Eastwood sorrowfully. "All the same, they're making a deal of money out of shipping."

"Fortunately they're not the only ones," Mr. Smithson remarked happily.

"It might have been a different story if the Navigation Act hadn't been repealed," said Stewart, hoping to make an impression. "I think we owe our prosperity to that."

"It undoubtedly helped," said Mr. Eastwood, "but I think the real reason was subsidies. Don't you agree, Mr. Smithson? If the Government hadn't started the Cunard off with a regular grant of £60,000 a year the Yankees might have got in on the trade we have today and we shouldn't be anything like so prosperous."

Brady shook his head gravely. "It was a risky thing repealing those Navigation Laws. It might have left us in a ticklish position."

"I cannot agree with you there, Captain," began the reporter solemnly; "my paper stands for Free Trade——"

"It didn't, I remember, in 1849," interposed Mr. Smithson slyly. "Your paper and every shipowner was up in arms about the repeal—remember, Eastwood?"

The coasting shipowner nodded his agreement. "I think, on the whole, Free Trade has proved itself."

"Free Trade," boomed the reporter, "means world trade, and that means ships. Protection, gentlemen, may be essential for an agricultural country that can live on its own produce, but for a country like Great Britain—the workshop of the world—there can be only one policy, Free Trade. That's how nature intended commerce to be conducted. Supply and demand the two basic factors, and no interference with natural prices. It's all a case of taking the long view, as Mr. Gladstone is always urging. It was a good day for this country when he became Chancellor. He's done more for our trade than any other man in history."

"You're forgetting his income tax, aren't you?" put in Brady warmly. "When we had Protection the tariffs paid for the Army and the Navy and everybody contributed, which was fair enough, but putting a tax on income, that's imposition!"

"Hardly that, Captain," suggested Mr. Eastwood mildly. "Under protection the poor man is taxed for his food whether or no he can afford it, whereas the duty of a country is surely to tax those who can afford it. Leave the poor man alone. Let him have his food and drink, poor devil, for that's about all in life he has got. I don't hold any brief for Mr. Gladstone, his political record is not my idea of honesty, but as regards trade I think he's right."

Captain Brady was in no mood to see good in any government. "There's far too much interference by the State," he grumbled; "laws for his, laws for that. It's a wonder ships manage to get round at all. Why——"

Mr. Eastwood tactfully turned to Susy. "I'm afraid this conversation cannot be very interesting to you, ma'am," he said politely.

"Indeed, it is," she said eagerly. "If I'd been a man I'd have gone to sea, I'm sure."

"You'd make a poor sailor," scoffed Stewart; "why, you get sick in a railway train." The moment he uttered those words he regretted them, but fortunately for him, before Susy could make her devastating reply, the reporter said gloomily:

"Thank your lucky stars, lady, you were born a female."

"At least you might marry a sailor or someone with shipping interests," said Mr. Eastwood, with a mistaken but mischievous glance towards Stewart.

"I wonder that isn't the height of every woman's ambition," Sam Sharp remarked; "plenty of money and a husband you rarely see. What more could a girl want?"

"Oh, you men!" cried Susy impatiently. "You think every woman lives for nothing else but getting married."

"Doesn't she?" Stewart asked, too innocently.

"No, she doesn't. Lots of women make good careers for themselves."

"Well spoken, Mrs. Bloomer," chuckled Captain Brady admiringly.

"Bloomer, Bloomer?" Stewart quizzed thoughtfully. "I seem to have heard that woman's name somewhere before."

"At any rate I think she has the right idea," said Susy haughtily.

"She seems to have disappeared from the news since that strange meeting at the Albert Hall in London when they all wore trousers. Nothing kills a movement so quickly as ridicule," observed Mr. Smithson.

Susy was energetic in her defence of the American woman, Mrs. Bloomer. The fact of the women wearing trousers on the occasion of that meeting was, she maintained, only a symbol. The trousers were meant to signify that they were not out so much for liberty of limb as respect of person.

"You're right, ma'am," said Mr. Eastwood, coming to her defence; "ladies must have opportunities to make careers for themselves outside of marriage. Indeed, it becomes a greater necessity year by year, for young men nowadays," he went on, with a meaning look at Stewart, "are apt to think that a man's career is smothered by a happy marriage and a large family."

"You do well to say, 'happy marriage'," said Sam Sharp bitterly.

"Well, you're wedded to the bottle and you're happy enough," said Captain Brady surprisingly. Everyone laughed at the reporter's reproachful glance.

"You'll have to hurry up, Susy," Stewart said jestingly, much to

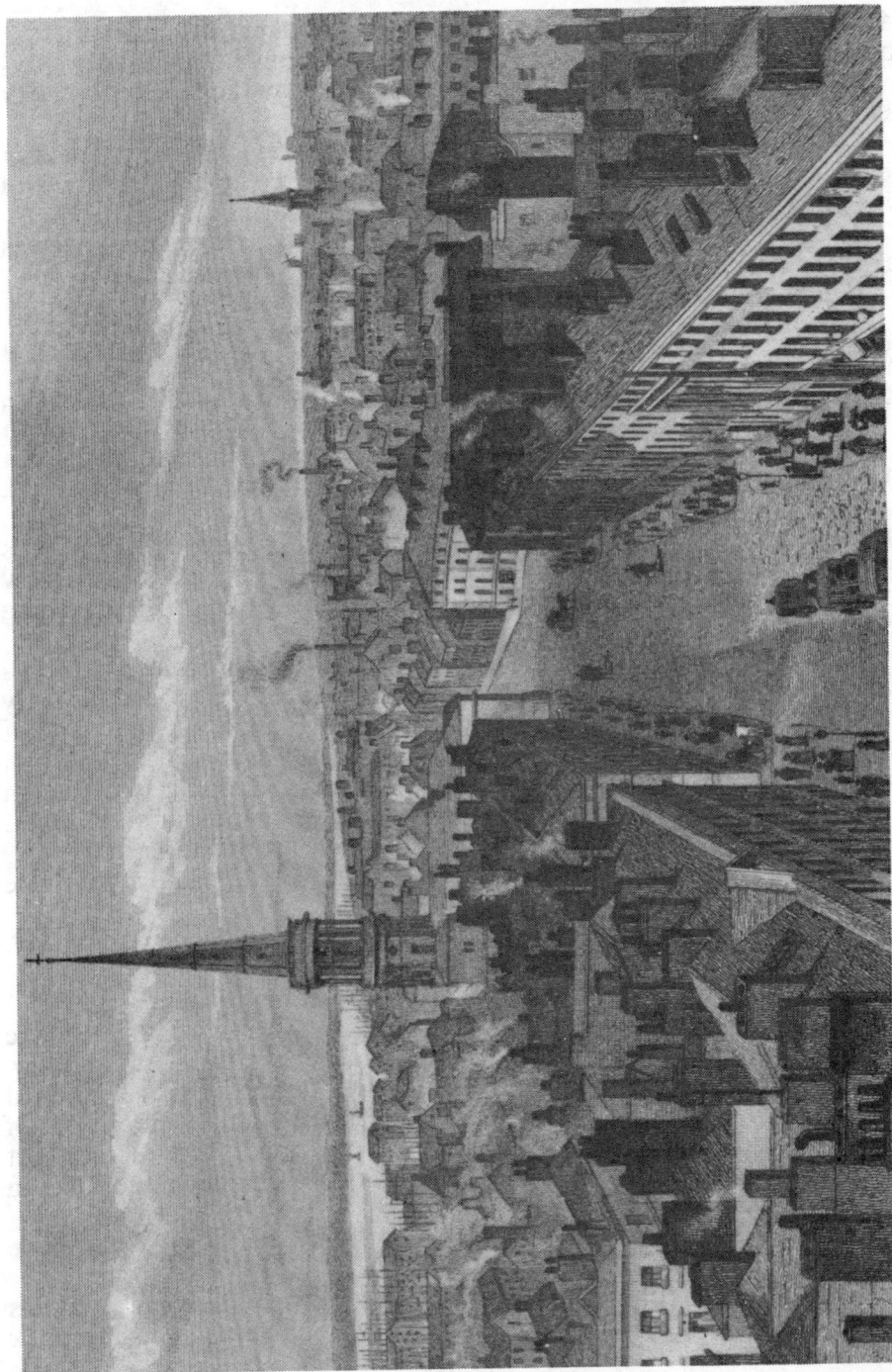

Liverpool from the Town Hall, looking towards the river

Mr. Eastwood's surprise, "I was reading in the paper this morning that the chances of a girl marrying at twenty-one are one in three; at twenty-five it's one in six; but if she hasn't managed it by the time she's thirty her chances drop to one in sixteen."

"When I think of you, Mr. Stewart," Susy said cuttingly, "I can't help feeling thankful that they've passed a divorce act. At least, it will give your future wife a chance when she finds out her mistake."

Mr. Eastwood began to grow alarmed. The course of true love was far from running smooth. He decided to change the subject.

"Have you bought any new pictures, Mr. Smithson?" he asked.

The other shipowner expanded visibly. Here was his favourite hobby, for, like most of Liverpool's rich men, he believed in culture.

"I was only remarking to Fred Leyland this afternoon," he began, "how few good pictures there are for sale. Somehow or other the modern artist doesn't seem able to paint. The daubs they turn out and ask a hundred guineas for are an insult to a collector's intelligence. At least, that's my opinion. Leyland is more tolerant; he thinks all this realism business has come to stay and he's trying to see it through Courbet's eyes, but he's finding it difficult enough, goodness knows. This new form of art is solely an excuse for the inability to paint anything comparable to the Masters."

Sam Sharp pricked up his ears, beckoned to the steward to fill his glass, and when that was done he said importantly: "Those are exactly the same sentiments that are being thought in France, sir, the home of all this so-called realism. A friend of mine who was in Zola's studio in Paris the other day, told me that a fellow called Cézanne raised a laugh there when he said that the time would come when a handful of apples painted honestly and competently would cause a revolution in art!"

Mr. Smithson gave him a friendly glance. "I didn't know you were interested in art, Mr. Sharp?"

"It is the duty of every journalist," returned the other pompously, "to take an interest in and encourage all the arts."

"I think pictures are lovely," sighed Susy romantically.

"Some of them are," replied Mr. Smithson, "providing you make the proper artistic allowances. But what art lacks today is stability. Take that young fellow Whistler. Leyland was telling me that he dashed off those two pictures of his 'Thames in Ice' and 'Demolition of Westminster Bridge' in three days! What can you expect of that sort of art? But just because the fellow is a bit of a character the folks in London think he's wonderful."

"What's Mr. Whistler like? asked Susy, with true feminine curiosity.

"Anything but romantic, I should say. He's small and dark and has a mop of black hair. They say he wears a monocle and a white duck suit."

"My, it must be hot in London," she said ingenuously, as though that were the other side of the world. "Do you know any real live artists, Mr. Smithson?" she asked, gazing at him respectfully.

"I'm afraid the only painter I know at all well is Rosetti, who unfortunately is figuring largely in the London newspapers these days, but not on account of his art. Perhaps he's not a great painter, but he's as well known in this country as Courbet is in France. I've always thought him a romantic figure in spite of his ugly square beard and ill-fitting clothes."

"The London papers aren't bothering much about his paintings just now," said Sharp significantly; "anyway, I always said he was a better poet than painter."

"Is that the fellow who's mixed up in that suicide case?" queried Stewart. "The papers say he's the head of some new cult."

"An aesthetic cult," said Mr. Smithson sadly; "beauty in everything. At least it's an original point of view. What do you think, Mr. Eastwood?"

"Rosetti has had a mysterious and tragic life," said Mr. Eastwood, reluctant to give an opinion on something he knew little about.

"Some scandal?" Susy asked, in a hopeful voice.

"I see that's what the newspapers are calling it, and I suppose this recent unfortunate business might be termed that."

"Do tell us the story," urged Susy.

"It's already been in all the papers," said Stewart, feeling superior.

"Rosetti loved a shopgirl," said Mr. Eastwood simply. "She was a pale, ghost-like creature, but there was something about her that inspired him and under her influence he produced the finest work he has ever done."

"Where he made the mistake," said the reporter sagaciously, "was in marrying her. We artists have got no right to try to serve two mistresses."

"Did he marry her, then?" asked Susy, enthralled.

"Yes, he did, and she died almost immediately."

"Where's the scandal, then?" said Susy; "that's only a sad story."

"The scandal," continued Mr. Eastwood evenly, "lies in the fact that some people said, mark you I'm not saying it's true, that she committed suicide by poisoning herself when she heard of her husband's infidelities."

"That's the trouble with women," said Sam Sharp gloomily, "once they've got you they want to bind you hand and foot. Still, I think Rosetti was a fool. He went and flung all the manuscript of his poems into the open grave at her funeral—and he was selling well at the time."

"What a lovely story," said Susy morbidly.

This talk of infidelities and hints at loose living was too much for Captain Brady; it was no sort of conversation to carry on in front of a young girl, but his guests had the bit of culture between their teeth and were not to be lightly swayed from the talk of art. Even young Stewart, who ought to have had more sense, was sitting listening to them as if he were for once interested in something else besides pounds, shillings and pence. All this talk of culture! The folks in Liverpool were getting too big for their shoes. Of course, the Greeks were to blame for it all. They'd come to Liverpool just as they'd gone to London, made a fortune out of Englishmen and then set up as patrons of the arts. As a result there were all these hard-headed shipowners and merchants falling over themselves to copy the Greeks' example. Lancashire men, too, who'd made fortunes, like Fred Leyland, all rushing to spend their money on pictures. It didn't make sense.

He sought to put these views before his guests. Mr. Eastwood smiled at him and asked how else were they to spend their money? Taxes were low, the National Debt negligible, and there was no point in piling up their money in the bank. "You must read John Ruskin, Captain, he'll explain it all to you."

"There's a man for you," said Sharp, waking up at the sound of the name.

"I don't much care for him," said Mr. Smithson, "he's altogether too dogmatic, too convinced in his own infallibility. Besides, his writings have dangerous tendencies. I actually read an article by him making out that the interest on money was wrong."

Mr. Eastwood sympathized thoughtfully with his friend's indignation. "He goes a little too far at times," he said, "though a great many of his arguments are reasonable enough."

"He's a heathen," said Mr. Smithson conclusively.

"What a liner!" murmured Sharp, drowsily envious.

"He's very industrious," agreed Mr. Eastwood. "Have you come across any of his writings, Mr. Stewart?"

"Could anyone help coming across them?" said the young man. "He's got something in every magazine and nearly every newspaper that you pick up. Can't say I like this theories about money."

"Enough about these free-thinkers," said Sam Sharp, hoisting himself drunkenly in his chair. "Did I tell you about the young Irish woman at the Customs barrier on the landing-stage? 'Have you anything to declare?' the officer asked her. 'No, nothing to declare,' she replied. 'What's in the bottle there?' he asked suspiciously. 'Holy water! Holy water from Lourdes,' she told him righteously. The officer pulled out the cork and smelt it. 'Why, it's whisky!' he cried accusingly. 'Praise the Lord!' cried the young woman, throwing up her arms. 'A miracle it is!'"

"You're incorrigible, Sam," said Mr. Eastwood, rising. "Come along, Smithson, when Sharp starts telling stories you always know it's time to go. My very best wishes to you and the brig, Captain, and you, too, Mr. Stewart. Don't forget the old Greek proverb, 'Take care of the shipments and the orders will take care of themselves'," and with that the party proceeded to break up.

"Want me to see you home, Susy?" the young man asked condescendingly.

"No, thank you, Captain Brady is coming with me," and she smiled sweetly.

"Oh! So you're becoming an old man's darling," he said, half-jestingly, half in earnest.

"What's wrong with Sam Sharp escorting the lady home?" interrupted that worthy, staggering to his feet.

"Stick to your bottle, Mr. Sharp, and thank you both, but I happen to prefer Captain Brady's company."

"Well spoken, lass," said the captain, delighted; "that would show some of these young whipper-snappers that every woman didn't think they were wonderful, eh?" He gave her a ponderous wink.

"A woman's place is in bed," said Sharp, with a Rabelaisian air of profundity.

"Are you going to stand there and see me insulted?" asked Susy sharply, turning to Stewart.

The young man, taken unawares by the unexpectedness of this attack, could only stammer and stutter.

"He's your friend. You brought him aboard, didn't you?" she demanded accusingly. "Then take him home, this minute." She looked so threatening that the two of them began to retreat nervously towards the companionway.

"She's a fair vixen when she's roused," mumbled Sharp, as he leaned heavily on Stewart's arm. "Can't think what's the matter with her; she never used to take that sort of remark amiss before."

Down below in the cabin, laughing together, were Susy and Captain Brady.

"You fair set their caps about their ears, then, Susy," he chuckled; "for a minute I thought you were going to box their ears."

"Not me," said Susy scornfully, "I know how to handle men all right, whether they're drunks like Sam Sharp or conceited young fops like Mr. Stewart."

"Young Stewart's not a bad sort, really," defended the captain.

"He's like all the rest of men—except you, Captain—and I think you're a dear," and she leaned lightly forward and kissed him on the cheek.

"Eh! I wish I was thirty years younger," sighed Captain Brady, and Susy, with a happy laugh, linked her arm in his and said:

"I bet you were a boy for the girls, Captain."

The old man said cheerfully, "I'm admitting nothing to you, young woman, or you'll be setting about me like you did those other two."

"It has been a nice party," said Susy, as she pulled on her gloves. "I liked those other two gentlemen. They were really educated, weren't they? I'd like to be able to talk about pictures and artists the way they did." She sighed wistfully.

"There's no reason why you shouldn't," said Brady encouragingly; "you can get it out of books like they did. All these Liverpool ship-owners and merchants fancy themselves on art—culture, they call it—but I'll wager that most of them have never had a better education than you've had. Their culture all comes from money, the *parvenue*, they call them in London town."

"That sounds a nice name," said Susy; "I'm going to become one of them."

"I'm afraid it's not meant to be as nice as it sounds," admitted Brady, "but all the same, there's no shame attached to it. None of us can help how we're born."

They walked along for a little while in silence and then Susy said thoughtfully: "You've been very kind to me, Captain. I've never had anyone be really kind to me before. I hope I make a fortune out of this public-house and then you can come and settle down with me and never go to sea again."

"That's all very well," chaffed Brady, "but what about the time when you marry? Your husband won't relish having an old man for ever sitting around the place."

"I'm never going to marry," said Susy, with conviction.

"Don't be foolish, girl. If you weren't always quarrelling, I'd suggest young Mr. Stewart as a likely man."

"Captain Brady," said the young woman furiously, "if you weren't such a good friend of mine I'd really be rude to you."

"Goodness gracious, Susy! you're a proper little spitfire tonight."

"I wouldn't marry Mr. Stewart if he were as rich as Mr. Leyland, nor if he was as good-looking as Mr. Benson, the play actor—which he isn't," she said venomously.

"All right, all right," Captain Brady said hurriedly. "I was only joking, you know," and so for the rest of the jurney there was little said between them.

The *Mary Jane* was due to sail at daybreak, just before the ebb started to make. The evening before Bidston Hill had semaphored a moderate north-east breeze outside, and so everything was auspicious for the sailing.

Stewart was early on board and sat drinking coffee with Captain Brady while they awaited the pilot. The mate joined them for a brief second to report the crew aboard and to get his instructions. Then he had gone out into that strange, eerie quietness which surrounds every dock in those early hours preceding the dawn. As the clock advanced slowly and the two partners sipped their coffee the distant whistling of steamers and tugs out on the river began to penetrate the quiet. The noises grew more peristent and audible as activity increased with the approach of tide-time. Dock-master's voices were faintly heard, crying out orders. A few footsteps sounded on the deck overhead. There was a gentle murmur of voices as the mate gathered together the carpenter, the cook and the deck-boy, then there was the vague, familiar rattle of a block, a hoarse shout nearer at hand followed by a loud, shrill blast from the steam-tug's whistle, and as the dock gates were opened the paddle-tug threshed importantly in and moored alongside the *Mary Jane*.

It was drizzling slightly, and the decks were greasy when the tug-master and pilot jumped on board the brig and clattered noisily down into the saloon.

"Sign this, Captain," demanded the tugmaster, thrusting his towage form in front of Brady.

"All ready, Captain?" asked the pilot, looking anxiously round for the rum bottle.

Stewart got up, prepared to go.

"You can get off at the lock-gates, Mr. Stewart," the captain invited.

"The rum bottle out, Captain?" quizzed the tugmaster, pockering his bill.

"Over there," indicated Brady. "No, not you, pilot," he said sharply, "you've got a job to do first."

"What! You call this cockleshell a job? Man alive, she's only the size of a rowing boat."

"All the same," said Captain Brady firmly, "you'll have to keep your drinking till the job's done."

"Come on, Jack," growled the pilot dolefully. "Let's get her out into the river."

"She's singled up, pilot," the captain told him, and leisurely reached for his peak cap, his only badge of office.

The breast ropes were slackened down, a longshoreman threw them off the bollards, and the riggers quickly hauled them inboard. The *Mary Jane* eased over slightly, the paddle-tug gave a series of sharp blasts and forged ahead, and the brig trailed after her, effortlessly. The gloom of dawn, a wet drizzling dawn, hung over them, the other ships in the dock showing up like ghosts as they were reached and passed. It was only half-light when they warped into the locks and waited for the tide to release the gates and let them out into the river.

"Good-bye and good luck, Captain," said Stewart, a trifle sadly, he didn't know why.

The old man seized him cheerfully by the hand. "I'll be back in a month," he promised. "See that you have a cargo ready."

Stewart flung his leg over the bulwark rail, hesitated a brief moment, then, disdaining the rope ladder, jumped on to the quay. As he walked towards the river end of the lock he almost collided in the gloom with an apparition standing sheltering under an umbrella.

"It's me, Mr. Stewart," Susy said.

"What on earth's brought you down at this ungodly hour?" he asked astonished.

"I've come to see Captain Brady's ship off. Where is it?" she asked, a trifle bewildered.

"She's in the top end of the locks. . . . She'll be down in five minutes or so."

Save for the dockmaster, the quay was deserted. It was the top of high water, and as the official looked at the tide-guage he gave a hail. A hoarse reply came out of the gloom, there was a clanking, ratcheting sound as the pawl turned over the capstan. Half a dozen men toiled slowly round and round, bending their weight on the capstan bars, and slowly the lock-gates swung open. There was a shrill blast from the tug's whistle, and her paddles threshed the water at an ever-increasing speed. As though anxious to get out into the open water, the brig surged quickly after her.

Susy's handkerchief was out, waving frantically, and as the brig drew abreast of them, Captain Brady, standing on the poop, recognized her, and with an unusual flourish swept off his peaked cap. Then the *Mary Jane* was past them, her stern, masts, and small fluttering ensign the only parts of her visible for a while. The tug squared her up in the middle of the river, there was a loosening and flapping of sails, and as the sheets were hauled home, the canvas bellied to the wind, the *Mary Jane* gathered her own way and the tow rope slackened. Figures scuttled up on to the fo'c'sle head, the top rope was thrown off and the tug drifted alongside the brig to take off the riggers. A few seconds later she was left alone, sailing proudly with gathering speed towards the bar.

The two on the quayside watched her out of sight in silence, and then Stewart said boastingly, "There goes £1500." But Susy wasn't listening, she was busy sniffing into her handkerchief.

"What on earth's the matter, girl?" he said testily. "Anyone would think you were saying good-bye to your sailor sweetheart."

"It's so sad and romantic. It's beautiful! I've never seen a ship set off before, and besides, Captain Brady is a special friend of mine. Surely a girl can cry if she wants to?"

"Dry your tears, then, and let's go and have some breakfast at Mother Simpson's." He shook his head, puzzled; women were beyond him.

They walked down to the Pier Head and through the ever-open doors of Mother Simpson's eating-house.

"Bacon and eggs for me, ma," said Stewart, but Susy would only have a cup of tea, and shortly afterwards she said she must be going, and since he made no attempt to dissuade her, she made her way back to the public-house.

The Royal Amphitheatre

CHAPTER 14

MISS SCRIPPS REFUSES

WITH the sailing of the *Mary Jane*, Stewart, for the first time in many months, found himself at a loose end with little to occupy his mind. There was all that junk in his storeroom to be disposed of, and the final cutting adrift from the ship-chandlery business. There were two courses open to him, one was to go on hawking the stuff round the docks, and the other was to sell it outright at a cut price to another ship-chandler. By hawking it round the ships he might eventually get rid of it at a small profit, but that would take time; it might take months. At that particular moment he felt the urge to get rid of it quickly. He hoped the tide of his fortune had turned and he wanted no pitiful reminder of the unsuccessful part of his life haunting him every time he set foot in his home.

He got out his ledgers and struck a balance. Then he went out and saw Bartlett's. When he returned, an hour later, he was a hundred pounds poorer, but he was much happier, for they had agreed to take all his stock at a hundred pounds less than cost price. And that was the end of his unfortunate ship's husbanding business.

The succeeding days were boring, he just could not get accustomed to doing nothing beyond paying a few routine visits to shippers. He searched diligently round for any other problems that might need clearing up. There was that unfortunate affair between Silas and Martha. Vaguely he felt sorry for Silas, but then, if Miss Scripps thought it necessary for them to marry, then they'd better get the banns up right away. It would please Miss Scripps, if no one else, and so he called Silas in from the courtyard.

The old sailor entered, the picture of dejection. He hobbled about with a stick now, bending forward painfully, while his free hand was spread out on the small of his back.

"It's no good, Silas," his employer said sternly, "all that play-acting won't get you out of this mess. If you really do feel like that now, what are you going to be like after Martha has had you for a week?"

"Belay, skipper, belay!" pleaded Silas, in no mood for Stewart's heavy humour. "I'm ill, skipper. It's me rheumatics. Something shocking they are. You ain't got any o' that there 'air oil left, I don't suppose?"

"Hair oil?" Stewart queried.

"Yes, that stuff you bought a couple o' months back. Wonderful stuff for rheumatics!"

"You mean that hair tonic?" said Stewart, realization coming to him. "Why, I've never used it. As far as I know the bottle's on the shelf there."

He got up and had a look, but it wasn't there. He turned, puzzled, towards Silas. "Anyway, it wouldn't be of use to you, you haven't a hair on your old head."

"It's like this 'ere, skipper," said Silas uneasily, "ever since I was in lodgings down Aigburth way I've suffered from rheumatics. I've spent pouns and pouns on medicine, but none of it's been any good. Then t'other day a drop o' that there 'air oil o' yours fell accidental on me elbow, and would you believe it, the rheumatics went away like magic. I admits it, skipper, I took that bottle and upon me oath it's the only stuff that's done my rheumatics any good. But the bottle's empty now, and I'm only a poor man, and I 'aven't been able to buy another, so my aches and pains are as bad as ever they was. You ain't upset, skipper?"

Stewart shook his head sorrowfully. "You know, Silas, I hardly feel it incumbent upon me to warn an old man like you of the serious dangers of evil-living, but if you will have your fun, then you must expect to pay for it. 'As ye sow, so shall ye reap,' and there are some persons, less kind than me, who'd say that you're only experiencing the results of a mis-spent youth. However, that is no concern of mine. I can't be responsible for your earlier years of indiscretion. You are my responsibility now, though, and that brings me to the trouble between you and Martha."

The old sailor looked at him uneasily. When the skipper took to talking in that fashion he didn't know where he was. All those long words showing off his education, he couldn't make out whether the skipper was in earnest or what! So he stood there self-consciously, his rheumatics forgotten.

"I think it only right and proper," continued Stewart, "now that we have the time to explore your irregular union with Martha, to come to a decision in the matter. You've got to make an honest woman of her, Silas. Needless to say, I feel humiliated at the treacherous way in which you have deceived this plainly trusting woman and unfortunately, as your employer, I feel some culpability in the whole sordid affair. It was in my house that you wrought this woman's undoing, and I would not sleep at nights if I thought you were free to continue this infamous conduct."

"Honest, skipper——" began Silas wretchedly.

"I could have understood a younger man being carried away by his passions, but not you, Silas. You, with your knowledge of the world and the frailty of womankind. Since your irresponsible attitude leaves me to believe that you will not voluntarily restitute the wrong you have done, I feel that my own good name and reputation demands that I take action. I am, therefore, going now to see Martha's mistress to make the final arrangements for legalizing the illicit bond you have contracted."

Silas gathered a most unfavourable impression of all this talk, but all his attempts to explain his conduct were waved aside by Stewart, and the next minute his young employer had departed for Duke Street. The old man scratched his head in puzzled bewilderment. This was a fine how-d'ye do, and all out of nothing. It was true Martha had spent the night there, but it wasn't his fault. He was a companionable sort of shipmate, and when Martha had told him that she didn't mind a nip of something warm he'd looked towards her as a kindred spirit. There'd been no harm done. One nip had led to another and before you could say 'Anchor's away' Martha was under the weather, or so she said, and refused to go home because they'd smell the liquor on her. She blamed him for leading her on, but it hadn't taken her long to turn him out into the courtyard to sleep, and locked, bolted and barred the door behind him. And now, here he was, really in serious trouble. The immediate future didn't bear thinking upon, and miserably the old chap wandered off in search of some of his old cronies and the sympathy he craved for.

Meanwhile his employer was resolutely striding up Duke Street, after first having carefully ascertained that Irish Higgins had set off on his nightly round.

His reception by Miss Scripps was painfully cool, and quick to sense the change, he searched around for the reason. But he was not very skilful where women were concerned, and her coolness left him mystified. He'd heard somewhere that a bold front was always necessary with women, so he took his courage in his hands and said determinedly, "I've come here to ask you to marry me right away."

The young woman stared at him in amazement. "Are you out of your mind?" she asked, and there was an angry glint in her lovely blue eyes.

"Very likely," said Stewart, smiling fatuously and not heeding the warning signal. After all, the last time he'd seen her it had been practically settled. He looked at her with a proprietary air. "I think I've been out of my mind ever since the day I first saw you."

Miss Scripps remained unmoved. This young man took things too lightly. "How do you propose that we should live?" she asked coldly.

"I've got a house and a share in a shipping business," he said optimistically.

"Yes, but how much does all this bring you?" she persisted.

"Oh! money doesn't matter," replied Stewart confidently. "So long as we love each other, there's no need to worry about little things like that."

"You surprise me, Mr. Stewart," said Miss Scripps tartly. "It may

not matter to you, living in the manner to which you're accustomed, but
I assure you that love in a hovel makes no appeal to me, even supposing
that I did love you, which I don't recall ever having said."

"But what about the other evening?" stammered Stewart, completely put off by this sudden reversal.

The young lady dismissed the happenings by ignoring them, and
her manner led Stewart to believe that it was only money which stood
between him and happiness with Miss Scripps, and she said nothing to
disillusion him.

"If we're to wait until I'm as rich as your uncle we may never get
married."

"At least you might show some signs of appreciating that no lady
with any self-respect would be delighted at the prospects you are
offering me," said Miss Scripps, determined that he should realize their
different social circumstances. "Where are all those wonderful schemes
of yours? You've been fond of telling me of what you intend to do,
and the name you intend to make, but I have seen nothing so far that
would indicate there is substance behind your words. If you really
loved me as you are so fond of declaring, I would have thought that
you would have applied yourself to your business. You can't say you
didn't have the opportunity. My uncle gave you every encouragement,
but no, you seemed to have preferred loose-living and idle talk to hard
work. I must say, sir, that I am surprised at your audacity in offering
me marriage without having any prospects of being able to support
me in a proper style. I don't think you properly appreciate the difference in our modes of living. Your proposal might sound very attractive
to that barmaid acquaintance of yours, but I can assure you it makes
no appeal to me."

Miss Scripps sat bolt upright in her chair, her indignation at the
calm, presumptuous way of this young man carried her far beyond what
she meant to say. Still, she was very angry, and her caustic reference to
Susy was like balm to her ruffled dignity.

"Fortunes aren't made in a night," said Stewart, properly abashed
by the young woman's attitude, "and I really am working as hard as I
know how." Realizing that he was not improving matters by talking,
he attempted to take her hand, but the young woman angrily jumped
to her feet, and they both stood stiffly there, silent.

Poor Stewart didn't know what to do next. He gazed at her lovely
auburn hair and clear blue eyes and the radiant colour in her cheeks
and tried to gain a little comfort from the fact that she hadn't actually
turned him out of the house. Perhaps it would be tactful to change the
subject, so he timidly ventured on to the topic of Martha and Silas.
But his ingratiating efforts here made no headway, for she dismissed
the matter by saying that she would never permit a decent woman like
Martha to marry such a dreadful old man as Silas!

Stewart was astounded, and protested that he had understood Miss Scripps to say that she insisted on their marrying.

"I've talked over the whole business with Mr. Puddicombe," she said haughtily, "and we're both agreed that on no account must Martha take this step. If the evening was spent as innocently as they both declare, then the need for marriage no longer arises," and for the first time since he had arrived, Miss Scripps showed some signs of losing her frigid self-possession.

"You've never been talking to that curate about such things?" said Stewart scandalized.

"And pray why not, sir?" she said, on her dignity again.

Quick to recognize the chill in her voice, he said anxiously: "Don't let's quarrel again. You know I love you."

But Miss Scripps was in no mood for reconciliation. "You talk glibly of your love," she said angrily, "and the very next minute you're off with some dreadful woman to Blackpool. The trouble with you, Mr. Stewart, is that you're unstable. Oh! it's no use you shaking your head. My uncle has opened my eyes to your true character these last few weeks."

"Your uncle's a fine one to talk," said Stewart bitterly.

Miss Scripps retorted quickly, "I won't stand here and listen to your abuse of my uncle."

Stewart, unable to keep his anger down, replied hotly: "If you think so much of your precious uncle, there's nothing more to be said. He doesn't like me and you may as well know that I don't like him. You can do what you like about it!" Without another word he picked up his hat and angrily left the house.

The cool night air calmed him down a little, but the bitterness of this final scene completely filled his mind as he strode along. He would have received a different reception had he been rich. But there it was, for all his angry words on leaving the house, he knew full well that he still wanted to marry her, and it seemed as though his only hope now was to improve his financial position as soon as possible. But how was he to manage that? He shook his head gloomily. The brig was not going to make their fortune overnight, that much was clear, not at the freight rates she was likely to get sailing between Liverpool and the Peninsula. She wasn't big enough for the colonial trade, and the civil war made it impossible to think of sending her to America. But did it? He recalled the visit of Captain Creesy, master of the *Uriah B. Heap*. He had made a fortune on that one trip alone. If the *Mary Jane* could make one successful trip to Galveston and bring a cargo of cotton back, all his troubles would be over. It was an idea.

Just then a hand smote him on the shoulder, and Sam Sharp stood wheezing beside him.

"Hullo, Sam," Stewart said, without enthusiasm.

Liverpool, 1860

"How's the courting going?" chuckled the reporter, placing the young man's crestfallen demeanour right away.

"Oh! go and jump in the river," said Stewart irritably.

"Nay, lad, that's no way to speak to a friend," remonstrated the other, in pained surprise. "You're not letting them get topsides of you, are you? I'd have sworn that it'd have taken more than a woman to upset you."

Stewart laughed sheepishly. "The trouble is, Sam, that it's just cost me £100 to wind up my ship-chandlery business."

"What's that to a smart young fellow like you?" Sharp said cheerfully. "But if you're short of cash let me stand you a drink. I can't bear long faces in young men, it isn't natural. How about the 'Pig and Whistle'?"

"Suits me," Stewart replied apathetically. He was so despondent that he thought it not a bad idea to get drunk.

"This place doesn't seem the same without that girl Susy. Somehow the sight of her made the beer taste better. You knew she'd left the 'Unicorn', of course? She's got a place of her own now, just off Vauxhall Road."

"A public of her own?" questioned Stewart, surprised.

"Aye, there's a girl that means to get on. Got her name outside as licensee, as she always said she would."

"But where did she get the money from?" asked Stewart.

"You'd better ask her that yourself. At any rate, she's scraped £200 from somewhere, and you know as well as I do that you don't find sums like that lying around in the gutter"; the old reporter gave him a significant wink.

"You mean . . ." began Stewart hesitantly.

"Nay, you be careful, lad. I'm hinting at nothing, and don't you get telling that young vixen that I was. She's a dangerous women when her morals are in question But didn't you know she'd moved?"

"I've other things to do besides collecting public-house gossip," said Stewart cuttingly.

Sam Sharp glowered back. "But are they as honest?" he asked righteously.

Stewart laughed ruefully. "Pay no attention to me, Sam, I'm in a foul temper today. Let's have a drink. You've no idea where she got the money from?" he asked.

"No idea at all, though between you and me I have my suspicions. What do you say if we take a walk round and see her?"

Stewart suddenly felt irritated. "Oh, this place is good enough," he said, and just then Sam Sharp caught sight of one of his many acquaintances. It was Mr. Gray, of George Forrester's Vauxhall Foundry. With him was the master of one of the so-called express liners, a Captain Hamilton Perry. They sat down after Sharp had completed the introductions.

"I'll wager that you were talking to the captain about that famous steering gear of yours," said Sam Sharp professionally.

The engineer laughed. "As a matter of fact, Sam, I was explaining how it steered the *Great Eastern*."

"Yes," said the reporter sagely, nodding his head, "I thought so. I wonder what you engineers will be astonishing us with next? But how's the Atlantic Ferry, Captain?" he continued pompously, turning solicitously to the seaman. This was just the society he delighted in. Let young Stewart see how conversant he was with the people and things that mattered in Liverpool.

"Still running," said Captain Perry politely, "though if there's going to be war with America, some of us may find ourselves out of a job."

"There'll be no war with America," said Sharp confidently.

"I don't know so much about that," said Mr. Gray; "if these politicians keep on the way they are doing, we'll be dragged into the business in no time. We'd have been in it already if it hadn't been for the Prince Consort."

"I'm not a Liverpool man," said Captain Perry, "and I can't say I feel the same about Gladstone as you do, but you must admit, Mr. Sharp, that he's violently on the side of the Southern States. The speeches he's making are dangerous from the point of peace."

"Yes, I'll admit that Gladstone and Liverpool are making a mistake there," said Sharp, "but you need have no fear, the people of Lancashire are just as strongly in favour of the Federal Government, even though it means that they can't get the cotton to keep their mills working. Why, in one town, the spinners refused to work when they found that the cotton came from a Southern plantation employing slaves!"

"Thank God for the common people of England," said Mr. Gray fervently.

"What about this privateersman Lairds are building for the Southern States?" asked Stewart suddenly.

Sam Sharp looked at him surprised, and then turned towards Mr. Gray. "You're friendly enough with the Birkenhead people," he said, "tell us what's happening about the *Alabama*."

"Nay, Sam," said Mr. Gray deprecatingly, "you're a newspaper reporter; it's you that should be telling us. All I know is that the cruiser's finished and they've got a crew of English reservists aboard. Whether the Government will let her sail is another matter."

"If the South is blockaded," said Stewart curiously, "how have they managed to pay for the building?"

"It's English money that's built her," said Mr. Gray dourly. "Paid for by bonds sold to English investors. And mark my words, if she gets out and sinks many ships, the English Government will be liable for a large indemnity when the war's over, for the South haven't a hope of winning."

Sam Sharp pooh-poohed the idea. "Why, if she got out," he said, "the Federal cruisers would make short work of her."

"You're alluding to these new ironclads of theirs, I presume," said Mr. Gray reflectively. "I've just been reading an account of the *Merrimac* and *Monitor* fight. Fired at each other all day, the account said, and the shots rippled off their sides like peas."

"You mean they were unsinkable?" asked Captain Perry, astonished.

"I mean that the protective iron covering on their sides is impervious to modern ammunition," replied Mr. Gray. "The construction of these two ironclads marks a new epoch in sea fighting. It makes the British Navy, for instance, obsolete. Shipbuilders will be making a lot of money in the future, replacing the present warships."

"Do you really think that, Mr. Gray?" asked the reporter eagerly.

"How will it affect the blockade?" asked Stewart anxiously.

"Blockade-running is not the same as a straightforward sea fight," said Captain Perry, who had just been appointed a lieutenant in the newly formed Royal Naval Reserve, and felt it incumbent on him to explain the elements of naval strategy.

"I can see that," Sharp remarked professionally, "the success of blockade-running depends on speed and cunning—not armour. All the same, it's a risky business."

"It may be," said Mr. Gray, "but so long as there's money to be made that way, there'll be people willing to risk their vessels. I heard of one shipowner this morning who boasted that his ship had made 700 per cent profit before she'd finally been sunk—just figure that out and remember the blockade's only been in force a year."

"Do you know anything about the blockade, Captain?" asked Stewart.

"Not very much, though I have come across both European and American blockade-runners. Some owners equip ships specially for the job, and a nice turn of speed they get, too. They need it! What is more, with the warships of the Union patrolling the coast night and day throughout the year, blockade-runners are getting fewer and fewer, for the Yankees seem to have got the business pretty well tied up. The hazards are reflected in the freights which are about 300 per cent higher than normal."

"What cargoes are they running?" the young man asked.

"They're so short of everything down there that the Richmond Government can't even raise paper to print its bills on," Captain Perry told him. "Iron and ammunition, I suppose, are what they need most. As for payment they say that bales of cotton that can't be shipped lie for miles and miles outside Galveston, and the ships help themselves to them. In 1860 the Southern States exported 200 million dollars worth of cotton, but this year they say that they'll be satisfied if their exports total four million dollars worth."

"It certainly sounds as though there's money to be made in running the blockade," said Stewart ruminatively. Under the influence of this thought and of the rum he had drunk, he began to cheer up visibly.

Sam Sharp also, now becoming loquacious, sought to impress the other two. He began to hold forth in great style about literature. Even Liverpool engineers aspired after culture and he found a ready listener in Mr. Gray.

It was all outside Captain Perry's interests though, and as soon as the talk veered away from ships and shipping he made his excuses and left.

"My old friend, George Augustus Sala, the wittiest and most enterprising daily scribbler of our time," Sharp was saying, "has just written and asked me to join him in London."

"Shall you go?" asked Stewart hopefully.

The reporter eyed him reprovingly: "And how do you think the *Albion* would get on without me? No, loyalty is my first name."

"I always thought it was, Samuel," Stewart remarked innocently.

"Surely, too," said Mr. Gray, who came of Scottish ancestry, "the money in London must be far better."

"The financial gain to me, of course, would be extensive, but at the moment I cannot consider it. Apart from my loyalty there is another reason. Gentlemen, I am writing a book!"

"A book!" said Stewart dumbfounded.

"Yes, a book!" said Sharp irritably. "There's nothing so remarkable in that, is there? The idea has been with me for some time now. This daily drudgery is too soul-destroying for the finer arts, and of course authorship is far more remunerative. But I am not embarking on the project for financial considerations, I can assure you, but because the literature of this country is deteriorating. The talent of composition is given to but few, and it is the duty of each one of us to render our best services to the country."

"I don't see how you can say that our literature's backward with Dickens, Thackeray, George Eliot and Wilkie Collins all contributing their quota," said Stewart, his tongue well-loosened now.

"That fellow George Eliot," said Mr. Gray reverentially, "writes the most wonderful novels I've ever read."

"Fiddlesticks!" interrupted the reporter rudely.

"Sir!" said Mr. Gray indignantly, "may I ask if you've read *The Mill on the Floss* published last year, and his latest work, *Silas Marner*, just out—and still say that those books are not the work of a genius?"

"Aye, I've read them both, and *Adam Bede*, too, but look at the male characters, Mr. Gray. They're nothing but women in men's clothing. Those books are written by a woman or else I'm a Dutchman."

"Still, you can't go against sales," protested Mr. Gray vigorously.

"Twaddle! only fit for romantic schoolgirls," said the reporter truculently. "Mind you," he went on, "the books sell all right. *Adam Bede* went to seven editions in a year—just think of it—16,000 copies sold in 1859! But it's only because there's nothing better for people to read. Dickens and Thackeray are written out and that's why I've decided to turn to real literature. I reckon if William Blackwood, astute publisher though he is, can afford to offer that woman £10,000 for her next novel without even seeing it, then there's money and reputation awaiting yours truly."

"You'd better stick to journalism," advised Stewart pessimistically. "At least, you get a lot of free liquor, but where will you be, Sam, if you have to buy your own beer? Why, you'd have to turn out more novels than Anthony Trollope!"

"I could do it," the reporter boasted; "look at the experience that lies behind me. In this bowed grey head of mine lie the seeds of immortal literature."

"I can well believe it, for I have yet met a man who could understand those leaders of yours," said Stewart doubtfully.

"Ah!" said Mr. Gray circumspectly, "that's the new art. Am I not right, Mr. Sharp?"

"Eh! What?" ejaculated the reporter, coming sharply out of a beautiful dream of fame and wealth.

"The new art," said Mr. Gray, "of writing. Just the same as in painting. The new impressionism, the beauty of words."

"What are you talking about?" said Stewart, a trifle tipsily. "Composition should mean what it reads."

"Don't my editorials do that?" said Sharp loftily.

"That's the argument," said Stewart, feeling full of intelligence and wit, "I'm telling Mr. Gray that I can't understand a word of them, and Mr. Gray says that no one's meant to, that's the new art. Is it true, Sam?"

"I'm not saying it is, and I'm not saying it isn't," the reporter said, "but there's certainly a message in what I write."

"Ah, that's the trouble," said Stewart gloomily, "what is it?"

"Naturally," answered the reporter, "my articles are written for the discerning. My message may not be visible the first time of reading, nor, perhaps, the second——"

"If you think that people are going to spend all day reading the *Albion* over and over again, trying to find your message, you're a bigger optimist than I thought you were, Sam Sharp."

"Besides," said Mr. Gray, "how are they to know that it will be the right message when they find it? Tell me that, Samuel boy," he wound up affectionately.

"Which side are you on?" asked Stewart indignantly.

"Both," said Mr. Gray sombrely.

"How can we have a good argument, then ?" complained the young man, appealing to the reporter, who sat steadfastly silent with a gravity of mien which did justice to the occasion.

"Tell me your problems and perhaps I'll give you an answer," said Sharp solemnly.

"Mr. Gray wants to know if his wife will be waiting up for him," began Stewart facetiously, "and I want to know what's the matter with my young lady," he went on in a rush of sentimental self-pity.

"Women, women, women !" the reporter looked at him disdainfully. "You harp on the female sex too much, young man. I fear you must be unbalanced."

"I c'n stand as straight as you c'n," challenged Stewart, making a vain effort to get up from his chair.

"Better marry than burn," quoted Sharp sententiously.

"I'd better be getting off home," said Mr. Gray, to whom the unhappy reference of a waiting wife aroused feelings of self-reproach.

"G'night," hiccupped Stewart happily. When the two were left alone, he said, "Well, Samuel, what are we goin' do now ?"

They sat drinking together for some little time, drawing closer in maudlin sympathy. Sharp's new love—authorship—and Stewart's old love—Miss Scripps—were discussed with the verbosity of liquor-loosened tongues. They revealed their troubles to each other and exchanged advice in melancholy fashion.

At last Sharp suggested that they might go and see Susy, and maintaining close mutual contact they reeled away.

Stewart remembered little of what followed, and when he regained consciousness it was broad daylight.

He stared around in puzzled bewilderment. He was in bed and his clothes were neatly folded on a chair. Of Sam Sharp there was no sign and there was no one else in the room to afford him any clue as to what had happened.

Where was he ? A sudden, sharp pain made him clutch his head, and dimly he began to recall some of the events of the previous night. His money ! What had happened to it ? He scrambled dizzily to his feet and searched frantically through his trouser pockets. His purse had gone. He sat down on the bed, a prey to the most bitter thoughts.

Then he heard light footsteps on the stairs outside, so he jumped quickly back into bed and pretended to be asleep, his brain a confused whirl of thoughts. At any rate he was still on dry land, so he couldn't have been shanghaied.

The door opened and a young woman looked into the room.

"Susy !" exclaimed Stewart, sitting up in bed so swiftly that the pain in his head was a full second late in catching him up.

"So you're awake at last," the young woman said, smiling. "I thought you were going to sleep the clock round."

"What am I doing here, and how did l get like this?" he asked urgently.

She looked at him slyly. "You've got a head on you, I'll bet."

"But how . . . but how did I get here?"

"One question at a time," laughed Susy. "You turned up in the public-bar last night with that drunken old man Sam Sharp. My! You weren't half-pickled. What ever made you get like that?"

"Go on, tell me everything," groaned Stewart.

"And then Mr. Tomkins, the printer, came in, fairly tearing his hair and took Sam Sharp off with him. He left you here. That's all there is to it," she said simply.

"But—but how did I get into bed?" asked Stewart, embarrassed.

Susy coloured under his questioning gaze.

"It's all right, I didn't take advantage of you, if that's what you mean. My barman put you to bed."

"Oh!" Stewart was relieved. The thought that he might have been put to bed by a woman was the crowning indignity. "What a fool I've been," he said miserably, sinking his head into his hands.

"Good lord! You do carry on. Anyone would think it was the first time you'd been drunk."

"Well, so it is," said Stewart harshly, and thinking of his vanished purse . . . "and the last."

"That's what everybody says," said Susy blithely, "but thank goodness they change their minds or else we'd be in a nice mess."

Stewart looked at her suspiciously.

"I hear that this is your own tavern?"

"Yes, I'm getting on, don't you think?" she said pertly.

"Where did you get the money from?"

"My! you ain't half curious. Well, if you really want to know, I've got a good friend."

His suspicions were confirmed. He looked at her angrily, and said accusingly, "So that's how you're getting on."

The clouds gathered on Susy's brow. "Mr. Stewart," she began primly, "if you're insinuating——"

"I'm insinuating nothing," said Stewart roughly, "the facts speak for themselves."

The young woman looked at him curiously and then said quietly, "I don't see what business of yours it is how I got the money."

"Of course you wouldn't," said Stewart bitterly, "but it's the business of any self-respecting man who sees a young woman heading for disaster."

Susy looked at him innocently.

"Disaster?" she said. "Oh! Mr. Stewart, you always try to frighten me. Do you think I'll be ruined?"

"You don't think a man's going to lend money to a girl like that for nothing, do you?" he asked, a look of wonder on his face at the girl's ignorance.

"Why not? There are some men who might."

"Come on, Susy," he said persuasively, "tell me who gave you the money and I'll see that he gets it back right away."

"You mean," said Susy, "that you'll lend me the money?"

"Sooner than see you fall into the clutches of someone who's only wish to help you is in order to get you into bed," said Stewart, with a directness which he thought the circumstances demanded. This young fool of a girl was going to get herself into trouble, indeed, if she hadn't already done so. It never occurred to him that any other reason could have prompted the loan.

"I think you're making me another improper suggestion," she said, bending her head so that he couldn't see her smile.

"You little fool," he said, half getting out of bed, and then realizing that he was clad only in a shirt, hastily pulled his feet back under the clothes. "Haven't you enough sense to know who your friends are? How much did you pay for the place?"

"Two hundred pounds," said Susy, catching her breath and still hiding her face.

"Phew!" exclaimed Stewart, wondering where he was going to get that sum from. What idiots women were. Fancy imagining for one minute ... but never mind, he had got to get her out of this mess.

"Pack your bag," he ordered authoritatively.

"What for?" she asked in amazement.

"Don't you see that you can't stay here?" he said patiently. The girl was plainly ignorant of the dangers of her position.

"But I don't want to leave," she said obstinately.

"Look, Susy," he said wheedlingly, "I've known you for the best part of a year now. I've seen you getting on in business. I've taken a liking to you and I don't want to see you end up like all the other girls. I'm your friend. Can't you trust me to do what I say? It's for your own good."

"I suppose that business at Blackpool was for my own good as well?" she said shrewdly.

"Oh, don't keep harping back to things that are dead and buried," said Stewart irritably. "I've apologized, and, anyhow, that was all a misunderstanding. This is a different matter altogether."

"Oh! is it?" said Susy coolly. "Well, I don't mind telling you I've no intention of leaving this tavern. It's licensed in my name and when I leave it'll be to take over a bigger and better place. I must say I admire your cheek coming here and starting to lecture an honest girl! Being in the hotel business may not be a great deal, but at least it's honest, and that's more than can be said for some of the business you've been mixed up in recently."

"What do you mean?" asked Stewart, dangerously quiet.

"If you don't know, I'm not going to tell you. But at any rate," she said, with a complacent expression, "nobody can accuse me of giving short measure!" and leaving him there fuming, she swept out of the room, humming a song merrily to herself.

He'd let himself in for that jibe, he reflected savagely. It all came of trying to help a girl. Well, she could go to hell as fast as she liked. He wouldn't stretch out a finger to help her, and he scrambled into his clothes as quickly as his throbbing head would allow. A clock was striking eleven, and he crept guiltily down the stairs, seeking to make an unobtrusive exit.

The combined circumstances of the previous evening and Susy's attitude that morning had made him very angry, and on top of that came the loss of his purse. All he'd got to show for it, on the other hand, was a temporary forgetfulness of Miss Scripps. Everything came back to him with full force now, and in spite of his anger he was strangely subdued.

As he slipped through the door, a voice called to him, "You've forgotten this." Susy stood in the passage holding out his purse. "There was four pounds twelve shillings and sevenpence halfpenny when you came last night, but I've taken out ten shillings for your night's lodging. You must patronize us again, Mr. Stewart," she said, smiling sweetly.

Stewart snatched the purse from her with a murderous look and made off without even stopping to count the contents. No wonder she was getting on in the world, if that was how she made her money! Ten shillings for one night's lodging! Phew! They only charged half that at the 'Angel' in Dale Street.

CHAPTER 15

SELLING THE CARGO

"WHERE'VE you been, skipper?" Silas greeted him anxiously. "I've been looking for you all over the town."

"Why, is anything the matter?"

"The *Mary Jane's* semaphored on Bidston Hill," the old sailor cried excitedly. "Just on a month since she sailed. Thirty days out and home."

Stewart waited to hear no more, but rushed down to the Custom House.

"Princes, half-tide, tomorrow morning," the official told him. "Expect her to be here long, Mr. Stewart?" he asked politely.

"She sails again in a fortnight's time, I hope."

"You'll want her to be on the loading berth a week, I suppose? The same one as last time in Salthouse Dock?"

"Thank you, that'll do fine. There's no chance of getting her discharged in the same berth?" he asked casually.

"I don't know," the official said doubtfully, "it's a bit unusual, but I dare say it might be arranged."

This young fellow was a nice sort of chap, he didn't come in bellowing and shouting and wanting to know what the Dock Board was for.

"Save you a bit of money if you haven't to shift ship," he said, with a smile, "just wait here a minute. It might be possible, mind you, I'm not promising anything, and if the berth is wanted urgently you'll have to move, but I'll make enquiries."

"Of course, of course," said Stewart diplomatically, "it's very good of you to consider it." Even Mr. Eastwood couldn't have been more tactful, he thought, as he walked back secure in the knowledge that he'd got the *Mary Jane* on the best possible berth with no trouble at all.

He wasn't the first person on the Pier Head the next morning to see the *Mary Jane* warped in, for Susy was there to welcome Captain Brady home, just as she'd wished him good-bye a month ago.

"What do you want down here?" Stewart asked her gruffly.

"I might ask you the same thing," she replied brightly.

It was no use trying to get a rise out of Susy, he decided, she was a bit too much for him. Still, she must be a good-hearted girl to get up at that time in the morning to greet Captain Brady, a man old enough to be her father. But was he really? Stewart glanced at her suspiciously. The sharp morning air certainly agreed with her. He'd never seen her looking so pretty. No, it was impossible. Captain Brady was nearly three times her age; he'd never be such a fool as to marry so young a

girl. You never knew with these old men, though, and as for Susy . . .
if she suspected the captain had much money, he thought bitterly, she'd
make no bones about it. The thought depressed him and took the edge
off his earlier enthusiasm.

It would be a fine how-de-do if he suddenly found Susy the wife
of his partner! He paced uneasily up and down with the girl, and
would dearly have loved to know what she was thinking. At one time
he'd rather thought that she was fond of himself, but the events of the
past few weeks had shattered that illusion.

"There it is!" cried Susy suddenly, excitedly, pointing down the
river towards New Brighton fort.

"That's a tug," said Stewart curtly.

"No, I mean behind the tug," she persisted, "I can see it plainly
now."

Dammit, thought Stewart morosely, she was right again.

"You mean you can see her," he emphasized cuttingly, "I thought
you were talking about a seagull."

"I can see her," she amended ; "I'm sure it's the same boat."

"You're sure she's the same brig," corrected Stewart. At any rate,
he'd show her she knew nothing about ships, even if she had got sharper
eyes than he had. He was pleased to see that now she turned deferentially towards him.

"The brig," she said carefully, "seems bigger now than when she
left."

"Probably grown a bit," said the young man sarcastically, "it's a
month since you last saw her, don't forget."

"She can't have got so much cargo in her," opined the girl a few
minutes later in a disappointed tone.

Fancy her tumbling to that! "Why, what do you know about
cargo?" Stewart asked, astonished.

"I do think you're unkind," said the girl, turning and looking at
him. "I know I don't know anything about ships, but you needn't poke
fun at me all the time. I'm just as anxious as you are about the *Mary
Jane*. Please, Mr. Stewart," she pleaded, "don't be angry with me."

"Oh, all right," said Stewart hastily. He always was confused when
a woman looked at him like that, and the next moment his confusion
was heightened as a small gloved hand crept under his arm.

Conflicting emotions swept over him, he didn't know what to say.
She was always taking the wind out of his sails, but he needn't have
worried, for Susy seemed to be unaware of his disturbed feelings and
she chattered brightly away as Captain Brady and the *Mary Jane*
drew nearer.

Stewart suddenly felt very happy, and went to great pains to explain
why the brig, towed by the tug, continued up the river past them before
she finally turned round. "The flood tide's still running, see ? And she

wants to stem it so she can steer better when she approaches the locks."

The *Mary Jane* lay out in the middle of the river, heading downstream, and they watched her, fascinated, as she slowly headed over towards them. Then, nearer at hand, they heard the clink, clink of a capstan and Susy turned round to see the lock-gates being slowly opened.

"Come ahead!" bawled the dockmaster through his megaphone to the tug, and lest his voice should be lost in the noise of the river, he went through an energetic pantomime with his arms.

"They're bringing her in now," Stewart explained, "although the flood's only been running for three hours. That's the value of having a shallow-draughted vessel. Get in and out at almost any state of the tide."

The tug came slowly ahead and the brig slowly followed. Now the tug was under the lee of the seaward quay and she forged ahead more quickly, trying to get the brig out of the swirl of the tide. A few seconds more and the brig had a rope ashore forward, then another aft, and soon she was inside the pier and free from the dangerous currents of the river.

"They've got to look alive," Stewart informed her professionally, "when they're docking a ship at this state of the tide; a moment's hesitation or indecision and the tide would catch her and sweep her out on to the sandbank just outside the channel there."

As soon as the lines were ashore the tow-ropes were cast off and the tug fussily backed out to sea again ready for another job.

"That isn't fair," cried Susy, "they haven't put her in the locks yet! How will she manage?"

"Easy," said Stewart; "the crew will warp her along themselves. See, they're going round the capstan now," and steadily the little vessel crept up to where they were standing.

Susy's handkerchief was out, and she was waving it delightedly to the captain on the poop. Stewart was equally excited and was flourishing the top hat which he had donned in honour of the occasion.

"What sort of a trip, Captain Brady?" he bellowed expectantly.

"Not bad, not bad at all," the captain replied noncommittally, leaning over his taffrail. "Hullo there, young woman!" he called out, catching sight of Susy. "How've you been behaving?"

He'd forgotten all about Stewart and the trip. Susy was radiant, and the young man felt a quick stab of resentment as he saw how engrossed they became, Susy, laughing and joking, slowly kept pace with the brig's progress up the lock. Neither of them had a word for him now. He fretted visibly. All this irresponsible chatter when he was wanting to know about the cargo.

"Have you got the freight-money, Captain?" he interrupted.

The captain turned to look at him. "For goodness' sake let's get into port before we start on business," he said irritably, and went on gossiping with Susy.

"Can we come aboard?" called Stewart, seeing a gangplank put ashore.

"You'll have to wait till the doctors and customs have finished," one of the locksmen told him, "but you've plenty of time. We've got three more ships to get in before we lock her into the dock. It'll be all of an hour yet."

They saw the doctor clamber aboard, followed by the customs officer, and with a parting wave of his hand the captain went below to the saloon.

Susy said to Stewart eagerly, "Do you think I can go on board with you?"

"You'll never be able to climb over the ship's rail with those skirts on," he said grudgingly. That was the worst of women, couldn't realize that there was business to do, always wanting to gossip. So long as Susy remained, the chances of pinning Captain Brady down to business were small.

"Look here, Susy," he said persuasively, "the ship's in port now, but the captain and I have got a lot of work to do. There'll be plenty of time for you to see him later."

"Is it very important?"

"Very important," replied Stewart.

She was disappointed, Stewart could tell, but dammit all, he thought, there's a time and place for everything, and business comes first. He saw her disappear out of sight, and then more cheerfully turned to wait for the doctor to come on shore again.

After a few minutes three men appeared on deck again.

"All right, Mr. Stewart," the captain hailed him, "you can come aboard now," and like an agile monkey the young man slipped over the bulwark rail and hastened aft to seize the captain by the hand. This was as it should be done, he thought. This was how he'd seen countless owners welcoming back their captains, no mawkish sentiment involving women. There was a time and place for everything, and a woman's place was decidedly not on board ship.

"Where's Susy?" was Brady's first remark.

"Oh, I've sent her home," replied Stewart lightly. "We can't have women around when there's business to be done, you know."

"Susy wouldn't have been in the way," said Captain Brady disappointedly.

"You're not getting too fond of her, I hope, Captain?" said Stewart chaffingly, but with a note of enquiry in his voice.

"Fond of her? Of course I am. Like as if she were my own daughter. There's more to that girl than you think."

"I agree she's pretty enough," the young man said.

"Who's talking about looks?" growled the other. "It's character that counts. She's worth ten of that doll of Irish Higgins," he said challengingly.

"Each to his own choice," remarked Stewart casually, as though he had no interest at all in the subject under discussion. "But now, Captain, how did you manage for cargo?"

"Not a spare cubic foot of space anywhere."

"But you were a deeper draught when you sailed," Stewart pointed out.

The old captain looked at him pityingly. "What of it? This isn't an india-rubber ship, you know, and when the holds are full, that's good enough for me. I said I wouldn't be hanging around, and no more I have."

"You certainly haven't done that, Captain! Thirty-two days out and home is splendid. She must be a regular little flier."

"She's all that. A bit wet for'd, as I expected, but otherwise perfect. We've got a bargain here. She'll make your fortune yet," he said.

"How about the freight?" Stewart could keep the question down no longer. "Did they produce it at the other end all right?"

"Yes, no trouble at all. A bit of difficulty getting a homeward cargo, though. You see, they weren't expecting us. Still, it's all fixed up now. I let them know that we'd be calling regularly from now on; told them to have the cargo on the quay and we'd be there every sixth week to pick it up. Olive oil and wine, my boy," he said, looking pleased. "A hundred and fifty tons regular consignment."

This sounded very encouraging, but Stewart still felt uneasy about the apparent lightness of the returning brig.

"Now, Captain," he said apprehensively, "what have you got in those holds?"

"Let me see," said Brady, rummaging amongst a heap of papers. "There's barrels of wine and seventy-five tons of mixed fruit—principally prime oranges," he continued brightly; "never tasted better. Here, try one for yourself, you'll not find sweeter nor juicier ones anywhere in England at this time of year."

"Not now, Captain," said the young man testily. "Let's hear what else you've got first."

"I think that's about the lot," he said slowly. "Oh! there's about thirty tons of cork."

"Who on earth's that for?"

"That's for you to find, my boy!"

"Why, what do you mean, Captain?" the young man asked, puzzled. "It's consigned to someone, isn't it?"

"Not yet, it isn't," replied Captain Brady cheerfully. "In fact, all the cargo in the hold belongs to you and me. Since we arrived unexpectedly there was no freight on offer, and sooner than hang around looking, I spent the outward freight money on the goods you see on this manifest."

"Good heavens !" Stewart cried, aghast. "You mean there's no freight-money ?"

"Not till you get off ashore and get the cargo sold."

"But, Captain, thirty tons of cork ! I thought we were shipowners ?"

"Yes," said Captain Brady cheerfully, "and you'd better hurry up and find customers for those oranges. They've just about reached their prime ; a few days more and they'll be on the turn."

"And you're the one who lectured me about gambling," said Stewart reproachfully. "What would have happened if you'd had contrary winds on the voyage home ? Bang would have gone all that outward freight-money—in rotten oranges."

Captain Brady seemed to be enjoying some huge joke with himself.

"It was like this," he said, with a laugh. "When a farmer in Oporto offered me these seventy tons of oranges outright, I stepped outside and had a look at the weather. Then I stepped inside again and had a look at the oranges. 'Right, lad, I'll take them'—and here they are, all in tip-top condition. But if you'll take a tip from me, you'll go and get the fruit merchants down right away."

"Goodness knows how I'm going to get rid of thirty tons of cork, though," said Stewart, worried.

"Get the fruit off your hands first," said Brady complacently.

"I don't even know what you paid for the cargo. But never mind now. I'm off to get the wholesalers down. You'll have to enter the ship yourself, Captain. You can see I'll be too busy today to help you," and feeling that Captain Brady had played him a shabby trick, he hurried ashore and set off in search of the wholesale fruit merchants.

His partner's business acumen was sharper than Stewart had imagined as he realized when he saw the small dried-up oranges that were offered for sale on the fruit-stalls. Still, even if they managed to sell the consignment, Captain Brady had no right to hazard the takings of the outward voyage on this venture.

Stewart cheered up a little when he found that the wholesalers were plainly interested.

"I'm auctioning them off on the quayside tomorrow morning," said Stewart, as though he had been accustomed all his life to such business. "The cargo is open for inspection this afternoon in the warehouse at Salthouse Dock," and then he hurried back on board to get the discharge started.

He arrived just in time to prevent an angry dock official from leaving after waiting an hour on board to see either master or agent about the disposal of their cargo.

Stewart apologized profusely.

"Captain entered inward?" asked the official gruffly.

"Isn't he back?" said Stewart in surprise. "I ought to have done it myself. You know what old dodderers these sea-captains are—they're not used to the Board's efficiency yet."

"Will you be warehousing or hauling the stuff right away?" asked the Dock Board official, slightly mollified.

"We'll need the warehouse if you can accommodate us. I'll be using dock labour too."

"You know the charges?"

"Of course. Can we make a start, then?"

"I suppose it'll be all right," the other said doubtfully.

"I'll accept full responsibility if anything is wrong," said Stewart placatingly.

"Agent?" queried the official.

"Owner," said Stewart, in what he hoped was a casual voice. Then he got his first real thrill at the change in the other's attitude.

"In that case, sir, I'll give the dockers the word to go ahead. Sign here, please. If you have any complaints, sir, I trust you'll let us know. We aim to satisfy owners."

"That's what I like to hear. The new Board is certainly justifying its existence."

"The cheapest and most efficient port in England, sir, that's what we aim to make of Liverpool"

"Do that, and I'll bring all my ships here," said Stewart magnanimously. "I'm sorry the captain hasn't got the hatches off for you."

"No trouble at all, sir. The dockers will have them off in no time."

"Care for one?" Stewart inclined his head towards the saloon.

"Don't mind if I do, sir. I'll get the men started and then join you, if I may."

The young man walked leisurely aft. Yes, tact paid; keep everyone sweet and good-tempered; besides, he wanted the crates of oranges spaced about the warehouse floor so that they could be easily sighted.

"I don't suppose there's any chance of stopping pilfering?" he asked casually, after having plied the official with a brimming glass of the captain's best rum.

"We're pretty good as a rule, sir."

"If you care for a couple of bottles of the best . . . I could draw them off for you," Stewart offered.

The official was properly horrified. "No, thank you, sir, it would be more than my job's worth."

"No offence, I hope?" remarked Stewart blandly.

"None at all, sir; but you can rely on me. I'll see the brig has a good turn-out."

"Thank you indeed . . . but here's the captain himself."

Town Hall, Liverpool

"I'm glad to see you've lost no time in getting started, Mr. Stewart," said Brady, as he came into the saloon mopping his brow.

"You don't know Mr. Johnson of the Dock Board, do you, Captain? I've just taken the liberty of dispensing your hospitality. Mr. Johnson has been very considerate towards us."

"Quite right," backed up the old man. "I'm proud to make your acquaintance, sir." They bowed formally.

"I see you're down for this berth till the 15th, Captain."

"That's our next sailing-date," interposed Stewart. "You'll not want us to move?" he asked, thinking of the expense.

"I think it might be arranged," replied Mr. Johnson, with a smile. It was pleasant to do business with such a gentlemanly young fellow.

When he had gone, Stewart turned to the old man. "There you are, Captain, I've got the high and mighty Dock Board eating out of my hand."

"Hm! you seem in a better frame of mind than you were a couple of hours ago. I suppose you've found a customer for these oranges?"

"I've got some buyers coming down this afternoon," said Stewart cautiously; "but I haven't had time to do anything about the wine, and as for the cork, I still haven't the faintest idea who might be interested in it."

"What about the shipbuilders, Royden, Evans, Potter, even Laird? Or you might try Jimmy Beck, the ships' furnishers, or old John Nicholson, the rigger—they all use cork, you know."

"But thirty tons, Captain!" complained Stewart.

"What do you want me to do—go and sell it for you? I could get rid of it in the twinkling of an eye!" The captain glared challengingly at the young man. These young folks wanted everything handed to them on a silver platter.

"Not at all," Stewart replied, "that's my end of the business and I'll deal with it . . . even if you have dumped it on me unexpectedly. Now about the accounts for the cargo. We've got to get that settled before we sell it. What did you pick up in freight in Portugal, and what did you spend on cargo?"

Captain Brady gave him a strange look, and then laughed surprisingly. "The freight picked up in Lisbon," he said slowly and distinctly, "was £150, and the cargo they're breaking out now, part shipped at Oporto and Santander, cost me £512."

"What!" gasped Stewart, standing up, agitated. "£512! Phew!" He looked at the old man as though he had taken leave of his senses. But there was no doubt about it. A second glance at Captain Brady's smug, unruffled features confirmed that he had heard aright. The young man sat down slowly again, and after a while he asked in a small voice, "But where did the extra £362 come from?"

"Well, now," said Brady, looking as pleased at punch, "you see the point of stowing a bit of spare cash below your bunkboard?"

"You mean that you paid the difference yourself?"

"How else do you think it was bought?" Brady was enjoying himself. "I paid £362 out of Brady's Bank, Unlimited," he said jocularly; "and mind you, Mr. Stewart, I want it all back plus five per cent interest."

Stewart, striving to keep a hold of the situation, managed to ask fearfully, "And how much do you think the cargo is actually worth?"

Captain Brady stretched himself luxuriously. "A keen young fellow that knows his job should get as near £1000 for it as makes no matter," he said lightly.

Stewart looked at him helplessly.

"It's the cheapest consignment of oranges that's arrived in Liverpool for years," the old man continued. "It's a good job I was on the spot to snap them up. You should pick up £700 on the oranges alone," and Stewart gaped at his confidence; "and as for the wine, it's not very good stuff, but it'll sell. If you're still worried about the cork, why! you might even give it away. I only shipped it for dunnage purposes."

His young partner had nothing to say, he could only sit and stare in amazement; so the older man went on, "Now I want to see you with £1000 in your hands before I clear inwards, and then I'll be satisfied with the voyage," and he relaxed into his chair and gazed calmly at the deckhead.

Stewart finally got a pencil fixed firmly in his hand. The old boy was talking as though £1000 was chicken feed. He began to jot down the expenses for the voyage, his most pressing concern being to learn the worst.

Captain and crew's wages..	..	..	..	..	£60
Port and harbour dues, Lisbon, Oporto, Santander				..	£40
Insurance and depreciation	..	..	..	..	£40
Captain's disbursements abroad ..		..	..	..	£10

"Was there anything else, Captain?"

The shipmaster reached across the table and looked serenely at the figures on the bit of paper. "You've missed out pilotage and towage, as well as Liverpool port and light dues," he said scornfully.

"I don't know the Liverpool charges yet," said Stewart; "and surely, Captain, you didn't take pilots and tugs abroad!"

The old man looked at him in disgust. "You don't think I'm going careering about in places like Oporto without a pilot or a tug, do you? Why, yon's one of the wickedest ports I know of. I'd have looked well trying to tow that brig in with my own long boat. In yon place the

Freshetts come roaring up on you without warning, and the next minute you're high and dry on some sandbank with never a hope of getting off."

"The Freshetts?"

"Aye," said the captain pityingly, "a kind of tidal bore that comes racing up the river. It's local knowledge you want in a place like Oporto, and I haven't got it, see! That's why I took a pilot and tug. Now, any more questions?" he asked fiercely.

"No, no," Stewart replied hastily.

"Well, then," said the captain, mollified. "If we're going to stay on this berth for twelve days, I reckon what with pilotage, tugs and light dues it'll all come to about £50, so put that down."

Stewart, strangely subdued, did as he was bid, thus bringing the voyage expenses to £200. The captain looked at the amount silently, and then said, "Now add £382, that being the cost of the present cargo over and above the receipts to hand."

"You mean £362, Captain," Stewart ventured to correct.

"Oh! I do, do I? And what about my five per cent. interest?"

Stewart sighed heavily and wrote down £382. Captain Brady apparently had his own way of keeping accounts.

"There you are then, Captain. We've spent £582, and all we've got to show for it is seventy-five tons of oranges, thirty tons of cork (God help us!) and 500 hogsheads of wine."

"And a very nice little lot too," said the captain complacently; "we should clear £500 net profit. How's that for business, my boy?"

But Stewart was unable to share the shipmaster's enthusiasm. "Let's stick to shipowning, Captain," was all he could say.

"Just as you like," said Brady, disappointed at this reaction. "But what's happened to you? I thought this was the sort of thing you fancied?"

"It's not what's happened to me, but what's happened to you, Captain," Stewart complained bitterly. "When you left a month ago, you lectured me on being too smart, and yet—here you are!" he ended up helplessly.

Brady laughed. He was well satisfied. He'd proved that the old 'uns were equal to the young 'uns. "Very well," he said, "if you feel like that, we'll stick to shipowning. Anyway, I don't suppose I'll ever get another chance of snapping up a cargo such as that again."

"Meanwhile," said Stewart gloomily, "I've got to raise £600 on what you have brought. What price should we ask for the oranges and the wine?"

"Nay, lad, that's your job. I'm only a master mariner, I know nothing about business, that's for you to work out." And that was all Stewart could get out of him.

The mainyard was creaking and groaning as the stevedores whipped the cargo ashore. "This 'ere's a back-aching job, mister," whined one of the lumpers.

"You're getting paid for it, aren't you?" Stewart answered curtly enough.

"Sixpence an hour, mister, I asks yer!" growled the labourer indignantly "what's that to keep a wife and ten kids on?" But Stewart's back represented only an indifferent interest. "I bet 'e 'as 'is wittels all right," muttered the lumper to his mate, but Stewart was peering down the holds, he wasn't concerned with the dockers' troubles.

The hold presented a chaotic scene, unintelligible to him, but he supposed it was all right. Perhaps he'd be better able to judge if he saw the cargo in the warehouse. He passed over the gangway, and just as he set foot on to the quay there was an almighty crash. Startled, he turned round and saw two crates of oranges lying smashed to smithereens, with oranges rolling everywhere. The stevedores were looking down, smiling triumphantly.

Stewart was horror-stricken. That was sheer wanton damage. But where was the foreman? He found him inside the warehouse. "Couldn't 'elp it, sir," he said, "accidents will happen. If you've got anything in the bottle it might encourage 'em to go a bit careful."

"I'll tell the steward to give you a bottle of rum," Stewart promised hastily, thinking fearfully of the casks of wine yet to be discharged. The Dock Board might be efficient, but they should pay their stevedores more. Sixpence an hour!

In the warehouse the crates of oranges were being spaced out carefully, and already several buyers had arrived to look them over. "How many crates?" someone asked.

"About 1400," Stewart replied. "What do you think of them? Not bad, eh!"

"You'll be lucky if you get ten bob a crate," said one of the buyers pessimistically, and the others standing by all agreed.

Ten shillings a case! For fully a minute Stewart didn't grasp the full significance, then he stopped and put out a hand to steady himself. That was a fortune! So Captain Brady had been right after all. The buyers were looking at him curiously, and seeing their glances he pulled himself together quickly. "I'm not giving them away, you know," he said, with a fair attempt at jocularity.

A fellow in a low-crowned beaver hat sidled up to him and whispered, "I'll give you 12s. 6d. a piece, mister, for the 1400 cases and, what is more, I'll pay all landing charges."

"Done!" said Stewart in a flash, and then, turning to the rest of the crowd, he called out: "The sale is off, gentlemen. The cargo has been disposed of by private arrangement." The buyers all swarmed round him angrily, and he began to regret having accepted the offer. It looked as though he might have got 15s. a case if he had sold them by auction; but it was too late now, he had given his word and the deal was made.

He dashed aboard, eager to break the news to Brady. "I've got rid of the oranges, Captain!" he shouted joyfully.

"How much?"

"Eight hundred and seventy pounds," said Stewart, doing a lightning calculation.

"Not bad. Feeling a bit better now?"

"I'm off to see the Customs about the wine," said Stewart energetically. "It will pay us to keep it on board until we find a customer, and the Customs may let us do that."

"Far better get rid of it right away," advised Brady. "Until it's stowed under bond I can't clear the ship inwards, you know."

"If we keep it on board it will save us high bonded warehouse charges."

"I'd sooner it was ashore; but have you tried to sell it?"

"Good heavens, Captain! give me a chance. I've only just managed the oranges."

"I'll tell you what," said the captain thoughtfully, "we might ask Susy, since she's in that line of business."

Stewart looked at him hesitantly. "I've been meaning to speak to you about Susy, Captain. I think you ought to be a bit careful there."

"Why! what's all this?" asked Brady, mystified.

"She's left Higgins' place and got a house of her own now!" Stewart said darkly.

"Well, what of it?"

"Where did she get the money from?" Stewart asked significantly.

"You're not suggesting . . ." began Brady, pretending to look shocked, though there was a twinkle in his eye which the other didn't see.

"I'm not suggesting anything," said Stewart righteously, "but the fact is that she's set up a tavern under her own name. I've warned her, but what do you think I got for my pains?"

"Aye, she's an independent young woman," the captain sympathized, careful to keep his face averted, "but what can I do about it?"

"A dockside tavern is no place for a decent young woman. You must speak to her about it, Captain; she seems to take some notice of what you say."

"You seem to be uncommonly concerned about her," said Brady mischievously.

"No more than I am about any other respectable girl," denied Stewart. "Susy may be a bit lively, but she's a good girl," he said solemnly.

"How do you know that?" the captain asked brazenly.

"Why, I know she is," he asserted lamely.

"And you think she's out of place in the Dock Road?"

"Of course I do. She's got some sort of a notion of relying on good liquor, food and honesty to bring her trade. Just fancy!—in the Dock Road, with every other public-house crowding its doors with trollops and no one paying any attention to the liquor so long as it makes them drunk. She doesn't stand an earthly chance."

"I don't know that her idea is so bad," said Captain Brady meditatively; "with everyone out to rob the sailor, a place such as she has in mind might become popular."

"It'll be a forlorn hope, Captain. It'll take more than one woman to clean up the Dock Road."

"Well, I'll see what I can do," promised Captain Brady thoughtfully. The young fellow was right. The Dock Road was no place for a woman on her own; he saw it now.

"I hope you don't mind my telling you all this," said Stewart apologetically.

"I wish you'd marry the girl and have done with it," the old man said crossly.

"Why, Captain, whatever put such a thought into your head?" said Stewart, astonished.

Brady looked across at him irritably.

"Why can't you make your mind up one way or t'other?" he asked.

"You're mistaken, Captain," Stewart replied coldly. "I like the girl—indeed, who doesn't?—but as for marrying her, I've never even thought of it. I hope some day," he went on, "to persuade Miss Scripps to be my wife."

Brady gave a snort of disgust. "Then what the devil are you worrying about Susy for?" he bellowed.

The young man did not deign to reply.

"You'll regret the day you ever married Higgins' niece," the old man went on angrily; "but if I know anything of the Higgins' blood, she'll never marry you until you've a lot more than two pennies to rub together."

Stewart flushed, that remark touched him on the raw, but he still refused to bandy Miss Scripps' name with Susy's.

"I suppose you think you're too good for Susy?" said the old man bitterly.

"After all, she's only a barmaid," said Stewart.

Brady looked at him curiously, a trifle sadly. "You've got a long way to go, my lad. Position isn't everything, it's character that counts."

"Oh, the girl's all right," condescended Stewart. "She can't help her parents or her upbringing—but there it is."

"I didn't know her parents were still alive," said Brady curiously.

"There's a drunken old slut of a mother somewhere up in Pitt Street," the young man replied.

Captain Brady spat expressively into the beautifully polished cuspidor. "Pshaw!" he exclaimed, "you almost make me sick. I suppose your parents were beyond reproach?"

The young man stiffened instantly. "My parents are dead, sir, and I'd be obliged if you'd keep their names out of this conversation."

The older man seemed to regret his words as soon as they were spoken. "Ah, well, we mustn't quarrel. I'll go and see what I can do about Susy, and if I were you"—a humorous glint came into his eyes—"I'd try and find a buyer for that cork!"

Stewart's remarks about Susy's mother had set Brady wondering, but first of all there was this question of Susy and the Dock Road to be considered. He went ashore to see how she was faring.

Susy hailed him with cries of affection when he ambled into the private bar. He looked round appreciatively. Everything was spick and span, beautifully clean, just as he'd imagined it would be, but there were woefully few customers about.

"Trade seems a bit slack," he observed casually.

"Yes," she said apologetically. "I'm not properly established yet, but they'll come in time. There's no women, you see, and that takes a bit of getting used to in the Dock Road."

"What's the exact position, lass?" asked Brady sympathetically.

She looked at him doubtfully. "I'm afraid we're living very much from hand to mouth—in fact, we're only selling just enough to cover our expenses."

"Well, so long as you're doing that it's not so bad."

"Yes, but I haven't been able to introduce any of the improvements that I'd have liked—unless," she added, with a laugh, "getting rid of the trollops might be called an improvement."

"H'm!" said Brady reflectively. "Do you think you've bitten off more than you can chew?"

"Oh, no!" she said, but not quite so confidently. "Takes a little time to get going, that's all."

"You know, Susy, I think you deserve something better than this."

"Are you very disappointed in me?" she asked sadly.

"No, lass, it's not that. It's only that I don't like to see you down in this part of the town."

"I've got along so far without any trouble," she said, slightly puzzled.

"Aye, I know you have, but wouldn't you be happier and more comfortable in a proper hotel in a decent district?"

"Of course I would," she said. "I've lost all my illusions about the Dock Road, but what you suggest would take money, and where am I going to get it from? People like you don't grow on trees." She gave him a happy, affectionate smile.

"I'll put up the money for you," he said ; "but remember, it must be a proper hotel. I won't have people calling you just a barmaid."

"I'm not ashamed of being a barmaid," she said frankly. "I've been honest and respectable, and you can't say more than that in any business."

"All the same," Captain Brady persisted, "I'd like to see you getting on in a better way, even if it's only to give young Stewart a smack in the eye."

"Oh, it's that way, is it ?" laughed Susy understandingly.

She thought for a moment, and then said : "If I move I'd like to get right away from Liverpool. In fact, I'd like to go to Blackpool. There's lots of money to be made there, what with trippers and Wakes and folks going to the seaside for their holidays."

"Money, money !" laughed Brady. "What's the matter with you young people ? Is it the only god you worship ?"

"There's nowt like a bit o' brass," said Susy happily, lapsing into dialect.

"But Blackpool," said Brady. "I've never heard of it."

"Nor have a lot of other people," said Susy, "but they'll hear plenty about it in the next few years. Hotels, as you like to call them, ought to be cheap too. But what about this place ?" she asked suddenly. "Perhaps we won't get what we paid for it."

"I don't mind if I drop £50 on it," said Captain Brady, who liked the Blackpool idea the more he thought about it.

And that was how Susy came to leave the Dock Road and take up residence in Blackpool.

CHAPTER 16

FINDING OUT ABOUT SUSY

STEWART, ignorant of these happenings, worked energetically, and within three days the *Mary Jane's* entire cargo was disposed of for £1257. A boat-builder had been induced to offer £35 for the cork, which was now badly crumbled. Luckily, it was just the thing he wanted for the construction of lifeboats for the three new liners of the National Steam Navigation Company.

As soon as the cargo had been dealt with, the new consignment began to arrive and was piled up in a corner of the warehouse. Stewart had to get the Jerque Note himself, for Captain Brady seemed to have disappeared completely. The last time Stewart had seen him was the day after the brig arrived in port, and the old captain had made it quite clear that he was leaving all the work to Stewart, and he had departed in high spirits, carrying one of the new Gladstone bags in his hand.

"The mate will tell you anything you want to know," he had called out from the quayside, and that was well over a week ago. No one knew where he had gone.

On the whole, Stewart preferred it like that, it left him free and un-hampered to attend to all the necessary business.

After the inward cargo had been discharged and the ship rum-maged, Stewart had started to chase up the new consignment, and he spent most of his time between the brig and the shippers, fretting at their delay in getting the cargo down to the docks. For a week the goods just dribbled into the warehouse, and one good sling a day would have seen them aboard. Then, two days before the advertised date for sailing, the cargo began to pour into the shed.

"It's always like this," said the foreman stevedore. "They've had nearly a fortnight to get their stuff down, but no, they read the sailing-date in the *Albion* and think the day before will do!" He wiped the sweat off his brow with his hand. "Some day they'll have to pay extra time after five o'clock, and perhaps that'll smarten their ideas up a bit."

But where was Captain Brady? Here they were, due to sail in forty-eight hours' time and still no sign of him. Stewart began to get anxious. There were quite a number of bills awaiting their joint signatures, there was the crew to sign on and a host of other problems requiring the captain's attention. Perhaps he was staying with Susy, and hopefully Stewart tramped down to the Dock Road to look for his erring skipper.

Susy had vanished as well, and the lettering over the door showed the name of a fresh licensee. Stewart was worried, and went inside to make inquiries, but the change had been complete and the staff were all new. No one knew what had happened to the former tenant.

To Stewart's fearful imagination this abrupt departure seemed mysterious and sinister, but although he pondered over the reason for Susy's disappearance he never thought to connect her with Captain Brady's absence.

However, the day before sailing, Captain Brady turned up again, looking smug and complacent to Stewart's aggrieved eyes.

"Got the hatches on, my boy?" said the captain breezily.

"No, I haven't," said Stewart shortly; "there's only half the cargo down, if you really want to know."

"Bless my soul!" said the old man, raising his eyebrows. "Whatever have you been doing?"

Stewart felt that really was the limit. Here he had been running about and working like a slave, and then to be asked what he'd been doing! There was no justice in the world! He choked back the angry words which threatened to master him and managed to reply quietly:

"There's a whole lot of business to see to, Captain. We'd better get off to the Custom House and then we can come back and go through those bills quietly."

So, slowly and sedately, in conformity with Captain Brady's newly acquired imperturbability, they set about visiting the various offices where the captain's presence was needed.

Back again in Chapel Walk, Stewart produced the accounts for the previous voyage. The sale of the cargo, he explained, showing the various credit notes, had realized the sum of £1257, and the tentative voyage expenses up to the time of clearing ready for loading were £715. These figures cheered him up and gave him confidence to tell the captain that he wanted to draw £100 on his own account from the profits of the voyage. The old man never asked him why, but readily agreed, and appeared to be in a most magnanimous humour. This necessity for signing each other's drafts, he suggested, might be abolished. Besides, the young man had to live somehow. Captain Brady proposed that the entire £716 should be paid into the bank and Stewart be at liberty to draw on it as he wished.

"We might as well start as we mean to go on," he said; "if we can't trust each other with the cash, we'd better find out now."

"That's the talk, Captain," Stewart agreed enthusiastically, wondering what had come over the old man.

This arrangement made the financial affairs of Stewart and Brady, as far as they themselves were concerned, much more elastic and convenient, though Stewart promised that he would keep careful and accurate accounts.

In spite of the young man's misgivings, the cargo was shipped and battened down some hours before the brig was due to sail, and so there was no delay in the *Mary Jane's* departure on her second voyage.

Susy was down on the Pier Head to see the brig off. Stewart greeted her with a mixture of surprise and suspicion. As they waited for the *Mary Jane* to enter the lock, they walked up and down, chatting fairly amicably, although Stewart's efforts to find out what she was now doing were fobbed off so obviously that a greater mystery than ever seemed to surround her movements.

It had been the same with Captain Brady. Every time Stewart referred to Susy he found that the conversation was turned neatly but firmly to some other subject.

Before he could ponder for any length of time on this double mystery, the inner lock-gates opened and the brig, along with several others, entered from the dock. The matter was forgotten in his pride of ownership.

It was sailing time, and on the quayside several more owners were casually pacing up and down. Stewart watched them covertly, studying their actions, and would have given a good deal for them to have spoken to him; to have raised their hats in recognition of mutual interests. But no, they chattered and laughed amongst themselves, apparently unaware that close beside them stood another shipowner whose activities they would do well to watch.

The river lock-gates opened, there was a sudden fierce tooting of tugs' whistles, the pantomime of the piermasters, and the hurried scrambling throwing-off of mooring-ropes from the shore bollards. A few minutes later a final flourish of Captain Brady's hand from the poop and the brig was out in the river, gliding easily in the wake of the tug. Stewart could see the men swarming into the rigging and the sails loosening on the yards all ready for the order from aft.

When he turned round Susy was gone. He was sorry, for he had anticipated taking her into Mother Simpson's and there attempting to find a solution of the mystery. Ah well, it would wait. She'd turn up again later on, and feeling smugly self-satisfied he went home.

There were many things to be seen to, there were a few papers to be filed, and lastly, there was Miss Scripps to think about.

In the bustle of the last fortnight he had had no chance to see her. Even the habit of Sunday church-going had had to stand aside while the *Mary Jane* was in port, and there had been nothing done to heal the breach which had sprung so violently open the last time they'd met. It made him unhappy to think of the misunderstandings which always seemed to crop up when they were together. Perhaps, he thought hopefully, she'd be more amenable if he were to go and apologize for his behaviour. For all the misery of his past recollections, he yet longed to be near her, hoping for a sympathetic word or glance. The fact was, of course, that Miss Scripps was rapidly tiring of him, yet, woman-like, did not see fit to cut him completely adrift. There had been something amusing and perhaps adventurous in that first acquaintanceship, but now it had become less interesting as she realized how impecunious he was. At first there had been something likable in his *gaucheries*, but that feeling had long since gone. His friends, too, were the most disgusting people—that horrid drunken reporter, that dreadful servant Silas and that loose young woman Susy. True, he went to church, but his attitude towards Mr. Puddicombe had made her blush for him at times. The whole affair was preposterous, but she had been flattered by the attentions of a young man who so obviously thought he was going to get on. Even now she was not too sure that one day he would not do all he said he would do, and it was that thought at the back of her mind that prevented her from sending him about his business once and for all.

So things progressed in the immediate weeks following the departure of the *Mary Jane*. As Miss Scripps realized that there was no hope of an early improvement in Stewart's financial position, her attitude became cooler and cooler, and at last it began to dawn even on the young man that the affection between them was very much one-sided. The final realization came one Sunday, when she refused the offer of his company on her homeward walk, and told him that she was going out to lunch with some friends at Wallasey, then, shortly afterwards, he'd seen her walking slowly down Prince's Parade on the arm of Mr. Puddicombe. Stewart followed them jealously to the bottom of Dale Street before he was convinced that her tale about going out to lunch had been merely an excuse to avoid his company. Miserably he turned back home, a prey to violent self-pity, and he sat down brooding, long and gloomily, as to why he should be treated in this fashion. If only he could make sufficient money, he felt sure that all would be well again; but between the business of shipowning, as defined by Mr. Eastwood, and his need to appear successful in Miss Scripps' eyes, there was a wide difference.

In vain he racked his brains in search of some scheme that would satisfy both, and he was still pondering over these worries as he stood on the landing-stage to watch the *Alabama* put to sea on her trials.

The thought might not have occurred to him even then had not the next day's papers been full of the story of how the privateer, under cover of 'trials', had eluded the authorities and vanished from the Mersey to become a prey upon the merchant ships of the Northern Federal States.

As Stewart read the account something stirred within him. He recalled the captain of the *Uriah B. Heap* and his story of the immense fortune amassed in a single running of the blockade. He remembered Captain Perry and his information about the blockade itself. "You want a fast ship," he had said, "to slip past the Yankee patrols at night."

The *Mary Jane* was a 'flier'. The prize was great; he let the newspaper fall to the floor unheeded. Here was a chance to make enough money in a single voyage to enable them to buy two more ships!

The thought was dazzling. The project would establish them amongst Liverpool shipowners, but it was the realization that success in the venture would finally bring Miss Scripps to him that decided Stewart to send the *Mary Jane* blockade-running.

For the moment he had forgotten Captain Brady, but before long the imponderable figure of the old man began to loom disapprovingly over all his plans. There seemed little hope of convincing the conservative old sea captain of the necessity for taking the *Mary Jane* on a blockade-running voyage. Yet there was a way. Susy could do it, if only Stewart could persuade her to help him. But where was she? No one seemed to know.

Anxiously, energetically, Stewart pursued his inquiries; but she had not been seen about for the past few weeks. Irritably he thought that it was just like her to stand between the success and failure of his scheme by disappearing at this stage.

Stewart sought Captain Evans Rees of the 'Pig and Whistle', but he had heard nothing of her, and after the way she had treated him he was not particularly interested. A girl with morals such as hers had no right to be in the trade, he had said sourly. As an afterthought, though, Captain Rees suggested that she might have joined the Band of Friends again!

Stewart was almost despairing when he caught sight of Sam Sharp. The very man! If anyone knew of Susy's whereabouts it would be Sam. Stewart approached the reporter tactfully. "How's the book progressing, Sam?" he asked.

The other looked at him in surprise. "Book, what book?"

"Why the book you were going to write to re-establish British literature; the book you were telling Mr. Gray and me about the other evening."

"Oh, that," said the reporter calmly. "I've got it all sketched out in my head. Sit down and I'll outline the first few chapters."

"I'd be glad to," said Stewart regretfully, "but just now I'm in a hurry and only popped in to see if you know what's happened to Susy. She's not been around for a month now and I really must see her."

The reporter cocked a significant eye. "You sound as if you're in a hurry. Don't tell me you've made up your mind to make her an offer?"

Stewart gave a noncommittal laugh, and the reporter, taking it for an admission, beamed all over his face.

"Why, this calls for a celebration," he said hopefully.

"Don't take me up wrong, Sam," said Stewart sharply. "I have an important question to ask her, but it's not——"

"I know, I know," interrupted Sharp, "the young woman's got to reply first, eh? Well, if that's the case I'll be delighted to assist. More than likely she's staying along with that female who calls herself her mother; but come along with me, we'll ask the landlord, he'll tell us where she lives. You leave it to me. If Susy's not there I'll soon find out where she's got to."

Stewart tried to explain, but the reporter cut him short and there was no further opportunity to clear up the position. As a matter of fact the misunderstanding rather suited Stewart's purpose, especially if it meant that Sam Sharp was willing to leave his beloved cups for an hour or two. Lightly he told himself that it would be easy to explain things to Sam later; meanwhile, it was essential that he should see Susy and get the promise of her help before Captain Brady returned.

A little later they wandered slowly up Pitt Street. The narrow roadway was hemmed in by a monotonous row of houses—grim, decrepit and dirty. Hordes of screaming, filthy children played in the gutter, whilst on the low doorsteps frowsy women squatted gossiping. The younger women were mostly suckling infants with their sagging breasts protruding unashamedly, whilst the older ones, grey-haired and scraggy, clothed in indescribable rags, sat smoking black, stubbly clay pipes. The scene was one of the deepest squalor, and Stewart paled at the thought of so much poverty and misery.

"What's the matter?" queried the reporter, looking at his face. "You aren't squeamish, are you?"

"It's always been dark when I've had to come this way before."

"Ah!" said the reporter, nodding his head, "you miss the beauty at night. Still, perhaps it's the best time to visit these parts. It may be more noisy when the drunks get home, but it's only noise then. This other," he waved his hand towards the garbage in the gutter and the slatternly women, "is out of sight."

They walked along in silence for a little way, both busy with their thoughts, but Sam Sharp was carrying too much liquor to be silent for long.

"Nightfall," he said dramatically, "is like a drug in these parts, the squalor, the dirt, the whining brats give way to the beautiful yellow rays of the street-lamps—to liquor and the only romance these poor devils know. Nightfall brings them relief from the hard, remorseless light of day—but lo! What is this?" He broke off his discourse suddenly to stop outside a tumbledown public-house. "See that notice there! 'Drunk for a penny, a blind for twopence.' This looks good to me. Shall we test the veracity of the publican?"

"Oh, come along, Sam," Stewart said impatiently. "Let's get out of this place. If Susy lives here, God help her!"

"As I was saying," went on his companion, catching up again, "nightfall to these poor creatures is nature's beauty. 'Drunk for a penny, a blind for twopence,' " he repeated, "and I suppose a gracious landlord throws the straw in as well. Can you wonder that every young woman you see nurses a suckling infant at her breast? Yet the doctors say that the young 'uns die off like flies. Aye, I reckon there's more bugs than babies in Pitt Street."

"What a life!" commented the young man.

Sam Sharp looked at him sardonically. "The greatest era in British history is now being played, and we may count ourselves fortunate in being among the players . . . I wrote that for this morning's editorial." He laughed bitterly and then continued: "Commerce and industry! What remarkable benefits they have bestowed on these islands of ours! That was in, too. 'Drunk for a penny, a blind for twopence.' You know, there's something I like about that advertisement."

Stewart looked at him puzzled. This was a Sam Sharp he had never before encountered. "It all sounds a lot of nonsense to me," he said irritably.

"So it is," said the reporter; "don't you see, the whole world is a lot of nonsense. Commercial prosperity and the foundation of an Empire on the one hand, and these poor devils on the other."

"You're wasting your sympathy," said the young man coldly. "They live here because they want to, because they're too shiftless to think of anything better."

The old reporter looked at him curiously. "It may be as you say, and yet sympathy costs nothing—even you might spare a little at that price! I'm afraid you're a hard young man, Mr. Stewart," and he shook his head pityingly.

"It's not a question of being hard," Stewart said cuttingly, "but of being soft. I don't mind admitting I mean to get on, and I haven't sympathy to waste on folks who won't help themselves."

The reporter shook his head gloomily. "That's true," he said, "the world is so busy getting on, that it has no time for those who don't. You either get on—or—well, I suppose there's a Pitt Street in every town. 'Drunk for a penny, a blind for twopence'—dammit, it sounds attractive. Why have I been going in fear and trembling of Charlie Tomkins all these years? The future is rosy. Pitt Street, I hear thee calling me!"

"Don't be a fool, Sam," said Stewart, disturbed in spite of himself at the half-serious tone of the reporter's words. "How much farther do we have to go?"

"No. 54 court, no. 4 alley, no. 3 house! There's an address for you, my boy! Far better than plain Duke Street or Gambier Terrace."

"How do you come to know it so well?"

"Ah! that's another story. It goes back to the days when the *Shipping Albion* was a little unknown news-sheet, striving to exist without the support of yours truly. I was commissioned by a gentleman to write a series of pamphlets on the Corn Laws, and what better hunting-ground could there be than Pitt Street ? That was how I ran across Susy's so-called mother, but she hadn't any children then."

"What do you mean, so-called mother ?"

"Figure it out for yourself. I first met the woman in 1845 and she had no children then. How old is Susy ?"

"Why, I think she said she was twenty-one."

"That means she was born in 1841. Well, I took down Belle Watkins' testimony in 1845, and as I was saying, she had no children, at least none that were living. I made a capital story out of that."

"Who is Susy, then ?" asked Stewart, perplexed.

"I don't know, my boy. As a matter of fact, I've never given it much thought before ; but leave it to me, I'll find out this afternoon."

At last they came to a narrow, dark tunnel with the number 54 printed over the entry.

"Here we are," said Sharp, and Stewart followed him silently into the sombre gloom.

They walked perhaps twenty yards before the tunnel gave way to a dreary courtyard off which ran numerous other entries.

"No. 4 alley," said Sharp. "Here it is," and on they went, pushing their way past screeching children to emerge in a smaller courtyard with three house doors on each side.

"It's all like a rabbit-warren," said Stewart.

"No. 3 house," said Sharp, and Stewart grimly noticed the broken windows and the foetid mud of the courtyard.

"Belle Watkins live here ?" bawled the reporter loudly.

"There's some fancy gents to see you, Ma," called out a neighbour, and the rest of the inhabitants of No. 4 court gathered round them curiously.

The door of No. 3 opened and an old woman with a shawl over her head came hobbling out. Sam Sharp took charge of the situation.

"Belle Watkins," he said in his most impressive voice, "we have some private business with you."

The old woman peered at him fearfully.

"I ain't done nothing wrong, mister," she whimpered.

"That's all right, mother," said Sharp soothingly, "we're not from the police. We've only come to find out the whereabouts of a young woman who calls herself Susy Watkins, believed to be your daughter. But let's go inside," and pushing past her, he stepped into the living-room, with Stewart close at his heels.

"I allus knew she would come to a bad end, mister, with 'er 'igh and mighty ways. What's she done ?" and she followed them eagerly inside, shutting the door on the buzzing, excited throng of neighbours.

"She's not done anything," said Stewart exasperated. "It's just that she's been missing for three weeks and we want to find out where she's gone."

"Please, Mr. Stewart," said the reporter, "I thought you agreed to leave this to me."

The young man relapsed into silence, the sordidness of the room beginning to oppress him.

"Now," said Sharp, turning pompously to the old woman, "where is she? It will be to your advantage to give us all the information you can."

"So 'elp me, mister. I ain't seen 'er for nigh on six months. A fine way for a girl to treat 'er old mother."

"Do you mean to tell me that you haven't heard from her recently?"

"Well, I gets me five shillings a week from 'er regler, and that's all I know."

The reporter looked at her calmly. "In that case I think you had better come with us to the police!" The one word, 'police' seemed to have the desired effect and the old woman cowered back.

"A fine thing for an old woman like me to get mixed up with the police," she moaned, frightened.

"Pooh! it won't be the first time," said the reporter, "but it looks as though you've forgotten me, Mrs. Watkins. Seventeen years is a long time, but I remember the police were pretty interested in you then."

A look of dread came into her eyes. "I don't know what you mean, mister," she mumbled.

The reporter gave Stewart a triumphant look, then, turning to Belle again, he said reminiscently, "I seem to remember a Bow Street runner who was anxious for news of a gang of baby-snatchers! But you wouldn't know anything about that, would you, Belle? You ought to remember me though. Seventeen years isn't a lifetime, and I used to pride myself in those days that women didn't forget my face!"

"Honest to God, mister, I never 'ad nothink to do with the snatchings," burst out the terrified woman.

"How did you acquire Susy, then?"

"She's me own child, sir."

Sam Sharp looked at her sorrowfully. "You remember the Corn Riots," he said significantly.

The old woman looked at him beseechingly. "It wasn't our fault, mister," she said, turning to the more sympathetic Stewart. "We were driven on to them riots by some gent writing and making speeches. We didn't know no better." Suddenly she stopped and turned back to the reporter.

"Now I know who you are, you devil!" she said. "It was you with your silvery tongue that drove us to it. It was you wot got my man transported to Australia, and might 'ave 'ad 'im 'ung for all you care!"

"Nonsense, my good woman," said Sharp urbanely. "The riots were the outcome of national discontent at the oppressive measures of the Government. That you and your husband were unfortunate to be apprehended in the act of taking food from a shop damaged in the riots has my hearty commiseration. But you remember my advice to you all was action without violence. Still, there's two things you might clear up for me. Firstly, how is it that you are back here after having been convicted along with your husband? Secondly, how do you come to have a daughter twenty-one years old? Last time I spoke to you, you told me that all your children had died through lack of food."

The woman gave a moan and buried her face in her hands.

"I never snatched 'er, mister, true as I'm standing 'ere, and though she ain't me own flesh and blood, I've looked after 'er as though she were me own." Then, haltingly and fearfully, she went on to tell her tale.

It amounted to the complete history of her life but Stewart motioned the reporter into silence when he attempted to cut her short. Eventually she came to the riots and described how they all lay in Walton Gaol waiting for the trial and certain transportation. And how a priest came up to her and promised to secure her release if she would agree to go to America.

She accepted, and shortly afterwards a young woman came to see her. The young woman and her husband were sailing for America to make a fresh start in life, and they had a small girl, little more than a baby, for whom the mother needed a nursemaid. Father O'Reilly had suggested Belle Watkins and spoke up for her at the trial so that she was acquitted, on condition that she went to America.

In order to make certain, Belle was kept in Walton Gaol until the day the ship sailed, and the priest himself was held responsible for seeing her safely on board. The two young people were kindness itself and did all they could to make her forget the unpleasant past.

After a fortnight at sea, Belle was awakened one night by a tremendous crash. The entire 500 emigrants streamed up on to the deck and panic reigned. At first, Belle had managed to keep near her employers, carrying the little girl, but as the panic grew, they became separated and she never saw them again. Somehow or other, in that terrible confusion, she had found herself and the child in a boat. It was overflowing with people, but she could not remember how she got there, nor how the boat, amidst all that maddened, frightened crowd of emigrants, got away from the doomed ship's side. In the darkness of the night, Belle saw the loom of a great iceberg. At first she thought it was land and took heart from the thought that in a few hours they would all be on shore again.

When day broke, both ship and iceberg had disappeared, and the only signs of the tragedy were a few drifting spars, with here and there a dead body floating forlornly.

The men in the boat disagreed as to what they should do. Apparently they were much nearer America than England, but one of the seamen said that they would never reach America with all the westerly winds, and there had been a lot of argument.

She did not know what they decided on in the end, only that it was getting colder and colder. The rising wind brought the spray dashing over their heads, battering their bodies and soaking their clothing. Belle protected the little one as much as she could by gathering her tightly into her arms and sitting with her back to the front of the boat.

For two days they kept afloat and were picked up on the third day by a ship bound for South America. These twenty-three people in that one small boat were the sole survivors of the original 500 who had set out from England.

When Belle realized that there was no hope of Susy's parents having been rescued, she decided to keep the child herself. She'd grown very fond of the bonny little girl and thought that if she didn't look after her, the little girl would have to go to the Poor Law Institution, for the mother had given her to understand that they had no relatives in England.

The British Consul gave her the choice of staying in America or returning to England, and she decided to go back to England, thinking that all the trouble over the riots would have settled down. It had all been forgotten until this gent had come today.

"Well, there you are," said the reporter, turning to Stewart. "That's all we can do."

"Just a minute," said Stewart curiously, "what was the name of the child's parents?"

"That won't serve any purpose," said Sharp. "You heard her say that there weren't any relatives in England."

"What's her real name?" persisted Stewart.

"Eastwood, sir," said the woman.

"What?" cried Stewart excitedly. "Are you sure?"

The old woman was startled by the young man's outburst and said nothing.

"Have you any means of proving it?" he went on. "Come on, answer me!"

"I meant no 'arm, sir. You won't send me to gaol," she said, terrified, and Stewart had to restrain his own excitement to pacify her fears before he could get any further information out of her.

"There was a little locket which the child had worn round her neck," Belle said.

"Where is it?" asked Stewart, trying to keep his excitement under control.

The old woman went hesitantly to an old tin box resting on the chimneypiece and emptied its contents on to the table. Out of a mass of old junk she took a small heart-shaped locket inscribed J.E. to E.M. 5.6.12.

Sam Sharp picked it up and held it in the palm of his hand.

"Gold!" he said. "Can't think why she's never pawned it."

Stewart took it from him firmly.

"Here's a sovereign," he said to the old woman. "I'll keep the locket."

"You're not going to give me in charge?" asked Belle pitifully.

"Great heavens, no!" said Stewart. "If what I think is true, you can say good-bye to Pitt Street, and look forward to a happy and comfortable future."

He saw by her bewilderment that she had not made sense of his remarks, so he added kindly, "We'll be back to see you when we find Susy."

"Well, just fancy that!" said Stewart, as he and Sam retraced their steps down Pitt Street.

"What's all the excitement?" asked Sharp gruffly. "You're still no nearer finding Susy, and it looks to me as though Belle Watkins may have been spinning another of her hard-time stories."

"It's good enough for me," Stewart said emphatically. "I believe every word of it. Susy is Joe Eastwood's grand-daughter."

It was the reporter's turn to look astonished, then, slowly, enlightenment dawned upon him.

"I seem to remember something about a son of his, now you mention it. Married against his father's wishes, didn't he? What a story this'll make for the paper!"

"Sam," said Stewart in a cold, determined voice, "if so much as a whisper of this creeps into that rag of yours I'll come and throw you in the river." He glared fiercely at the reporter.

"All right, lad," said the other hastily, "no offence meant. If you want to keep it dark that's good enough for me. But see, there's that sign again 'Drunk for a penny, a blind for twopence'. What about it?"

Stewart smiled indulgently. It had been a splendid day.

"I don't mind," he said, so thrusting open the door, they walked into the bar in high good humour. The long, low room was empty except for a few tippling women with shawls over their heads, and straggly wisps of hair hanging over their faces.

"Landlord," called out Sam Sharp majestically, "we've called about the sign in your window."

The landlord, a greasy individual in shirt-sleeves and dirty apron, came up to them with an uneasy smirk on his face.

"What can I do for you, gents?"

"There's a notice in your window which says, 'Drunk for a penny, a blind for twopence'. As humble representatives of truth in advertising," said the reporter, "my friend and I have stepped in here to see if you mean what you say."

The landlord's smirk vanished and was replaced by a look of suspicion.

"My 'ouse ain't for the likes o' you," he said.

Sam Sharp drew himself up and said : "If you hold the magistrates' license, sir, then by law you are compelled to accept our custom." He placed two pennies on the counter. "Proceed, landlord. Let us taste the tipple."

The publican gave them an evil look and without another word turned away to draw the mixture.

"Do you think it's quite wise, Sam ?" Stewart whispered doubtfully.

"Don't worry," said the reporter. "The whole thing's a fraud. We'll show him up."

A few seconds later the landlord was back with two dirty mugs, which he placed before them. Sam Sharp's eyes sparkled with anticipation.

"It smells like gin," he said, wrinkling his nose. "Well, here goes to the great adventure," and while Stewart watched him apprehensively, he lifted the mug and poured half its contents down his throat. Suddenly he began to cough and choke, tears came into his eyes ; unsteadily he put the half-drained mug on the counter, and in a spasm of sneezing vainly endeavoured to find his handkerchief.

Stewart sympathetically thumped him on the back. "It must have gone down the wrong way, Sam."

When at last the reporter could speak, he said to the publican, "Is that the tipple ?" and there was a vast respect in his eyes.

The landlord shrugged his shoulders contemptuously. "Wait till you spend your twopence on the 'blind'," he said significantly.

"Come on," said Sharp urgently, "let's get out of here while I'm still conscious," and without further argument he lurched into the street, where it seemed as though he couldn't gulp in enough fresh air.

"What's the matter, Sam ?" the young man asked maliciously. "Surely you're not admitting you're beat ?"

Sharp looked at him self-consciously. "I'm admitting nothing of the kind," he said. "There's a time and place for everything and just now I remembered we had important business to do. It was for your benefit I left, not because of the liquor."

"Never knew you to be so considerate before. What do you think was in the drink—gunpowder ?"

"It tasted to me like methylated spirits," said Sam unguardedly. "Raw methylated spirits. If you were to put a match to my breath now I wouldn't be surprised if I went up in flames."

"The landlord's advertisement was probably true then," Stewart said.

"Aye!" said the other, and gave such a hiccup that Stewart had to laugh.

Soon they were back in Dale Street and they separated. Sam wanted to go into the 'Pig and Whistle' to wash the taste out of his mouth, but Stewart was anxious to find Mr. Eastwood. He hurried up the few steps leading to the shipowner's office and without troubling to knock, burst into the room.

There was the usual somnambulant air over the whole place, the old clerks were bent silently over their desks, and the two brothers were silently engrossed in their dominoes. At the noise of the young man's entry they all looked up resentfully.

"Mr. Eastwood," said Stewart urgently, "may I have a word with you in private?"

"What's this, more trouble?" the old shipowner asked resignedly. "Sit down, young man, and let Fred and me finish the rubber," and the two brothers turned placidly to resume their game again whilst the old clerks returned to their ledgers. Stewart was left there standing awkwardly, almost bursting with his news. Silence reigned completely; after all it was twenty years since Mr. Eastwood had heard of his son, so what did an extra half-hour matter! Stewart sat down and waited.

"Domino!" cried Fred triumphantly at last, and his elder brother scratched his head ruefully.

"You had the luck with you there," he said.

"Oh, come, Joe, there was skill as well. Anyway, that's twopence-halfpenny you owe me. You know," he said slyly to his brother, "I don't think your young friend here likes being kept waiting," and they both turned round, amused, to look at Stewart fiddling with his hat.

"I believe you're right, Fred," said Joe, feigning surprise. "Well, I mustn't keep the young gentleman any longer."

In the privacy of the little inner office, Stewart brought out the pendant. "Have you seen this before, sir?"

Mr. Eastwood bent forward and then jerked sharply upright.

"How did you come by this?" he asked.

"You recognize it?" the young man said anxiously.

"Recognize it? Of course I do. It's the very first present I ever bought for my wife. It bears the date I first met her. This is strange, very strange," and he sat down heavily in his chair.

As he listened to Stewart's story he gazed fixedly out of the window, seeing nothing, and only the occasional nervous twitching of his hand showed that he was conscious of Stewart speaking. At last the story was finished, but the old man continued to stare out through the window on a river that presented a pageant of activity. Ferry-boats crossed and recrossed; steam-paddle tugs threshed fussily about, rousing the air with their short shrill whistles. One of McIver's boats hauled out from the landing stage, a picture of dignity and concealed power, whilst under her stern glided silently and effortlessly the finest sailing ships, newly come home, their paintwork shining and their yards neatly squared by the lifts and braces.

But Mr. Eastwood saw none of this.

"What is she like?" he asked, breaking the long silence.

"You met her on board the *Mary Jane* at that little supper party which Captain Brady gave just before he sailed."

"Of course, of course, how could I be so blind? But, a barmaid I remember you calling her. Dear, dear, we must get her out of that."

He called his brother in and Stewart had to tell the story all over again. Fred was more indignant than his brother and was all for prosecuting Belle Watkins, although he admitted that she had probably meant well when she adopted Susy. He could not help but feel that if Belle had made a correct report to the authorities Susy would have had a chance of being properly brought up and spared all these years of misery.

"Hardly misery," Stewart smiled. "If you knew Susy you wouldn't think that. She's enjoyed every minute of being alive."

The two old men looked at him reproachfully. How could he say a thing like that when they knew how and where those years had been spent?

"All I can say is that you'll appreciate Susy's character only after you've known her for a while."

"You must arrange everything, Fred," said the elder brother. "She must come and live here and I hope we can make some sort of amends for the past."

"Just a minute, sir," interrupted Stewart coolly, "first of all we've got to find her."

His remark threw the brothers into a state of alarm.

"Find her? But we thought she was working in some wretched tavern in the Dock Road?"

"So she was until month ago. She's vanished completely since then."

"The police must be informed," said Fred sternly, taking charge of the whole business.

"I don't think that's advisable, sir," Stewart said hastily. "I think her disappearance has something to do with Captain Brady. I'm not certain, but I think that when he turns up with the brig, Susy will come to life again. At any rate, it would be wise to wait until he arrives; he seems to have constituted himself her guardian. And apart from all that, Susy would probably be annoyed if she thought the police were seeking her. You see, sir, she's a young woman with very determined ideas of her own," he said apologetically.

"But she might be in serious trouble?"

Stewart laughed, he couldn't help himself, but he did manage to convince them that it would augur better for their future relations with Susy if they did nothing in the matter until Captain Brady came home; he was expected any day now.

Stewart finally left them, talking eagerly to each other, planning how they would rearrange their lives, how they'd make up for their past mistakes.

He felt very pleased with himself as he went slowly down to his basement, and his pleasure was sweetened by the thought that it would be himself who would tell Susy about her newly acquired relations. He pictured her gratitude as he revealed the story to her. After that, it was going to be easy to get her to influence Captain Brady to take the *Mary Jane* blockade-running. Sheer gratitude must make her do that.

Exchange Buildings — 'The Flags'

CHAPTER 17

BLOCKADE RUNNING FROM BIRKENHEAD

EVERYTHING was turning out very nicely. One successful trip to Galveston would establish their fortune on a firm footing. Stewart planned to sail in the ship on that voyage to make perfectly certain that nothing should go wrong.

He now began to wonder how soon he dare attempt the venture. It was too short notice to put the brig on to it as soon as she got back from Portugal. Besides, there were the cargo commitments already entered into for the next voyage. Perhaps he might manage the attempt in about two months' time. He would have to find an opportunity to explain it all to Susy and to secure her co-operation.

Things were going so well that he decided to try and find out locally if there were any chance of obtaining a contraband cargo.

As night fell he took the ferry to Birkenhead and walked up towards Laird's shipbuilding yard at Green Lane. He entered a public-house, the 'Shipwright', just opposite Laird's rigging loft.

It was the landlord's habit when a stranger entered his house and if business would permit, for him to go across and invite him to have a drink—that is, if he looked a respectable sort of fellow. "The 'ospitality of the 'Shipwright's'," the landlord called it. That evening, trade was slack and he soon found his way to the little table at which Stewart was sitting.

"I don't seem to remember you 'aving graced me 'ouse before," he began unctuously, and his little beady eyes travelled slowly but in-offensively over Stewart.

"No, I don't often get across the water," Stewart replied amicably; "it's a bit off my track. All the same, sir, if I may say so, you seem to have a nice house here and the beer is the best I've tasted on Mersey-side. You must have a pretty good cellar, I'm thinking."

"There's no finer kept beer within twenty miles," affirmed the landlord proudly, "I drains the pipes and the engines out myself, and I washes 'em with sweet, 'ot water and a touch o' soda. I've never yet 'ad a complaint about my beer," he ended with justifiable pride, for it was an age when Englishmen were connoisseurs of beer. "If you leaves a job like that to the cellarman, what can you expect? It's only natural 'e'd 'ave one of the lasses down there to 'elp 'im, and you know as well as I do, mister," he added with a coarse leer, "the beer-engine's pipes wouldn't get the attention they need! No, the 'Shipwright' 'as got a reputation for its beer, and it deserves it. I'll tell you a secret of the trade, mister, look after the cellar yourself."

"Thanks for the tip, I'll keep it in mind for chance I go into the

241

business," said Stewart affably. "I suppose most of your trade comes from Laird's yards?"

"It do and it don't. Before breakfast and during the dinner hour they keep us busy, but at night time I reckon it's the sailors from the docks that bring in the money."

"Did you ever get any of the *Alabama* crowd in?" Stewart asked casually.

"Did we not!" answered the landlord; "every night right up to the time they sailed. The 'Shipwright' was their favourite public-house. I was in the know there all right. The newspapers would have given me something for the story I could 'ave told 'em. I knew when she went out on 'er trials that she wasn't coming back! None o' the crew knew, and as for the captain, a closer man you never met. But I knew she was going. It makes me laugh when I read all the fuss the newspapers and Parliament are making."

"But how did you find out?"

The landlord looked round furtively. "See that American gent over there?" he whispered. "Well, 'e tipped me the wink."

Stewart looked cautiously at the man indicated, and then he said, "Who is he?"

" 'E's a gent who don't encourage questions, but 'e gave me the tip because 'e didn't want me to go giving the sailors credit and leave a bad impression behind 'em when they didn't turn up again. A real gent I told 'im 'e was, but 'e only laughed and said it was a matter o' politics, though I couldn't see that myself." He leaned closer to Stewart. " 'E's Mr. Wills, see? The unofficial representative of the Southern States, 'e calls 'imself."

"Do you think I might meet him?" said Stewart, striving to keep the excitement out of his voice.

"Oh, I don't know about that," said the landlord, drawing back in alarm. "I don't want Mr. Wills to think I go gossiping about 'is business."

"It's only for a drink," persuaded Stewart.

"Well, if I do bring 'im over, don't you go letting 'im know that I told you about the *Alabama*!"

"Trust me," said Stewart reassuringly, "I know when to treat a conversation as private."

Thus pacified, the landlord withdrew to return a little later with the American. After a few drinks, the landlord returned to his work and the two men sat talking companionably together. Stewart let it be known gradually that he was a shipowner but an hour elapsed before Mr. Wills became communicative. By that time they had consumed a considerable quantity of beer and Stewart had put on record that he was an ardent sympathiser with the Southern States, that he had the greatest admiration for the *Alabama* and the task she had set out to do, and that if the opportunity arose he would jump at the chance of sending his brig through the blockade. But, he explained, he was first of all a business man, and as the Americans were fond of saying, "You can't let sentiment govern business."

He sat back after that and looked at Mr. Wills expectantly. He had put all his cards on the table and it was the other's move now. To Stewart's delight, the American began to question him casually as to what trade he was in, about the brig herself, her speed, and the argo she could lift. Finally, secretively, Mr. Wills mentioned that he knew a certain party who might be interested, and he might put Stewart in touch with them.

Stewart was anxious to bring matters to a head and said, "To-night?"

"Sure! Finish your drink and come with me. You'd better be on the level though, these are dangerous times and we intend this business to be kept quiet—understand?"

This dark threat did not unduly disturb Stewart, and a few minutes later they were threading their way past gaunt, deserted warehouses, infrequent gas-lamps lighting the darkness ineffectually.

At length they came to a tall, dark building. Mr. Wills, whose pace had been growing steadily slower, stopped outside a huge wooden gateway. He took a quick glance up and down the street and then, beckoning Stewart to follow, slipped through a small door cut in the main entrance.

There was not a sound to be heard save for the scurrying of rats in the inky blackness. Stewart felt strangely excited. Mr. Wills lit a candle and the flickering little flame cast eerie shadows over neatly stacked crates, cases and barrels which filled the shed. A narrow walk was left between them.

Without a word they followed the sharply twisting passage until they came to some rickety wooden steps which groaned and creaked under their footsteps. After three more flights of steps they reached the top floor, but still Mr. Wills showed no signs of stopping. Rounding a corner they found themselves in a clear space where a few timbers had been knocked together to form an office. A narrow strip of light shone beneath the door. As the American pushed it open Stewart saw a man seated comfortably at a table, placidly munching food, stopping now and then to take a swig of beer from a flagon. An oil hurricane lamp stood on a table alongside.

He greeted the American in an undertone. "They're expecting you," said the watchman, or whatever he was, and he nodded his head in the direction of a tier of hogsheads which formed one side of his makeshift office. Mr. Wills went straight over to the tier, and the next moment Stewart was astonished to see the half round of one of the casks swing open exposing an iron ladder. Motioning to the young man to follow him, Mr. Wills started to descend. The ladder led them into a large room lighted by a candle stuck in a bottle on a table. Four men sat round playing cards. They looked up casually at the newcomers, and at the sight of Stewart stopped playing and put their cards down on the table.

Mr. Wills quickly explained who Stewart was and then introduced him to a burly, rough-looking individual who held the title of marine superintendent.

"Does he know how to keep his mouth shut?" the marine superintendent asked.

Stewart smiled faintly, all this secrecy seemed to him to be a bit overdone.

"Well," the superintendent explained tersely, "we're running contraband. It's illegal, but your Government is reasonable, and so long as we don't make too big a song and dance about it, they're prepared to keep their eyes shut."

"Why all this secrecy then?" asked Stewart.

It was the Federal Government, he was told. Their agent in Liverpool was on the lookout for such business, and it was to hide the contraband from his knowledge that all these precautions were necessary. So long as he laid no specific charge to the British Government they were safe enough.

"Do you mean to say that all those cases and barrels I saw were contraband goods?" asked Stewart unbelieving.

Not all, they told him. The ones lining the alleyways were dummies, behind them lay the real contraband, cases of rifles and barrels of gunpowder.

They laughed at his incredulity. Someone found an empty box for Stewart to sit on; the cards were swept away and they settled down to talk business. Finally, he was promised £6000 over and above his expenses if he managed to get 200 tons of contraband through to Galveston and bring a cargo of cotton back.

No questions asked, no cash required, and all the shipping and paper formalities fixed up for him. They wasted very few words, and after putting the proposition to him they sat back silently and waited for his reply.

"I'm contracted to make another voyage to Portugal, but I'll be free to put the brig at your disposal, say in six weeks' time. How will that do?"

The marine superintendent looked disappointed, he had thought the brig was available right away.

"It's your brig," he said laconically, "there's the offer and it's open to anyone who's got the guts. But if you ain't got a ship right now, you'd better come and see the boss here when you have," and having said that he picked up the cards disgustedly and began to deal again.

Mr. Wills got up, and Stewart followed him outside. Then, with a parting word of warning against mentioning anything that he had seen, they parted on the understanding that Stewart should seek out Mr. Wills when the brig was free.

The prospect of £6000 dazzled Stewart, and all the way home he pictured what he would do with it. In a buoyant frame of mind he strode the deck of the ferry that carried him back to Liverpool. He looked at his watch and for a moment his confident spirit almost persuaded him to call on Miss Scripps and tell her all his plans. But it was nearly ten o'clock and he decided to leave it till morning.

The next day his optimism was less pronounced, perhaps it would be better to wait until this glittering prize was really in his grasp before he put his suit to the test again. Though he longed to redeem himself in her good graces, his better judgment warned him that deeds rather than words were the way to her heart.

He spent the next few days pacing the Pier Head in the hopes that Captain Brady would turn up with the brig. Frequently he stopped to train the long glass on Bidston Hill, but there was never a sign of his own burgee amongst the constant stream of owners' flags that fluttered from the yard-arm.

Seamans 'Floating Church', 1862

CHAPTER 18

MR. EASTWOOD FINDS A RELATIVE

OVER a month had gone by since Captain Brady sailed, and as the fifth week drew to a close Stewart began to feel uneasy. His advertisement of the next sailing in ten days' time had already appeared in the *Shipping Albion* and he kept an anxious watch on the signal station.

It was fortunate that a small brig like the *Mary Jane* would not take long to discharge in a modern port like Liverpool. All they really needed was two clear days, one for discharge and the other for loading. It would mean working right through the forty-eight hours, but it could be done and there was no real need for him to get anxious yet. All the same, he wished he had some idea how far away Captain Brady was.

On Saturday morning, Silas came running into the bedroom to tell him that their flag was up on Bidston Hill, and on the last of that day's flood, the *Mary Jane* came racing up the river and managed to scramble into the lock, the last ship for the day.

"You almost gave me a heart attack, Captain," called out Stewart cheerfully from the lockside. "I thought we were going to miss our next sailing date."

"Can't expect fair winds all the time. As a matter of fact, head winds in the Bay kept us dodging about for a week."

"Well, you're here, Captain, that's the main thing. What sort of a trip?"

"Can't grumble. Nothing so profitable as last voyage, but a nice cargo and plenty more left behind us to pick up next time. But come aboard, the Customs are just finishing."

Stewart skipped aboard and paced the poop with Brady while the tug towed them into Salthouse Dock again.

"Tomorrow's Sunday," Stewart reminded him. "Do you think we should try to get a gang to discharge her?"

"Not worth the expense, my boy. As it is you'll find extra bills for berthing Saturday afternoon, but I thought it better to come straight in rather than lie out in the stream over the week-end. The cargo lumpers can make a clean start on Monday morning. Got a cargo for my next voyage?" he asked.

"As much as you can lift, and more."

"If business goes on at this rate we'll be needing another ship," said Brady chaffingly.

"We'll need to get some more capital first," Stewart said pointedly, "but let me have your papers, Captain, and I'll deal with them. You'll be wanting to get ashore for a decent meal."

"Any idea how the trains are running?" the old man asked suddenly.

"Oh, much as usual, Captain," Stewart replied facetiously.

"Be serious, boy. What time is the next train to Blackpool?"

"Blackpool!" cried Stewart, at a loss. "Now, Captain, my name's not Bradshaw. But why Blackpool? Won't Manchester do? I can give you three trains there before midnight. Or what about a trip to London? Leave Lime Street at ten tonight and arrive ten o'clock Monday morning."

Captain Brady gave him a cutting look. "Stop fooling," he ordered, "and find out as quick as you like the next train to Blackpool. The Custom House is closed and there's nothing I can do before Monday morning, so I think I'll spend a quiet Sunday there with Susy."

"With Susy!" gasped Stewart. "What on earth is she doing there?"

The captain laughed at the young man's astonishment.

"What do you think? She's in business. On your orders," he continued maliciously, "I persuaded her to give up the Dock Road tavern, and I've a mind to see how she's getting on. Not that I've really any cause to worry. That girl would make her living if she were the only Gentile in a Jewish market place."

"But you never told me anything about all this," complained Stewart.

"And indeed, why should I?" exclaimed the old man, surprised. "So far as I know our partnership only covers the *Mary Jane*. Of course, if you've got other ideas . . ." he went on heavily.

"We've been searching high and low for Susy for weeks past," said Stewart in an aggrieved tone. "Nobody knew what had happened to her. I do think it was inconsiderate, Captain."

The old man's mouth fell open, but before his rising indignation could find expression, Stewart went on to say that if he'd known where she was he would have been able to tell her something to her advantage.

"Don't talk in riddles," said Brady testily. "If you've got something to say, say it! Don't be for ever hinting at mysteries."

"Well," said Stewart, confident of the surprise and amazement he was going to cause, "we've found out who Susy's parents were."

He waited expectantly for the gasp of amazment which never came. Captain Brady was looking thoughtfully out of the saloon port.

At last he said: "What of it? That's no news to Susy or me. I found it out before I sailed a month ago."

"You mean to say that you knew that she was Mr. Eastwood's grand-daughter?"

At that, he did succeed in causing some measure of surprise. Although Captain Brady had found out Susy's real name from Belle Watkins, he had not been able to trace any of her relatives.

Stewart felt a little mollified at the other's interest, and explained how he had found out the whole story, and also that Mr. Eastwood was anxiously waiting to welcome Susy to his house.

Captain Brady shook his head doubtfully. "I don't know how she's going to take all this. Still, I'd better be off and break it to her."

"If you're going to Blackpool, I'm going with you," said Stewart with determination. "After all, it's my duty to tell the girl."

Captain Brady looked at him as if he were going to speak, then he turned away to conceal his expression. "If you really think it's your duty, Mr. Stewart, come along then. We'll both go together."

The brig was forgotten and an hour later they were both in the train rolling away towards Blackpool. It was dark when they arrived and Stewart followed Captain Brady unquestioningly, his mind busy with memories of his former visit. Soon they came to a respectable, newly-built house on the sea-front. It stood back from the road and was fronted by a fairly large courtyard with two solid gas-lamps giving an air of importance to the entrance.

"It's a sizeable place," said Stewart, impressed.

"You wait till you see it in daylight," said Brady proudly. As though he was responsible for it all, thought Stewart.

The next moment they were pushing their way through the crowd of holiday-makers who still thronged the place, although the daily trippers must have been gone an hour ago.

"By jingo!" said Stewart in spite of himself. "She seems to be making a good thing of it."

Just then they caught sight of Susy, a highly attractive, cool person coming down the stairs. Captain Brady called her name and she gave a delighted start of surprise and flew over to him. To Stewart's consternation she hugged the old man close and then kissed him heartily on the cheek. She did not appear to have noticed the younger man standing there.

"I am here, you know," said Stewart sulkily.

"Oh, it's you, is it," said Susy, turning a calm, appraising look on him. Then she continued to talk more animatedly than ever to Captain Brady, her cheeks slightly flushed.

"I must say you don't seem over pleased to see me," said Stewart petulantly.

The other two laughed, and Susy said: "If you'd done as much for me as Captain Brady has perhaps it would be different. Who do you think lent me the money to buy this place? Why, Captain Brady, of course!"

"Now, Susy," admonished the old man, "I thought you promised to say nothing about that."

"Never mind," said the girl, with an apologetic laugh. "It's out now. But don't you worry. I'll not let him get any more money out of you."

"Look here," began Stewart angrily, "if you think I've nothing

better to do than worm money out of Captain Brady's pockets——"
their laughter drowned the rest of his protests.

Susy jumped for joy when she heard that they were staying the
night.

"I suppose you'll charge a sovereign each for a night in this palace?"
said Stewart, a trifle maliciously.

"Now stop quarrelling, you two," said Captain Brady, "and let's
hear how everything is going on."

Susy gave him a detailed account. The hotel was packed full every
night. She was fully booked up to the end of September and could
have let twice as many rooms. More and more people seemed to be
coming every day. Blackpool had certainly caught the imagination of
industrial Lancashire, and there was nothing like sufficient accommodation to be had.

"You'd make your fortune quicker here, Mr. Stewart," she
twinkled, "than you will in ships out of Liverpool."

"What are you doing about accommodation?" Captain Brady
interposed gravely. "It seems a pity to turn away money."

"I've managed to rent the next two houses," said Susy. "But if I'd
rented all the houses in Blackpool, there would still not be room enough
for all the people who want to come."

In the excitement of their arrival, Stewart had temporarily forgotten
the reason of his visit. Suddenly he remembered and whispered to
Captain Brady, "Do you think I should tell her now?"

"Bah!" said the old man impatiently, "leave it for tonight. Time
enough for you to tell her when I make myself scarce for an hour tomorrow morning." So they stayed up till well past midnight, chatting
away, and Stewart listened to Susy's ambitious plans with increasing
dismay.

After a time he said, "If you're turning people away, Susy, how are
you managing to put us up?"

"I'm putting you in the maids' room."

"Well, I hope that's all right with them," Stewart said ambiguously.

"Yes," she said coolly, "I've arranged for them to go home tonight."

Captain Brady turned to the young man with a look of pride. "See!
she thinks of everything." He glanced regretfully at his watch. "I think
it's about time we were thinking of bed."

The last of the customers had departed and the barman had turned
out all the lights except in the room in which they were sitting. He came
in now with the keys jingling, the shutters were up and the doors were
locked.

"I'll let the girls out when they've finished washing up, but meanwhile I'll show you gentlemen where you are sleeping," said Susy,
taking the keys from the barman. "Good night, Fred."

The sun streaming through the windows of the maids' room woke

Stewart long before his usual time. He sat up in bed and looked at the green fields stretching into the distance. Birds sang lustily, and Stewart sat for a while enchanted with the contrast between this and the Liverpool mornings. He felt as cheerful as the birds outside, perhaps there was something to be said for this Blackpool air after all. It was much too fine to stay in bed, so he jumped up and decided to go for a walk before breakfast. The front door was already open and as he stepped outside he involuntarily took a deep breath. The wind coming in straight from the sea filled his lungs and gave him a feeling of exhilaration. It was wonderful, and he turned northwards with resolute steps.

Before long, the last house was left behind and Stewart tramped strenuously across the sand dunes. Not a soul was to be seen and the only sound was that of the sea breaking off the shore and the wind gently soughing through the coarse grass of the sandhills. The wind was stronger than he had thought and it caught his hat and carried it away, to disappear over the top of the next sand dune. With a crazy laugh (there certainly was something strange about him that morning) Stewart sprang to the chase, yelling like a madman and taking a childish pleasure in hearing his voice rising above the wind. With a ridiculous whoop, he came bounding over the top of the sandhill and then, with a cry half-uttered, he stopped. There, in the shelter of the sandhill, a few feet from his fine beaver hat, sat Susy with a book open on her knees. She gazed at him in astonishment.

"Oh, hullo!" said Stewart awkwardly. "Lost my hat—see," he gave a self-conscious laugh. "Just come to find it."

"My, what's come over you?" said Susy, when she had recovered from her surprise. "You're very bright and gay this morning."

"Mind if I sit down?" he asked nonchalantly.

"Please yourself, it's not my beach."

"You sound as if you're angry about something?"

"Now, why should you think that? Haven't I always been sweetness itself to you?"

"Oh, give over, Susy! Let's be friends." He picked up the book she had been reading. "*John Stuart Mills,*" he read. "My! you aren't half going it, Susy. What's it about?"

"You wouldn't understand," snapped the young woman, who for some reason did not seem to be in the sweetest of tempers. "It's all about liberty and freedom for women."

"But they're already free enough, aren't they?" said Stewart puzzled.

"There, I told you you wouldn't understand. Give it back to me, please."

"Do you always come out here so early in the morning?"

"I do if it's fine."

"Like it?"

"I wouldn't stay if I didn't, would I?" she answered, not relaxing an inch.

But Stewart persevered. He had his own reasons for wanting an amicable understanding. "We've missed you in Liverpool. When are you coming back?"

"When the season is over here."

"Oh, then you are coming back?"

"Of course I am. I've got to live somehow."

"Don't you wish you could finish with all this business of earning a living?" he asked earnestly.

"Oh, Mr. Stewart——" Susy pretended to look coy, "I do believe you're going to do it again."

"Do what again?" Stewart looked puzzled.

"Make me an offer," said she, relapsing into helpless giggles.

Stewart looked at her exasperated. "You little idiot," he said, but Susy only giggled the more.

At length she stopped and turned towards him. "I'm sorry," she said, "but you take yourself so seriously and it always makes me laugh," and she began to giggle helplessly again.

Stewart looked at her coldly. "If you'll restrain your amusement a moment you may be interested to learn that I've discovered who your grandfather is!"

"My grandfather!" she said, sitting bolt upright. "Do you mean that you know about my mother and father?"

Stewart inclined his head gravely, took out the cheroot he had saved for just that occasion, and with painful deliberation began to light it. It was the first cheroot he had ever endeavoured to smoke, but he fancied that it gave him an air of dignity.

"Put that filthy thing out," said Susy sharply, "I don't remember having given you permission to smoke."

To his own surprise he obeyed her somewhat hastily.

"Now, young man, what is it that you've got to tell me?" and a forceful young person seemed to have taken the place of the usually light-hearted Susy.

Stewart felt disappointed. He hadn't planned things like this, with himself on the defensive. The young woman was impatiently pressing for an explanation, so he said as importantly as possible, "After much labour and searching I've found that Mr. Eastwood, the Liverpool shipowner, is your grandfather."

"You mean that dear old man I met on the *Mary Jane*?" she cried excitedly. "Why, that's lovely! But are you sure?"

"So sure that Mr. Eastwood has asked me to take you to him as soon as possible," Stewart replied tartly.

Susy snuggled up to him and pressed his arm invitingly. "Don't look so upset," she said. "I really am grateful for the trouble you must have taken."

"Why, Susy," said Stewart, melting, "it was nothing really, I'd do far more for you than that if I had the chance."

She looked at him silently for a time and then smiled happily in a way that thrilled him strangely. "I really believe you would," she said, and then, jumping to her feet she laughingly stretched out her hand to help him up. He took the proffered help and forgot to let go of her hand until Susy eventually withdrew it as they reached the road. On the way back, Stewart related the full story of how he had pieced together Mr. Eastwood's reminiscences and Belle Watkins' admission.

The 'Winsmere' was just beginning to show signs of life when they got back. The wind had whipped colour into Susy's cheeks and her eyes sparkled as she outrageously carried her bonnet in her hand. Stewart's eyes followed her appreciatively. "You look ten times prettier," he said admiringly.

Susy turned the full force of her gaze on him. "You do say the nicest things," she said demurely.

The next moment they were being greeted heartily from the stairs by Captain Brady. He had just enjoyed the best night's sleep he had ever had and was anxious to get started on a large breakfast. Going to the door, he took in several deep breaths of the sea air.

"It's like wine," he said, turning to Susy. "I've travelled on every sea and been to most foreign parts, but I've never yet come across air so bracing as this. No wonder Blackpool is becoming popular. Why, it's as good as a tonic. If you could manage to bottle some of this, Susy, you wouldn't need to serve liquor to thirsty sailors."

"Mr. Stewart's just told me about my grandfather," said Susy.

"And what are you going to do, lass?" asked Brady, suddenly becoming grave.

"Do? There's nothing to do, is there?" she questioned, puzzled.

"I mean," said Brady carefully, "they want you to give up your business and settle down with them in Liverpool."

"Oh, I'm not going to do that," she said with conviction, "I'm not going to let you down, if that's what you mean."

"It's not a case of letting anyone down," said Stewart. "It's just a case of your own kith and kin wanting you to live with them. I am sure Captain Brady will agree with me that it is your duty to go and live with Mr. Eastwood."

"Is that what you really think?" she asked, turning to the captain.

An air of despondency seemed to have settled on the old man. "Yes," he said, far from enthusiastically, "that seems the proper thing to do."

"Of course it is," said Stewart. "There can be no question about it. Besides, a woman's got no place in business, Susy—leave that to the menfolk."

It was an ill-advised remark at that stage for an angry glint came into her eyes and she said, "That settles it, then."

"Good!" said Stewart. "I'll see about getting the business sold for you."

"You'll do nothing of the kind," she said calmly. "I intend to stay here."

"But," said Stewart aghast, "you can't do that."

"Can't I?" said Susy. "Just you wait and see."

"You speak to her, Captain," Stewart said disgustedly.

"Nay, lad, you know as well as I do, if she's made up her mind to do a thing, neither you nor me nor her grandfather will make her alter it."

Stewart, perhaps rashly, tried to argue with her. Had she no sense of duty? What was he going to say to Mr. Eastwood?

"You won't have to say anything to Mr. Eastwood because I'm going to Liverpool myself, and judging from what I saw of him on the *Mary Jane*, he won't try to persuade me against my will."

"Of all the ungrateful, perverse——" began Stewart, who hadn't bargained for this.

"Steady, young fellow! I won't have a word spoken against the girl. She's old enough to know her own mind."

"It's strange," said Susy thoughtfully, "that Mr. Eastwood has suddenly arrived at the decision for me to go and live with him. I must say he's been a long time making his mind up."

"He never even knew of your existence," said Stewart, "as it was, he went his brother over to New York directly he heard of the loss of the *Savanna*."

"I don't think he can have been very concerned about my father, either, else he wouldn't have turned him out the way he did. If Mr. Eastwood thinks that all he's got to do is to lift his finger and I'll come hurrying back to him, he's very much mistaken," said Susy, standing on her dignity.

"You don't understand," said Stewart patiently. "It was all due to obstinacy on your father's side as well as Mr. Eastwood's. Your grandfather is anxious to make amends for the unhappy incidents of the past."

"It's a pity he didn't think of that earlier, instead of compelling my mother and father to leave the country," she said bitterly.

"There's nothing to be gained by all this argument," said Captain Brady gently. "It's a matter for Susy and Mr. Eastwood to decide between themselves. Let's leave it at that and enjoy ourselves while we're here."

After a while, Stewart realized that there was nothing to be gained by attempting to force his opinions upon her. If her mind was made up and she preferred to stay as she was, then he had better accept it, and try to persuade her to influence Captain Brady to take the brig over to Galveston with a contraband cargo. It did not really matter what Susy did and it was ridiculous to be disturbed by her decision. It was her influence over Captain Brady that really counted.

After breakfast, the three of them set out for the foreshore to watch the bathers. It was novel and amusing; a sight which Susy, at any rate, found vastly entertaining.

"Look at that fat old man," she whispered laughingly to Stewart, as a very portly old gentleman waded cautiously into the water, encased in a large horizontally striped bathing garment.

"Ssh!" reproved Stewart, "refined young women are not supposed to look too closely."

"But what else can I do?" she persisted, giggling helplessly, "if they keep coming out like that?"

"There's no need to laugh at the men," exclaimed Stewart; "look at that ridiculous frump of a woman just coming down the steps of her machine. She looks as though she's wearing a tent."

Gingerly, the lady in question came down a few steps of the ladder and dipped a tentative toe in the water. With a shriek of dismay she withdrew it quickly, but there were others behind her, and vainly protesting in half alarm, she edged into the water.

"God bless my soul!" said Captain Brady profoundly, as he watched these strange figures. "Who'd have thought I'd have lived to see such public displays?"

"Why, Captain," said Susy delightedly, "I do believe you're shocked. And you a man of the world!" she mocked.

"Never seen anything like this," the old man exclaimed bewildered.

> "A nymph, a naiad or a Grace
> Of finer form or lovelier face,"

Quoted Stewart as the shivering bathers scuttled past them.

Susy looked at him respectfully. "I do wish I could think of things like that to say," she sighed wistfully.

"I cannot tell a. lie," said Stewart facetiously, "those lines were written by Sir Walter Scott."

"But you could make them up if you wanted to, couldn't you?" she asked almost reverently.

"Well . . . er . . . I might, you know."

"It must be lovely to have poetry written specially for you."

"Pidgin-English," said Brady disgruntled. He did not like all these semi-naked people frolicking around, and as for poetry, it was all more or less immoral talk clothed in strange language! "I think we'd better be moving on," he said uneasily, and resolutely turned his back on the bathers.

The other two exchanged an amused glance and then followed silently in his wake. Stewart caught hold of Susy's hand and was surprised and delighted when she made no effort to withdraw it. Captain Brady stopped and waited for them to catch up. He saw them unashamedly holding hands, and he sniffed disgustedly. There must be something about the place that made folks lose their senses altogether.

The sun blazed down upon them, the newly washed sand was crisp and hard beneath their feet, and the wind blew freshly in from the sea so that it was impossible for anyone to remain out of temper for long, and Captain Brady soon regained his good spirits. The spectacle of the bathers and the dangerous talk about poetry were forgotten, and the rest of the day passed all too quickly.

That night, at seven o'clock, they all climbed into the train and were whisked off back to Liverpool. As they neared the Mersey the holiday spirit seemed to leave Stewart, and much to Susy's annoyance he began to question Brady about the brig's cargo. The captain, sensitive to Susy's disapproval, was uneasy and vague. He suggested that they wait till Susy had left them before they began discussing business.

Susy decided that it was too late to think of venturing to Mr. Eastwood's that night, and suggested that Stewart might take her round in the morning.

"That's right," nodded Brady approvingly, "we'll fix up a room for you in the 'Angel', Susy, and young Stewart here can come and call for you in the morning."

"But, heavens above!" protested the young man, "we'll be so busy tomorrow morning clearing the brig and getting the cargo started that I'll not have a minute to spare."

"Nonsense," said the old man sternly, "leave the ship's business to me, and as for the cargo . . . well, there's a mate on board, that's what he's there for."

"All right," said Stewart resignedly, "I'll find the time."

"Isn't he obliging?" Susy remarked coldly.

"Now, now, you two," began Brady anxiously, scenting trouble; "of course he's a lot to do, and he's worried about the brig," he explained to Susy. The old man wiped his brow. He could not understand the ways of these modern young people. One minute making public exhibitions of themselves walking hand in hand through the main streets, and the next minute or so quarrelling amongst themselves fit to beat the band. He shook his head gloomily, it was all very strange.

Susy was eventually settled in a room at the 'Angel', and then Captain Brady and Stewart sat down to discuss business over a couple of glasses of rum.

"It'll be all right to start discharging before I've cleared her inwards?" asked Captain Brady.

"Certainly," replied Stewart with confidence, "I've been down to the Customs House every day this week, giving them notice of your arrival."

"What about the consignees?"

"If you'll only give me their names and particulars of shipments, I'll get round them first thing in the morning. I don't suppose you brought the Bills of Lading. No? Well, I suppose all the cargoes F.O.B.? Yes? Then I'll tell the mate to use the warehouse storage accommodation. I warned the Dock Board we'd very likely be needing it. The outward cargo should start coming down on Wednesday. You should have your Jerque Note by Tuesday night, if all goes well, and it'll be in order to start loading the following day."

"Yes," said Captain Brady drowsily, the mixture of Blackpool air and West Indian rum being too much for him, though not for Stewart, who went on talking vigorously and energetically, describing the parcels which were certain to be there on the quayside on Wednesday morning, and others that couldn't be relied upon till late Friday night. He went on to talk of collecting the freight and of balancing the voyage accounts, and then suddenly he stopped. "Hey! wake up," he called disgustedly, shaking his partner by the shoulder.

The old man wearily opened his eyes for a second. "All right," he said sleepily, "call me when she swings!"

Stewart got to his feet. Where would the firm of 'Stewart and Brady' have been, he thought, but for him? He shook the old man again. "Time to go aboard, Captain!" and without further demur, Captain Brady struggled to his feet. Stewart saw him safely back to the brig, and eventually he arrived home well after midnight.

CHAPTER 19

MISS EASTWOOD PLANS AHEAD

IT seemed as if the pillow had hardly touched his head before Silas stood before him, holding a cup of thick, black-looking fluid, which he called tea. "Eight bells, skipper, you're sleepin' worse'n a middle-watchman," he grumbled.

"Eight o'clock! Good heavens, I meant to be down the docks a couple of hours ago. Why didn't you call me?"

"Nay, skipper, if I've called you once I've called you a dozen times, but no matter, the minute I left you, there you was, snoring your head off again."

Stewart dressed hurriedly. There was just time to slip down to the Salthouse Dock and see how things were going, then deliver the particulars of the consignments and see if the cargo agents had got the bills of lading. Two hours later he was back and he went upstairs to warn Mr. Eastwood that his grand-daughter would be calling on him in about an hour's time. This information put the two brothers into a panic. They plied him with questions. Where had she been? How had she received the news?

"There's too much to tell," said Stewart. "I'm afraid I haven't the time to explain everything. Anyway, you'll hear it all from Susy in a short time," and with that the two old gentlemen had to be content, for Stewart was off to collect Susy.

He arrived at the 'Angel', but as if time were of no account, Susy sent word down to him that she would not be ready for another half-hour at least. When she did finally come sweeping down the stairs, she took his breath away.

"Great Scott!" he exclaimed in amazement. "Do you think you're going to a wedding?"

She gave him a deep curtsey. "Do you like my new dress, sir?" she asked. "I only bought it this morning."

"What on earth for?" he asked, surprised, "There was nothing wrong with the one you were wearing yesterday!"

"You don't find a grandfather every day of the week," she informed him, "and even though I do think he's been neglectful, I want to make a good impression."

"You'll certainly do that," remarked Stewart fervently; "still, it's more respectable than that bustle you once wore!"

"It is rather nice, don't you think?" Susy asked, pirouetting vainly. "Of course it's dreadfully old-fashioned, but that's why I bought it. It would never do to go there looking like a fast young woman."

Stewart felt quite proud of her as they went out of the 'Angel' together. "Do you think we'd better have a cab?" he asked suddenly, thinking of the new dress.

She glanced at him mischievously. "I do believe that you're afraid of being seen with me."

"Of course I'm not—here, madam, take hold of my arm!"

As it happened by one of those strange freaks of circumstance, one of the first persons they met in Dale Street was Miss Scripps, accompanied by the faithful Martha. Susy saw them first and said primly, "Here comes a friend of yours, Mr. Stewart!" and shortly Miss Scripps was abreast of them, only the heightened colour in her cheeks betraying the fact that she had recognized them.

Stewart felt a strange thrill and was surprised to find that was the only emotion that came upon him, he didn't care a bit. The only person who appeared to be interested was Martha, and her eyes were nearly popping out of her head.

The young man swept off his hat with an exaggerated flourish, but as far as Miss Scripps was concerned he might not have been there. By not so much as the flutter of an eyelid did she acknowledge him.

Susy looked at him curiously. "You've done it now," she said, but Stewart was feeling neither elated nor depressed. He could not understand himself.

The rest of the journey was accomplished almost in silence. The young woman was delivered into the welcoming but apprehensive arms of her grandfather, and Stewart thoughtfully went down to his basement premises. He wanted to get the whole thing straightened out. It was not that he did not love Miss Scripps, he assured himself over and over again, and in an effort to stimulate his fervour, he recalled her beautiful auburn hair and her blue eyes; but somehow, the thought of them no longer gave him that former ecstatic thrill. He asked himself why it was that the encounter had failed to rouse any emotional feeling in him. It was very odd. Another time he would have cut off his hand sooner than let it happen, but that particular morning he just did not seem to care.

There must be some explanation, but for the moment he could see none. The sooner he got on with this blockade-running and made enough money to appear presentable in her eyes, the better. Things could not be allowed to continue in the present unsatisfactory state.

Had he been upstairs in the room with Mr. Eastwood and Susy, his eyes might have been opened.

Mr. Eastwood with bitter self-recriminations and Susy with forgiveness, had come to see eye to eye over many things. At first, the old man was very disappointed at her decision to stay in Blackpool. "I'm not a rich man, my dear, as fortunes go these days, but I've sufficient to keep you here in comfort and let you do all the things a young woman of your age will want to do. The business may not be very profitable, but it's sound."

"I'm sure it is," she said sweetly, "but it wouldn't be fair to let Captain Brady down after all he's done for me, and besides, I've got other plans." She looked at him mischievously for a while. "I'll let you into a secret," she said, smiling, "I'm going to be married very shortly."

"Good gracious me!" exclaimed the old man, starting back in astonishment. "I understood from young Stewart that you were as yet fancy free."

"Oh, he said that, did he?" said the young woman nodding.

"I know I've no right to question you, my dear, but——"

"You want to know who it is? Well, if you'll promise to keep a secret, I'll tell you. It's that conceited young man who rents the basement from you."

"Gracious me!" was all the old man could say. Events were moving too fast for him.

"Aren't you pleased?"

"Of course I am, my dear, but I'd no idea he felt like this about you. I'm delighted. But when did all this happen? I thought he intended to marry a Miss Scripps."

"Oh, that red-haired——" she began, but suddenly remembered to maintain her ladylike behaviour in front of her grandfather. "No," she continued mildly, "he doesn't know it yet, but he's going to marry me."

Poor Mr. Eastwood sat down, or rather collapsed into a nearby chair. This last piece of information was altogether too much for him. "I hope, my dear," he said in a wavering voice, "that things turn out as you hope," and he cast his eyes doubtfully towards her.

Susy laughed lightly, and moving over to his chair placed a hand affectionately on his shoulder. As she bent down and brushed his forehead with her lips she murmured, "I always get what I want, Grandfather; and now," she said purposefully, "I intend to stay in Liverpool until Captain Brady sails again. Have you got any room for me here?"

"Of course, my dear," the old man replied. "As soon as I heard you were alive I had a special room made ready for you, but you shall look round all the rooms and choose for yourself."

She decided to have the room which had been originally prepared for her. It looked over the river to the Welsh hills, rising splendidly in the distance. An old-fashioned four-poster bedstead occupied the central position.

"It's the bed your father was born in," Mr. Eastwood informed her.

Susy looked round her in delight and almost wished she had not to go back to Blackpool. "Never mind," she said, clapping her hands with glee, "I shall be here for the winter."

They all got on famously and for the rest of that week the two brothers were in a heaven of delight. In spite of her protests, they persisted in waiting on Susy hand and foot. Her every wish was law to them and when Susy's grandfather confided to his brother that Susy was set on marrying young Stewart, they decided that such things must not be left to chance, and something must be done about it.

They made a practice of inveigling Stewart into their premises, but somehow this scheme of throwing the young people together did not seem to work at all well. On most of the occasions, Susy was bright and cheerful, but Stewart was gloomy and taciturn.

The old men, watching with dismay, decided that things were not going well for Susy's plan, though she seemed to be happy enough.

Stewart, whilst conscious of Susy's presence, was more occupied in wondering how to persuade Captain Brady to take the *Mary Jane* on a venture to the blockaded Southern States. He had hinted vaguely about other blockade-runners, but the old man's reaction had been unsatisfactory. He was very much on the side of the Yankees, and their slavery policy was, to him, the sole consideration of the war.

After a few days, the two brothers began to feel a little more hopeful about the affair of Stewart and Susy. They noticed that Stewart frequently looked at Susy speculatively, and one day even Susy caught him out. She horrified the two brothers by saying, "Young man, I don't like the way you look at me." Then she calmly turned her attention to the food she was eating, the only unruffled member of the party, apart from Captain Brady, who grinned delightedly.

Stewart's look of despair convinced them he would willingly make her an offer if once he found the chance. That was the trouble, they decided, the two young people were never left alone together for five minutes on end. Captain Brady hovered round Susy like a faithful shadow.

So the two brothers got together and devised a scheme which would remove Captain Brady and themselves for a few hours. It was not so difficult as they thought, for when they told the captain that they would like his opinion on a little schooner which was lying at Rock Ferry, he enthusiastically agreed to go with them and look at the vessel.

Early that evening, feeling highly pleased with themselves, the Eastwood brothers set off with Captain Brady. As they passed out into the street, Susy's grandfather whispered to Stewart, "Now's your chance!"

"What?" asked the astonished young man.

"Ask her while we're out," hissed the old man fiercely.

"Thank you very much, Mr. Eastwood, I will." That was very queer, thought Stewart. However did the old man know that he was going to ask Susy to persuade Captain Brady to go blockade-running? It was most disturbing, for if Mr. Eastwood knew of his intentions, so might the others. He sat silently, wondering how best to approach the subject.

"You're very quiet," Susy said curiously.

"Am I? I'm afraid it's because I've got nothing to say."

"Do you like my new dress?"

Stewart looked at the voluminous skirt, the leg-o'-mutton sleeves, the incredibly slender waist. "It seems all right," he said gruffly. Then his eye lighted on two large curls hanging carelessly over her left shoulder, whilst the rest of her hair was gathered tidily into a net at the back of her neck. "Your hair is a bit untidy. Some of it has slipped out of place."

Susy looked at him contemptuously. "That's the new fashion," she told him coldly; "this style is the very latest thing. My hairdresser arranged it only this afternoon. It's called the 'waterfall' style," she added.

Stewart examined it more closely. It was quite pretty hair, he decided, and took on a most beautiful lustre with the sun shining through it. Something of all this must have been perceived by Susy, for she turned her face away, in such a manner that the rest of her hair came in for his full inspection.

"I think you are most rude, the way you stare at a girl."

"I'm sorry," said Stewart penitently; "honestly, I didn't know I was embarrassing you."

A long silence followed, then Susy said, "You certainly are a great hand at entertaining a lady."

"I'm sorry," said Stewart helplessly.

"Can't you say something else besides 'I'm sorry'?" she flashed back at him.

"Look here, Susy," pleaded Stewart, "why are you so short with me these days? Have I done anything to offend you?"

She gave him a withering look. "I think you flatter yourself, Mr. Stewart. I was unaware that my attitude had undergone any change."

"It has," he assured her. "You're more distant, cold. I can't explain it," he went on, getting flustered, "but there it is. At one time we used to be the best of friends, but now, if I so much as try to joke with you, you turn on me like a tiger." He was bewildered.

"I'm sure you're imagining things," she returned haughtily, "I've never given you two thoughts."

"And after all I've done for you," he said bitterly.

"If we're going to quarrel, I think it would be better if you went for a walk."

"Susy," he said, "what's happened to you? Ever since you learned that your name was Susanna Eastwood you've been a different person. Why can't we be friends like we used to be?" And he looked so upset that her heart softened a little towards him.

"But I do feel the same towards you," she protested. "You're one of my friends, just like Captain Brady."

Stewart didn't know whether to be pleased or not at this classification, but before he had time to think any further she went on:

"Of course, I'm grateful to you for finding out about my grandfather."

Stewart drew a deep breath. This, he felt, was his opportunity. "Do you really feel grateful?" he asked hopefully.

"Of course I do. It might have been months before Captain Brady could have found out for me."

"Oh!" said Stewart, "you think that Captain Brady could have solved the mystery? I'm sorry I gave up so much of my time to the matter. It might well have been employed to better advantage."

The young woman smiled across at him. "You are a silly. You seem determined to misunderstand me."

She came across to him, the colour high in her cheeks and her eyes bright with feeling as she looked up at him. She clasped one of his hands in both of hers coaxingly, and Stewart's heart, much to his surprise, began to beat very fast. This must be the opportunity.

"Will you do something for me, Susy?" he said, in a sudden burst of companionship.

She withdrew her hands, stepped back a pace and her eyes began to twinkle. "I'm still a good girl," she warned him.

"Oh, be serious for a moment," he urged. "I want you to help me with Captain Brady."

Once started, he rushed on like a river bursting its dam. He explained all about their business, how slowly it was progressing, the last voyage they'd only cleared £58. It was essential for them to obtain more capital so that they could buy more ships in order to run a regular service and become properly established as shipowners. At the rate they were progressing, he exaggerated, it would be years before they could obtain even another ship.

As Susy remained silent, Stewart became more and more eloquently enthusiastic about his scheme. There was only one way, he assured her, in which he could earn £6000 in a single voyage. Indeed, he had already been promised that sum, and the only stumbling-block that remained was Captain Brady's consent to the undertaking.

"Go on," she said quietly, "what is this scheme?"

He went on to tell her of his meeting with the men who had promised him £6000 over and above expenses if the *Mary Jane* would undertake one trip to Galveston and back.

"Surely, if Captain Brady knows about this, he'd be only too eager to do it?" she said.

Stewart looked at her sadly. "That's just the point," he said. "If I put it to him he'll object out of hand."

Unloading recent arrivals on the Dock Road

"Why?" she asked, mystified. "It's just a simple, straightforward voyage, isn't it?"

"Exactly," he agreed too hurriedly, "but that's just why he's likely to refuse."

"But why should he? Have you asked him?"

"No—I was hoping," he said diffidently, "that I might persuade you to speak to him first. You know, he'll do anything for you."

"But why," she persisted, "do you think he would refuse you?"

"I don't know." Stewart shrugged his shoulders helplessly. "These old men are often very obstinate."

Susy looked at him shrewdly for a minute, a tiny suspicion of a frown on her face. "I don't think he's obstinate. I think he's very reasonable."

"Yes, I know he is with you," said Stewart, "but in business matters I often have a terrible job with him."

"Are you sure there's no other reason?" she asked.

"There may be some sentimental reason about helping the Southern States," blustered Stewart.

"Southern States?" repeated the young woman, puzzled. "What have they got to do with it? I thought you said the voyage was to Galveston?"

Stewart looked at her pityingly. "Galveston is a port in the Southern States of America," he said slowly, with emphasis.

The girl laughed. "I thought it was in South America." Then suddenly she hesitated and the smile left her face. "But I thought the seas around the Southern States were blockaded by Yankee warships," she said.

"Pooh! just one or two old gunboats," scoffed Stewart. "Captain Brady would probably never see a single one," he went on optimistically.

Susy said nothing for a while, and went and sat down in a chair near the fire. The young man watched her anxiously, and after a while he said tentatively, "With you saying you were grateful to me, I thought that maybe—perhaps"—he floundered—"you might possibly persuade Captain Brady to undertake the voyage."

She flashed him an indignant look. "What would happen if a Yankee cruiser saw the *Mary Jane*?"

"But she's hardly likely to," he protested.

"But just suppose that she did?"

"Why, I suppose they'd take her as a prize."

"And what would happen to Captain Brady?"

"Listen, Susy, there's not one chance in a hundred of a fast little brig like the *Mary Jane* being caught."

"That's all I wanted to know," said the young woman calmly. "And now may I tell you something? I think you're the most mercenary, selfish and cold-blooded person I've ever met. If you think for one minute that I'd try to persuade Captain Brady to risk his life for you to get rich quick, you're sadly mistaken.''

"I propose to sail with the brig as well," said Stewart quickly, in self-defence.

"Then not only are you a rogue, but a fool as well!"

She was on her feet now, angry colour in her cheeks and her eyes blazing. "Captain Brady," she went on, "is one of the few people I really love. If I thought there was any danger to his life in sailing even so far as Portugal, I'd make him give up going to sea."

Stewart was amazed at her indignation. "Why, if I'd known that you felt like that about it, Susy, I'd never have asked you," he said, distressed.

His protestations were unavailing, and Susy, getting into her stride, really told him what she thought. It was a very chastened Stewart who heard her finally exclaim, "Sometimes I think you're not human!"

An hour later they were still sitting there as far apart as possible. The conversation was very sparse, but Susy's anger seemed to have dwindled, and they had become reasonably amicable after Stewart had sworn that he would never mention the idea to Captain Brady.

Well, there went his scheme for getting rich quick, and far from feeling depressed about it, he was surprised to experience a very definite feeling of relief.

He would never now find himself in the position demanded by Miss Scripps, at least not for years ; and in any case, there was that damned curate for ever hanging around.

In a sudden revulsion of feeling, he thought, 'She's welcome to him,'' and decided to devote himself entirely to the business of shipowning. Captain Brady was right, stick to ships and they'd repay your interest over and over again. There was something true and faithful about them, none of the fickle shallowness of women.

The steps of three men were heard coming down the deserted street, their cheerful voices mingling reassuringly as they approached. Stewart hastened to the door, eager to escape from Susy's chilling company.

Captain Brady and Fred passed him with a hearty greeting, but old Mr. Eastwood hung back with the air of a conspirator. "Well," he asked eagerly, "did you ask her?"

"Yes," replied Stewart shortly.

"What did she say?"

"No," reponded Stewart laconically.

"What?" exclaimed the old man, dumbfounded. Stewart closed the door, and Mr. Eastwood, muttering, "Dear, dear!" went in to join Susy and the others.

Whatever could have happened? thought the old man. He was perplexed to see his grand-daughter laughing and joking with the captain and Fred, apparently in the highest of good humours.

Stewart, however, was dour and gloomy and shortly after he excused himself. He descended into the solitude of his basement and sat down at the table with his head in his hands. He felt that life was treating him shabbily. Goodness knows, he'd worked hard and been conscientious in everything he'd done. What more did you need to do to become successful?

It was getting on for a year now since he'd landed in Liverpool and set out to be his own master, but what had he accomplished? His original £200 capital, earned so laboriously on the Indian Coast, had disappeared. As he surveyed his fluctuating fortune he wondered what successful young men like Leyland and Ismay had got that he lacked. He thought back over this crowded first year in Liverpool. There was little satisfaction to be gained from the memory, apart from the purchase of the *Mary Jane*, and that didn't really count for much, for he was only a part-owner.

There was the pathetic ship-chandlery business and its ignominious end. It had brought him into contact with Miss Scripps, but, bearing in mind all the uneasy, unhappy moments she had cost him, he wasn't sure whether her acquaintance had been a debit or a credit.

It was something, anyhow, that he could sit there and calmly analyse his feelings for her. A few weeks ago it had been so different. Then he had been in an agony of apprehension about her, and yet, when he had been in her company, he had longed to be somewhere else.

Well, that was love, he supposed. Thank goodness he had got over it. He concluded that he had got over it, or else he would have been far more upset over the latest breakdown in his plans to amass a lot of money quickly.

Looking back, there had been one or two good moments during the past year. There was the re-insurance of the *Bangalore*, but that had been more due to good luck than good business. He had been lucky not to lose all his gains on the Shipping Exhibition. Women again! If it had not been for Miss Scripps he would never have been involved in that affair which had so nearly proved disastrous.

He got up and went to the mirror which hung on the wall, he would not have been surprised to find that the affair had given him a few grey hairs; but he searched in vain.

Actually, although the Shipping Exhibition had not been a great financial success, it had earned him a certain reputation. But even the modest success of the Exhibition had been due rather to Mr. Eastwood's efforts than Stewart's. Had it not been for the fortuitous appearance of the *Great Eastern*, bang would have gone the £1000 he had made on the insurance of the *Bangalore*. Even there with the *Great Eastern*, the women had bothered him again and endangered his plans with their protest meetings on the landing-stage.

So there he sat in the autumn of 1862, and miserably he cast around in his mind for something to mark his progress. Of all the things he had attempted, the only one which had brought him any real happiness was his part-ownership of the brig *Mary Jane*, and even in that partnership he did not feel too sure of himself. If it had not been for the restraining hand of Captain Brady, he might have played ducks and drakes with the brig herself in his desperate plans to make a fortune overnight.

Stewart sat on in a thoroughly chastened mood, the autumn dusk closing around him. He had reached the lowest depths of self-pity when a light knock sounded at the door, but he was too wrapped up in his bitter mood to hear it.

The next moment Susy had slipped quietly into the room and said, "What, sitting all alone in the dark?" and she lightly placed her hand on the young man's shoulder.

He looked up suddenly. "I'll light the gas," he said.

"No, don't bother. Grandfather asked me to come down and see if you were all right. He thought you might be feeling ill by the abrupt way you left us."

She moved away and sat down on the sofa at the other end of the room.

Stewart said: "No, I left because I was feeling a bit depressed. I didn't want to dampen the others' enjoyment."

"You'd better sit down here," said Susy, patting the sofa alongside of her. Stewart, as though mesmerized, obeyed.

After a while she broke the heavy silence by saying, "You're not angry with me because I refused to help you with Captain Brady, are you?"

She was so close to him that his arm kept brushing her leg-o'-mutton sleeve, and unthinkingly he slid his arm along the sofa back behind her.

"What did you do that for?" she asked.

"It's out of the way there," he said nervously.

"Then put it back where it belongs," she said, and without waiting for him to move, dragged his arm back. In this manœuvre their arms became linked and there they sat in silence.

Stewart was almost in a trance. He had never dreamt that Susy's presence could affect him so strangely. It seemed unbelievable that barely an hour ago she had called him a rogue and a fool, and now here she was with his arm in hers, and making no effort to release it.

"You're not angry with me?" she repeated.

Stewart looked at her. She seemed very close to him now. He noticed her slightly parted lips and the dark lustre of her hair, and on her shoulder those two fascinating, amazing curls. His heart seemed to expand. Something was happening to him.

"No," he whispered huskily, "I could never be that," and was rewarded by a happy laugh and a slight pressure on his arm.

"It wouldn't have been fair on that dear old man," she continued, looking at him in a way that made his senses reel.

Stewart was speechless. He wanted time to think, to analyse these new, powerful emotions which were welling up inside him. The silence continued.

"Do you remember the last time I was here?" she said, with a laugh.

Like a flash it all returned to him how, in pestering him for something to do in the Exhibition, she had revealed the shapeliness of her legs.

"You don't reply," Susy persisted.

Stewart sighed heavily. "I was thinking of those legs," he said.

Susy had the grace to blush, and hastily turned the conversation. "It seems years ago," she said reflectively, "since I used to look forward to you coming to the bar of the 'Pig and Whistle'."

"You looked forward to me coming?" he said, astonished, and half turning towards her.

Susy realized her mistake and sought to temporize by saying that she had looked forward to every customer; but it was too late, the damage was done. In turning towards her, Stewart had again caught sight of those two maddening curls on her shoulder. He stretched out his hand to put them at the back of her neck with the others.

She gave a brief cry of protest, but the next moment, he never really knew how it happened, his arms were round her and he was crushing her to him. Stewart's mind was a riot of confused thoughts. He glanced down at her head resting without demur against his chest. She seemed to be taking it very calmly.

"Susy," he said anxiously, "you're not angry with me for this, are you?"

She lifted her face to his and her eyes were limpid pools.

He heard a soft laugh and a whisper, "It just depends what your intentions are!"

Stewart bent down and kissed her gently on the lips. Susy drew back slightly, but he was intoxicated and kissed her again and again. "I love you, my dear," he breathed into her hair.

"Please, please," Susy laughed happily, "give me time to get my breath."

But Stewart's courage had returned. He was masterful, dominant, his depression had given way to exhilaration. This was love! It was all-possessing. He allowed her to draw away a little, and sat devouring her hungrily with his eyes. What a blind fool he'd been.

Some time later they began to take a more rational view of life. Susy was enchantingly provocative, but Stewart knew where he was now. He put one arm round her waist and with the other grasped both her hands.

LOOK OUT FOR

Getting to Know...
THE RIBBLE VALLEY
ISBN 1 872226 45 0   £4.95

Getting to Know...
PENDLE
ISBN 1 872226 46 9   £4.95

Getting to Know...
THE LAKE DISTRICT
ISBN 1 872226 47 7   £4.95

These books are a walker's guide, a good pub guide, a tourist's companion and a nature notebook, all combined in one volume. A look into the secrets of these well-loved areas.

...

CAMMELL LAIRD — the golden years
(Dave Roberts)
More than just a history of this famous shipyard.
Well illustrated
ISBN 1 872226 48 5

A HISTORY OF LANCASHIRE COOKERY
Tom Bridge takes us deep into Lancashire's culinary past to reveal the classic dishes of the region.
ISBN 1 872226 25 6   £4.95

LIVING MEMORIES OF MERSEYSIDE
Over 100 photos showing people and places of Merseyside after the war, with captions.
ISBN 1 872226 19 1   £4.95

PORTS OF THE NORTH WEST
(Catherine Rothwell)
History of ports from Birkenhead to Cumbria (incl. Merseyside)
ISBN 1 872226 17 5   £4.95

Look out for special bargain...
A HISTORY OF YE OLDE LIVERPOOL
First published in 1927 by the *Liverpool Daily Post*
ISBN 1 872226 02 7   Now only £1.00

"You've been a long time making up your mind," she said, leaning against him.

"Pooh!" boasted Stewart. "It doesn't do to let everyone know your intentions."

Susy looked at him slyly. "You've known all along, then?"

"I think you're the most lovely girl in the world," hedged Stewart, burying his lips in her hair, and then added, as though jealously; "I feel sorry for Captain Brady."

Susy laughed happily. "Do you remember that time I came and sang to you?"

"Yes. What was it now—'Champagne Charlie'. That's it!" he said enthusiastically, and they both began to laugh again at the memory.

"How did it go?" he asked thoughtfully, and as Susy started to sing he joined in with his deep bass voice, "'Champagne Charlie, good for any game at night, boys.'"

They sang the chorus through idiotically, and then lapsed into roars of laughter.

"Just once again, Susy," he pleaded, and they raised their voices in unison.

This time they had got no further than the first line when the door flew open with a crash, and there in the doorway with a hurricane lamp held high above his head stood Silas.

Susy and Stewart did not move. They remained where they were, giggling helplessly at the old sailor's shocked countenance.

Silas was outraged. That young woman again, with her hair all anyhow. It was more than he could stand.

"I don't 'old wi' such goings-on, skipper. This 'ere's a respectable 'ouse, but if you're going to take up wi' such young women as 'er, you'd better pay me off."

"Why, you wicked old man!" cried Susy indignantly. She jumped to her feet and flew towards the door with such speed that Silas, startled, backed hurriedly out of the room. Stewart rocked helplessly with mirth.

Susy came back thoughtfully. "I can see that I'm going to have trouble with that old man of yours," she said.

Stewart got up and grasping her tightly in his arms, said gravely: "There's only one way to quieten Silas's conscience, and that's by making an honest man of me. Will you?"

THE END

NORTHERN CLASSIC REPRINTS

Hobson's Choice (the Novel)
(Harold Brighouse)
The humorous and classic moving story of Salford's favourite tale. Well worth re-discovering this enjoyable story. Illustrated edition. Not been available since 1917, never before in paperback.
ISBN 1 872226 36 1   £4.95

Poems & Songs Of Lancashire
(Edwin Waugh)
A wonderful quality reprint of a classic book by undoubtedly one of Lancashire's finest poets. First published 1859 faithfully reproduced. Easy and pleasant reading, a piece of history.
ISBN 1 872226 27 2   £4.95

Stories and Tales Of Old Merseyside
(Frank Hird, edited Cliff Hayes)
Over 50 stories of Liverpool's characters and incidents PLUS a booklet from 1890 telling of the city's history, well illustrated.
ISBN 1 872226 20 5   £4.95

The Lancashire Witches
(W. Harrison Ainsworth)
A beautifully illustrated edition of the most famous romance of the supernatural.
ISBN 1 872226 55 8   £4.95

The Best of Old Lancashire
— Poetry & Verse
Published in 1866 as the very best of contemporary Lancashire writing, this book now offers a wonderful insight into the cream of Lancashire literature in the middle of the last century. Nearly 150 years later, edited and republished, the book now presents a unique opportunity to read again the masters of our past.
ISBN 1 872226 50 7   £4.95